THE LONG GLASGOW KISS

Also by Craig Russell

Lennox

The Jan Fabel Series:

Blood Eagle
Brother Grimm
Eternal
The Carnival Master
The Valkyrie Song

THE LONG GLASGOW KISS

CRAIG RUSSELL

Quercus

First published in Great Britain in 2010 by

Quercus
21 Bloomsbury Square
London
WC1A 2NS

A CIP catalogue record for this book is available
from the British Library

ISBN 978 1 84724 968 5 (TPB)
ISBN 978 1 84724 969 2 (HB)

10 9 8 7 6 5 4 3 2 1

Printed and bound in Great Britain by Clays Ltd, St Ives plc

For Marion

THE LONG GLASGOW KISS

CHAPTER ONE

Some concepts are alien to the Glaswegian mind. Salad. Dentistry. Forgiveness.

Until the night Small Change MacFarlane died, I had no idea just how unforgiving Glasgow could be. My education in vindictiveness was about to be completed.

It was mid-heat wave hot and sticky and I had an even hotter and stickier date with Lorna MacFarlane the night her father was murdered. I had parked my Austin Atlantic up above the city on Glennifer Braes, from where you could see Glasgow stretched out below, dark and sullen in the muggy night; but, to be honest, we didn't take in much of the view. Looking back, it's ironic to think that two members of the MacFarlane family had been on the business end of a blunt instrument at roughly the same time.

Lorna was quite a bit above the usual Glasgow standard: she was pretty, with strawberry blonde hair and a knockout figure. Like most lowlifes made good, her bookie father was always striving for a touch of respectability and had sent Lorna to a fancy boarding school in Edinburgh. The aim had probably been to turn her into a proper little lady, but whatever languages were taught there, I had found out in the back of my Atlantic that when it came to French, Lorna was a natural linguist.

If I had to describe my relationship with Lorna at that time, the word *shallow* would fit best. Mind you, it was an adjective that could have been applied to almost all my relationships with women. Lorna and I were, however, *particularly* mutually undemanding. She was killing time until she landed the right type of husband material, and me ... well, I was just doing what I always did. If events hadn't taken the turn they had that night, I think we would have drifted apart without acrimony. But that night, up on Glennifer Braes, we had no idea what was ahead of us.

My ignorance was especially blissful. I was completely unaware that a blood debt was about to be extracted, or what a *Baro* or a *bitchapen* were. And if someone, on that humid, too-hot summer evening had mentioned the name John Largo to me, I would have assumed they were talking about a character in a Wild West movie. Which would have been apt, in a way: the West didn't get any wilder than Glasgow.

But John Largo was no cowboy. He was what the French would call an *éminence gris*. A shadow. A very dangerous shadow with a long reach.

After our back-seat tango, I drove Lorna home to Pollokshields. Glasgow had its own social geography, meaningless to anyone from outside the city but all-important to its minority of middle classes. Glasgow, by and large, was a classless sort of city where the only thing that counted for anything was how much money you had. The Glasgow accent was common across social boundaries; intelligibility or, more correctly, the comparative lack of unintelligibility, was the only indicator of status. The result was that social prestige tended to be determined by geography, or more subtle social indicators such as proximity to a toilet that flushed or whether your grandmother still lived in a slum.

When it came to the accounting of turf, Small Change had done well over the years, better than almost any other bookie in Glasgow, but he hadn't earned the kind of cash or respectability to spring him over the Clyde, out of the Southside and up the Glaswegian social ladder. The MacFarlane residence, therefore, lay in Pollokshields, on the south side. The house itself was large, detached, and the usual unimaginatively sturdy, Scottish, Victorian sandstone villa in a street of near-identical unimaginatively sturdy, Scottish, Victorian sandstone villas, all following the usual Presbyterian imperative to temper prosperity with anonymity. In a search for some kind of distinction, almost all the houses in the street had names, not numbers, and when we reached *Ardmore*, there was a knot of black police Wolseleys blocking the drive.

That's usually my cue to see how far and how fast I can travel in the opposite direction, but Lorna started to panic and, parking on the street, I went with her up to the house. It was clear something deeply unpleasant would be waiting for us. It was: six-foot-six of tweed and oxblood brogues that went by the name of Detective Superintendent Willie McNab.

'What's going on?' I asked and McNab ignored me.

'Miss MacFarlane?' He spoke to Lorna solicitously and I was impressed at how convincing his human being act was. 'Could you come with me please?' He steered her into the lounge, first casting a 'and don't you fucking move' look over his shoulder at me.

I smiled. It was nice to be noticed.

I was left standing with the cop doing guard duty on the front door. He was a big lad, a Highlander, like ninety per cent of the uniforms in the City of Glasgow Police. Highlanders were recruited for size not intellect and they were easy to bewilder with shiny beads or electricity: it only took me a couple of minutes to wheedle some information out of him. Small Change MacFarlane, Glasgow's most successful bookie and Lorna's father, was, apparently, lying stretched out on his study floor, ruining the Wilton with several pints of O-negative.

'Whee think he whass chust in the door from the races,' my new Hebridean copper chum confided musically. 'He whas a bhookie you know. Somewhone clobbered him whith a statue hof his favourite greyhound . . . *Billy Boy.*'

I frowned my dismay. 'What are the odds of that?'

When McNab reappeared in the entrance hall, I was still on the threshold but could see past him, through the door and into the living room. Lorna was sitting on the sofa, distraught, and being comforted by her stepmother. I took a step into the house but was halted by McNab's huge hand on my chest.

'And what *exactly* was your involvement with Jimmy MacFarlane?'

I decided to continue our communication by glares and I gave McNab my best 'Take your fucking hand off me' look. It was as effective as if I'd spoken to him in Nepalese and the restraining hand remained planted on my chest.

'Small Change? None,' I said. 'I'm a . . . a *friend* of his daughter, that's all.'

'How good a *friend*?'

'Well, let's say we're seeing a lot of each other at the moment.'

'And that's your only connection with James MacFarlane?'

'I've met him a few times. Mainly through seeing Lorna,' I said, omitting to mention that Small Change had promised me a couple of tickets to the forthcoming big fight between local boy Bobby Kirkcaldy and the German Jan Schmidtke. The fact was that the first thing I'd thought about on hearing of his demise was whether Small Change had managed to earmark the tickets for me *before* getting his head pulped. I decided that expressing such sentiments would expose one of the less appealing aspects of my nature. There again, it maybe wasn't that bad: my second thought had been to wonder how long it would be after her father's death before Lorna would be in the right frame of mind for some more back-seat wrestling.

'No other business?' asked McNab. 'You haven't done any work for him? Snooping?'

I shook my head, suddenly feeling sullen. I looked down at the hand on my chest. A stout fist uncoiled. Thick fingers, flaky knuckles. Crisp white shirt cuffs beneath tweed.

'We'll see and make sure to keep your nose out of this, Lennox,' he said. 'This is police business.'

'I've no intention of getting involved.' I frowned; I was confused by McNab clearly feeling the need to warn me off. 'What was the motive?'

'Well let's see . . .' McNab rubbed his chin with his free hand in mock thoughtfulness. 'MacFarlane was one of Glasgow's richest bookies and greyhound breeders. He just came back from the races with a bag full of cash which we can't locate . . . let me think . . . Got it! Crime of passion.'

'You should stick to what you're good at, Superintendent, and leave the sarcasm to me.'

'And you leave the police work to me. This is a simple robbery. We'll get this one all by ourselves, Lennox. A couple of days and we'll have the bastard in custody.'

'Ah,' I smiled, and nodded appreciatively. 'The Scottish legal system at work. A model of fairness and justice where every man is considered innocent until proven Catholic.'

I could picture the scene. Housebreakers, as burglars were called under Scottish law, tended not to use violence. I imagined a procession of the usual suspects having the crap beaten out of them at police headquarters. In the movies, police detectives were always reassuring people they questioned that it was 'just routine'. I wondered if that was the line the City of Glasgow Police used: *'We won't keep you long . . . it's just routine. A few more boots in the ribs then you'll be able to pick your teeth off the floor and leave . . .'*

'Can I ask you a question?' McNab interrupted my musings.

'You're in the business of asking questions, Superintendent,' I said, without adding that usually the answers were beaten out of the mug being asked. 'Go ahead.'

'Why don't you fuck off to Canada?'

'Is that a question or the new slogan of the Canadian immigration bureau? It's catchy, I'll give you that.'

'You're quite the wag, aren't you Lennox?' He looked past me, or over me, out beyond the garden, as if he wasn't fully focussed on our conversation. Then, suddenly, he locked his eyes with mine and leaned in. His face in mine, his hand on my chest, there was no question about his focus now. 'Do you remember our last little chat in St. Andrew's Square?' McNab referred to the City of Glasgow Police HQ.

'How could I forget? You, me and that charming lad from the Hebrides with the wet rag wrapped around his fist.'

'If you don't cut the wisecracks I could arrange a reunion . . . Keep your lip buttoned Lennox. Answer my question: why *don't* you fuck off back to Canada?'

'I like it here,' I replied, ignoring the logical pickle of answering his question with my lip buttoned. 'The Glasgow air agrees with me. If I were to leave, my pleurisy would probably clear up – and it's taken me such a long time to perfect it.' I sighed and gave a shrug. 'I don't know, maybe one day I might go back. When I'm ready.'

'I'd give it some serious thought if I were you.' He dropped the hand from my chest. It had been there so long I felt the warm, heavy ghost of it through my jacket and shirt. Point made and taken. Superintendent Willie McNab could put his hand on anyone in Glasgow, any time and for as long as he wanted. 'There's a lot of people I know who don't like you, Lennox. People who still think you know more about the McGahern case than you let on.'

'Then they're wrong.' I threw a hasty, fake smile over my discomfort at McNab once more digging up dead history. Very dead history. 'I keep telling you, Superintendent, there's a lot less to me than meets the eye. Can I go and talk to Lorna now?'

'Just remember to keep your nose out of this business with MacFarlane.' Lighting a Player's, McNab took a long draw, then blew a jet of smoke out into the muggy Pollokshields night. 'Or I'll arrange a change of scenery for you myself. Am I clear?'

'Crystal ... If there's one thing I can say about your veiled threats, Superintendent, it's that they're all threat and no veil.'

Maggie MacFarlane poured me a Scotch while I sat and consoled her stepdaughter. Lorna's real mother had died ten years before and Jimmy 'Small Change' MacFarlane had remarried. Maggie, his second wife, couldn't have been any more than ten years older than Lorna.

When some men achieve a certain age, provided they've also achieved an appropriate bank balance, they give up the family saloon for a flash sports car, all sleek lines and curves, and an exhilarating ride that makes them feel for a moment that they're young again, even if they can't quite cope with the horsepower. Second wives can be like that; Maggie MacFarlane was definitely like that, and at our initial meeting, the first time I called to pick up Lorna, Maggie had somehow given me the clear impression that if I ever wanted to take her for a quick spin, then that was just fine by her.

'How are you holding up?' I asked Maggie. Truth was she was holding up just fine. A little too fine.

'I just can't believe it,' she said, handing me the Scotch and pouring herself one. 'Poor Jimmy. Who would do such a thing?'

I took my Scotch and put my arm around Lorna and persuaded her to take a sip of the whisky. She was at that stage where the crying had stopped and she simply sat ashen and still. She coughed and screwed her eyes tight as she swallowed the Scotch. The fire in the whisky seemed to catch light in her expression and she glowered at Maggie.

'I have a few ideas,' said Lorna in a low, spiteful mutter. Happy families. I was upset for Lorna's sake; but I glanced at my watch: it was past closing time. And it was fast getting past the time when my secret knock could get me into the Horsehead Bar.

I decided to break the tension. 'Did you find the . . . I mean, was it you who found Mr MacFarlane?' I asked Maggie.

She sat down on the chesterfield opposite us, crossing her legs with a hiss of silk on silk. It was, of course, the most inappropriate time for me to take a look at her legs and I made a great effort not to. As usual, I failed. Her lips were deep crimson around the cigarette she lit: some fancy foreign brand with filters and a band of gold paper.

'I was at a friend's place in Bearsden,' she said, holding me in a steady blue gaze. 'I got back about an hour ago. When I got here I knew something was wrong because the front door was ajar. Then, when I went through to Jimmy's study . . .' She dropped her eyes and took a long slug of Scotch.

'What did the police say?'

'Not much. Just that they think it was a robbery. Someone who knew Jimmy would be coming back with the night's Shawfield takings.'

'Have the police mentioned any names?'

Maggie was about to answer when McNab came into the living room without knocking. Knocking was something other people did.

'Miss MacFarlane, could I ask you a few questions?' He looked at me pointedly before adding: 'In the kitchen might be best.'

Maggie waited until Lorna and McNab had gone before answering. 'No. No names. But I would imagine they have some ideas.'

I gave a low laugh. 'They're not ideas people, the police. Thinking has an annoying habit of getting in the way of a conviction.'

When Lorna came back from talking to McNab she was in tears; an effect his company often came close to having on me. I went back to dutifully comforting her, and stayed with daughter and stepmother without as much as once asking if Small Change had happened to mention anything about boxing tickets before his untimely demise. I was nothing if not a gentleman.

From what I could pick up it looked like McNab was probably right: Small Change had had his brains bashed in for the night's takings he had brought back. It would have been a tidy sum all right, but not so tidy as to be worth hanging for. And if McNab was personally involved in the case, then someone would definitely hang. I actually found myself grateful that I had the most solid of alibis.

I hung around until about two a.m., by which time the police had gone. I promised to ring in the morning and left.

CHAPTER TWO

The streets I drove through to get back to my flat were deserted and I reflected that there were probably cemeteries more lively than Glasgow at two in the morning. That was probably why I was so aware of the headlights in my rear mirror. I wasn't sure if they had been with me since Pollokshields, but they had certainly been there for long enough for me to become suspicious. I didn't pull over outside my flat – instead I drove along Great Western Road and turned into Byres Road, taking a random right into a silent residential street lined with sandstone tenements and semi-detached houses, soot-stained darker than the night sky above them. The lights in my mirror held back as far as they could without losing me, but nonetheless followed my arbitrary route. Again completely at random, I pulled up outside a tenement, stepped out of the Atlantic, locked the door and walked with a sense of purpose into the tenement close.

The car drove past. An Austin. One of the big jobs. Black or dark grey. The kind the police cruised around in. I saw a driver and passenger, but I couldn't make out either figure other than that one of them had shoulders to make Atlas jealous. Small Change MacFarlane was a big enough fish all right, but I didn't see why his case warranted so much attention. I didn't see why I warranted so much attention from the police, given my tangential involvement. The car cruised around the corner and I heard the synchromesh get a grinding as it did a three-point some-where out of sight. Stepping out of the shadows, I went back to my car and leaned against the wing, my arms folded, patiently waiting for the unmarked police car to drift around the corner. Sometimes I can be too smart for my own good.

The Austin reappeared and pulled up next to me. It was a Sheerline; too fancy for the police. Something vast and dark unfolded from the passenger seat and cast an improbably large shadow in the lamplight.

'Hello again, Mr Lennox . . .' Twinkletoes McBride said in his earth-rumbling baritone and smiled at me. I straightened up from the wing of the Atlantic. This was interesting.

'Twinkletoes? What are you doing here? I thought it was the police. Why are you tailing me?'

'You'll have to ask Mr Sneddon that,' he said earnestly. 'I'm sure he can elucidate you.' Twinkletoes pronounced every syllable deliberately: *ee-loos-ih-date*.

'Still reading the *Reader's Digest* I see,' I said amiably.

'I'm improving my word power . . .' Twinkletoes beamed. I imagined how much more interesting his expanded vocabulary would make the experience of having your toes lopped off with bolt cutters – Twinkletoes' speciality as a torturer and the origin of his nickname. Or *ehh-pee-thett* as he would probably call it.

'An expressive vocabulary is a true treasure,' I smiled.

'You're not fucking wrong there, Mr Lennox.'

'Mr Sneddon wants to see me now?' I asked. I unlocked my car. 'I'll follow you.'

Twinkletoes stopped smiling. He swung the back door of the Sheerline open. 'We'll bring you back to your car. Afterwards. If that isn'ae *in-con-veen-ee-ent.*'

'Okay,' I said, as if he was doing me a favour. But the thought did run through my head that I might return unable to count to twenty on my fingers and toes.

Twinkletoes McBride may have been sadistic and psychopathically violent to order, but at least he was a friendly sort of cuss. The same couldn't have been said of the driver of the Humber, a thin, meagre and nasty-looking thug with bad skin and an over-oiled Teddy Boy cut. I'd seen him before, lurking menacingly in the presence of Willie Sneddon. To give him due credit, lurking menacingly was something he did extremely well and it made up for his lack of conversational skills.

We drove out of the city, west, passing through Clydebank and out along the road to Dumbarton. The only car on the road. The ugly tenements eventually gave way to open country and I began to feel uneasy. A free taxi ride from Twinkletoes McBride in itself was enough to make you wary, but knowing who had summoned your presence was enough to start the lower parts of your digestive anatomy twitching. Twinkletoes was one of Willie Sneddon's henchmen. Willie Sneddon was the King of the Southside – one of the so-called Three Kings who ran almost all the crime worth running in Glasgow. Willie Sneddon was bad news of the worst kind.

When we turned off the road and headed up a narrow farm track, I started to think that the news was about to get worse. I even found myself casting an eye over the car door handle, reflecting that at this speed jumping from the car wouldn't be a break-neck job. Getting caught by Twinkle and his taciturn chum, though, probably would be. Willie Sneddon was the kind of social host to become piqued if you declined his invitations: once I'd started running, if I wanted to hang on to my teeth, toes and maybe even my life, I'd have to keep running until I was back in Canada. We jolted over a pothole. I calmed down.

It made no sense that Sneddon had anything unpleasant planned for me other than his company, which, in itself, would fill my unpleasantness quota for the month. I had done nothing to offend Sneddon or either of the other two Kings. The truth was, I had tried to avoid doing work for them as much as I could over the last year.

I decided to sit tight and take my chances.

The farm track ended, as you would expect, at a farm. The farmhouse was a large Victorian granite job, suggesting a gentlemanly sort of turf-turner. Beside the house was a huge stone barn that I guessed was not being used for its original purpose, unless it was home to an equally gentlemanly breed of cattle: the two small windows in its vast flank were draped in heavy velvet that glowed ember-red in the night and yellow electric light shone from under the heavy wooden barn door.

Twinkletoes and Happy Harry the driver conducted me from the car to the barn. I could hear voices coming from inside. A lot of voices. Laughter, shouting and cheering. Twinkle pressed an electric bell push and a peephole slid open as we were checked out by whoever was on the other side.

'I've never been to a milk bar speakeasy before,' I said cheerfully to my less-than-cheerful driver. 'Does Sneddon have an illicit buttermilk still in here?'

He replied by lurking menacingly at my side. Twinkle pressed the bell push again.

'Maybes we shou' try da *udder* door,' I said in my mock-New York gangster voice and smiled. It only served to confuse Twinkletoes and deepen the menace of his companion's lurk.

I had half expected the doorbell to be answered by a heifer in a dinner suit. As it turned out, I wasn't far wrong: a bull-necked thug swung open the door. Stepping across the threshold was like diving into a pool; we were immersed in a humid fug of cigarette smoke, whisky fumes and sweat. And the faint copper smell of blood. A simultaneous wave of noise and odour-heavy warmth washed over us: men shouting in anger-edged eagerness, the odd female voice shrill and pene-trating. The barn wasn't exactly full of people, but they were elbow-jostle crowded in a circle around a raised platform upon which two heavily muscled men were beating the bejesus out of each other. Both were stripped to the waist, but they wore ordinary trousers and shoes rather than boxing gear. And no gloves.

Nice, I thought. Bare-knuckle fighting. Unlicensed, unregu-lated, illegal. And more than occasionally fatal. I had never really understood the need to pay to watch a bare-knuckle fight in the West of Scotland. In Glasgow particularly, it seemed to me redundant, like asking a girl out on a date in the middle of an orgy.

Twinkletoes put his hand on my shoulder and I nearly buckled under the weight. 'Mr Sneddon says we was to get you a drink and tell you to wait till he was ready.'

A girl of about twenty with too much lipstick and too little frock stood behind the crepe-draped trestle table that served as a bar. Unsurprisingly, she had no Canadian Club and the Scotch I took as a substitute had the same effect on the lining of my mouth that I imagined it would have on paint. I turned back to the fight and took in the audience. Most of the men wore dinner suits and the women were all young, showily dressed, and anything but wife material. The look of the men turned my gut: that pink, scrubbed, fleshy-faced look of accountants, lawyers and other lower-middle-class Glaswegians out slum-ming it. This was their little charabanc ride to vice. I guessed there were more than a few Glasgow Corporation bureaucrats and even a copper or two here by personal Sneddon invitation.

The stench of venality mingled with the sweat and booze-tinged air.

A cheer from the crowd drew my attention back to the fighters. I didn't mind a boxing match myself, but this was not sport. No skill other than using your face and head to break your opponent's knuckles. The face of each fighter was the mirror image of his opponent: white skin puffed and swollen and smeared with spit, sweat and vivid streaks of blood; eyes reduced to slits, hair sweat-plastered to their scalps. And both faces were expressionless. No fear or anger or hate; just the emotionless concentration of two men engaged in the hard physical work of doing harm to another human being. Each punch had the sound of either a wet slap or an ugly, dull thud. Neither man made an attempt to dodge his opponent's blows; this was all about beating the shit out of each other until someone fell down and didn't get up. Both fighters looked exhausted. In bare-knuckle there are no rounds, no breaks for rest or recovery. If you were knocked to the ground you had thirty seconds to get back up to 'scratch', the scored line in the centre of the fighting area.

There's something about bare-knuckle fighting that holds your unwilling attention, and I found myself focussed on the brutality on the raised platform. The fighters seemed oblivious to everything around them. Probably everything before them and after them. I remembered the feeling from the war. In combat you have no past, no history, no future; no connections to the world outside. You're not even connected to the men you kill in any human way. I recognized the same dislocation in these two men. One was slightly smaller but heavier-set than the other. Blood from his nose was back-of-the-hand smeared across his upper lip and cheek and one distended eyelid was purpling up and threatening to close over his eye. It looked as if it was only a matter of time before his larger opponent would be able to take advantage of his compromised vision, but the smaller man suddenly swung an ungainly but brutal left hook. It connected with the bigger fighter's cheek with a sickening snap. Even across the barn and through the cigarette haze I could see the big man had stepped out of his body for a moment and his arms hung limp at his side.

The spectators roared delight and fury, depending on whom they'd placed their money, and the smaller guy slammed a nose-breaking jab into his opponent's face. Blood cascaded over the big man's mouth. More roars from the crowd. This was the end. The smaller fighter had the smell of victory in his bloody nostrils and tore into his adversary, his bare-fisted punches slapping loudly into the bigger man's ribs and gut. Another roundhouse left sent a viscous arc of blood and saliva through the air and the big man dropped like a felled tree.

There was no congratulation for the winner or commiseration for the loser; the serious business of settling bets got underway and there was another jostle around Sneddon's illegal bookie and a couple of enforcers. Sneddon would be happy: the disgruntled faces hanging back outnumbered the beaming, eager grins of the winners.

After a while, everyone made for the bar and I eased back into a corner with my gut-rot Scotch and contemplated the success I had made of my life. It had so very nearly gone wrong. A few different choices and I could have ended up wealthy and contented three thousand miles from Glasgow, missing out on the edifying experience of watching two bruised apes beat the crap out of each other in a Scottish barn.

Twinkletoes returned with a shortish, compactly built and hard-looking man wearing a suit that was well tailored and expensive without being flash. His blond hair looked freshly barbered and there was a brutal handsomeness in the face. Unfortunately, the ugly deep crease of an old razor scar on his right cheek clearly dated from a time before he could afford the kind of expert needlework evident in his clothes.

'Hello, Mr Sneddon,' I said.

'Do you know where you are, Lennox?'

'Hernando's Hideaway?'

'Aye . . . very fucking funny,' Sneddon said without a smile. 'This is my newest little sideline. You see the fight?'

'Yeah. Lovely.'

'Pikeys . . .' Sneddon shook his head in wonder. 'They fight like fuck for pennies. They would do it for the love of it. Mad fuckers.'

'And you run a book on it . . .'

Sneddon nodded. 'It's been a good night.'

'I'll bet . . .' I said. Old Ben Franklin once said that the only certain things were death and taxes. But that was before Sneddon's time, otherwise it would have been death, taxes and Willie Sneddon's hand in your pocket.

'I've had the place six months. It took a while to fix it up. I got the house, the barn, the whole fuckin' farm because some toff bet more on the ponies than he had in readies. Wanker. It's quite poetic that I run a wee gambling thing here, considering I got it because of gambling.'

'Aye Mr Sneddon, that's *eye-ron-ic*,' said Twinkletoes at Sneddon's side.

'Was I fucking talking to you?' Sneddon glowered up at Twinkletoes who loomed above his boss. Twinkle made a hurt face and Sneddon turned back to me. 'Anyway, I've kept this place pretty quiet. I don't even think Cohen and Murphy know about it yet. So keep your mouth shut.' Sneddon referred to the other two Kings: Handsome Jonny Cohen and Hammer Murphy.

I took a moment to ponder why everybody felt that they had to tell me to keep my mouth shut all the time. 'If they don't know about it, then I'm sure they soon will,' I said. 'This is a village masquerading as a big city. Nothing stays quiet for long.'

'Like Small Change MacFarlane getting his coupon smashed to fuck . . .' Sneddon smiled. Or moved his face around in an attempt. The result was something cold, hard and careless.

'Yeah . . . just like. My God, it doesn't take long for word to get around. MacFarlane's not cold yet. Is that why you had Twinkletoes and smiling lad pick me up?'

Sneddon cast a glance over his shoulder at the crowd. 'Let's go over to the main house. It's quieter . . .'

I'd been to Sneddon's house in Bearsden, a mock-baronial mansion with manicured gardens, a few times. This place was totally different. As soon as I stepped into the entrance hallway I knew that this was a business premises. From the outside it was a Victorian farmhouse; inside it was a Victorian brothel, all thick velvet crimson drapes, chaises-longues and Rubenesque tits in frames on the walls. The living room of the house had been converted into a bar with scattered sofas. On one a working girl sat with a bored expression as a drunken customer drooled and pawed inexpertly at her. Mel Tormé crooned from a record player in the corner, and the bar was manned by another girl in her early twenties who, too, had applied too much make-up and too little frock.

'What do you think?' asked Sneddon in a tone that suggested he didn't give a toss what I thought.

'Nice ambience. Brings out the romantic in me.'

Sneddon snorted an approximation of a laugh. He tapped

Twinkletoes on the chest and nodded in the direction of the drunk and the girl. Twinkletoes obliged by conducting them out of the lounge.

'So what's a nice boy like me doing in a place like this?' I asked. Sneddon told the girl behind the counter to pour us a couple of whiskies and I noticed she brought a single malt up from beneath the bar. The good stuff.

'You was at Small Change's place tonight. What business do you have with him? Was he getting you to do a bit of sniffing for him?'

'The only sniffing I've been doing has been around his daughter. All pleasure, no business.'

'You sure?' Sneddon narrowed his eyes. It made him look all brow, which was an advantage in Glasgow. Athens had been the cradle of democracy, Florence had given the world the Renaissance, Glasgow had refined, to a precise art, the head butt. The Glasgow Kiss, as it was affectionately known amongst the nations of the world. 'I would be *put out* if you was being less than square with me.'

'Listen, Mr Sneddon, I would think a long time before I'd lie to you. I know Twinkletoes didn't get his name because he dances like Fred Astaire. I'm attached to my toes and I like to think it's a mutual arrangement. And anyway, I was asked the same thing tonight by Superintendent McNab.'

'McNab?' Sneddon put his glass down on the bar. 'What the fuck is he involved for? I thought it was a robbery gone wrong.'

'It's a big case, I guess. Small Change was high profile,' I said, hiding how impressed I was with the speed and accuracy of Sneddon's intelligence-gathering operation. Then I realized I was part of it. 'Anyway, he took a lot of convincing that I wasn't involved with MacFarlane.'

'So you had nothing to do with Small Change or his business?'

'Like I said, I'm seeing his daughter, that's all. What's the problem?'

Sneddon waved his hand at me as if he had been flicking away an annoying fly. 'Nothin'. It's just that I had some business going on with Small Change.'

'Oh?'

Sneddon gave me a look. 'Listen, Lennox, if you're hanging around MacFarlane's place, you can maybes help me out.'

'If I can ...' I said and smiled, hiding the sinking feeling in my gut.

'Keep me up to date on what the coppers are getting up to. And, if you get a chance, see if you can find anything like Small Change's diary. Appointment book. Whatever he kept details of meetings in. Or maybe a log book with events and stuff in it.'

'May I ask why?'

'No you fucking can't.' Then he sighed, as if relenting to a child's demand for ice cream. 'Okay ... I had a meeting with Small Change this afternoon. A *project* we was working on together. I'm moving into the fight game ... not like tonight – something more than a couple of pikeys knocking the shite out of each other. Real boxing. I was talking to MacFarlane about a couple of fighters. Things could get *complicated* if the police found out.'

'And what was Small Change bringing to the table?'

'It's not important. Listen, this deal was nothing big. I just don't want that kind of police attention. I never want police attention. But specially not if that fucker McNab's heading the case. Can you check it out for me or not?'

I made a big deal of thinking it over. 'I'm not trying to be funny, Mr Sneddon, but if I had an appointment with you, I don't think it's the kind of thing I'd put in a diary. I mean ... that could be evidence, like you say. I don't think MacFarlane had the kind of business that he would want recorded some-where.'

'That's because you don't think the way me and MacFarlane do. I have a diary. Every fucking appointment, every talk I have with Murphy or Cohen goes into it. Like you say, evidence. King's Evidence if I ever need it. Cohen and Murphy do the same thing. Insurance. And I know that MacFarlane had a mind like a fucking sieve . . . only when it came to things like that. As a bookie he could tell you what was running where and when and what the odds were, right off the top of his head. But stuff like meet-ings he'd have to write times and dates down or he'd forget.'

'I don't think I can help. The coppers took away boxes of stuff from his study. I'd guess they've already got their hands on his diary.'

'You're smarter than that, Lennox.' Sneddon fixed me with a hard stare. 'Small Change wouldn't keep his diary somewhere obvious, and the coppers are too fucking stupid to look anywheres that's not obvious. You know something, if I had a suspicious nature I'd start wondering if you don't want to help me. I would maybes even start to think you've been trying to avoid me. Maybes even Murphy and Cohen too. What's the matter, Lennox . . . getting too good for us?'

'I've done more than my fair share for you, Sneddon . . .' I put my glass down on the bar; I was maybe going to need my hands free. If only for Twinkletoes to lop my fingers off. 'If I remember rightly, it was me you called when you were hauled off down to St. Andrew's Square last year. I don't think you, Murphy or Cohen have anything to complain about. But you're not my only clients.'

Sneddon looked at me with a sneer. 'Okay, Lennox. You're a tough guy – I get it. Find Small Change's appointment book – or whatever he used to keep that kinda stuff in – and deliver it to me and I'll pay you three hundred quid. Whether my name's in it or not.'

'I'll have a look if I can.' I had told Sneddon I'd think long and hard before I lied to him; when it came to it I did it in the bat of an eyelid: I had no intention of snooping around the MacFarlane house on his behalf. But there again, three hundred quid was three hundred quid. It was best to keep my options open. 'Was that all you wanted to see me about?'

'There was something else.'

I fixed my smile with glue. Sneddon saw through it.

'That's if it isn't fucking beneath you to do a job for me, Lennox,' he said maliciously.

'Of course not.'

'Anyway, you don't need to worry, you won't get your hands dirty. It's a legit job.'

'What is it?'

'Like I said, I'm getting into the fight game. Me and Jonny the kike have each got a share in a fighter.'

'You and Handsome Jonny Cohen?'

'Yeah, me and Cohen. You got a problem with that?'

'Me? Not at all. It's very *ecumenical* of you.'

'I'm not prejudiced. I'll do business with anyone. Absolutely anyone.' He paused. 'Except Fenians, of course. Anyways, this young fighter we've got shares in . . . he's going places. He has a coupon-mashing right hook. The thing is, he's been getting a bit of grief.'

'What kind of grief?'

'Fucking stupid stuff. A dead bird put through his letterbox, paint on his car, that kinda shite.'

'Sounds like he's upset someone. Has he spoken to the police?'

Sneddon gave me a look. 'Aye . . . seeing as I have such a cosy relationship with them, that's the first thing I said he should do. Use your head, Lennox. If the polis start sniffing about then they'll sooner or later end up on my doorstep or Jonny Cohen's. We'd both rather keep our investment quiet. It was Cohen what said we should get you to look into it. Discreet, like.'

'Discretion,' I said sententiously, 'is my middle name. So who has he pissed off enough to start a vendetta?'

'No one. Or no one that he can think of. I mean, he's hurt a few in the ring, but I don't think that's what this is all about. I reckon that someone has put a stash on him to lose when he fights the Kraut and they're just trying to put the wind up him before the fight. You know, like chucking a fish supper into a greyhound's kennel the night before the race.'

'Wait a minute . . . you said before he fights the Kraut. By Kraut do you mean Jan Schmidtke? Is your boxer Bobby Kirkcaldy?'

'He's not *my* boxer. I own a piece of him, you could say. So what?'

I blew a long, low whistle. 'That's a wise investment, Mr Sneddon. Kirkcaldy's tasty. And you're right, he is going places.'

'Oh . . .' Again Sneddon smiled the only way he could. Sneeringly. 'I am so fucking pleased that my business decisions meet with your approval. Cohen and me both lost sleep worrying that we'd gone ahead without your okay.'

I had to admit, Sneddon was *much* better at sarcasm than McNab. But still nowhere near as good as me.

'I'm just saying that Kirkcaldy is hot property,' I said. 'The stakes are high with him, literally. You got any idea who's trying to spook him?'

Sneddon shrugged. 'That's your job. You find out . . . if you do, don't let them know you're onto them. You want the job?'

'Usual fees?'

Reaching into his hand-tailoring, Sneddon pulled out his

wallet and handed me forty pounds in fives. It was more than most people made in a month but didn't seem to lighten Sneddon's wallet too much. 'There's another hundred in it for you when you give me a name for who's behind all this malarkey.'

'Fair enough.' I took the money with a smile. It was part of my customer relations policy. There again, smiling when people gave me money came pretty naturally to me. It was a clean job. Legit, like Sneddon had said. All I had to deliver was a name, but I tried not to think too much about what would happen to the face behind the name once I'd delivered it.

'You said you were talking to Small Change MacFarlane about a couple of fighters. Was Kirkcaldy one of them?'

'Fuck no. No, it wasn't nothing in that league. Just a couple of potential up-and-comers, that's all. Small Change didn't even know of my interest in Kirkcaldy. You've got to fucking watch what you say to bookies. This is Kirkcaldy's address.' Sneddon handed me a folded note. 'Is there anything else you need?'

I made a show of a thoughtful frown, even though the idea had come to me as soon as I had heard mention of Kirkcaldy's name. 'Maybe it would be a good idea if you could spring me a ticket for the big fight. Means I can check out anyone dodgy.'

'I would sincerely fucking hope that you've got to the bottom of this before then. But aye ... I can manage that. Anything else?'

'If there is, I'll let you know,' I said, inwardly cursing that I hadn't thought of a reason to ask for two tickets.

'Right. You can fuck off now,' said Sneddon. I wondered if the freshly minted Queen followed the same court etiquette. 'And don't forget to have a sniff about for Small Change's appointments book. I'll get Singer to drive you back to your car. You know Singer, don't you?' Sneddon beckoned across to the Teddy Boy who'd driven me and Twinkletoes out to the farm.

'Oh yeah . . . we chatted all the way over here.' I leaned forward conspiratorially. 'To be honest, I found it difficult to get a word in edgewise . . .'

Sneddon gave me another of his sneers-or-smiles. 'Singer' certainly didn't seem to like my witticism, I could have been becoming paranoid, but I thought I detected even more menace in his lurking.

'Aye . . .' said Sneddon. 'Singer's not much of a conversationalist. Not much of a singer either come to that, are you, Singer?'

Singer interrupted his lurk long enough to shake his head.

'You could say Singer is a man of action, not words.' Sneddon paused to take a cigarette from a gold cigarette case so heavy it threatened to sprain his wrist. He didn't offer me one. 'Singer's Da was a real bastard. Used to beat the shite out of him when he was a kiddie. Knocked his mother about too. You know, more than normal. But Singer had this talent. He got it from his Ma. He had a cracking wee voice on him. Or so people tell me. Never heard it myself. Anyways, at weddings and shite like that Singer and his Ma was always asked to stand up and give a song. Not that he took much asking, did you, Singer? He used to sing all the time. The only thing the wee bastard had . . .'

I looked at Singer who returned my stare emptily. He was obviously used to Sneddon discussing his most intimate personal history with a complete stranger. Either that or he just didn't care.

'But it used to wind up his Da no end. He'd come home drunk and no one was allowed to make a sound. Any peep out of Singer and his Da would kick the shite out of him. Literally, sometimes. Then one day Singer's old man comes back with a really black one on. Wee Singer is innocently chirping away with his Ma in the kitchen, but his Da gets the idea that there should be a meal on the table for him. He goes fucking mental. He grabs Singer and starts to beat the shite out of him. So his Ma comes to try to defend the wee fella. So do you know what he does?'

I shrugged. I looked at Singer: I had a good four inches on him, but he was a hard-looking bastard. Vicious-looking. But I didn't like listening to Sneddon rejoicing in his misery.

'He cut Singer's Ma's throat,' Sneddon answered his own question. There was a hint of awe in his voice. 'Took a penknife – a penknife mind – and cut her throat from ear to ear, right in front of the wee fella. So Singer's never sung – or spoken – since.'

'I'm sorry,' I said to Singer because it was the only thing I could think to say. He looked at me expressionlessly.

'Aye . . . a bad bastard was Singer's Da. They hung the fucker at Duke Street and Singer was put into an orphanage. Then a kind of funny farm because of him not talking and that.' Sneddon looked at Singer knowingly. 'But you're not mad, are you, Singer? Just bad . . . all the way through. I found out about him because Tam, one of my boys, did time with Singer. Shared a cell. Will I tell him what your speciality was, Singer?'

Singer, unsurprisingly, said nothing. But he didn't nod or move or blink.

'Someone grassed him up to the police for a robbery he did. But without the witness there was no evidence. But Singer didn't kill the bastard. He cut his fucking tongue out. All of it. Kind of poetic, isn't it?'

'Yeah . . .' I said. Singer's face was still impassive. 'Positively Audenesque.'

'Anyway,' said Sneddon. 'I like having Singer around. D'you know the ancient Greeks liked to have mutes around at funerals? Professional mourners. Anyway, I look after Singer now, don't I, Singer?'

Singer nodded.

'And Singer looks after me. And my interests.'

I was acutely aware of Twinkletoes' absence in the car on the way back into town, as if he had left twin voids of space and silence. I took a Player's Navy Blue and offered the packet to Singer, who shook his head without taking his eyes off the road. He was that kind of guy. Focussed. I had forgotten exactly where I'd left the car, but Singer found his way to it first shot.

'Thanks,' I said as I got out of the car. Singer was about to drive off when, on an impulse, I tapped on his window. He rolled it down.

'Listen, I just wanted to say . . .' What? What the hell was it I wanted to say? 'I just wanted to say that I'm sorry about the wisecracks I made . . . you know, about you not talking. I didn't know about . . . well, you know . . . that was a shitty break . . .' I fell silent. It seemed best considering I seemed to have lost the ability to string a coherent sentence together.

Singer looked at me for a moment, in that cold, expressionless way he had, then gave a nod. He drove off. I stood and watched the Humber disappear around the corner, wondering why the hell, after all of the other shit I had done and seen in my life, I had felt the need to apologize to a cheap Glasgow hoodlum. Maybe it was because what had happened to Singer had happened when he was a kid. It was the one thing I found tough to take: the crap that happens to kids. In war. In their own homes.

Not for the first time, I considered the colourful life I had forged for myself here in Glasgow. And the interesting people I got to meet.

CHAPTER THREE

It's funny: at the time, I didn't think of the week after Small Change's murder as 'the week after Small Change's murder'. I had other things to think about, other things to do. It's often only in retrospect that you see the significance of a particular moment in your life. At the time it's just the same old crap, and you just stumble along oblivious to the fact that you should be keeping a scrapbook, or a diary, or photographing the minutiae of your life; that at some time in the future you would look back and think, if only I'd known what the fuck was going on.

Obviously, I saw Lorna every day that week. And obviously I kept my hands out of her underwear – I am nothing if not a gentleman – and, anyway, experience had told me that the ardour of even the most enthusiastic of mattress companions diminishes with grief. Not with death; with grief. I'd learned during the war that death and violence tend to be powerful aphrodisiacs for both genders. Suffice it to say, I became the most solicitous and least lecherous of suitors.

To be honest, I had other distractions.

They say Eskimos have a hundred words for snow. Glaswegians must have twice that many for the different kinds of rain that batters down on the city year-round. In winter, Glasgow lies under an assault of chilled wet bullets; in summer, the rain falls in greasy, tepid globs, like the sky sweating on the city.

Completely atypically, Glasgow was experiencing a dry and searingly hot summer. Half of the city's population spent most of that summer looking up, squinting at the sky and trying to form the word *blue*.

I found the hot weather disconcerting. Usually any sunlight in Glasgow was mitigated by a sooty veil thrown up by the factories and tenement chimneys; but that summer there were disorientating moments when the sky cleared and the heat and the light reminded me of summers back home in New Brunswick. It was only ever a fleeting illusion, though, repeatedly shattered by the fuming, dark-billowing reality of the city around me.

At least I got to wear lightweight suits that hung better. When it came to material, the Scots had a year-round preference for tweed, the scratchier and denser the better. A Scottish acquaintance had once tried to reassure me that tweed from the Isle of Harris was less scratchy, explaining that this was because it was traditionally soaked in human urine. I could have been accused of being picky, but I preferred couture that hadn't been pissed on by an inbred crofter.

I had spent three days getting all the gen I could on Sneddon's fighter. Bobby Kirkcaldy had been born in Glasgow but raised in Lanarkshire, first in an orphanage and then by an aunt. Both his parents had died prematurely from heart attacks when Kirkcaldy was a child. Tragic, but not unusual: if cardiac disease had been a sport, then the entire British Olympic team would have been made up of Glaswegians.

Young Bobby Kirkcaldy had used his fists to fight his way up and out of the Motherwell slum that had been his adoptive home. To put his success in context, Motherwell was the kind of place anyone would fight like hell to get out of. I'd been able to track down a couple of businesses that Kirkcaldy had invested in and it was clear he was getting good advice on cashing in on his success when he eventually hung up his gloves. Either that, or he was as nifty with investment as he was in the ring. In fact, for someone approaching the height of his boxing career, he seemed to have his mind, and money, on other things.

My office was three floors up, across Gordon Street from Central Station, and by Thursday I had done just about all I could do on the 'phone and was going to take an afternoon trip out to see young Mr Kirkcaldy. I decided to drink a coffee and read the newspaper before I left. I like to keep up with things. I never knew when Rab Butler or Tony Eden would ask for my advice.

All the news was gloomy. Britain wasn't the only nation struggling with the loss of an empire: the French were having the stuffing kicked out of them in Indochina by the Vietminh. There had been a clash of razor gangs in the Gorbals. A man had been run over by a train on the outskirts of the city. The police hadn't issued a name. The only thing that cheered me up was an advertised assurance that, apparently, taking an Amplex chlorophyll tablet each day guaranteed breath and body freshness; obviously an attempt to break into an underexploited market.

I was in the middle of *Rip Kirby* when I got a pleasant surprise. A very pleasant, five-foot-three, blonde surprise. I recognized her as soon as she walked into my office, despite the fact that we had never met before. She dressed with an elegance that Glasgow didn't stretch to. Cream silk blouse, figure-hugging powder blue pencil skirt, long legs sheathed in sheer silk. Her throat was ringed with a necklace with pearls so big the diver must have had to bring them up one at a time. Earrings to match. She wore a small white pillbox-type hat and white gloves, but had a jacket that matched the skirt draped over the same forearm as a handbag that, in a previous life, had swum in the Nile or the Florida Everglades.

I stood up and tried to prevent my smile from resembling a leer. It probably just looked goofy. But Sheila Gainsborough was probably used to men smiling at her goofily.

'Hello, Miss Gainsborough,' I said. 'Please sit down. What can I do for you?'

'You know me?' She smiled a famous person's smile, that polite perfunctory baring of teeth that doesn't mean anything.

'Everybody knows you, Miss Gainsborough. Certainly everybody in Glasgow. I have to say I don't get many celebrities walking into my office.'

'Don't you?' She frowned, lowering her flawlessly arched eyebrows and wrinkling a fold of skin on her otherwise flawless brow. Flawlessly. 'I would have imagined . . .' Shrugging off the thought and the frown, she sat down and I followed suit. 'I've never been to a private detective before. Never seen one before, come to that, other than Humphrey Bogart in the pictures.'

'We're taller in real life.' I smiled at my own witticism. Goofily. 'And I call myself an enquiry agent. So why do you need to see one now?'

She unclipped the sixty-guinea crocodile and handed me a photograph. It was a professional, showbizzy shot. Colour. I didn't recognize the young man in the picture but decided in an instant that I didn't like him. The smile was fake and too self-assured. He was wearing an expensive-looking shirt open at the neck and arranged over the collar of an even more pricey-looking light grey suit. His chestnut hair was well cut and lightly oiled. He was good-looking, but in a too-slick and weak-chinned sort of way. Despite his dark hair, he had the same striking, pale blue eyes as Sheila Gainsborough.

'He's my brother. Sammy. My younger brother.'

'Is he in show business too, Miss Gainsborough?'

'No. Well, not really. He sings, occasionally. He's tried every other kind of business though. Some of which I'm afraid haven't been totally ... *honourable*.' She sighed and leaned forward, resting her forearms on the edge of my desk. Her skin was tanned. Not dark, just pale gold. The cute frown was back. 'It's maybe all my fault. I spoil him, give him more money than he can handle.' I noticed that she had a vaguely Americanized accent. I spoke the same way, but that was because I'd been raised in Canada. As far as I was aware, Sheila Gainsborough had never been further west than Dunoon. I guessed she had been voice-trained to sink the Glasgow in her accent somewhere deep and mid-Atlantic.

'Is Sammy in some kind of trouble?' I too leaned forward and frowned my concern, taking the opportunity to cast a glance down the front of her blouse.

'He's gone missing,' she said.

'How long?'

'A week. Maybe ten days. We had a meeting at the bank – he's overdrawn the account I set up for him – but he didn't turn up. That was last Thursday. I went to his apartment but he wasn't there. There was two days' mail behind the door.'

I took a pad from my desk drawer and scribbled a few notes on it. It was window dressing, people feel comforted if you take notes. Somehow it looks like you're taking it all that little bit more seriously. Nodding sagely as you write helps.

'Has Sammy done this kind of thing before. Gone off without letting you know?'

'No. Or at least not like this. Not for a week. Occasionally he's gone off on a bender. One ... two days, but that's all. And whenever I'm in town – you know, not on a tour or in London – we meet up every Saturday and have lunch in Cranston's Tea Rooms on Sauchiehall Street. He never misses it.'

I noted. I nodded. Sagely. 'You said his account is overdrawn – have there been any more withdrawals since he went awol?'

'I don't know . . .' Suddenly she looked perplexed, as if she'd let him down – let me down – by not checking. 'Can you find that out?'

''Fraid not. You say you were supposed to attend the meeting at the bank with him?'

'I'm a co-signatory,' she said. The frown still creased the otherwise flawless brow. With due cause, I thought. Her brother sounded like a big spender. A high liver. If he hadn't been trying to pull cash from his already overdrawn account, then he wasn't spending big or living high. Or maybe even simply not living.

'Then you can check,' I said. 'The bank will give you that information, but not me. Even the police would have to get a court order. Have you been to the police, Miss Gainsborough?'

'I was waiting. I kept thinking Sammy would turn up. Then, when he didn't, I thought I'd be better getting a private detective . . . I mean enquiry agent.'

'Why me?' I asked. 'I mean, who put you in contact with me?'

'I have a road manager, Jack Beckett. He says he knows you.'

I frowned. 'Can't say . . .'

'Or at least knows *of* you. He said . . .' She hesitated, as if unsure to commit the rest of her thought to words. 'He said that you were reliable, but that you had contact with – well, that you *knew* people that were more the kind that Sammy has been mixing with.'

'I see . . .' I said, still trying to place the name Jack Beckett and making a mental note that if I ever did come across him, to thank him appropriately for the glowing character reference.

There was a silence. A taxi sounded its horn outside on Gordon

Street. A river-bubble of voices rose up from outside and through the window I had left open in the vain hope it would cool the office. I noticed a trickle of sweat on Sheila Gainsborough's sleek neck.

'So exactly *what* kind of people was Sammy mixing with? You said he had gotten involved in less than honourable businesses. What do you mean?'

'Like I said, Sammy isn't really in show business as such. But he does do the odd singing job. He's not great, if I'm honest, but good enough for Glasgow. He's been singing in nightclubs and mixing with a bad crowd. Gambling too. I think that's where a lot of the money has been going.'

'Which clubs?'

'I don't know . . . not the ones I started in. There was one he went to a lot. I think he sang there too. The Pacific Club down near the river.'

'Oh . . . yes,' I said. Oh fuck, I thought. Handsome Jonny Cohen's place.

'You know it?'

'I know the owner. I can have a word.'

'Have you ever heard of the Poppy Club?' she asked.

'Can't say that I have. Why?'

'When I went to his flat there was a note by the telephone that said "The Poppy Club". Nothing else. No number. I looked up the 'phone book but there's no "Poppy Club" listed in either Glasgow or Edinburgh.'

I wrote the name down in my notebook. Reassuringly. 'What's Sammy's full name?' I asked.

'James Samuel Pollock.'

'Pollock?'

'That's my real name. Well, it *was* my real name. I changed it by deed poll.'

'So you were Sheila Pollock?'

'Ishbell Pollock.'

'Ishbell?'

'My agent didn't think that Ishbell Pollock had the kind of ring to it that a singing star's name should have.'

'Really?' I said, as if confused as to why anyone would be blind to the charms of a name like Ishbell Pollock. They had done a good job on her. A Glasgow club singer, one amongst thousands. But they had had great raw material to work with. Sheila Gainsborough had the looks – she certainly had the looks – and the voice to stand out from the crowd. She'd been talent-scouted. Groomed. Repackaged. Managed. She maybe had the looks and the voice but the name Ishbell Pollock and the Glasgow accent would have been dropped faster than utility-mark panties on VE Day.

I wrote Sammy's full name in my notebook. 'When did you last see Sammy?'

'Lunch at the Tea Rooms, a week past Saturday.'

'What about friends . . . girls . . . people he used to hang around with? And you said he has been associating with a bad crowd. Can you put any names to them?'

'He has this friend, Barnier. A Frenchman. Sammy mentioned him a couple of times. I *think* they were friends, but it could have been a business thing.'

'First name?'

She shook her head. 'Sammy always just called him Barnier. There can't be that many Frenchies in Glasgow.'

'I don't know,' I said. 'They probably come here in their droves for the cuisine.' We both smiled. 'Anyone else?'

'I was at his flat one day and he got a telephone call from a girl. They sounded intimate. All I got was her first name. Claire. But there were a couple of guys he knew who I really didn't like the look of. Rough types.'

'Names?'

'Sorry. I only saw them once, waiting for Sammy outside the club. They had the look as if . . . I don't know . . . as if they didn't want to be seen. But they were a shiftless sort. Late twenties, one about five-eight with dark hair, the other maybe an inch shorter with sandy hair. The one with the dark hair has a scar on his forehead. Shaped like a crescent.'

I sat and looked at her, deep in thought. She looked back eagerly, obviously reassured that she had provoked some deep, investigative cogitations. What I was really thinking about was what it would be like to bend her over my desk.

'Okay. Thanks,' I said once the picture was complete. 'Would it be possible for us to go to your brother's flat . . . have a look around?'

She looked at her watch. 'I need to be on the sleeper to London tonight. I've a lot to do beforehand. Could we go now?'

I stood up and smiled. 'My car is around the corner.'

The Atlantic had been sitting in the sun and I rolled down the windows before holding the door open for Sheila Gainsborough to get in. I found myself casting an eye up and down the street in the desperate hope that someone – anyone – I knew was there to see me let this beautiful, rich and famous woman into my car. Two youths passed without noticing, followed by an old man wearing a flat cap and, despite the temperature, a heavy, thick, dark blue jacket and a neckerchief tied at his throat. He paused only to spit profusely on the pavement. I didn't take it as a sign of his being impressed.

Even with the windows open, the car was stifling; the air heady in its confines: hot wood and leather mingled with the lavender from Sheila's perfume and a vague hint of a musky odour from her body.

Sammy Pollock's flat was on the west side of the city centre, but not quite the West End. We drove without speaking along Sauchiehall Street to where the numbers started to climb into the thousands and she told me to turn right. A ribbon of park broke up the ranks of three-storey Georgian terraces. There were some kids playing on the grass and mothers, prams parked beside them, sat indolently on the park benches, beaten listless by summer heat and motherhood.

Pollock's apartment was actually over two levels of one of the semi-grand stone terraces. At one time the terrace would have gleamed golden sandstone. A once brightly coloured arch of stained glass and lead work sat above the door, almost Viennese: Charles Rennie Mackintosh style or similar. But Glasgow was a city of ceaseless work. Dirty work. The unending belchings of smoke and soot had blackened the stone and dulled the glass. It was like seeing a parson in frock coat and breeches after he'd been sent down a mine for a few shifts.

'You've always had a key?' I asked Sheila as she unlocked the door.

She sighed. 'Look, Mr Lennox, I can tell you've guessed the set-up. I own the flat. I own it, I furnished it and I let Sammy stay in it. I also give him an allowance.'

'How old is Sammy?'

'Twenty-three.'

'I see,' I said. I thought of a twenty-three-year-old being handed everything by a sister who, herself, had yet to hit thirty. I thought about when I had been twenty-three, fighting my way through Europe with only a vague hope that I'd make it to twenty-four. Sammy Pollock was only thirteen years younger than me, but he was a completely different generation. Lived in a different world.

She read my mind. 'You disapprove of Sammy's way of life?'

'I envy Sammy's way of life. I wish I'd had it when I was his age. You're a very generous sister.'

'You have to understand something . . .' Letting her hand rest on the door handle, she looked at me earnestly with the bright blue eyes. 'I'm five years older than Sammy. Our parents are both dead and I'm . . . well, I feel *responsible* for my brother. And I've been lucky. Got the breaks. And that's put me in the position to help the only person I care about in the world. Sammy's not a bad kid. He's just a bit silly at times. Immature. I'm just worried that he's got himself in with a bad crowd. Got into trouble.'

'I understand.' I nodded to the door she still held shut. 'Shall we?'

'Someone's been here.' It was the first thing she said when we walked into the living room. Sure enough, the place was a mess. Some of the mess was clearly bachelor living at its best – over-full ashtrays, sticky-bottomed beer bottles, and whisky glasses bonding maliciously with the expensive walnut of the side tables, a jacket tossed carelessly on an armchair, a couple of dirty plates and a coffee cup. It was a vernacular I was familiar with myself. But there was another dimension to the disorder, a third-party, purposeful element. Like someone had been looking for something, and in a hurry.

'Sammy?' Sheila called out and moved urgently across the living room towards the hall. I took a couple of steps and halted her progress with a hand on her arm. The skin was warm; moist beneath my fingertips.

'Let me have a look,' I said. 'You wait here.' I had already closed my hand around the leather-dressed spring-steel sap I carried in my pocket. When I was in the hall and out of Sheila's sight, I took the sap out.

'Mr Pollock?' Nothing. 'Hello?'

I moved along the hall. An ivory-coloured telephone sat on a chest-high hallstand, another full ashtray beside it. I noticed some of the butts were filters, not something you saw a lot of, and they were rimmed with crimson lipstick. I slipped one into my pocket. I moved on, checking each of the rooms as I passed. The flat was bright and expensively furnished, but each room had been turned over, with papers and other debris scattered all over the floors. I climbed the stairs and found the same on the upper floor. I came to Pollock's bedroom. More clutter strewn across the floor. Something shiny caught my eye, glittering in the sunshine. Once I was sure we were the only ones in the flat, I called down and asked Sheila to come upstairs.

'You said you were sure someone has been in here. I take it the flat wasn't like this when you were last here?'

She shook her head. 'Sammy was never house-proud, but not this . . . this looks like he's been burgled.'

I nodded to the bedside cabinet. There was a lead crystal ashtray and a brick of a gold table lighter. 'No house breaker is going to leave without that in their pocket. This hasn't been a burglary, this was a search.' I bent down and picked up from the floor the shiny item that had caught my eye. It was a small, polished, steel-hinged box, lying open on the floor. I looked around my feet and found the contents that had spilled out.

'Does your brother have any medical condition I should know about?' I placed the syringe and needle back in the metal box and held them out for Sheila to see. 'Is he diabetic?'

Sheila looked at the box and her expression darkened. 'No. He doesn't have any medical condition.'

'But this means something to you?' I asked.

She looked at me hard for a moment before answering. 'I've been around a lot of musicians. It's part of my job. Musicians and artists . . . well, they experiment with stuff.'

'Narcotics?'

'Yes. But I don't think . . . or at least I've never had any reason to think that Sammy would be involved in that kind of nonsense.'

For a moment, we both gazed silently at the metal syringe box in my hands, as if it would surrender its secrets to us if we stared at it long enough.

'It could have been Sammy himself, of course,' I said. I could have sounded more convincing. 'Maybe he came back to collect stuff. Pack a bag.' I pocketed the syringe box.

'I'll check his wardrobes and drawers,' she said dully. 'Maybe I'll notice something missing. If he's taken clothes . . .' She stepped past me. The room was hot and stuffy and as she passed, I again picked up a whiff of lavender and musk: the dressing and the flesh. Oh boy, Lennox, I thought, you've got it bad this time.

There was a sound from downstairs and we both froze. Someone was opening the apartment door. Sheila had closed the snib over behind her and that meant whoever was coming in had a key. Again I stopped Sheila as she made her way to the bedroom door, clearly to call out her brother's name. I put a finger to my lips, slipped past her and moved as quickly and quietly as I could back down the stairs, again unpocketing the spring-handled sap. I reached the bottom of the stairs just as a young man with black hair and a dark complexion opened the vestibule door and stepped into the hall.

'Hello,' I said with a friendly smile, keeping the sap out of sight. The dark-haired man looked at me, his eyes wide with surprise.

'Who are you? What are you doing here?' The eyes narrowed as surprise gave way to suspicion. I kept smiling and tightened my grip on the sap.

'You know in these films,' I said, 'where someone says "I'm

asking the questions here"? Well, that's me. Let's start with why you have a key for an apartment you don't own or rent and seem to come and go as you please.'

'Are you a cop?' he asked.

'Let's just say I'm investigating the disappearance of Sammy Pollock.'

'But you're not a cop . . .' His eyes narrowed further. Suddenly he looked unsure of himself. 'You sent by Largo?'

'Largo?'

He looked relieved, then the hardness came back to his eyes. His head lowered slightly into his shoulders and he slipped a hand into the side pocket of his jacket. Playtime.

Upstairs, Sheila Gainsborough must have crept towards the stairs. A floorboard creaked. My dark-haired chum's eyes cast in the direction of the sound and he looked less sure of himself. He clearly thought I had reinforcements in the wings. I was a little piqued that he thought I'd need them to deal with him.

'If you're not a cop, then fuck you.' He turned and went back into the small tiled vestibule, moving swiftly but without panic.

'Oh no you don't . . .' I reached out and grabbed his shoulder. 'Just hold on a minute . . .'

He was about three or four inches shorter than me and he misjudged the vicious backward jab with his elbow. Instead of hitting me in the face or throat, it slammed painfully into my chest and sent me backwards. It gave him time to open the front door and he was stepping through it when I ran for him. I slammed the door shut on him with the flat of my foot. All my weight behind the kick. The edge of the door caught him on the shoulder but glanced off and smashed into his cheek, jamming his head between the door edge and the jamb. He was stunned. A thick bulge of blood swelled up on his cheek, then turned into a torrent down the side of his face and neck, staining his shirt crimson.

'Oh, sorry,' I said. 'Did I catch you with the door?'

His hand made for his pocket and whatever was in it, but his movements were sluggish and unfocussed. I snapped the sap at him hard. Twice. The first blow cracked something in his wrist and the second caught him on the nape of his neck. His lights went out and he went down, half in and half out of the door. I grabbed him by the back of his shirt collar and dragged him back into the flat.

I turned to see Sheila standing halfway down the stairs, her eyes wide and a hand to her mouth.

'Did you have to do that?' she said, once she had recovered sufficiently.

'He had a go,' I said. 'And he's got some kind of weapon in his pocket. He was going for it.' I bent down and pulled out a switchblade. I flicked the release and held the knife up for her to see. 'See ... self-defence.'

'You seem to relish defending yourself, Mr Lennox.'

I shrugged and pulled the slumped figure to his feet. He was still groggy but looked at me maliciously. I didn't like that so I gave him the back of my hand. Twice and hard across the uninjured side of his face. Setting boundaries.

'For God's sake, that's enough, Lennox ...' Sheila stepped forward staring hard at me. She was right. It was enough. It was too much. I had that hot, tight feeling in my chest. The desire to hurt someone else that I learned during the war slept in me. I could see Sheila didn't like the person she was looking at. At least we had that in common: I didn't like me much either.

I steered our visitor back into the flat and dropped him into the armchair. Sheila followed us in and leaned against the wall.

She lit a cigarette and smoked it urgently. Other than that she was calm and collected. Impressive. I gave the man in the chair the once-over: mid-twenties, the double-breasted blue pinstripe not cheap but not expensive, same for the shirt and tie. I noticed his shoes were not the newest and brown leather. I felt like giving him another slap just for that: black or burgundy shoes with blue pinstripe; not brown.

'What's your name?'

'Fuck off,' he said sullenly, cradling his injured wrist.

'There's a lady present,' I said, grabbing a fistful of pinstripe Burton. Watch your mouth or you'll get a little more pampering from me.'

He looked across at Sheila and muttered something apologetic.

'So what's your name?'

'Costello.'

'Very funny, I expect Bud Abbott is outside on lookout.' I gave his mid-price tailoring a twist in my fist.

'It's true. Paul Costello. That's my name.'

I let him go and straightened up. 'You Jimmy Costello's boy?'

'Yeah. That's me.' He looked suddenly sure of himself. 'You've heard of my Da? Then you'll know that he won't like it much when I tell him you did this to me ...' He held up his wrist and turned his cheek to me.

'Why do you have a key to this flat?' I asked.

'Mind your own business. I'm going to 'phone my Da and he's going to sort you out for this good and proper.'

I nodded. 'Miss Gainsborough, could you wait for me in the car?' I held out my car keys to her but she didn't take them.

'What are you going to do?' she asked, her tone simultaneously injecting disapproval and suspicion.

'Don't worry,' said Costello. 'He's not going to do anything.

He didn't know who he was dealing with. Now he does and he's going to try and talk his way out of it. Except he won't.' He sneered at me.

'Like Mr Costello says, we have a bit of a disagreement. I need to talk to him in private.' I shook the car keys as if I was ringing a bell. 'Please.'

She took the keys sullenly and left, slamming the door behind her. After she'd gone, Paul Costello glared at me maliciously.

'Shiteing yourself now, aren't you? You know who my Da is all right. You should check who you're dealing with before you start throwing your weight about.' He winced, cradling his injured wrist with his other hand. 'I think you've fucking broken it.'

'Let me look at it.' I bent down and Costello looked at me suspiciously. 'Seriously, let me look at it.'

He held out his hand and I gingerly felt the wrist joint. He yelled out.

'It's not that bad,' I said. 'I think I've cracked a couple of bones, that's all.'

'That's all? Wait till my Da finds out.'

'You're right,' I said, still examining the wrist. 'You should always know who you're dealing with before having a go. Take me . . .'

Costello winced again as I found a sensitive spot on his wrist. It was beginning to swell up. Maybe there was a more significant break after all.

'As I was saying, take me . . . I do know who your father is.' I dug my thumb hard into Costello's swollen wrist. He screamed. 'And I don't give a crap. D'you think that your pig-arsed Mick father is someone I should be scared of?'

He tried to pull his hand away and I rewarded him with another vicious squeeze. More screaming.

CRAIG RUSSELL | 45

'Truth is, I work for the Three Kings. You know the Three Kings?'

Costello nodded, staring wildly at the wrist he could not free from my grip.

'Well, I work for them all, on and off. I do know your father and he's nothing in the scheme of things. A nobody. If Hammer Murphy decided to squash him he could, as easy as a bug. So you run to Pop with tales and I'll do the same with Hammer Murphy. We understand each other?' I punctuated my question with another vicious squeeze of his wrist. His face contorted and when I eased the pressure he nodded violently again.

'Okay,' I continued. 'Now that we understand each other, I think we should have our little chat. Now . . . why do you have a key to this flat?'

'Sammy gave me one.'

'Why?'

'We're friends.'

'What do you mean "friends"? Good-mate friends or knob-jockey friends?'

'What the fu—'

I interrupted his profanity with a light squeeze.

'I'm no poof,' he protested when he got his breath back. 'Sammy and me are just friends.'

'Now you're going to find this a tad difficult to believe,' I said self-deprecatingly, 'but I have a lot of friends myself, and none of them have a key to my place. Try again, Mr Costello . . . *Junior.*'

'That's the truth. Sammy lets me crash here every now and again. I work at the club too.'

'What club? The Poppy Club?'

'Poppy Club? I've never heard of it. I work at the Riviera . . . my Da's place. Sammy sings there now and again.'

'The Riviera?' My laugh came out a snort. 'Very glamorous. And on what particular part of the Ligurian coast does your father's club reside?'

Costello looked at me as if I was talking Japanese. In Glasgow it paid to keep your cultural references simple. 'Where's the Riviera Club?'

'Partick. Near the river,' he said.

This time my snort came out a full-blown laugh.

Costello looked offended. 'It's a classy place.'

'I'm sure it is. It must be high on every VIP's itinerary. I would guess you see a lot of Princess Margaret.'

'Fuck you.'

'Now, now, Junior. Don't get tetchy or I'll hold your hand again. Speaking of holding hands, why are you so cosy with Sammy Pollock? I wouldn't have put you two together.'

'We've got ideas. Business ideas. He's fed up of just being Sheila Gainsborough's brother and I'm fed up being thought of as just Jimmy Costello's son.'

'Please stop. I'm getting all teary. When did you last see Sammy?'

'A couple of weeks ago. I was out of town.'

'Where out of town?'

'What's it to you?'

I smiled and squeezed. He winced and glowered.

'London . . .' He strained it through his teeth. 'I was down in London for a couple of weeks.'

'So you didn't know he was missing?' I let go of his wrist and lit a cigarette.

'You fucking enjoy this, don't you?' He smiled maliciously through his pain. 'Hurting people. You really do enjoy it, don't you?'

'Oh, please don't generalize . . .' I looked offended, then smiled ingratiatingly. 'I don't enjoy hurting *people*, I enjoy hurting *you*. Let's just say it's our thing. Now ...' I let the smile drop as I leaned forward. 'Did you know Sammy was missing?'

'Missing? Is he missing? I know he's not about. That doesn't mean he's missing. I tried to get him on the 'phone a couple of times from London. I just thought I'd missed him, been unlucky. That's why I came around today.'

'What kind of business?' I blew smoke into his face.

'What?'

'What kind of business are you and Sammy thinking about getting involved in?'

'Just ... I don't know ... artist management. We were going to represent some of the musicians who work the pubs and clubs. The better musicians. We know a lot of them. So we thought we'd offer management.'

'Are you sure you're competing with Bernard Delfont and not ICI?'

'What?' Costello gave me an irritated frown.

'I wondered if you were thinking about getting into the pharmaceutical business.' I took the metal syringe box from my pocket, opened it and held it out for Costello to see.

'Is this supposed to mean something to me?'

'I was just wondering if you and Sammy were thinking about supplying more than career advice to your musician chums.'

'You've lost me, mister ...' If Costello was lying then he was hiding it well. Although most of his expression was tied up with pain. I got the feeling his cheek was now competing with his wrist for his attention.

'Who's Largo?'

'What?'

'You thought I was a cop, then you thought I'd been sent by someone called Largo.'

'Largo? Nothing. I mean nobody. Someone I owe some money to. I thought he'd sent you round here to see if I'd show up.'

'Does Sammy know Largo? Does he owe him money too?'

'No ...' Costello kept my gaze. He didn't look like he was lying, but with a slimy piece like him it was difficult to tell.

'You didn't answer me. Who is Largo? I've never heard of him.'

'Just a guy.'

'Just a guy who sends people to collect his debts, apparently.'

'Listen, Largo's got nothing to do with Sammy. They don't know each other.' He winced and eased his wrist closer to his chest with his other hand.

'Give me the key,' I said, pocketing the syringe box again.

'What?'

'Give me the key. Sammy Pollock doesn't own this flat and you sure as hell don't. So hand it over.'

After he handed me the key with his good hand I hoisted him up and escorted him out of the flat. The heat hit us as soon as we were on the street.

'You've not heard the last of this.' Costello glowered at me, clutching his injured wrist. I took a step towards him and he scuttled off in the opposite direction.

Sheila Gainsborough was standing by the car, the sun catching the gold in her hair.

'Well, did you manage to beat the truth out of him?'

'Listen, Miss Gainsborough, I think we need to understand one another. Young Mr Costello, whose acquaintance we've just made, is a less than desirable type. I know his father, or at least know of him. Jimmy Costello is even less desirable. He's a gangster and a thug. You've come to me with a problem: your brother has gone missing and the first thing we find out is that his flat has been turned over by someone. Then Costello junior arrives with a key to the flat you pay for and seems to come and go as he pleases. I'm sorry if my methods seemed a little *direct* but, having made young Mr Costello's acquaintance, I am now a lot more concerned about your brother's disappearance than I was an hour ago.'

Sheila Gainsborough did her cute frown again. 'Did Costello explain what he was doing there and why he had a key?'

'Well, to start with, he doesn't have one any more.' I handed her the key and it was swallowed by the alligator. 'Costello claims they were friends and potential business partners, but he was pretty vague about what type of business. Representing musicians. Does your brother know anything about working as a talent agent?'

'Sammy? Not a thing.'

'I doubt if Costello has taken a course on it either.' I started the car but paused before moving off. 'Does the name "Largo" mean anything to you?'

'What, the place in Fife?'

'No, this isn't a place. It's a person. Costello thought I had been sent by someone called Largo.'

Sheila stared ahead for a moment, thinking. The scent of her hung in the small, humid silence. 'No,' she said eventually. 'I don't know anyone called Largo. And I can't say I've ever heard Sammy mention anyone by that name.'

'Okay,' I said, and smiled. 'I'll take you back into town. I'd recommend you continue with your plans and travel down to London. I'll have a sniff around. Is there somewhere I can get in touch?'

Snapping open the alligator, she pulled out a visiting card. 'This is my agent's number. His name is Humphrey Whithorn. If you need to get in touch, he can always find me. But what are you going to do? You've got nothing to go on.'

'I've got the clubs where he worked. I can start there.' I took the card. The name Sheila Gainsborough sunk silver grey into thick white vellum. Whithorn's name was at the bottom right, smaller. Like everything else about her the card shouted quality and money. I tried to imagine the name *Ishbell Pollock* on the card. It didn't take. 'In the meantime, it would be good if you could check with your bank to see if Sammy has made any attempts to withdraw more money.'

I drove her back to my office where I asked more questions about Sammy's lifestyle. After we ran out of straws to clutch at, I promised to do everything I could to find her brother. Stretching out a hand for me to shake, she nodded and stood up. I walked her to the door – not much of a walk in my tiny hot-box office – and promised her that I would keep in touch. Watching her as she made her way back down the stairwell, I noticed how she seemed to glide, rather than walk, her gloved hand hovering above the banister and her high heels light on the stone steps. Sheila Gainsborough had a grace I hadn't seen in a woman for a long time. It reminded me, for a moment, of someone else and the memory hit me in the gut. Someone else was someone dead.

When Sheila disappeared from view, I turned back into the heat of my office. I sat at my desk for a long time trying to pinpoint the source of the uneasy feeling that was beginning to gnaw at me.

My digs were on Great Western Road. It was a good enough place, the whole upper floor of a typical Glasgow Victorian villa.

It's not uncommon to come across a place to stay by happen-chance: someone knows someone who knows somebody else who has a room to let. The happenchance that had led to my flat becoming available was a German U-boat fortuitously hitting a Royal Navy Reserve frigate directly midships. The frigate had gone down faster than a Clydebank whore on a payday docker, and took with it a young junior officer called White. No big deal: just one of the millions of brief human candles that had been prematurely snuffed out during the war. This insignificant statistic, however, had been a universe-shattering tragedy for the pretty young wife and two daughters of the junior naval officer. A future that had once shone so brightly now lay rusting at the bottom of the Atlantic with the hulk of the broken frigate.

I had encountered the fractured White family when looking for a place to stay. Mrs White had advertised the place in the *Glasgow Herald*. With only a Navy widow's pension to survive on, Fiona White had come up with a drastic but practical solution: she had the upstairs of the house converted into a more or less self-contained flat and put it up for rent, with an insistence that the successful tenant be able to display exceptional references. My references had been the most exceptional you could buy from a forger and Mrs White had accepted me. What I couldn't quite work out was why she had let me stay, given that I had had a couple of late night visits from the local constabulary over the last couple of years. But, there again, the place wasn't cheap and I was sedulously prompt with the rent each week. The truth was that I could have easily moved on to a better place, but I had become fond of the little White family. Anyone who knew me wouldn't have been at all surprised that my first thought when I had met the pretty young widow was that maybe I could console her. And she was the type of woman you really wanted to console. But, as time went on, something unpleasantly chivalrous had crept unbidden into my attitude towards her and I felt somewhat protective of the sad little family downstairs.

There was a wall 'phone on the stairs that we both shared and when I got back to my digs I 'phoned Lorna. I had hoped to satisfy her with a call but she was insistent that I come round.

Doing the gentlemanly thing was getting to be a bad habit and I drove across to Pollokshields. When I arrived at the house, I was surprised to find my Hebridean chum back on guard duty at the front door, 'chust forr the laydees peace hoff mind' he sang reassuringly to me.

I sat between Lorna and Maggie, the atmosphere so charged that I expected to be struck by lightning at any time. I comforted. I soothed. I made my talk as small as it was possible to make it, avoiding anything that might remind us all that we were just twenty-four hours on from a brutal murder. Maggie made some tea and offered me a cigarette from a hundred-box on the coffee table. I noticed the brand was Four Square, made by Dobie of Paisley.

'That's not what you were smoking the other night,' I said. 'The fancy cork tips.'

'Oh those?' She shrugged. 'Jimmy got me them. It's not my usual brand.'

Reaching into my jacket pocket, I pulled out the stub I'd lifted from Sammy Pollock's hall stand ashtray. I held it out to Maggie so she could see the twin gold bands around the filter. She frowned.

'That's them all right. Where d'you get that?'

'It's a case I'm working on. Missing person.'

'Is the missing person French?'

'Not that I'm aware. Why do you ask that?'

'Montpellier, that's the brand. French. Jimmy got half a dozen packets from someone. Probably smuggled. Maybe that's why you've found someone else smoking them. Maybe someone's smuggled a lorry load in.'

'Could be.' I turned to Lorna. 'Have the police got any news? Have they said anything about the investigation?'

'Superintendent McNab has been back,' she said. Her eyelids looked heavy and settled-in grief had dulled her expression. 'He asked some more questions.'

'What kind of questions?'

'Who Dad had seen over the last few weeks. If anything unusual happened.'

I nodded. Willie Sneddon was right to keep his meeting and dealings with Small Change quiet. 'And did anything unusual happen recently?'

'No.' It was Maggie who answered. 'Not that either of us knew about. But Jimmy played his cards close to his chest. He kept anything to do with business to himself.' She paused for a moment. 'There was only one thing . . . not worth mentioning . . .'

'Go on . . .'

'Someone left a box for him. A delivery.'

'I remember that,' said Lorna, frowning. 'It was strange. A wooden box with nothing in it but a couple of sticks and a ball of wool.'

'Wool?'

'Yes,' said Lorna. 'Red and white wool all bound up together.'

'Doesn't sound significant,' I said. 'Did the police go through your father's stuff again? I mean in his office?'

'No. Why?'

'I just wondered.' I shrugged and sipped my tea. 'Did your dad keep an appointment book at home?'

'Why are you asking?' It was Maggie who cut in, more than a hint of suspicion in her voice. The thing about suspicion is that it can be infectious and I found myself wondering why she felt the need to be cautious.

'Like I said to you before, the police aren't the most imaginative bunch. Maybe they didn't think to check for an appointment book at his home.'

'Jimmy didn't need one,' said Maggie. 'He kept everything up here ...' She tapped a demi-waved temple. 'He didn't need an appointment book.'

'That's what I thought ... Never mind.'

'Do you think it would help?' asked Lorna, without any of her stepmother's suspicion.

'Maybe. At least we would know who he had seen on the day he died.' I decided to drop it. Maybe Maggie's answer would be enough to get Sneddon off my back.

I stayed for over an hour. Or at least until I felt I had fulfilled my duty as consort to the bereaved daughter. Lorna saw me to the door and kissed me as I was leaving. It was a desperate kind of embrace and her fingers squeezed tight and hard on my arms. It made me feel sad. Sad because she really needed something from me and I really wanted to give it to her. But I couldn't, because it wasn't there in me to give.

Lorna and I had been in it for the laughs, nothing more. And that was the way our little diversion should have played. But now, with her father murdered and finding herself alone, she was looking for something that neither of us had signed up for.

She seemed to sense its absence and drew back from me. Something cold had formed in her eyes: a frost of realization and resentment.

'Listen Lorna ...' I began.

'Save it, Lennox,' she said.

When I came out of the mouth of the drive, a car turning in was forced to brake. I waved my thanks but the driver ignored me, heading up the drive as soon as I was clear. He didn't even look in my direction, but I took a long look at him. The car was moderately fancy, a nearly new, maroon Lanchester Leda or Daimler Conquest, polished to gleam like a sleek droplet of fresh blood. The driver himself looked pretty polished: he was driving hatless so I could see he was around thirty with black hair and a pencil moustache. Neat. Tailored, as far as I could see. I pulled up at the kerb and considered going back up to the house to see what he wanted. He wasn't a cop. Too well-turned out and expensively carriaged. I got out of the car and walked a little way up the drive, ducking behind a bush to take a surreptitious look. He was at the door and I could now see I was right about his suit. It was expensive. He was tall, maybe a couple of inches on me, which was rare for Glasgow. Maggie opened the door and let him in. She knew him, that was clear and they both unconsciously took a look back down the drive, as if checking no one was watching. Or maybe he had mentioned our brief encounter at the bottom of the drive. They couldn't spot me behind my euonymus camouflage and disappeared into the house. There had been something about the way they had greeted each other that lay somewhere between the intimate and the professional. Maybe they had some business together.

There was, of course, a limit to how surreptitious they were being: Lorna was still in the house. Unless. I had a less than charitable thought about my recently bereaved sweetheart and dismissed it almost in the same instant it occurred to me. No conspiracy here, Lennox. And even if there is, I told myself, leave it alone. You've been warned. And anyway, while there might have been a moral imperative to help bring Small Change's killer to justice, I had paying cases to work on.

And I was never much one for moral imperatives.

Chapter Four

It was getting late but I thought I'd call into the Horsehead Bar for a snifter before heading home. The Horsehead had become my unofficial second office. At one time my main office, but recently I'd been trying to make at least a half-hearted stab at legitimacy and had been spending less time there.

When I arrived, Big Bob the Barman grinned at me. I grinned back. He was a good sort, Big Bob. I'd often wondered if he'd become a barman for the alliterative effect; that if he had been known as Fat Fred he would have become a fireman. Whatever Big Bob had been before his time behind the bar, he was a tough son-of-a-bitch now. So close to the war, there was a bit of an unspoken rule: you recognized other men who'd been through the mincer and you didn't talk about it. You identified each other as a common breed, but you didn't talk about it.

'Well fucking well.' Bob poured me a Canadian Club. 'Where have you been? I thought you'd fucked off back to Canada.'

'You working for the New Brunswick tourist office too?' I asked, he frowned. 'I've been busy, Bob. Anyone been asking for me?'

'Naw ... just Little Bollocks over there.' He nodded in the direction of a youth at the end of the bar. I beckoned for him to come over.

'I take it he's been nursing that half all night?' I asked Bob, who gave a knowing look and nodded. 'Give him a fresh pint.'

'How's it going, Mr Lennox?' Davey Wallace beamed at me as he came round to my end of the bar and Big Bob handed him his beer. Davey was about five feet-seven, as fresh-faced as the Glasgow atmosphere would allow, and dressed in a too-big second-hand suit that had been expensive once. A war and a generation ago.

'Hi, Davey,' I said.

'Business good?' he bubbled with enthusiasm. 'Any new cases?'

'Same old stuff, Davey,' I answered with a smile. Davey Wallace was a dreamer. A good kid, but a dreamer. For many within its boundaries, Glasgow was as much a prison as a home. The bars that confined them were the class system and, in almost every case, the lack of any viable alternative to a life of manual labour. The shipyards and the steelworks devoured the city's young: I'd often wondered if Rotten Row, Glasgow's appropriately named maternity hospital, simply put 'apprentice' instead of 'boy' on birth certificates.

Davey was an apprentice – an apprentice welder – working the morning shift in the shipyard. Started at fifteen and would most likely work there until he was sixty-five, by which time he would have given up his passion for Rock'n'Roll, probably because he'd be deaf from the constant riveting before he hit forty. But now, Davey Wallace, seventeen years old, parentless at seven, in an orphanage until fifteen, unmarried and with no kids yet to bind him further to an ineluctable industrial fate, escaped into the cinema every afternoon and Saturday night, where he would meet up with a different gang: Bogart, Cagney, Mitchum, Robinson, Mature.

When Davey had found out that I was a real-life enquiry agent, he had approached me in the bar like a Greek shepherd approaching Zeus. Since then, he had taken every opportunity to remind me that if I was ever looking for help ...

'Thanks for the pint, Mr Lennox.'

'You're welcome, Davey. Shouldn't you be in bed? What about your early shift?'

'I sleep in the afternoons, mostly.' Then, as if correcting himself: 'But I'm always available ... you know, if you needed any help on one of your cases, Mr Lennox. I'm always here.'

I exchanged a look with Big Bob, who grinned.

'Listen, Davey,' I said. 'It's not like you think it is. It's not like in the movies. There's nothing glamorous about what I do for a living.'

His expression dulled. 'You should try working down at the shipyards. Anything's glamorous compared to that.'

'Really,' I grinned. 'I would have thought it was riveting ...'

Davey either didn't get or didn't appreciate the gag and stared at his pint glumly. It was, I had noticed, a Scottish tradition. I sighed.

'Listen, Davey, I can't offer you a job because I don't have a job to offer. I struggle to pay my own way at times. But here's the deal ... if anything comes up where I need an extra pair of eyes, or need any kind of help, I'll give you a shout. Okay?'

He looked up from his beer and beamed at me. 'Anything, Mr Lennox. You can rely on me.'

'Okay, Davey. Why don't you finish your beer and get off home. Like I say, I'll get in touch if I need anything.'

I let him hang on my elbow till he finished his drink. After he was gone, Big Bob came back and poured me another Canadian Club.

'You realize I only keep this pish in here for you,' he said. 'Why can't you drink Scotch like everybody else?'

I cast my gaze around the bar, trying to penetrate the blue-grey cigarette haze. A knot of older men in flat caps sat huddled around a table in the corner playing dominoes and smoking scrappy roll-up cigarettes. Swirled in cloud-like tobacco smoke, they paused from their game only to sip their whisky and laid their dominoes on the beer-ringed table top with the joyfulness of grim Titans toppling graveyard headstones. Glasgow at its most Goyaesque.

'I don't know, Bob,' I said wistfully. 'Maybe it's a delight I'm saving myself for . . .'

'Oh for fuck's sake . . .' Bob said, suddenly distracted and looking over my shoulder. I turned and saw that four young men had come in through the side door of the public bar.

'Tommy . . . Jimmy . . .' Bob called to the two other barmen and the three of them stepped out from behind the bar with a squared-up purposefulness and crossed to the young men. I noticed that the newcomers were dressed in rough work clothes; one wore a heavy leather armless tabard over his jacket and all four were wearing rubber boots. I noticed that their hair was longer than the usual and the guy with the tabard had thick, black, curling locks. They had the sunburned look of men who spent more time outdoors than in.

'Fucking pikeys . . .' Bob muttered under his breath as he passed me. 'Okay you lot . . . fuck off out of it. I've told your mob before you're not welcome here.'

'All we want is a drink,' said Curly, with a dull expression and a hint of Irish in his accent. It was clear he was accustomed to welcomes like the one Big Bob was offering. 'Just a drink. Quiet like. No trouble.'

'You'll get no drink here. You lot don't know how to have a quiet drink. I've had the place wrecked before by your kind. Now fuck off.'

One of the others stared hard at Bob. He had the ready stance of someone thinking about kicking off. Curly put a hand on his shoulder and said something to him I couldn't understand. The tension went from his frame and the three walked out silently, but not hurriedly.

'Fucking pikeys . . .' Bob repeated after they were gone.

'Gypsies?' I asked.

'Irish tinkers. They're over here for the Vinegarhill Fair in the Gallowgate. They've pitched up camp by the old vinegar works.'

'They seemed reasonable enough to me,' I said.

Big Bob crossed his Popeye forearms across his massive chest. 'Aye, they seem that way now, but a few drinks in them and they go fucking mental. By the end of the night I'd be picking the furniture up for firewood if I start letting knackers drink in here. Drink and fight, that's all these bastards know.'

'Yeah . . . drink and fight,' I repeated, trying to work out how this fact distinguished them from the usual Glaswegian customer. 'It's funny, I was at a pikey fight the other night.'

'Aye? I bet there was blood and snotters all over the place. Fucking mental.' Bob shook his head in a way that reminded me of the awe Sneddon had displayed when talking about his tinker fighters.

I got back to my digs about ten. As I passed her door, I heard Fiona White switch the television off. I had bought a set six months before, when my cash flow had been going through one of its sporadically positive periods. I had come up with the pretence that the television would be better in their lounge. More room. Some crap like that. The truth was that I had no great interest in television: I still couldn't see it replacing radio. One of my greatest disappointments had been to see the actor Valentine Dyall for the first time on television. The face behind the voice behind the 'Man in Black' on radio's

Appointment with Fear turned out to look like a dyspeptic bank manager.

I had told Mrs White that I could watch it at any time, if that was okay with her, but she was to feel free for her and the kids to watch it whenever they felt like it. I knew they did, but she had a habit of switching it off when I was in my flat. She had told me, when I had assured her that it was really okay with me for them to watch as much TV as they wanted, that she was worried that she would 'wear the tube out'. The truth, I knew, was that she didn't want to feel she owed me anything. She didn't want to owe anyone anything. It was a drawbridge that had been drawn up a long time before I had first encountered her. Fiona White was an attractive woman, still young, but I really couldn't recall ever having seen her smile.

I went up to my rooms and listened to the Overseas Service for a while before tuning into the Home Service. There was an item on the news about the forthcoming fight between Bobby Kirkcaldy and Jan Schmidtke. It was one of the most anticipated fights in the city's boxing history, despite the fact that the result was a foregone conclusion: the German slugger Schmidtke was universally considered to be outclassed and outgunned by the stylist Kirkcaldy.

I grinned smugly at the thought that I'd managed to spring a ticket for the fight, after all. The grin faded though, when I thought about how big-league Willie Sneddon's and Jonny Cohen's ambitions were becoming. Taking a slice of Bobby Kirkcaldy was stretching them beyond Glasgow. I started to feel uneasy about getting mixed up in whatever dodgy dealings were going on behind a sporting event of national significance.

But, there again, that was the business I was in. Dodgy dealings.

*

That summer, and for about a year leading up to it, ever since I'd gotten involved in all kinds of shenanigans down at the docks and ended up with holes in me where there shouldn't be any, I had been trying to get myself straightened out. It was difficult to frame a description of my life without resorting to profanity and it was true to say that my life was truly fucked up. I guessed that was what people said about me: 'Oh, there goes Lennox. Okay guy. Fucked up though.' I had made a great effort over the last twelve months to diminish the fucked-upness of my life. I had one over-arching ambition: that one morning while shaving, I could look in the mirror without disliking the person who looked back at me.

The truth was I had been a straightforward, bright and as enthusiastic-as-all-hell, all-Canadian kid growing up on the shores of the Kennebecasis, with rich parents and an education at the upper-crusty Rothesay Collegiate College. Nothing fucked-up there. But then a little Austrian corporal decided to fuck up more than my world and I found myself an officer in the First Canadian Army and four thousand miles from home and up to my knees in mud and blood. The First Canadian, or at least those who led the First Canadian, had an enthusiasm for throwing my countrymen into the mincer. Normandy, Dieppe, Sicily. Wherever there was a serious-ordnance-ripping-through-human-flesh party, we tended to get the first invite. My excursion started in Sicily and lasted all the way through Italy, Holland and Germany. It was somewhere along the way during my Grand European Tour that the Kennebecasis Kid became yet another casualty of war. Whoever it was I became during the war, he fitted right in, right here in Glasgow.

And it had been while I stood in Glasgow, wearing a demob suit that I otherwise wouldn't have been seen dead in and holding a ship ticket to Halifax, Nova Scotia, that I had first encountered the Three Kings.

There's this misconception that all gangsters are the same. That all coppers are the same. Some people even believe, sometimes with a fair amount of justification, that all gangsters and all coppers are the same. The truth is that the underworld is a community like any other, with the same range and variety of personality, physical type and character that you find in any walk of life. You can't even say that they are united in dishonesty or immorality. Some villains have a very strict moral code. Some don't.

The Three Kings were a good example. What Willie Sneddon, Jonny Cohen and Hammer Murphy didn't run in Glasgow wasn't worth running. In 1948, Glasgow's three leading crime lords had sat down over lunch in a civilized manner in the elegant surroundings of the Regency Oyster Bar and discussed the future. The upshot was that, while they sat and divided the lunch bill equally between them, they had done pretty much the same to Glasgow.

There had been nothing elegant or civilized about what had preceded their lunch. A vicious gang war, Sneddon and Cohen on one side, Murphy on the other, had threatened to wipe them all out. Added to which, the first casualty of war was profit. By the time Sneddon, Cohen and Murphy emerged from the Regency, a coronation had taken place: the three crime lords had become the three crime kings.

But, like I said, no one is the same, and the Three Kings were very different people. Willie Sneddon was a truly nasty piece of work. Devious and malignant. Sneddon, the Gorbals hard man, had robbed, murdered and tortured his way to the top. But he was smart. Even subtle.

Subtlety was not something you associated with Hammer

Murphy, in much the same way you wouldn't associate camels with the Antarctic. Michael Murphy had gained the epithet 'Hammer' after pulping the skull of rival gang boss Paul Cochrane with a lead barrel-headed builder's mallet, in front of the assembled members of both gangs. Murphy was a man of limited intellect but possessed a viciousness as truly, awesomely monumental as the chip on his shoulder. He had embraced his new nickname with enthusiasm and was known to wield a hammer against knees, elbows and skulls whenever a suitable opportunity arose. It was, he had once confided in me, good to have a trademark.

Jonny Cohen, the third king, was a perfect illustration of the variety of personality and type within the criminal fraternity. Known as Handsome Jonny because of his film-star looks, Cohen was a decent kind of guy and a devoted husband and father who lived a quiet life in Newton Mearns – Tel-Aviv on the Clyde, as it was known in Glasgow. Or at least he was a decent, quiet-living kind of guy when he wasn't holding up banks, organizing jewel robberies, running illegal bookies, that kind of thing. It was also true to say that Jonny had moved a few souls closer to the Lord in his time, but they had all been competitors or active playmates in the big Glasgow game. No civilians. I liked Jonny. I had good reason to: he had saved my neck. And when I first arrived in Glasgow, it had been Jonny who first suggested he and his *colleagues* could perhaps make use of my skills.

Don't get me wrong. I had known exactly the kind of people I was getting involved with. And I had known that some of the *enquiries* I carried out for them took me very close to, and often over, a very fudged border between the legal and illegal. I'd gotten involved in some seedy and unpleasant shenanigans and, as time had gone on, I had felt like I was sinking deeper and deeper into a personality that I really didn't care for. That's why, over the last twelve or thirteen months, I'd been making a real effort to straighten myself out; and that meant having less to do with the Three Kings. Instead, I had been doing fine upstanding work for the community, mainly staging infidelities in seedy hotels for divorce cases. But the two cases I was now working on threatened to drag me back into the cosy embrace of Glasgow's most dangerous men.

One thing that unites the criminal fraternity is that they don't tend to keep banker's hours. Extortion with menaces, vice, armed robbery and running brothels takes it out of you, and your average gangster tends not to be a morning person. So I decided to wait until the following afternoon before paying Jonny Cohen a house call, even though I knew that he, of all the Kings, had the closest to a normal daily schedule. I gave him a ring after lunch and we arranged to meet, conveniently, at the Pacific Club that evening about five.

I stood before the Pacific Club and contemplated glamour. It's a funny thing, glamour. The word itself was as Scottish as they come, meaning a spell or an enchantment cast over someone to enrapture them. It was odd that, having invented the word, the Scots were totally at sea with the concept. Whenever they strived to achieve it, it just came out all wrong. No, that wasn't entirely true. There were exceptions: Sheila Gainsborough had glamour in spades. Naturally and effortlessly. A rare achievement, given the lack of it in her origins.

The Pacific Club was intended to be glamorous. It failed. More than that, its failure was the kind that would have helped Neville Chamberlain feel better about Munich. The Pacific Club was the ground floor and basement of a soot-blackened building on Broomielaw, down on the north bank of the Clyde as it dissects the city centre. It was a gloomy place even in daytime, being almost tucked under the latticed ironwork of the rail bridge over the river. The sun was still blazing when I got there and it was a relief to step into the club's clammy coolness, like walking into a subterranean cave.

Officially, the Pacific was a private, members-only club, a legal wriggle that allowed Handsome Jonny Cohen to circumvent most of the licensing laws. Like all such night-time venues, it had that depressing tacky look during the day. Like a seaside resort off-season. The air in the club was clear but the greasy odour of stale cigarettes clung to every surface. There were two dozen chair-stacked tables, a small stage and a bar in the corner. The nautical theme was represented mainly by ship life rings, emblazoned with 'SS PACIFIC CLUB', on the walls, and by some netting half-heartedly arranged over the stage. The small curved bar had a driftwood sign above it stating that it was the 'HAWAIIAN HULA BAR' and some more netting draped around it. There were crab shells dotted about the netting. Maybe it was just me, but I couldn't image anywhere within the known universe and probably several parallel ones that could possibly be further away from some sun-drenched, azure-sea tropical island than the Broomielaw in Glasgow.

Although, I had to admit, the Pacific Club was probably as good a place as any to catch crabs.

I got there about ten before five just as the staff were arriving to unstack the chairs from the tables and start preparing for a long night of overpriced drinks, under-clad girls and mediocre jazz. Handsome Jonny was already there. He beamed a searchlight grin of perfect teeth above the Cary Grant cleft in his chin. He looked clean, cool and fresh. I am definitely no slouch at turning myself out, but I had the distinct feeling that Jonny's tailor and barber had gotten together to conspire to give me an inferiority complex. I was suddenly aware that my shirt was clinging to my back with sweat. Jonny's thick, dark hair had been immaculately cut and for a second I wondered how feasible it would be to travel to Hollywood from Glasgow once a fortnight for a trim. I decided to keep my hat on for the moment.

'Stands Scotland where it did, Lennox?' He reached out his hand and I shook it.

'Wrong character.'

'What?'

'You've got the wrong Macbeth character. MacDuff asks Ross: "Stands Scotland where it did?" The character of Lennox doesn't say anything much to anybody. Just sticks by his king and ends up getting killed for it.'

'Is that the kind of Lennox you are? The question is which king would you stick by?' Jonny didn't wait for an answer and grinned. 'You know what I like about you, Lennox? Talking to you is always an education.'

'It's the company I keep. I've been hanging around with Twinkletoes McBride. Sometimes it's just like the Brains Trust when we get together. Anyway, I think it's fair to say you and I have learned a few things from each other . . . *about* each other . . . don't you, Jonny?'

Jonny's smile stayed in place but changed a little, like a wisp of cloud passing across the sun. 'What can I do for you, Lennox?'

'Well, I've got two cases on at the moment and you're involved in both, in a way.'

'Oh? I take it one is the Bobby Kirkcaldy carry-on.'

'Willie Sneddon has asked me to speak to Kirkcaldy. Looks like someone's trying to spook your fighter.'

One of the staff started to vacuum and Jonny winced at the noise. He beckoned for me to follow him and we sat at a table right at the back of the club, on an elevated section that overlooked the small stage. It was odd seeing Handsome Jonny Cohen here: he could not have looked more out of place; which was even more odd because it was, after all, his place. If you had seen him here as a customer, with his looks and expensive hair-cuts and tailoring you paid for in guineas, not pounds, you would say to yourself: 'That guy's slumming it.' But he wasn't a Pacific Club customer: he was the owner. And Jonny the busi-nessman knew that he didn't need to lavish his good taste or better cash on the place.

I took my hat off and ran a smoothing hand through my 'Pherson's cut. The finest one-and-sixpence could buy you in Glasgow. But it still wasn't Hollywood.

'Just a minute . . .' He got up again and went across to one of the girls preparing the bar. He sat down again and once more hit me with his searchlight smile. 'I've got a treat for you.'

The girl came back with a bottle and two glasses.

'Thanks, Fran . . .' he said and took the bottle from her and held it towards me, cradling it in both hands as if presenting me with an award.

'All the way from Bardstown, Kentucky. Heaven Hill Bourbon. I know you prefer ryes to Scotches. Go on, try it.' He poured me a glass and I took a sip.

'Perfect . . .' I said. And it was.

'You know Sneddon and I both have a share in Kirkcaldy?'

'Yeah. But Murphy hasn't?'

Jonny shook his head as if I'd suggested he sell me his sister for sex. 'Not likely. And it's best he doesn't know anything about this. He's always moaning that we leave him out of stuff. Well, this time we did. He'd start throwing his weight about and there are other people involved with Kirkcaldy who'd run a mile if they took one look at Murphy.'

'I know the feeling,' I said.

'Sneddon's got this bee in his bonnet about Kirkcaldy being got at,' Jonny said with an almost sigh.

'I can see his point.'

Jonny shook his head. 'Something's not right about it, Lennox. It's not just a spook job. All of this shite . . . nooses left on his doorstep.'

'Nooses?' I put my drink down. 'Sneddon didn't say anything about nooses. He said Kirkcaldy had had paint poured over his car and a dead bird put through his letterbox.'

'Yeah,' said Jonny. 'Those too. But someone laid out a hangman's noose on his doorstep. And did Sneddon tell you about the paint on the car? The colour, I mean?'

I shook my head.

'Red. Blood red. And the dead bird wasn't just a sparrow or shite like that. It was a dove. A white dove. Now what the fuck's all that about?'

'Put it all together and it looks like someone's making some kind of death threat,' I said. 'I'd say that would fit with warning him off winning this fight.'

'Naw . . . something doesn't feel kosher about it all,' said Jonny. 'It was me who suggested to Sneddon that we put you on to it. There's more to this than some kind of half-arsed attempt at fight fixing. You know what I mean?'

I shrugged. 'I'll explore every avenue, as they say in all the best cop movies.'

'You said two.'

'What?'

'You said there were two cases you were looking into that I was involved in some way.'

'Oh . . . yes. Well, not you so much as this place,' I said, looking around me. 'You know the singer Sheila Gainsborough?'

''Course. Glasgow girl made good. Nice singing voice.'

'And the lungs to go with it,' I said. 'Anyway, her brother has gone missing.'

'Oh yeah. Sammy Gainsborough.'

'Sammy Pollock. Gainsborough is her stage name. She's legally changed it now to Gainsborough but it was Pollock. Her brother is Sammy Pollock.'

'I've got news for you. He goes by the name Gainsborough now, at least professionally. Cashing in on Big Sis's success, I'd guess.'

'So you do know him.'

'Sure. He's sung here a couple of times. He's nothing to write home about. Okay voice, but he's no match for his sister.'

'When did he last sing here?'

'About three weeks ago.' Jonny took a cigarette case from his pocket and offered me one. We both lit up. 'Sammy was filling in for a cancelled act. Last minute thing. He wasn't a regular booking here. Haven't seen him since, even as a customer.'

'Was he a regular?'

'Reasonably. That's why we were able to get him to stand in for the act that cried off sick. He wasn't just available: he was *here*.'

'Did you know that he's involved with Jimmy Costello's son?'

'Paul Costello?' Jonny frowned. 'No I didn't. Now that is one greasy little shite. Now that you mention it, he's been around the club a few times. I wouldn't have linked him with Sammy though. I don't think I've ever seen them together. Not here. Do you think young Costello has something to do with Sammy Gainsborough's disappearance?'

'I don't know, Jonny. He says he didn't even know that Sammy was missing. Maybe he isn't. Could be he's off on a bender somewhere and he'll wash up in a couple of days or so.'

'If he *is* missing, I would take a long hard look at Costello. If he's anything like his old man he's a twisted wee bastard trying to squeeze cash from anything he can lay his hands on.'

'I'll bear that in mind. How well do you know Costello? I mean Costello senior?'

'I haven't had a lot of dealings with him. He runs a bookie and a pub in the East End. Pays tribute to Hammer Murphy and Murphy calls on him for stuff now and again. Borrows extra muscle, that kind of thing. Murphy really does run his patch as a kingdom. Or a fiefdom. Costello does as he's told, pays what he's told and is left to do his own thing so long as Murphy's kept in the know.'

'That's pretty much what I thought. And is Costello Junior learning the trade from his old man?'

'Costello has two sons. Paul and his older brother, Michael. I don't think Costello has much time for either of them. Paul is a wanker and Michael turned out to be a real disappointment to his old man.'

'Oh?'

'Yeah ... imagine the shame of your son turning out honest when you've devoted your life to thieving. Must have been a huge blow to Costello to see the fruit of his loins turn out to be law-abiding. Michael even considered the priesthood, apparently, but instead moved to Edinburgh and works as a civil servant.'

'Shit ...' My tone and expression registered my sympathy for both father and son. 'A civil servant in Edinburgh. No one deserves that. Do you know of a Frenchman called Barnier?' I asked.

'Alain Barnier? Sure. What's he got to do with anything?'

'According to Sheila Gainsborough, he's been hanging around with Sammy Pollock.'

Jonny smiled. 'Alain Barnier doesn't hang around with anyone. They hang around with him. He's a smooth operator.'

'Who's he with?'

'No one.'

'Come on, Jonny, everyone who's got a piece of action in this town is aligned with you, Murphy or Sneddon.'

'Barnier is mainly legit. Sure, I think he's got a few tasty deals on the side, but nothing that we would be interested in. I do the odd bit of business with him.'

'What kind of business? What's his line?'

'Officially he's an importer. He imports wine, mainly. And spirits. He also brings in stuff from the Far East. Furniture, ornaments, that kind of shite. He's lived here for about a couple of years and he supplies some of the fancier restaurants in town. Edinburgh too. But if there's anything else you need brought in, he probably can arrange it for you.' Jonny poured us another each and tilted the Heaven Hill bottle's label in my direction once more. 'Barnier was my contact for this stuff. Cognac too.'

'Let me guess, he doesn't like to put the customs man to any trouble?'

'He's very considerate that way. Saves our hard-working public servants a lot of paperwork. But the stuff he brings in has always been at the quality end, you could say. Nothing you'd find at Paddy's Market. Word is that side of his operation isn't as good as it was. Rationing coming to an end has been bad for business.'

'What about cigarettes? Does he smuggle those too? Fancy French brands?'

Jonny shrugged. 'Doubt it. Suppose it's possible, though.'

'Have you ever heard of the Poppy Club, Jonny? It's maybe got something to do with Barnier. It definitely has something to do with Sammy Pollock.'

'Poppy Club?'

'It's not listed in the 'phone book. Maybe it's not licensed.'

'Never heard of it, Lennox.' By the time he poured the third Bourbon, I was beginning to glow. I reappraised the Pacific Club, but the glow didn't catch: it still looked depressing.

'Where would I be able to find Barnier?' I asked.

'He's here if we've got a good jazz act on. Fridays. But not every Friday. You're best trying to catch him down at the river. He has an office of sorts down there. More a shed. Near the bonded area.'

'Is that where he liberates his goods from bondage?'

Jonny shrugged. 'Wouldn't know. If he does, it will be through bribery. The odd brown envelope to a watchman, copper or taxman. Barnier is no out-and-out crook, like I said. Just sails close to the wind. Law wise. You two should get on.'

'I better go,' I said, draining the glass. 'Thanks for the whisky.'

Jonny saw me to the door and, after the gloom and Bourbon of the Pacific Club, we stood squinting for a moment in the bright sunlight.

'Lennox?' said Jonny, shielding his eyes with his hand.

'Yep?'

'This other case. Sammy Pollock. I know you have to follow it up, but don't let it get in the way of finding out what the fuck is happening with Bobby Kirkcaldy. Sneddon's getting as antsy as hell. The fight's in just over two weeks' time. And, like I say, there's something about the whole thing stinks as far as I'm concerned.'

'I'll see him tonight. Thanks again for the Bourbon.'

Jonny had, of course, been right. Whenever I thought of the Sammy Pollock case, I smelt grief; whenever I thought of the Kirkcaldy case, I smelt money. There was a lot of it riding on Kirkcaldy and I guessed Jonny Cohen and Willie Sneddon would be in a big bonus mood if I got it all sorted out for them. And

I had, to a certain extent, done the sniffing about that I'd promised Sheila Gainsborough I'd do. But there was something about
the thing with Sammy that was nagging away at me. Anyway,
I hadn't had a chance to practise my French for a long time.

Chapter Five

The British Empire, the most avaricious piece of land theft since Genghis Khan saddled up a pony, was a remarkable thing. What made it particularly remarkable was that it had been carried out by the British, probably the most apologetic race on the planet. I always imagined them as some kind of impeccably well-mannered, latter-day Vikings, frightfully embarrassed about all the raping and pillaging. I suppose my interest in the globe-spanning collection of Raj, colonies, dominions, mandates and protectorates lay in my being very much a product of it: I was born in Glasgow but shipped off with my folks when I was still a baby and Canada was still 'the Dominion' as far as everyone was concerned. Then, after twenty-one summers, the 'Mother Country' of which I had had no direct contact, or even recollection, suddenly and urgently needed my assistance. Four thousand miles away.

And now, sixteen years on, I was living in the Second City of an Empire on which, despite classroom assurances to the contrary, the sun was most definitely now setting. For a century and a half, Glasgow had been the Empire's industrial heart. But the War had screwed all of that up. Britain had ended the conflict all but bankrupt: if the United States had not come along in 1946 with a close on four billion dollar-loan, then the sceptr'd isle would have gone bankrupt. Now, former enemies were fast becoming new competitors in shipbuilding and heavy industry. Things were changing fast in the world. They were changing faster in Britain. And fastest in Glasgow.

Not that you would have guessed it from the activity in the docks as I drove past them. It was ten-thirty in the morning and already hot. I had both the Atlantic's windows rolled down, and as I drove past the quays the sound of metal being hammered, clashed, seared and cut rang dull but loud in air so muggy and thick with grime you could have strained it. It was as if the temperature was being increased by the activity itself.

To my left a forest of cranes jostled at the water's edge, swinging ceaselessly, loading and unloading docked ships or supplying vast sheets of heavy-gauge steel to the yards. I drove on past the huge red-brick dockside bonded warehouses, five storeys high behind tall fences. I parked on the street and went to the gatehouse and asked where Alain Barnier had his offices. The gateman was the usual retired cop with the usual I-couldn't-give-a-fuck attitude, and the best I could get out of him was directions to some other smaller shipping offices where they might have a better idea. It took me half an hour of asking around before getting a pointer to Barnier's office. By the time I got down there it was after eleven.

As Jonny had said, it was more of a shed than an office, one of a rank of semi-cylindrical Nissen huts, like a row of Sequoia logs half sunk into the earth. The sign above the door said *Barnier and Clement Import Agents*. I knocked and went in. As soon as I did, I could see that this was no front but a genuine working office: there was the kind of ordered chaos that's impossible to fake. A counter separated the main body of the hut from the reception area. There was a push bell on the counter and next to it a paper spike piled high with impaled shipping bills; there were three desks behind it, half-a-dozen filing cabinets and a woman.

The woman was about five-one and dressed in a businesslike grey suit that strained a little at the waist and bust. She had a pale round face and black hair coiled in a perm so tight and unyielding it could have withstood an A-bomb test. She had a small thin-lipped slit of a mouth that she had tried to flesh up with red lipstick.

'Can I help you?' she asked, coming around from behind her desk and to the counter. She stretched the thin lips in a weary, perfunctory smile.

'I'm looking for Mr Barnier.'

'Is this about the key lan?' she asked.

'The key lan?' I frowned. 'What's a key lan?'

She ignored me. 'Mr Barnier's not here at the moment. Did you have an appointment?'

'No. No appointment. When will he be back?'

'You'll need an appointment to see Mr Barnier.'

'My eyes work just fine without an appointment. When will he be back?'

She had large, round, green eyes set into her round face and she used them to stare at me as if I had been a congenital idiot. 'An appointment . . .' She came close to the kind of syllable by syllable pronunciation favoured by Twinkletoes McBride.

'The sign says Barnier and Clement. Is Mr Clement here?'

'*Monsieur Clement*,' she said, correcting my pronunciation, dropping the hard 't' at the end of the name and sounding it out as '*Clemmong*' in the way that only the Scots can murder the French language, 'does not work here. He is based in our French office.'

'I see . . .'

There was the usual hinged lid arrangement on the counter

and, swinging it open, I stepped through the counter and onto her side. The round green eyes grew rounder.

'You're not allowed in here . . .'

'I'll wait,' I said, and sat down behind one of the desks, pitching my hat onto a pile of papers. 'Probably best, seeing as you can't tell me when he'll be back or where I could find him.'

My dumpy girlfriend with the round eyes and thin lips lifted the hatch on the counter, as if holding it open for me. 'You can't wait.'

'There you go underestimating me again. I *can* wait. I've done it before. Lots of times. In fact, between you and me, I'm rather good at it.'

She picked up the telephone on her desk and dialled a number. She turned her back on me and spoke into the mouthpiece in a hushed but agitated voice. After a moment she turned and held the receiver out to me wordlessly.

I smiled cheerfully at her: we were getting on so well.

'You are looking for me?' The voice on the other end of the line spoke perfectly articulated English. The French accent was distinct, but not heavy.

'Mr Barnier? I wondered if we could have a chat.'

'A chat about what?' No suspicion or guardedness. Just impatience.

'I'm trying to get in contact with someone. You may be able to help me find them.'

'Who?'

'I'd rather we discussed this face-to-face. And as soon as possible, if you don't mind. Where could we meet?'

'For whom are you looking?' he asked again, with the acquired perfect grammar of a non-native English speaker.

'Sammy Pollock. You maybe know him as Sammy Gainsborough.'

There was a pause at his side of the connection. Then, in the same contraction-less, formal English: 'There is something about this which suggests to me your interest is professional rather than personal, yet you did not identify yourself to Miss Minto as a police officer.'

'That's because I'm not. If I had it would have been impersonation. I'm not very good at impersonations. Except Maurice Chevalier, but I'm sure, as a Frenchman yourself, you'd be able to see through that one.'

'I do not have the time for this. What is your name?'

'Lennox. You do know Sammy Pollock, don't you, Mr Barnier?'

'I do. However, I do not know him well. Insufficiently well, in fact, to know anything about his whereabouts.'

'I'd still like to talk to you, Mr Barnier.'

'I am afraid I am too busy for this. I cannot assist you with your enquiries. And these are enquiries, are they not? I take it you are some kind of private detective?'

'I'm just helping someone out, Mr Barnier. Sammy Pollock has gone missing and I'm trying to ascertain his state of health and whereabouts. I would be obliged if you could spare me a few minutes. There may be something you know that seems insignificant to you but that could help me track Sammy down.'

'I am sorry. As I said I do not have the time . . .'

'I quite understand. I'll explain to Mr Cohen. It was he who suggested I speak to you.'

I got what I wanted: a small silence at the other end of the line. Barnier was putting things together in his head. Whether they came together in an accurate picture or not, I didn't really care.

'Do you know the Merchants' Carvery in the city centre?' he said at last, a sigh spun through it.

'I know it,' I said. The Merchants' Carvery was a no-riff-raff kind of bar and restaurant. In a riff-raff kind of city. Barnier obviously had style and the cash to back it up. I couldn't see someone like that being involved with Sammy Pollock. Even less with scum like Paul Costello. But it had to be checked out.

'Meet me there at eight p.m.,' he said. 'In the bar.'

'Thank you, Mr Barnier. I'll be there.'

I drove back towards the town but before I got to the centre turned up the North road towards Aberfoyle. My head hurt, a dull, persistent throbbing in the temples and behind my eyes. Glasgow had pulled a curtain over the sun, a thin, dark-flecked veil of cloud. The temperature stayed hot, however, and the air around me seemed denser, heavier. I knew that the pain in my head was a warning of a storm coming. Getting out of the city didn't do much to ease the oppressive air that was now playing my sinuses like an accordion. After about fifteen minutes I was up around the Mugdock area where Glasgow yielded to open countryside and scattered, expensive houses. The sun had broken through again, but the pre-storm heaviness continued to hang in the air and the sky to the west was the colour of shipyard steel.

Bobby Kirkcaldy's place wasn't the most expensive, but it was a huge step up from his origins in Motherwell. But then again, having a toilet indoors, and one that you didn't have to share with four other families, was a huge step up. Truth was I quite admired Kirkcaldy as a boxer. He had started off welterweight, later moving up to middleweight but retaining a certain grace and lightness on his feet. I had seen him fight twice and it had been like watching two completely different boxers. Kirkcaldy was one of those boxers who, while probably no mental giant in any other way, seemed to possess a profound physical intelligence: a constant process of interpretation and fine re-calibration to match every move his opponent made. It was as if he could read any fighter within the first minute of a round and adapt his style to suit: if he was up against an infighter, Kirkcaldy subtly increased his range, forcing his opponent to stretch outside his preferred zone; if Kirkcaldy was up against an outfighter, he closed in with tight jabs, forcing his opposite number always backwards and onto the ropes.

One of the fights I had seen had been against Pete McQuillan. McQuillan was a slugger and bruiser; a stump of a man who struggled to stay in the middleweight bracket and in terms of style was just one step up from the pikey bare-knuckle boys. McQuillan winning a fight – and he had remained undefeated until then – depended either on a knockout, or his doing so much devastation to his opponent's face that the referee stopped the match. Then he had been matched with Bobby Kirkcaldy. It had been an amazing thing to watch: McQuillan viciously scything empty air while Kirkcaldy had danced around him, placing stinging jabs with absolute precision. It took McQuillan to a place he'd never been before: the distance. Kirkcaldy had been the unanimous points winner. Now he was the clear favourite for the European Middleweight Championship and would be meeting the West German Jan Schmidtke.

And I would be there. I had a ticket.

The house was roughly the same size as MacFarlane's in Pollokshields but was more recently built, maybe in the Twenties or Thirties, and it benefited from a more prestigious geography. It had also benefited from whitewash, which made it look bright and foreign in the sunlight. The front door faced south but was shielded by a Deco arch edged in earth-red brickwork. The white-wash walls beneath the red tiles and the terracotta brick detailing was an ambitious attempt to give the house an almost Mediterranean look, which in Scotland was an achievement akin to making Lon Chaney look like Clark Gable. I wasn't sure how much of the credit should go to the architect and how much to the alien climate that seemed to have invaded the West of Scotland.

The door was answered almost instantly when I rang the electric push-bell. I got the idea that they had heard my Atlantic crunch its way up the drive. They were looking out for visitors, welcome or otherwise, I guessed. It wasn't Bobby Kirkcaldy who answered the door but someone probably even more pugnacious-looking, an older man in a dark suit and thin woollen tie. He was lean and mean-looking and he had the appearance of something assembled from the toughest material; he had white bristle for hair and a deep-lined, leathery face that was more than weather-beaten. It looked as if anything capable of giving it a beating, weather or otherwise, had had its turn on his face. His flattened nose had that thick, rubbery, formless look that suggested it had been broken so many times that there was no cartilage left to give it any kind of meaningful shape. The damage wasn't just visually apparent; when he spoke he sounded muffled and nasal. Even more than the average Glaswegian did.

'What do you want?' he asked.

'A quiet life, money, a beautiful girl and a sense of inner peace.'

He looked at me blankly. Along with the crap, he had clearly had the humour beaten out of him.

'I'm here to see Bobby,' I sighed. I was not appreciated here. 'My name is Lennox. I'm expected.'

He looked me up and down. I mirrored his examination. It was difficult to age him. He could have been a battered fifty or a fit seventy. It was obvious he was an ex-fighter, but I reckoned as much damage had been done to his face outside the ring as in it. I tilted my head and smiled impatiently. The old warrior stood to one side to let me in. I was going to hand him my hat but he didn't look the Jeeves type, so I hung on to it and followed him down a long hallway with terracotta tiles on the floor and tasteful art, some original, on the wall. I guessed that a Motherwell-raised boxer like Kirkcaldy would probably have about as much good taste as my elderly companion with the devastated nose would have a sense of smell; I put the domestic aesthetic down to a good decorator.

He led me into a large lounge with big French windows that looked out over a massive expanse of landscaped garden to the green hills beyond. It was a nice place. The kind of nice you had to pay for. Again, what struck me most was the way it had been furnished. Glasgow was, generally, a make-do-and-mend kind of city; Britain was a make-do-and-mend society, mainly because until recently the country's very survival had depended on it. Post-war near-bankruptcy had added inertia to the pendulum swing from austerity to prosperity. Added to all of this was Scottish social conservatism. I had seen a few homes that had been decorated in the Contemporary style – Jonny Cohen's, for example – but generally Modernism was distrusted. And when it was used as décor, it was normally done half-heartedly or clumsily overdone.

All of which is why Bobby Kirkcaldy's home would have looked to the average Scot like a Hollywood set. This was all good stuff. If the furnishings weren't original Bauhaus or le Corbusier or Eames, they were pretty good copies. There was a wall filled with books. I had the uncharitable thought that Kirkcaldy the boxer must have told his interior designer to make him look smarter. Just like in the hall, the art on the lounge walls looked original. Most of it was modern and edgy – abstracty stuff – but there was something about that kind of art that appealed to me. Like the furniture, it was new. And for me, New was Good. Again, I put it all down to an overpaid interior decorator.

Bobby Kirkcaldy stood up when we came in. He had been sitting on a leather lounger by the big windows and when he got up and crossed the room to us, he did so with the same easy grace with which I'd seen him move in the ring. He had thick, dark hair and, unlike the old guy at my side, there wasn't the usual evidence in Kirkcaldy's face of a boxer's career. His nose didn't look as if it had ever been broken and there was only a hint of the high-cheeked angularity of a fighter's face. He was wearing an open-necked shirt and lightweight trousers. The look was casual but had Jermyn Street all over it.

'You Lennox?' asked Kirkcaldy. He didn't smile but there was nothing overtly hostile in his manner, either. Just businesslike.

'I'm Lennox. You know why I'm here?'

'To look into this nonsense that's been going on. You've been hired by Willie Sneddon. To be honest, I think all this shite bothers Sneddon more than it bothers me.' Kirkcaldy's voice was light, almost gentle, but he managed to inject a hint of distaste when he articulated Willie Sneddon's name. He spoke with a quiet confidence and had less of an accent than I had expected. When you saw him up close, as opposed to the distance a boxing stadium compels, there was an intelligence in the eyes. But there was something else that I couldn't define. And it stopped me liking him.

I turned and looked at the punch bag who had shown me in, and then back at Kirkcaldy.

'It's okay,' Kirkcaldy said. 'You can talk in front of Uncle Bert. Uncle Bert has coached me since I was a kid.'

Uncle Bert looked at me expressionlessly. But, there again, he'd probably had the mobility to form an expression beaten out of his face years ago. I found myself silently questioning his qualifications as a boxing trainer, seeing as no one seemed to have taught him the meaning of the word 'duck'.

'Okay,' I said. I looked around the room in the way you do when you've got to that point where you should have been invited to sit but haven't. 'Nice place. Like the paintings. I'm never sure where Abstract Expressionism ends and Lyrical Abstraction begins.'

'These are neither,' said Kirkcaldy. 'I don't trust "isms". Political or artistic. I just buy what I like and what I can afford. And the only reason I can afford it is because of the fight game.' He picked up that we were still standing and pointed to a sofa that hovered just clear of the polished wooden floor. I lowered myself onto it: there was a lot of lowering involved. Kirkcaldy certainly didn't talk like the average street-to-ring pugilist and I started to suspect the books on the shelves weren't just for show. There was a certain type of working-class Scot who, deprived of it in their childhood, treated learning and knowledge as if they were bullion. I thought I was above making snobby judgements; I'd just proved to myself that I wasn't. It was clear to me now that the impression of physical intelligence Kirkcaldy showed in the ring was part of something bigger.

'Do you know much about art, Mr Lennox?' he asked, and sat down on the Eames chair opposite. Uncle Bert remained standing. It was probably force of habit: staying upright had cost him dearly in the past.

'Some,' I said. 'I was interested in it before the war. Then it was kind of expected of me to get interested in the war. But I still like to visit the odd gallery.'

Kirkcaldy smiled and nodded. There was nothing to the smile in the same way there had been nothing to Sheila Gainsborough's smile. 'You know this is a lot of nonsense, don't you?'

I shrugged. 'It sounds to me like someone is trying to spook you before the big fight. There are a lot of people betting a lot of money, one way or the other, on this fight. And some of those people aren't above dodgy dealings to protect their investment.'

'It's obviously somebody trying to spook me, but it's not working. I don't spook easily, and anyone who's had anything to do with me would know I'd quit the ring before throwing a fight.'

'Has anyone approached you about it? 'Phone calls, notes under the door, that kind of thing.'

'No. Nothing. Like you say, just a spook job. Trying to put me off my preparation for the fight.'

I nodded and noted. Maybe it would get back to Sneddon that I had nodded and noted. This was a wild goose chase, just like the thing with Small Change's appointment book. The only thing that surprised me about it was Kirkcaldy's willingness to accept it was someone trying to queer him for the fight. Like Jonny Cohen, I got the impression this was about something else. I decided to run the idea past him.

'Is there anything else – anybody with a grudge, or some dispute you've got going – that might explain this?'

He pursed his lips and thought it over for a moment. 'No . . . I can honestly say I can't imagine anyone doing this for personal reasons.'

'I see,' I said. It was interesting that he had to think about it before answering. As if he had never before considered the possibility. We talked for another half hour, during which I noted down each of the things that had happened, the dates, the times. Kirkcaldy gave me the information in a going-through-the-motions manner. I asked if I could see the car that had been splashed with red paint: it had been repainted. The noose had been thrown out as had, obviously, the dead bird.

'What kind of bird was it?' I asked.

'What? I don't know. A bird. A dove or a pigeon, I think. But I do know it was white. Pure white. So probably a dove.'

'How did it die?'

'I don't fucking know.' He became agitated and the Motherwell in his voice became more pronounced.

'What will you do?' he asked wearily.

'Well, I've nothing to go on. You've no idea of who might have a personal grievance against you . . . There's not a lot I can do other than watch your back for a while.'

'I can watch my own back,' he said and cast a meaningful look at Uncle Bert.

'Well, if you don't mind, I'll keep an eye on things. Of course I can't be here all the time, so if anything happens, you can get me on one of these numbers normally.' I scribbled down my office and home number, as well as the number for the 'phone behind the bar at the Horsehead.

By the time I left Kirkcaldy's place, the ship-iron sky had turned even darker and the air even more oppressive. It was damp-hot and I could feel the pressure like a band around my head. I had only been driving for a couple of minutes when the weather broke.

If there's one thing Glasgow can do well – better than anywhere else I know – then it's rain. There were a couple of bright, ugly flashes in the sky and the rain hit my windscreen before the deafening thunder rolled over me. It didn't just rain – it was as if there was a pent-up fury driving the thick, heavy bullets of rain that rattled and drummed furiously on the roof of my car and mocked the best but feeble efforts of my windscreen wipers. As I approached Blanefield and headed into Bearsden, I had to slow the car to an almost crawl, unable to see more than a few feet in front of me.

I had time on my hands before I met the Frenchman so I drove down to Argyle Street. The torrential rain hadn't stopped but I was lucky enough to get parked a thirty-second dash away from the corner tearooms. I went in, shook the rain off my hat and moaned to the waiter I handed it to about the sudden change in the weather. There were only a couple of other tables occupied and I sat in gloomy silence. When I'd finished my lamb chop and mashed potatoes I drank a coffee and smoked, gloomily contemplating the rain through the window.

A fool's errand. No matter how long I thought it over, the Bobby Kirkcaldy job remained a fool's errand. Willie Sneddon was thrashing about in the dark trying to protect his investment. Other than sit outside Kirkcaldy's house all night, there was very little I could do. And if it came to a twenty-four-hour surveillance job, then it would cost Sneddon dear. He'd be better getting Twinkletoes McBride to park himself outside. Or Singer. This was a muscle job. I was going to have to tell Sneddon so.

After I'd settled my bill at the cashier's desk and collected my hat, I went back out into the rain. It had eased considerably, and with its easing it had taken some of the stale heat out of the air. But Glasgow was Glasgow again, dressed in rain and shades of grey.

It took me only a couple of minutes to get to the Merchants' Carvery in the city's business district. It meant that I was early and I decided to wait in the car until just before eight. The Merchants' Carvery was Glasgow's attempt at class: it sat looking out over a square of park in the middle of a grid of Georgian and Victorian terraces. As the Carvery's name suggested, the city's wealthy traders and industrialists had once occupied the surrounding houses; now most had been converted into offices. Sitting parked outside, I made a little wager with myself that

I would be able to pick out Barnier when he arrived. As it turned out, the only people I saw going into the restaurant was a middle-aged couple. Both dressed in tweed.

The Merchants' Carvery was one of those places designed, or more correctly decorated and furnished, to intimidate. A place you were meant to feel out of place. To me, it was overdone; way overdone. The plush red leather of the booths was just that little bit too plush and much too red. If the Carvery had been in Edinburgh, it wouldn't have been quite so overdone.

I went in and handed my hat over again, this time to an attendant in a white waist-length jacket and pillbox cap. He was, without doubt, the most geriatric bellboy I'd ever seen and I worried that he would buckle under the weight of my fedora. I told him I was there to meet with Mr Barnier and he nodded towards a tall man standing at the bar with his back to me. It was going to take us an age to cross the lounge so I thanked my elderly hop and gave him a two-shilling tip: I reckoned that the weight of half-a-crown would tip him in more ways than intended.

'Monsieur Barnier?' I asked the man's back and he turned to face me. Alain Barnier was not what I had expected. For a start he was tall and light-haired, not quite blond, with greenish eyes. To me he looked more like a Scandinavian or German than a Southern Frenchman. His skin tone wasn't dark either, although I knew he had lived in Glasgow for at least a couple of years; but there again, no one could be as pale as a Glaswegian. Scots were the whitest people on the planet; and Glaswegians came in pale blue tints, except for those who had been burned scarlet by unaccustomed exposure to the big fiery ball in the sky that had, until a couple of hours ago, made a mysterious appearance that summer. Barnier was a striking man, hand-some, with deep creases under his eyes that suggested a lot of smiling, but there was something a little cruel in his features. I estimated his age to be about forty.

Other than his slightly golden skin tone, there were a couple of other things that gave Barnier away as a foreigner. His clothes were expensive but not showy. And not tweed. His suit was extremely well-tailored in a pale grey, lightweight flannel, run through with a faint white pinstripe. It didn't look like a British cut. Added to that, he was immaculately groomed and wore a neatly trimmed moustache and goatee beard that gave a point to his chin. My first thought was of a Cardin-coutured fourth Musketeer.

'My name is Lennox, M. Barnier,' I said in French. 'We spoke on the telephone this afternoon.'

'I was waiting for you. Drink?' He beckoned to the barman with a casual authority that Scots find difficult. 'Two cognacs,' he said in English.

'Please . . .' he said, reverting to his native tongue and indicating one of the plush leather booths at the back of the lounge bar. We sat down. 'You speak French very well, M. Lennox. But, if you don't mind me saying so, you have a strong accent. And you speak slowly, like a Breton. I take it you're Canadian?'

'Yes. New Brunswick. The only officially bi-lingual province in Canada,' I said, and was surprised at the pride in my voice.

'But you're not a Francophone yourself?'

'That obvious?'

Barnier shrugged and made a face. He was French. I expected it. 'No . . . not particularly. But you have a strong accent. I assumed English was your first language.'

'Where are you from yourself, M. Barnier?'

The drinks arrived. 'Toulon. Well, Marseille originally, then Toulon.'

I sipped the cognac and felt something warm and golden infuse itself into my chest.

'Good, no?' he asked. A smile deepened the creases around the eyes. 'I supply it. It is one of the best.'

'It tastes it. I had some of the bourbon you supplied Jonny Cohen. That was excellent too.'

'Ah, yes . . . you mentioned you knew M. Cohen . . .' Barnier looked at me over the rim of his brandy glass. 'By the way, you rather annoyed my Miss Minto.'

'Really?' I said, raising my eyebrows and trying to look as innocent as I had been at sixteen when my father had interrogated me about some missing cigarettes and whisky. 'We seemed to be getting on so well. I learned a new word – key lan – or is it two words?'

There was something in the mention that stung Barnier. He quickly hid it. 'I can't have you upsetting her. Miss Minto is a very . . . *determined* lady who is essential to the efficient running of the office.'

'Why did she ask me if it was about the *key lan*. Am I pronouncing it right?'

'She was referring to an item we've recently imported. Miss Minto probably thought you wanted to see me about it, that's all.'

'I'm flattered that Miss Minto thought I was rich enough to buy it.'

'She didn't. The item's gone astray in transit. It's more than likely been incorrectly crated and labelled, that's all. Miss Minto probably thought you were from the insurance company.' Barnier's smile had dropped and his tone now suggested that the small talk was over. 'What exactly is it you want from me, M. Lennox?'

'I've been engaged to look into the disappearance of Sammy Pollock. You may know him as Sammy Gainsborough.'

'I hardly know him as either. M. Pollock was an acquaintance. Nothing more. My dealings with him were so infrequent that I'm struggling to remember the last time I saw him. Why is it that you are asking me about Pollock?'

'Can you? Remember, I mean?'

Barnier made a show of running through a mental inventory. He pulled gently at his goatee, smoothing it into an inverted peak.

'It would have been about two or three weeks ago. A Friday. He was at the Pacific Club at the same time I was. It is a dreadful place . . . please don't tell M. Cohen I said so – he is a valued customer after all. But it really is an awful place. I go there because, ironically, M. Cohen does tend to get rather good jazz acts on Fridays. Anyway, I saw young M. Pollock there. He did a turn . . . sang a few songs to fill in for a no-show act. He was there with a girl, if I remember correctly. But we didn't speak that night.'

'And you haven't seen him since?'

'Listen, Mr Lennox . . .' Barnier reverted to his flawlessly articulated, grammatically perfect English. 'I really have no idea whether I have seen him since or not. Sammy Pollock is not someone who features in my consciousness much. It may be that I have seen him and not noticed. Now, I repeat my question: Why are you asking me about this young man?'

'You must excuse me, M. Barnier, but it's my day for straw clutching. I was told that Sammy Pollock was seen in your company on occasion. The truth is that he really does seem to have gone missing and I'm more than a little concerned for his welfare. So far I've not been able to come up with the slightest hint of where he is.' I looked at the Frenchman's face. There was nothing to read in his expression. Maybe it was just that my I'm-all-at-sea act didn't wash. Or maybe he just wasn't interested.

'Did you have any business dealings with Pollock?' I asked.

'No. None.'

'The occasions where you saw him . . . did you know the people he was with?'

'Again, no. Listen, I don't mean to be rude, but I really don't think I can help you any further.' He drained his glass. It was a gesture of punctuation – our conversation had come to a full stop.

'Thanks for your time, M. Barnier,' I said in French.

I left Barnier in the Carvery, picked my hat up from the geriatric bellboy and headed out into the street. The rain had stopped but the sky still looked bad-tempered. It wasn't alone.

It had been a fruitless day and I was too tired to go up to Sneddon's Bearsden house or even to ring him. Telling Willie Sneddon that you really can't do his bidding is something done face-to-face and in the right frame of mind. I didn't get into the car straight away but went to the telephone kiosk on the corner, fed it some copper and called the number Sheila Gainsborough had given me in London. The English accent at the other end told me that he was her agent and she wasn't there.

'I know,' I said. 'She gave me this as a contact number.'

'I see. Are you Lennox?' His voice was a tad too high and slightly effeminate. I gave a small laugh at the thought that I obviously expected theatrical agency to be one of those robustly masculine professions, like steelworking or mining.

'That's me,' I said.

'Tell me, Lennox . . . do you have anything to report?' Oh boy, he was losing my affection big time with that tone.

'That's why I'm 'phoning,' I said.

'Well?' he asked. He spoke to me as if I was the hired help; to be fair, I was. But, there again, so was he.

'Miss Gainsborough told me she could be contacted through this number. I take it you're Whithorn ... Will you be seeing her this evening?'

'I see Miss Gainsborough almost every evening,' he said. Proprietorially. 'She'll be here in about half an hour.'

'Tell her Lennox called. And that I will 'phone again this evening. About ten o'clock. If she could make sure she's available to take the call.'

'Why don't you just tell me what you have to report and I'll pass it on.'

I gave another small laugh. Louder this time, for him to hear. 'Client confidentiality, friend. I would have thought that would have been a concept you'd be familiar with.'

'I'm not just Miss Gainsborough's agent, Mr Lennox. I'm her advisor. Her friend.'

'I'll 'phone back at ten.' I hung up. I decided to make a point of putting a face to the voice that had been at the other end of the line. I had already decided I would dislike Humphrey Whithorn's face as soon as I saw it.

I walked back to where I had parked. I didn't pay much attention to the Wolseley parked three cars back from my Atlantic until an unnecessarily large man in a formless raincoat and a too-small trilby planted himself on the pavement, squarely in my path. Another appeared at my side, smaller but still robust, and with the kind of face you would avoid looking at in a bar. Or anywhere else. I felt the second guy's firm grip on my upper arm, just above the elbow. I could tell right away that these were no policemen. They were somebody's goons.

'Okay, Lennox,' said the raincoat. 'Mr Costello wants to see you. Now.'

I felt relief. Of sorts. Having to deal with any muscle is tiresome, but normally compliance comes from knowing who's behind the muscle. Costello didn't carry that kind of weight and I made a bored, irritated face.

'Does he now?' I said. For some reason, the image of Barnier's homely, insistent little secretary came to my mind and I decided to follow her example. 'I'm a busy kind of guy. Tell Costello to make an appointment.'

The fingers around my arm tightened and I turned to the second guy and smiled. They were hard men. Men who were in the business of hurting. But Jimmy Costello was not famed as a criminal mastermind and his lack of genius extended to the quality of goon he recruited. They had probably been following me all day and I wouldn't have spotted them in the rain. There had been a dozen suitable places for them to have made their move on me. This was not one of them. A stupid choice of place to pick me up off the street. We were in the middle of the business district, admittedly at eight forty-five in the evening, but outside a well-respected eatery. And there was a district police station two blocks away. No, this was as dumb a choice as they could have made and the ideal place for me to kick off. But they were too stupid to realize it and the goon with the vice grip on my arm looked as sure of himself as his partner did.

'Now,' he said with a vicious-looking grin. 'Are you going to come quiet or come the cunt?'

There was something I found out about myself during the war. It was something I could have done with not finding out for the rest of my life. Something ugly and dark. I lay awake at nights wondering if the war had created it, or if it had been there all the time and it might never have been awoken if the war hadn't come along. As I stood there with two violent thugs trying to coerce me into a car, I felt it begin to stir deep inside; and greet me as an old friend.

'Listen, guys,' I said in a friendly voice, but quiet. Quiet so they had to strain to hear it. 'I'm not coming with you. And if you try to make me, someone's going to get hurt. Tell Costello if he wants to see me, he can pick up the 'phone like everybody else. If he's peeved because I smacked his kid about, then tell him sorry . . . but I don't give a crap.'

'Whadyou say?' The big guy in the raincoat frowned and leaned forward, which is what I wanted him to do. I only had one arm free so I swung a kick at the spot on his raincoat where I reckoned he kept the family jewels. My reckoning was dead on and he folded. The guy with my arm yanked me backwards, again what I expected him to do. I went with it. Keeping your distance from your attacker isn't always the best strategy in a street fight and I rammed into him, bending him backwards onto the bonnet of the Wolseley. I fell on top of him, face-to-face. He got a punch in and jarred my head with it, making black and white sparks dance for a split second across my vision. With my free hand, I had grabbed my hat as it came off from the punch. I pushed it into and over his face, covering his eyes and pulling it away just as my brow slammed into his nose.

I was just mentally complimenting myself on my excellent management of the situation when a mule kicked me to the right of my spine, just above the kidney. I heard two lungfuls of air pulse out of me and I was in that panicked, winded place where filling your body with oxygen fills the universe. The big guy in the raincoat who had kicked me grabbed my arms and pulled me back from his bonnet-sprawled partner. I was still struggling to catch a breath but knew if I didn't pull myself together I was in for a kicking. Suddenly the big guy let go of me and I leaned forward, my hands resting on my knees, and pulled long deep breaths into my emptied lungs. I turned to see something that didn't make any sense, then turned my attention back to my bloody-faced chum who was pulling himself up from the bonnet of the Wolseley. I now knew I only need concern myself with him: the thing that hadn't made sense when I had turned around was seeing Alain Barnier behind me, very efficiently beating the crap out of the rain-coated thug.

But I still had my hands full and kept focussed on my chum who was now pulling himself upright from the bonnet of the Wolseley. I took a step forward, ready to hit him when he came up. He wasn't as stupid as I had taken him for, because he read my movement and, bracing his elbows on the bonnet, he swung his foot out and up. It was a vicious kick but it missed its target and I was able to grab his ankle. I gave his leg a hard yank and his body slid off the car's bonnet like a ship being launched from a slipway. He came down onto the pavement hard and there was the sickening sound of his skull against the kerb. He lay still and for a moment I was genuinely worried that I had killed him. He put my mind at rest by giving a low moan.

I heard the commotion continue behind me: Barnier and the other guy. Also shouts coming from the direction of the Carvery. I turned to see what was happening. The big man in the rain-coat looked the tougher of the two goons and was certainly the bigger. I reckoned he would be more than a handful for Barnier, but when I turned around I saw that the undersized trilby had been knocked off his head. There was blood coming from a cut on his temple as well as from the mess of his mouth. It was Barnier who fascinated me: he stood back from his opponent; almost calm. I could see his eyes move, constantly checking the big guy's hands, feet, face, as if reading every intention, antici-pating every move. The big guy staggered forward and swung a clumsy, desperate hook at Barnier, who stepped back grace-fully as if allowing an elderly lady to pass him on the *boulevard*. It was then I saw how the Frenchman had been doing so much damage to his opponent. He seemed to lean his entire body back and his leg swung round and up, the side of his foot like a scythe through the air. It slammed into the side of the big man's head. Costello's goon toppled like a felled tree.

I took a few backward steps until I stood shoulder-to-shoulder with Barnier, both of us ready should our playmates get up from the pavement. There was a huddle of people behind us on the steps of the Carvery and in the distance I heard the urgent trilling of a police car's bells.

'I 'phoned them,' Barnier said to me in French and without turning to me. He was a cool one all right. 'So we better get our story straight.'

The goon whose head I had cracked on the pavement hauled himself upright, leaning on the wing of his car. He looked across at Barnier and me. His eyes were still a little glazed but he was focussed enough to see that we were ready to deal with any more fun and games and clearly decided that the playtime bell had rung. He picked up his pal's trilby and poked him with his foot, muttering something about the police. The two goons clambered clumsily into the Wolseley and drove off.

'Who were your chums?' asked Barnier, again in French.

'Dissatisfied customers,' I said.

'You best come back inside and get cleaned up.'

I nodded and started to follow him into the Carvery, ignoring the arrival of a black police Wolseley 6/80. When we got to the front door, Barnier delivered me into the care of the geriatric bellboy who escorted me down some red carpeted stairs to the gents' toilets. There was an attendant there who looked shocked, so I guessed that my face must have been a mess. However, when I looked in the mirror above the wash-hand basins, it didn't look too bad and I asked for a wet towel to hold against my cheek to keep it from swelling up and bruising too much. While I waited for the towel, I washed my hands and face, cupping some cold water and running it over the back of my neck. I had to ease myself up slowly from the basin, pressing a hand gingerly into the small of my back, where the raincoat had kicked me. I was getting too old for this.

I dried myself off, straightened my collar and tie and got my elderly bellhop in the monkey jacket to dust down my jacket before helping me on with it.

'Perfectly dreadful, sir,' he said with genuine dismay. 'Perfectly dreadful that one can't mind one's own business without being accosted and robbed in the street.'

I nodded and smiled wearily. That was obviously the story Barnier had given them when he told them to call the cops. I pressed the damp towel to my cheek. The old hop disappeared back up the stairs and came down a minute later with ice wrapped in a napkin. I was impressed he could move so fast. I leaned against the porcelain tiled wall and held the ice to the side of my face. After a few minutes I tipped both the hop and the toilet attendant and headed back up the red-carpeted stairs to the lounge. When I got there, Barnier was at the front door talking to the two police constables. It was the tenor of the place that the uniforms had to stay at the front door, not even being allowed to conduct their interview in a staff room or office. Whatever it was that Barnier had said to them, they were clearly satisfied with it and they headed off back to the car without taking a statement from me. The one thing I noticed about Barnier was that there wasn't a mark on him and the impeccable grey flannel was still impeccable. He came over to me, slapped me on the shoulder and grinned.

'I think you could do with another cognac, no?'

'I could do with another cognac, yes,' I said.

We went back and sat at the same booth. 'What did you say to get rid of the cops?' I asked.

'I told them that you were my cousin from Quebec and that you couldn't speak a word of English. I told them that the two guys outside had tried to rob you and that I and the manager in here had seen the whole thing. I gave them a phoney description of the car and sent them on their way.'

'They didn't want to speak to me?'

'I told them you spoke only French and that you were going home in a couple of days and that you did not want the complication of pressing charges or having to delay travelling.'

'And they were satisfied with that?'

'This is the police we are discussing, my friend. Dealing with a foreign national who is about to head off home is complicated. And if there is one thing I have learned about policemen the world over, it is that they do not like complications. Now, why not tell me what that was really all about. Has it some connection to young Mr Pollock's disappearance?'

'Yes. Or at least in a way. Sammy Pollock was hanging around with Paul Costello. He's the son of Jimmy Costello. Have you heard of Jimmy Costello?'

Barnier gave another Gallic shrug and shook his head.

'Costello is a crook and a thug. Small-time stuff, but he has a small gang. Our two dancing partners would be paid-up members. Costello also has a waster of a son. It takes something to be such a wash-out that you're a disappointment to the underworld, but that's what young Paul is. Anyway, he was hanging around with Sammy Pollock before he went missing. He also had a key for Sammy's apartment. I took it from him and we had a frank exchange of views. So frank that I think I may have cracked the odd bone.'

'And Papa Costello is not pleased?'

'It would appear not. But, to be honest, I don't think he gives a shit. That outside was him going through the motions. He maybe doesn't really care about me giving his son a slap, but he has to be seen to take exception. Big people for appearances, our criminal fraternity chums . . .'

'Well, I think you may receive a return visit from your friends. Or their colleagues.' He arched an eyebrow.

'Maybe I should hang around you. That was pretty fancy footwork.'

'*Savate*. French Foot Fighting. It is sometimes called the *jeu Marseillais* because it became very popular in Marseille in the last century. Sailors, you see. The idea is that if you are fighting on a ship at sea, then it is better to have a hand free to hang onto something if the ship is pitching.'

'Yeah . . .' I said. I'd heard of *savate*, but what I'd seen outside had been something more. 'But I thought that *savate* was a type of street fighting. Dockers and sailors. If you don't mind me saying, you don't strike me as someone who spent his youth brawling in the backstreets of Marseille.'

'Do I not?' Barnier replied. 'Perhaps not. But if there's one thing I have learned in life, it's that people are very seldom who we think they are. Anyway, *savate* has become a little gentrified over the years. A sport. Alexandre Dumas *fils* studied it.' I watched the Frenchman's cruel, handsome face. The smile he framed with the trimmed moustache and goatee beard had something knowing about it. And something melancholic. He struck me as a weary, sad Satan.

'Well, whatever its origins,' I said. 'I was glad of it. Thanks for your help out there. And with the police.'

Barnier gave a small shrug.

There seemed to be nothing more to say to each other and my feet took me back out onto the street and to my car. This time there were no heavies waiting for me. For the moment. I would have to deal with the Costello situation sooner or later.

As I opened the door of the Atlantic, I looked back towards the Merchants' Carvery. Barnier was at the window of the lounge bar, watching; just as he must have done when he saw Costello's men jump me.

Barnier bothered me. I had no reason to doubt what he had told me about his relationship, or lack of it, with Sammy Pollock. What was bothering me probably had nothing to do with that at all. It was just that there was something about the Frenchman. Some shadow he dragged around with him. And for a wine merchant, he certainly knew how to handle himself.

I called in at Lorna's on the way back to my flat. I had hoped that the cold compress had stopped the side of my face swelling up and bruising too much, but it was still tender to the touch and Lorna noticed it as soon as I arrived.

'What happened?' she asked as she let me in, but her concern was grief-dulled and she was content with a dismissive shrug and a mumbled 'It's nothing . . .'

We sat in the living room, alone. Maggie MacFarlane was out. Making arrangements, she had told Lorna. I wondered how many of those arrangements would involve the matinee idol I saw pull up the day before.

Lorna looked tired and her eyes were red-rimmed from crying. I spoke softly and soothingly and did all of the right things that a sensitive suitor should do. After a while, and when the moment seemed to open up and allow it, I asked her about the visitor in the Lanchester–Daimler. She looked at me blankly for a moment.

'Tall, dark hair . . . moustache,' I prompted.

A look of dull enlightenment crossed her expression. 'Oh yes . . . Jack. Jack Collins. He was Dad's partner. And he's a family friend.'

'Partner? I didn't think that your father had a partner.'

'Oh, no, not in the bookie business. Jack Collins is involved with boxing. He arranges matches. I think he's like an agent or promoter for some of the fights. He and my father were putting together some fights. They had set up a company together. Jack and my dad were ... *close*. Jack really is like a member of the family.'

'They weren't involved in arranging this Kirkcaldy–Schmidtke fight, were they?'

'No ... nothing as big as that. Why are you asking?'

'Just curious,' I said. 'Why was he round here yesterday?'

'He's been helping sort out some of the business stuff.'

'I see. Helping your stepmother?'

Lorna looked at me puzzled. Then it dawned on her. 'Oh no. Nothing like that. Trust me, I wouldn't put it past Maggie. I wouldn't put anything past Maggie. But I don't think Jack is in the slightest bit interested. Apparently he has a string of glamorous girlfriends.' She made an attempt at a mischievous smile, but her sadness washed it away as if it had been drawn in sand. 'Like I said, Jack and Dad were very close. There's no way Jack would ...'

'What did he want? Last night, I mean?'

'Just to see if he could help. And he was looking for some papers that Dad had.'

'Did he find them?'

'No, I don't think so.'

I had a drink with Lorna and she clung to me again when I was leaving. I fought down the sense of irritation that seemed to well up inside me. Again Lorna was breaking our contract of being mutually undemanding. I was, I thought to myself, a real piece of work.

When I got back to my apartment, I used the 'phone in the

hall to call Sheila Gainsborough at the number she had given me for her agent. The same light, effeminate voice answered. I asked to speak to Miss Gainsborough: there was a sigh and a silence, then she came on the line. I went through the progress I had made, which didn't take long.

'Have you heard from Sammy at all?'

'No,' she said. 'Nothing.' The transatlantic voice sounded tired and strained. 'I was hoping . . .'

'I'm still looking, Miss Gainsborough. I spoke to the Frenchman, Barnier. He doesn't seem to know Sammy that well after all.'

'Doesn't he?' She sounded surprised. But only vaguely. 'Sammy mentioned him a couple of times. I thought they knew each other.'

'Oh, he does know Sammy. Just not that well.'

We talked for another few minutes: there was little more she could tell me and there was less I could tell her. I promised to keep her fully informed of progress.

After I hung up I felt something dead and leaden in my chest. Every time I thought about Sammy Pollock, the picture darkened a little.

CHAPTER SIX

When the war ended, Britain had committed itself to a more equitable society. Maybe that was why, when Beveridge and company were planning the Welfare State and a fair deal for all, Willie Sneddon, Jonny Cohen and Hammer Murphy were coming up with the Three King deal. The whole idea had been to divide up Glasgow equally between them. Fair shares.

The cake may have been cut up equally, but somehow Willie Sneddon had managed to grab most of the icing. Of the Three Kings, Sneddon was by far the richest. No one really knew – but many suspected – how he had managed to amass just quite so much wealth. It was a quandary that had no doubt cost Hammer Murphy more than his fair share of sleepless nights trying to work out. Truth was that, if you knew Willie Sneddon, it wasn't that much of a mystery. There was something dark, cunning and devious about his nature, even more than you would expect from your average crime lord. Sneddon was a wheeler and dealer. More than just a criminal, he was a criminal entrepreneur, always seeking out that extra angle; always trying to find some new way of squeezing a penny out of a situation.

I knew – although I never discussed it with him – that the bulk of Jonny Cohen's money did not come from his clubs and other rackets. The main source of Jonny's income came from large-scale criminal acts: robberies mainly, break-ins, long firm frauds, the odd bit of extortion. With Jonny Cohen – and Hammer Murphy, for that matter – the bulk of their earnings came from big hits which yielded large sums of cash. The big score. Willie Sneddon was in the same line of business, but everyone knew that he had so many other deals and rackets running at the same time that he had a steady, constant cash harvest. Added to all of this there was the other dimension of his activities: Willie Sneddon the businessman. Sneddon had displayed genuine acumen for legitimate business, even if it had been founded on stolen, extorted or counterfeited cash. Like most big league crooks, he had started a number of seemingly legitimate concerns, fronts through which to launder dirty money. Where Sneddon had distinguished himself from the usual robber barons was in the way he had been able to turn these fronts into genuinely successful and legitimate businesses.

But it never took much scratching to expose the brass crook under the gilt veneer. The fact was that wherever there was a shilling to be made, crooked or legit, Sneddon had the nose to sniff it out.

All of this meant that Sneddon, unlike the recently deceased Small Change MacFarlane, had been able to make it across the social Rubicon of the Clyde. And then some. The Sneddon residence, a large mock-baronial mansion on a plot of land so big it could have had its own Lord Lieutenant and council, was in the leafiest and most upmarket end of leafy and upmarket Bearsden. I knew that he counted a High Court judge, a couple of shipyard owners, and several other captains of industry amongst his neighbours. I wondered how the judge felt about sharing a laburnum and privet border with Glasgow's most successful criminal. But there again, Willie Sneddon had attained the level of wealth and influence within the city where some of the people he had dealings with no doubt thought it bad taste to bring up some of the more dubious origins of that wealth.

And, of course, the odd brown envelope stuffed with cash would have helped. Glasgow was a city where anything could be bought. Even respectability.

I couldn't put off seeing Sneddon any longer. He would be looking for news and the only news I had for him was that putting me on the Bobby Kirkcaldy case was a waste of time and that Maggie MacFarlane had confirmed that Small Change never kept a secret appointments diary.

It wasn't raining. There was a more than half-hearted sun behind a milky veil of cloud and the air wasn't heavy and oppressively humid as it had been. I got up, shaved, and dressed in a pale blue silk shirt with dark burgundy tie and a two-button two-piece: deep blue with a touch of mohair spun through it. It had no weight and hung well and had cost me an arm and a leg. Deep blue socks and burgundy Oxfords. I brushed the shoulders of the suit jacket, donned it, and straightened my tie in the mirror. I put on my new hat, a skinny-brimmed Borsalino, and checked myself in the mirror. Damn, this suit hung well. It seemed such a shame to bag it down with the weight, but I was expecting that I would, sooner or later, run into Costello or a member or two of his robust entourage.

I habitually carry a sap with me: six inches long, spring-steel with a lead ball on the end, all encased in stitched leather. But I was a slave to fashion and I didn't want it bagging my suit. Fortunately I had a slimline equivalent: a nine-inch blackjack. Basically the same principle, but flattened out, only the width of a wallet and almost like a small version of a barber's leather razor strop. It was an elegant-looking thing, slim and black, like something Chanel would have designed for Al Capone.

I slipped the blackjack into my inside jacket pocket. On the left, where I could pull it out with my right hand. The leaden weight of it tugged that side of my jacket, but I decided to live with it. A flat blackjack is often missed when someone frisks you: it feels like a wallet. And I didn't feel like going out onto the street without some insurance.

I 'phoned Sneddon to arrange a meet. He told me he was tied up all day and couldn't I give him the information over the 'phone. I said I'd rather talk to him face-to-face, and anyway it wasn't the kind of thing to discuss over the 'phone, or some shit like that. He bought it and told me to call round in the evening, about eight-thirty.

I had 'phoned him first to make the point that calling and arranging a mutually convenient time was preferable to being lifted from the street by Twinkletoes McBride. Added to which, unlike the farmhouse out by Dumbarton, the place in Bearsden was Sneddon's home, as well as business headquarters. Maybe I could even persuade Jimmy Costello to follow the same diary etiquette. Though I doubted it.

Before I went out, I stopped at the hall 'phone and called Lorna at home. She was bearing up well, it seemed, but her voice still sounded tired and grief-dulled. I somehow got by with a promise to 'phone her later, without calling in at the house. I did ask her if the police had been around to ask anything else and if Jack Collins had been around again. No to both questions. Then we had one of those long silences where we each waited for the other to say something. Something meaningful or comforting. Something to take us out of our depth: shallow.

'I'll hear from you later then,' she said eventually, her tone still colourless, and hung up.

I drove out to the East End, to Dennistoun. Like many of the fine districts of Glasgow, it was a great thing to be able to claim that you came from Dennistoun. It was ever going back there

that was to be avoided. Dennistoun was a warren of old tenements, dressed in grime that had belched from chimneys when
Victoria had been a lass. As I drove into it there were gaps and
clear spaces where some of the more derelict slums had been
cleared. Shiny new blocks of flats were already in residence on
a couple of the cleared sites.

I drove to the far side of Dennistoun, to an incongruous green
patchwork square of allotments. Behind those, an equally incongruous building, made out of corrugated metal sheets bolted
together and which looked like it belonged in a shipyard.

I parked and went in through a door under a sign that told
the world this was *McAskill's Gymnasium*. Inside, there were two
practice rings, the ropes sagging and the canvas grey, and several
punch bags hung unpunched from the ceiling. It was quiet in
the gym. The only person was an old man in a turtleneck sweater
and flat cap sitting over in the far corner on a battered old
armchair, reading a newspaper. He looked up when I came in,
carefully folded the newspaper and came over to me.

'Hi, Lennox . . .' Old McAskill smiled at me. It was a weary
smile on a weary face that had also had more than its fair share
of encounters with a gloved fist. He jerked his capped head in
the direction of the office at the back. 'He's in there . . .'

I went through to the office. A lean man with a too-long face
was sitting behind the desk, smoking. He looked about forty
but I knew he was ten years younger than that. He had put his
hat on the desktop and I could see it was the kind of wide-
brimmed fedora that had been out of fashion for half-a-decade.
I dropped my skinny-brimmed Borsalino on the desk next to it.
To make a point.

'Mr Lennox . . .' The man smiled and stood up. He was tall.
No surprise: the City of Glasgow Police had a minimum height
requirement of six feet, hence the fact that at least two-thirds

of their number came from outside Glasgow. He shook hands with me. Now, it has to be said that City of Glasgow cops were not in the habit of calling me 'Mister' or shaking hands with me, unless it was to snap a pair of cuffs on me. But Detective Constable Donald Taylor was different. We had an arrangement.

'Thanks for coming, Donald. You on duty?'

'Backshift. Start at two.'

'Did you find out anything about what I asked you?'

He shook his head. 'Not much, I'm afraid, Mr Lennox. Bobby Kirkcaldy isn't Glaswegian. He was born in Motherwell. To sniff around any more I'd have to contact the Lanarkshire County Police. That would start questions.'

'But you would at least be able to check out whether he has a record or not.'

'Oh aye . . . I did that. Nothing. And from what I can gather there are no rumours about him. He seems to be straight.'

'What about the other thing? Small Change MacFarlane?'

'Sorry . . . no joy there either. I'm not on the case and, again, if I start asking too many questions, the gaffers'll get suspicious. I did talk to the evidence sergeant though. Conversational, like. He said they took tons of stuff away from MacFarlane's place. With his missus's say-so, like.'

'Nothing else?'

'Couple of things. Inspector Ferguson was asking about you.'

'He knows you know me?'

'No, not really. Well not that we . . . well, do *business*. Inspector Ferguson doesn't go in for that kind of thing. It was just that he knew that I'd interviewed you about that business last year. When you was away abroad.'

I nodded. Jock Ferguson had been my main contact in the police. Not paid for. A straight copper. Or so I had thought. I hadn't spoken to him in six months.

'What was the other thing?' I asked.

'It's just one of the reasons I couldn't ask too many questions about the MacFarlane thing. There's been all kinds of top brass sticking their noses into it. It's like there's something more to it than just a simple robbery.'

'And . . .?' I said impatiently. I knew Taylor was building up to something. Or building something – or nothing – up. He knew that I only paid for results.

'There was a Yank in St. Andrew's Square. He was in with Superintendent McNab and the DCC.'

'An American?'

'Think so. I passed them in the corridor. He talked like you.'

'I'm not American. I'm Canadian.'

'Yeah . . . his accent was stronger. He was a big man. Big as McNab. Loud suits.'

'So what's this got to do with me?'

'Well, you know what tarts are like. The typing pool and the women police constables were swooning all over the place because of his accent. He was the talk of the steamie. I'm friendly with one of the girls who works up in the DCC's office. She says they asked for all the files on MacFarlane's murder.'

'So this guy's an American cop?'

'Don't know. Someone said he was a private detective. Like you.'

'Okay . . .' I thought for a moment. 'Anything else going on?'

'Just this other murder.'

'What other murder?' I asked.

'The guy they found by the train tracks.'

'I thought that was an accident.' I lit another cigarette, pushing the pack across the desk for him to help himself. 'What are you Einsteins up to? You going to arrest the train driver?'

'Superintendent McNab is as mad as hell about it. Everyone

was happy that it was the train that killed him. I mean, they had to use *spades* to get all of him gathered up. But the pathologist who did the post-mortem said the guy was dead before the train ran over him. The other thing is he had two busted fingers and knuckles skinned to fuck. The quack says it looked to him like the guy'd been in a fight and was beaten to death, then dumped. The train mashed him up to buggery and the thinking is that whoever killed him dumped him on the tracks.'

'Makes sense,' I said. 'There was a good chance that no one would question that the injuries were caused by anything other than the train. Who was he?'

'No idea. No one's reported anyone missing that fits and he didn't have any identification on him. This pathologist is some new hot-shot with fancy tricks. He put in his report that from the stiff's build, the calluses on his palms and his colouring, he reckons he was a manual labourer of some sort. It fits with the clothes.' Taylor laughed. A thin, mean laugh. 'I think the pathologist's going to be our next murder victim. Superintendent McNab is really pissed off that he's been lumbered with another killing. Doesn't like paperwork, does the Superintendent.'

I nodded. I could see McNab prioritizing deaths. Nobodies, somebodies and, right at the top, coppers. If you killed a policeman, then McNab would be harder to stop in his tracks than the train that had mashed the labourer's corpse.

Taylor talked for another ten minutes without saying anything, again trying to justify his fee. When he was finished I thanked him and gave him the number of the wall 'phone in the hall at my digs.

'Give me a ring if you hear anything else. It'll be worth your while.' I opened my wallet and handed him three tenners. Coppers didn't come cheap.

After Taylor had gone I went back out into the gym. A couple of youths had arrived and had changed into boxing shorts and white singlets. They looked skinny and too pale. Both were working the punch bags and Old McAskill was leaning against the wall watching them disinterestedly.

I walked over to the old man and slipped him a fiver. 'Thanks for the loan of the office, Mac. Do you know much about Bobby Kirkcaldy?'

'Not much. He's a great wee mover. He's going to malky that Kraut next week.'

'You reckon?'

'No doubt about it.'

'But you've never come across him? I mean through the boxing.'

'Naw. He wouldn't pish on a place like this if it was on fire. Anyways, he's a country boy. No' Glasgow.'

I smiled at the thought that McAskill pictured Motherwell as some bucolic paradise. I suppose, in comparison to Dennistoun, it was.

'He's got a minder. Says he's his uncle. About your age. Calls him Uncle Bert.'

Old McAskill seemed to be concentrating. It took a lot of effort. He was clearly trying to retrieve something from a brain that had been rattled about in his skull by years of punches. It must have been like trying to pick a specific ball out of a spinning bingo cage.

'What does he look like?'

'Like he's used his face to break toffee.'

'Fuck . . .' He'd clearly found the ball he'd been searching for. 'Albert Soutar. Is he Kirkcaldy's uncle?'

I shrugged.

'Is his nose all busted to fuck?'

'I don't think *to fuck* covers it adequately. He could sniff his ears with it.'

'That sounds like Soutar all right. And he had family out in Lanarkshire. That's one bad wee fucker. Or was.'

'In what way?'

'In the late Twenties, early Thirties, he went professional, but he was shite. A slugger who stopped too many punches with his head. Did a lot of bare-knuckle too. Then he went inside.'

'Prison?'

'Aye. He was in with the Bridgeton Billy Boys. Razor gang. He was supposed to have cut up a copper. He kept his razor in the peak of his bunnet.' McAskill touched his own flat cap. 'He was a bad, bad bastard. He abused the privilege of being a cunt, as my old Da would say.'

I smiled, picturing the cozy fireside scene of young son on father's knee being inducted into the world of abusive epithets.

'So you think that Uncle Albert is the same guy?'

'Could be.' McAskill shook his head slowly. 'If it is, then he's so crooked he pisses corkscrews. I'd be surprised if young Kirkcaldy would have anything to do with him.'

I drove out of Dennistoun and had lunch – if you could call it that – at the Horsehead Bar. I ordered a pie and a pint and while I was proving valid the scientific principle that oil and water don't mix, I spotted Joe Gallagher, a journalist friend, at the other side of the bar. I use the word friend loosely, not just in terms of this guy, but generally for the acquaintances I had made in Glasgow since I first arrived in the city. Drinking buddy would have been a better description in Joe's case.

The price of information from journos is much cheaper than cops on the take. Usually a pint and a whisky chaser opens the channels of communication, so I made my way round to Joe's side of the bar and asked him what he was having.

I left half an hour later. My newspaper chum had told me that he had interviewed Kirkcaldy on a couple of occasions. Smart kid, in Joe's opinion. He had mentioned the battered old minder who seemed always to be at Kirkcaldy's shoulder.

'Yeah . . . calls him his uncle, I believe . . .' I had said.

'Some uncle,' Joe had muttered. 'That's Bert Soutar. Bad sort.'

It was eight-thirty on the dot. I pulled into the long, uphill drive that led through gardens dense with thick, glossy-leaved shrubs and trees and up to Sneddon's mansion. It was a pleasant evening. The deepening blue of the sky didn't seem to suit as a backdrop for the Victorian architecture of Sneddon's place. Gothic and the normal Scottish climate – and the Scottish character – were meant for each other. Even Sneddon's black Bentley R-type seemed to lurk on the drive; I parked behind it and went up to the house, half-expecting Vincent Price to answer the door and ask me in to see his waxworks. Vincent Price would have been good: my ring of the bell was answered by Singer opening the door and silently standing to one side to let me into the hall.

Sneddon didn't do his usual trick of keeping me waiting and I was led into his study. The bookshelved walls were heavy with learning and the room had a rich smell of walnut and leather. I somehow didn't think that Sneddon spent much time in here acquainting himself with literature.

'You got something for me already?' Sneddon sat down behind a tree-and-a-half of desk. I'd seen smaller aircraft carriers. He was wearing a well-tailored blue pinstripe three-piece with a handmade white and blue striped silk shirt, and a pale and plum red tie. It could have been the outfit of a Surrey stockbroker, but all it did was emphasize the razor scar and the hard, vicious face behind it.

'I saw Kirkcaldy yesterday,' I said.

'And?'

'There's nothing for me to go on. He can't tell me anything. This is a watch and wait job. You've got to catch whoever's doing this in the act.'

'So watch and wait.'

'I can't be there twenty-four hours a day. And I would have thought that you'd maybe want a couple of your guys to be there to mete out some *extempory* retribution when they do show up again.'

'I hired you because I want you to find out what's going on. I mean what's *really* going on.' Sneddon's hard blue-grey eyes were fixed on mine, as if trying to communicate a deeper meaning.

'I see. So Jonny Cohen's not the only one who thinks there's something more to this.'

Sneddon looked over my shoulder and past me, jerking his head in a gesture of dismissal. I turned and saw that Singer had been standing, silently of course, by the door. I had thought he'd left us alone after he'd shown us in, so if he'd been lurking for my benefit, then it had been a wasted effort.

'I've got a lot of fucking money riding on Kirkcaldy,' Sneddon said after Singer had left, closing the heavy door behind him. 'More than you can imagine. What did he tell you?'

Referring to my notebook, I ran through the facts as Kirkcaldy had related them to me. When I had finished and closed the notebook, Sneddon kept his hard eyes on me. He raised a questioning eyebrow.

'Okay,' I said. 'You want to know what I think, rather than what I found out. All right . . . Bobby Kirkcaldy went out of his way, several times, to tell me that I was wasting my time. That it was no big deal. He positively leapt on the notion that this was all just some bollocks to put him off his game before the big fight. And he reassured me that it would do no such thing.'

'So?'

'It was like he wanted to brush the whole thing off. Brush me off. How did you find out about this anyway? Did Kirkcaldy tell you?'

'No, he didn't. His manager told me.'

'And Kirkcaldy had complained to him about it?'

'No, as a matter of fact.' Sneddon's face remained impassive. 'His manager turned up at the house and saw the car covered in red paint. He asked Bobby what was going on and got the same tale you did.'

'Yeah . . .' I offered Sneddon a cigarette. He shook his head impatiently. I took my time lighting mine. 'Kirkcaldy is very dismissive about the whole thing. I asked him if it could be something personal – a grudge, an old enemy from the past, that kind of thing, and not related to the fight – he made a big show of thinking about it before telling me he couldn't think of anybody. Now if it were me and someone was leaving dead birds, nooses and crap like that on my doorstep, I think I would already have done a lot of thinking about anyone who might have an old grudge to settle. I don't think I'd need someone to come along and put the idea to me first.'

'So you think he knows what this is all about?'

'I'm not saying that, but let's face it . . . Jonny Cohen smells something fishy about the whole thing, so do I. Now you seem to smell a rat. What do you know about Kirkcaldy? I mean apart from his abilities in the ring?'

'Not as much as I'd like. You seen him fight?'

'Couple of times, yeah.'

'I know enough about the fight game to know that being a winner – I mean a *real* winner – is as much about what you've got up here as how hard you can hit.' Sneddon tapped his temple with his forefinger. 'And Kirkcaldy has got it all. He boxes clever. But more than that, he's ambitious.'

'Well, I thought you would have wanted that in a fighter you're backing.'

'Aye . . . I do. But what worries me is how much ambition he's got *outside* the ring.'

'Listen, Mr Sneddon . . .' I leaned forward and rested my elbows on my knees. 'There's no point in you being elliptical . . .'

'What the fuck does that mean? You been at the *Reader's Digest* with Twinkletoes?'

'It's clear to me that you have suspicions that you're not sharing. The other thing is, you could have dealt with all of this with your own men, sitting it out until whoever is doing this shows up to pull another stunt. But you got me involved to see if I smelt the same rat that you and Jonny Cohen clearly have. So why don't you tell me what it is you *really* want me to find out?'

Sneddon moved his mouth into the ugly shape he took for a smile. 'Maybe I like being epileptic . . .'

'Elliptical . . .' I corrected, and wished I hadn't. The coarse approximation of a smile dropped from Sneddon's face. 'Bobby Kirkcaldy has a shadow with him all the time. An old guy with a mashed-up face. Kirkcaldy calls him Uncle Bert. I've checked him out and it turns out he's an ex-razor gangster called Bert Soutar. Bridgeton Billy Boys back in the Thirties.'

'I remember the Billy Boys,' said Sneddon. I had no doubt that he did. The Billy Boys had been a Protestant sectarian gang, organized along military lines. Sneddon had only one weakness in business, one gap in his calculating objectivity.

He was a bigot to the bone. 'But I've never heard tell of a Bert Soutar.'

'He did time.'

Sneddon made a face and shrugged. 'Cutting up a few Fenians doesn't make him Al Capone. You think it's significant?'

'It suggests Kirkcaldy perhaps isn't as up-and-up as he seems. Maybe *Uncle Bert* is connected to dodgy dealings. It could explain the warnings.'

'Okay,' said Sneddon. 'Keep on it and see what you can turn up. I asked you about something else. Small Change's appointment book. Have you looked for that?'

'I asked Small Change's wife . . . widow . . . she said he didn't keep one. She said he did keep everything in his head. The police took some stuff away with them.'

'They warrant it?'

'No . . . no warrant. Maggie MacFarlane gave them the okay. By the way, she's already had a gentleman caller. Jack Collins. You know him?'

'Oh aye . . . I know Collins. Small Change had him as a partner in one of the bookie shops. And small-time fight arranging.'

'Is there any reason that I should be looking at Collins for anything?'

Sneddon laughed in a way that suggested he was out of practice. 'You could say that. Why don't you look at Collins for a family resemblance . . . MacFarlane used to do business with Collins senior. He was a greyhound breeder and racer. A successful one. Truth was Small Change was supposed to have been doing more business with Collins's mother, if you know what I mean.'

'Small Change is Jack Collins's father?'

'Aye. And he knows it. Rab Collins died of a heart attack twenty-odd year ago. Since then Small Change paid for Jack to go to a fancy school, all that crap.'

'I see.' I made the kind of face you make when you've tried every combination but you still can't get the safe open. There was a silence and Sneddon studied me for a moment. I hadn't realized until then that scrutiny can be aggressive. Something was going through his head. Something was always going through his head, but this was tying up his attention and his expression.

'Okay,' he said eventually. 'Here's the thing . . . I told you I met with Small Change earlier that day.'

'The day he was killed?'

'Yes. Well, you know the way Small Change wasn't totally legit, but he was more legit than not. Kinda the way you are. Well, like you, Small Change would do the odd deal with me, or Cohen or Murphy. He never did nothing that would get him lifted by the police. Nothing that he could be tied in directly, like. He was as slippery as snail shit in the rain. He liked to be the middle man. The one who arranges everything, and then he'd get an arranger's fee or a percentage of what came out of it.'

'And he was fixing you up with something to do with the fight game. That's what you told me.'

Sneddon made a face. 'I know. And to start with I thought it was. We were supposed to be meeting to talk about Bobby Kirkcaldy.'

I raised my eyebrows. It was all coming together. But what was coming together still wasn't clear. 'I thought you said that Small Change had nothing to do with Kirkcaldy. He wasn't in that league.'

'Aye. Aye . . . right enough. That's what I thought. But he wanted to talk to me about some deal he wanted to broker. He said Bobby Kirkcaldy was involved. Not as a fighter. As an investor.'

'So, you went to see Small Change. What did he say the deal was?'

'That's the thing. I went up to Small Change's place . . . just as arranged. Got Singer to drive me and wait outside in the car. But when I got there Small Change was shiteing himself. He was white as a fucking sheet. He tried to cover it up but when he poured me a drink his hands were shaking like fuck. Then he comes out with all of this shite about being sorry to have cost me a wasted journey, but the deal he wanted to set up had gone south.'

'Did he tell you what the deal had been?'

'No. Or at least he spun me some shite about Kirkcaldy setting up a boxing academy in the city but that the finance on his side had fallen through.'

'And you don't believe that? Sounds possible.'

Sneddon shook his head. He spread his hands out on the walnut desk top, fingers splayed, and looked at them absently. 'You know the business I'm in, Lennox. The bookies, the protection, the whores, the bank jobs, the fencing. You know what my business really is? Fear. It's fear what keeps the whole fucking thing together. I have spent most of my life filling my pockets by making the other guy fill his pants.' He leaned back in his chair and stared hard at me. 'So when I say that Small Change MacFarlane had had the frighteners put on him, I know what I'm talking about.'

'So did you challenge him?' I asked. 'Did you ask him what was really going on?'

'No. There was no point. I could tell that it would have done fuck all good. Someone had done a real job on MacFarlane. I could have brought Singer in from the car and he would still have kept shtoom.'

I nodded. It was a good point. If someone had been able to

out-menace Sneddon and out-lurk Singer, then there was something serious going on. Sneddon had a cigarette box on his desk:
it looked solid silver and was so big it should have had fifteen
pirates sitting on it. He flipped it open, took out a cigarette and
nudged it across the walnut aircraft carrier in my direction. I
helped myself and used the matching silver desk lighter to light
us both.

'And he ended up dead the same night,' I said.

'Yep.' Sneddon screwed his eyes up against the smoke. 'That's
why I want that appointment book.'

'Not just to keep the cops from knowing you saw Small Change
the day he died. You want to know who he saw before you.'

'Aye. It's maybes not even in the diary. And you say his wife
says he doesn't keep one anyhow.'

'That's what she said. Now I get why you wanted me to sniff
around.' I paused for a moment. I was like the clown in the
circus standing dumbly till the plank the other clown is
swinging around hits him on the back of the head. It hit me.
'Oh yeah ...' I said. 'Now I get it. That's why you've got me
involved with the Bobby Kirkcaldy crap. It's the same deal, isn't
it? You want me to find out if Kirkcaldy is tied up with whatever deal Small Change was brokering.'

'Aye. And my guess is that it's fuck all to do with boxing academies or shite like that. Especially with what you've said about
this dodgy fucking uncle he has in tow.'

'And the nooses and stuff?'

'Maybes it's connected – with the deal I mean, and nothing
to do with the fight what's coming up.'

'I see ...' I drew on the cigarette and contemplated the silver-
grey writhes of smoke. 'Now this takes me into dodgy territory.
You too, for that matter. The police are all over Small Change's
murder and I was left in no doubt by Superintendent Willie

McNab that his wife will be wearing my balls as earrings if I start sniffing around.'

There was the sound of aged wood on wood as Sneddon pulled open a desk drawer. He reached in, took something out and tossed it onto the desk in front of me. It was a large white envelope. It was tucked shut, not sealed, and it was stuffed thick. Rewardingly thick.

'Buy yourself some new balls.' Sneddon nodded to the envelope.

I picked it up and slipped it into my inside jacket pocket without opening it. It tugged satisfyingly at the material of my jacket, balancing the weight of the blackjack in my other inside pocket. I was going to have to start taking a satchel to work.

'You're right, the police are all over MacFarlane like flies on a turd.' Sneddon exposed his talent for colourful metaphor. 'And I ask myself why the fuck that is. He was an important bookie, but the cops on the case are too many and too high-up.'

I nodded. It fitted. I had wondered about McNab's involvement myself. 'So you think the police are onto whatever deal it was that Small Change was setting up?'

'If that's the reason, then it's something really fucking big. And if it's really fucking big, I really fucking want to know about it. You've got contacts in the police, haven't you?'

'Yeah . . .' I said reluctantly, wondering how much Sneddon knew about my arrangement with Taylor. Then the tug of the heavy envelope in my jacket pocket reminded me not to be too reluctant. 'So do you. Probably better than mine.'

'Listen . . .' Sneddon leaned forward and narrowed his eyes. Again he was all brow. 'I've already fucking told you: I don't want to be connected to this. That's why I'm going through you. You want the money or not?'

Taking a last, long draw on the cigarette, I stubbed it out in a boulder of crystal ashtray, picked my hat off his desk and stood up.

'I'll get onto it.' I turned towards the door then checked myself. 'You know everybody who's got a racket going in the city.'

'Just about.' Sneddon leaned back in his green leather and walnut captain's chair. A pirate captain's chair, probably.

'Have you ever heard of anyone called Largo?' I asked.

He thought for a moment then shook his head.

'Okay ... thanks. I just thought I'd ask.'

Industrial pollution can be a beautiful thing. When I came out of Sneddon's I stood by my car for a moment, looking out over to the west. Sneddon's house was elevated in more than a social sense and I could see out across the treetops and past the edge of the city. Glasgow's air was of the granulated variety and it turned sunsets into vast, diffused splashes of colour, like gold and red paint strained through textured silk. I stood and gazed westward, filled with a sense of contentment.

But that had more to do with the wad of cash weighing down my suit jacket than the sunset. I climbed into the Atlantic and headed back down into the city.

I should have been more on my toes. This time there was a little more subtlety and a lot more brains employed.

I was driving back from Sneddon's and was passing along the curve in the road where Bearsden notches down the social ladder to become Milngavie, when I saw a blue 'forty-eight Ford Zephyr Six up ahead, pulled into the kerb. The driver had the hood up and he was standing next to it on the road. He was about thirty-five, with dark hair, and from what I could see smartly dressed. I say from what I could see because he was doing what every true man does when his car breaks down: he was standing on the roadway, one hand on his hip, the other scratching his head. And like every true man, he had had to take his jacket off and roll up his sleeves to do the head-scratching. It was a pose of helplessness mitigated by stubbornness: you've tried everything and you're asking for help only as a last resort.

I muttered a curse when I saw he had noticed my approach and was vaguely wafting a hand about to wave me down. It's a rule: you don't look too desperate for another man's help; you're signalling in another member of the same auto club to provide the assistance that you would provide him, in the same circumstances.

Despite my efforts to the contrary, I am a Canadian. That means, no matter how hard I had tried to cure myself of it, I suffer from the congenital, chronic and truly Canadian ailment of politeness. I may have gotten lippy with gangsters and cops, slapped the odd uppity hooligan, and I may have fornicated, cursed and sworn on occasion, sometimes the same occasion; but I had helped so many little old ladies across the street that the Boy Scouts had taken out a contract on me.

This guy clearly needed help. I had to stop to help him. I was being so Canadian that it didn't occur to me for a second that this could have been a more discreet and subtle attempt by Jimmy Costello at abduction. There again, discreet and subtle were not traits you associated with Costello.

'Having trouble?' I asked as I pulled up next to him and rolled down the window.

He smiled. 'Thanks for stopping.' He opened the door of the Atlantic and dropped into the passenger seat before I could say anything. It was then I noticed the small crescent-shaped scar on his head. I was doing a split-second inventory in my head, trying to remember where I'd filed who had mentioned a five-eight man with dark hair and a crescent-shaped scar on his forehead, when he produced a gun from his trouser pocket. I recognized it as a Webley point-three-two Pocket Hammerless. The youngest it could have been was 1916. It could have dated back to the turn-of-the century.

'This is some kind of joke, right?' I said, with a derisive eyebrow raised at the revolver. But at the same time I was assessing my chances of coshing him with the flat, spring-handled blackjack I had in my inside jacket pocket. When people point guns at me, I get tetchy. I decided it was best to go along with my new chum for the moment. There would be time to discuss my attitude towards being held at gunpoint. Later.

'There's nothing wrong with this gun, pal.'

'There's nothing wrong with my eighty-two-year-old great-uncle Frank, but I wouldn't bring him along on an abduction.'

'Trust me, Lennox. This Webley fires just fine.'

'I'm sure it did when Mata Hari used it to scare off the Kaiser when he was chasing her around a banquet table. Where are you taking me? An antiques fair?'

The dark-haired goon sighed. 'Listen, Lennox, let's not put it to the test. Mr Costello wants to talk to you and the last time you got an invite you cut up rough.' He was better spoken than the average Glaswegian. He was also a cool enough customer. My efforts to rile him and stall until another car came along weren't working. I could see over his shoulder that a second goon had come out of hiding and was dropping the hood on the Zephyr Six.

'What's your pal got? A flintlock blunderbuss?' I said, cracking the joke with a smile to hide the fact that I was weighing up my chances of breaking his neck before he could pull the trigger.

'He's going to follow us. You can drive out to the pub to meet Mr Costello. Mr Costello told me to tell you to take it easy. There's no need to kick up a fuss. You got all heated up and messed up Tony and Joe and it was all unnecessary. This isn't what you think.' He gave an angled nod to indicate the road ahead. 'Let's go.'

I looked at the gun. It could still do the job, right enough. A bullet is a bullet, even if firing it would probably take off a couple of his fingers. 'So you're telling me this isn't all about Paul Costello?'

'You'll have to talk to Mr Costello about that, but no. Or not in the way you think.'

'Okay,' I said and sighed. 'Where to? The Riviera Club?'

'No . . .' My passenger grinned at me; his teeth were nicotine yellow and pitted. 'We're to take you out to the Empire. Just for a talk, like. Nothing heavy. So don't make trouble.'

'Me?' I said in an offended tone. 'I'm like Rab Butler . . . I'm all for consensus.'

My passenger directed me across the Clyde and we drove into Govan. Black tenements loomed on either side and he told me to park outside a public house emblazoned with a sign that declared this was the Empire Bar. The sun was now hiding behind the tenements and dressed in a winding-sheet of thin grey cloud. But gloom was something you associated with Govan.

'Oh look,' I said cheerily as we got out. 'The sun *is* setting on the Empire.' My companion replied by jerking his head towards the bar. The gun was pocketed now but he rested his hand in the same pocket. The Ford Zephyr Six pulled up behind us and the second guy got out. He was about an inch shorter than his colleague, with hair the colour of dirty sand. Both of them were just the way Sheila Gainsborough had described them.

We walked into the bar. It was noisy and it stank. The air was thick with cigarette smoke, stale sweat and whisky fumes. A woman with unnaturally black hair was making shrilly unpleasant sounds in the corner, accompanied by an out-of-tune piano. The Empire Bar was the kind of place you would have described as spit-and-sawdust; if they had bothered with the sawdust. I allowed myself to be guided to a corner table, guessing that Prince Rainier and Grace Kelly wouldn't be waiting for me there. They weren't: a short, fattish man in an expensive but ill-fitting suit was at the table, looking at me glumly as I approached with my escort. He had thick Irish-black hair that needed a cut and a pencil-moustache over a slack, ugly mouth.

'I believe you wanted to speak with me,' I said without a smile and sat down without being asked. Unlike Sneddon, Cohen or Murphy, Jimmy Costello didn't warrant a respectful tone. But, there again, it was exactly that kind of attitude that had gotten me into some of my stickier moments over the last couple of years.

'You want a drink?' Costello asked, his tone neutral.

'Whisky.'

Costello nodded to my dark-haired abductor, who headed off through the fug and throng to the bar, leaving us alone. Maybe this wasn't going to be the adventure I thought it would be. The singer over by the piano seemed to enter a paroxysm of passion. She was a thick-bodied woman in her fifties, about as curvaceous as a beer barrel, with a round, white face, small eyes, hair that was too dark and too long and lips that were too red. She was clearly a singer of the traditional sort, insofar as she was following the age-old Glasgow tradition of adding an extra syllable to every lyric and then singing them through her nose. A Glasgow pub is the place to be if you have an aversion to consonants. The singer informed me and anyone else within a five-mile radius that – apparently – the pipes, the pipes were calling *Dhmnnaa-anny Bhee-hoy.*

My escort arrived with two whiskies and a pint of stout, then left us alone again.

'You gave my boy Paul a hiding,' said Costello. No anger. He sipped his stout and looked at me with little interest.

'He asked for it, Jimmy. He went for a blade. Is this what this is all about?'

'No. And that's not why I sent Tony and Joe to pick you up the other day either. All of that shite . . . it was *unnecessary*.'

'Like I told your monkeys, if you want to talk to me, pick up a 'phone.'

'Listen, Lennox, don't fuck about with me. I'm letting the thing with Paul go. I'm letting the thing with Tony and Joe go . . . and believe me, Tony and Joe don't want it let go . . . So stop talking to me like I'm a piece of shite. You've made it clear what you think of me, but you're on my ground now. I could hand you over to the boys and send you home with your nose out of joint.'

I was about to answer when the singer in the corner reached new heights of volume and tunelessness. '*Dhmnnaaany Beh-ho-oy . . . dnhe beh-ipes, dnhe beh-ipes harr caw-haw-hing . . .*'

'You could try,' I said. 'I'm working for Willie Sneddon. And that's one nose you don't want to put out of joint. So let's cut the crap. What do you want?'

'Why did you beat up Paul?'

'I thought this wasn't about that.'

'It isn't. Not directly. I just need to know why you and him had words. Was it about this Gainsborough boy?'

'Sammy Pollock is his real name. Yes it was, as a matter of fact.'

'He's missing?'

'Yes.'

'So's Paul.'

There was a moment's silence. Or there would have been if Govan's answer to Maria Callas hadn't continued to pipe up.

'*Fuh-hum glemn to glemn ... hend de-hown dnhe mowmn-teh-ain say-hide ... dnhe suhmner his ge-hon, hend hall dnhe flouw-wurs fawh-haw-ing ...*'

'What do you mean missing?' I asked.

'What the fuck do you think I mean? He's missing. He's not around and no one's seen him for three days.'

'And you think I've got something to do with that?'

'No. That's not why you're here. I want you to find him.'

'I'm busy.'

'Aye ... and one of the things you is busy with is finding the Gainsborough boy. It's all connected. Paul was going around with him. They had big ideas. Fuck knows what, but they had big ideas.' Costello's ugly mouth drooped even further beneath the moustache. 'That's all Paul has ... is big ideas. No fucking guts or brains to make anything of them ideas.'

I sipped the whisky. In comparison, the stuff they had served at Sneddon's pikey fight was nectar.

'*Diss heyoo, diss heyoo ewho mnuss ge-ho, hend heye mnuss stuh-hay ...*'

'And you have no idea where he's disappeared to or why?' I asked.

Costello shook a sullen, ugly head.

'The two monkeys who brought me here ... what are their names?'

'What?' Costello looked confused. 'The dark-haired one is called Skelly. His pal is called Young. Why?'

'Did you tell Skelly to stick a gun in my ribs to get me here? I take exception to people pointing guns at me.'

Costello looked at me dourly and shook his head. 'He's a fucking bampot. I told him to make sure you came here. None of my crew should have shooters unless I say so. I'll sort him out.'

'It's okay,' I said. 'I'll have a word with him. I think it's better coming from me, if you know what I mean. But that's not why I was asking about Skelly and Young. I was told they were hanging about Sammy Pollock before he went missing. If it wasn't them, it was their twins, going by the description I got.'

'They're younger than the rest of my people. They hang around with Paul a lot. Maybe they think that he's the future. Some fucking hope. But that's all there is to it: Paul hung around Sammy, and Skelly and Young hung around Paul.'

I made to take another sip of the whisky, then put the glass back down again, deciding I'd rather keep my stomach lined. 'I'll tell you what,' I said. 'I'm still looking into this Sammy Pollock business. If I find out anything about Paul, I'll let you know.'

'I'll pay you . . .'

'No need. But you'll owe me a favour. The other thing is I need you to forget about what happened between me and Paul. And with your other three monkeys.'

'I already said . . .'

'There's more . . .' I looked across at the bar where Skelly was talking to his sandy-haired chum. 'I'm a man of principle, you could say. One of those principles is I don't let people point guns at me.'

'Aw . . . for fuck's sake . . .' Costello looked over to Skelly at the bar then back at me. 'Couldn't you let it go? I can't have you slapping all of my people around.'

'That's the deal.'

Costello paused for the clapping and raucous cheering that accompanied the conclusion of *Dhmnnaaany Beh-ho-oy*. I felt like cheering myself. When the applause died down, Costello nodded, acquiescing in the only way he knew how: sullenly.

'Now, back to young Paul,' I said. 'The first thing I would have thought you would have done is to speak to this guy Largo?'

'What? Who the fuck is Largo?'

'You don't know anyone called Largo?'

'Should I?'

I leaned back and sighed. 'No reason you should. Everybody I've asked about Largo has never heard of him. When I came across Paul at Sammy's flat, he started off thinking I was a copper.'

'He took you for polis?'

'Yeah ... I know,' I said with a sigh. 'I'm making a formal complaint to my tailor. Anyway, when he realized I wasn't, he asked if Largo had sent me. When I asked him who Largo was, he gave me the brush-off, but he did say it was somebody he owed some money to.'

Costello looked at me. His was the expressionless kind of face that was difficult to read. 'I don't like the sound of that,' he said at last. 'Why would Paul be borrowing money from someone? And if he did, how come I've never heard of this fucker Largo?'

'I caught Paul on the hop. It could be that this thing about owing Largo money was just the best explanation he could think of on the spur. Anyway, like I said, I'm looking into who this Largo might be because he could be connected to this thing with Sammy Pollock. And Paul dropping out of sight is probably connected, as you've already guessed.' I paused for a moment. 'What about the "Poppy Club" . . . that mean anything to you?'

Costello shook his head. 'Has that got something to do with Paul?'

'Maybe,' I said. 'Maybe to do with Sammy Pollock. Maybe nothing to do with anything.' I stood up and picked up my hat.

'Okay, would you tell your monkey to give me my keys back. I'll be in touch if I find out anything about Paul.'

'Tell me something, Lennox,' said Costello. 'This thing with Sammy Pollock ... and now with Paul ... are you looking for people or bodies. It doesn't look good does it?'

I shrugged. 'Them disappearing doesn't mean they're dead, Jimmy. I'm beginning to suspect they were doing a bit of business on the side, probably with this guy Largo who no one knows anything about. It could be that he's after them for money and they've both had to take a powder for a while. Who knows.'

'He's my boy, Lennox. My son. He's a waster and a wanker, but he's my son. Find him for me. I don't care what you say, I'll make it worth your while.'

I nodded. 'Okay, Jimmy. I'll see what I can find out.' I put on my Borsalino. 'I'll be waiting at the car, tell Skelly to bring my car keys out to me.'

Fresh air was a relative term in Glasgow, but it was good to get out of the Empire and onto the street. I ignored the grubby tenements and looked up above the roofs and smoke stacks. It was past ten but the sky was still reasonably light. Scotland's latitude made for long summer evenings. There was a burst of noise behind me as the pub door swung open. I turned and saw Skelly come out; his stooge Young was at his side.

'Here's your keys, Lennox.' Skelly smiled his yellow-toothed smile and held them out to me.

'Thanks.' I took the keys in my left hand. 'And I've got a tip for you ...'

I reached inside my jacket pocket with my right hand. For a minute, from the expression on his face, I think Skelly really thought I was going to hand him a ten-bob note. I pulled out the flat, spring-handled blackjack and in a continuous, back-hand movement, whacked him in the side of the mouth with it. The sound was somewhere between a snap and a crunch and he dropped like a stone. His friend took a step towards me and I held out my hand, making a beckoning gesture with my fingers for him to keep coming. Young clearly decided to decline the invitation and backed off.

I leaned over Skelly. He was coming round. His face was a mess of blood. From the look of it, I had done him a favour: he clearly wasn't too keen on toothpaste and I reckoned he would have a few less teeth to clean in the future. I patted him down with my free hand until I found what I was looking for, reached into his jacket pocket and took out the small Webley Three-Two.

'Here's your tip, Skelly . . . never, ever pull a gun on me. Even an antique like this. If you ever pull a stunt like that again, I'll kill you. That's not just an expression: I'll stop you breathing. Got it?'

He made an incoherent moaning sound behind his broken teeth. I took it as his assent. I pocketed the Three-Two and turned to the sandy-haired goon.

'If I see your face again, it'll end up in a worse condition than his. Have *you* got *that*?'

He nodded.

'Have a nice night, girls,' I said amiably, then I climbed into the Atlantic and drove off.

CHAPTER SEVEN

I spent the next couple of days paddling hard and getting nowhere. Nowhere with what had happened to Sammy Pollock. Nowhere on what was going on with Bobby Kirkcaldy. I was considering changing the name of my business to Sisyphus Investigations. The one good thing was I was able to leave a message with Big Bob at the Horsehead for young Davey to get in touch. I would maybe have something for him to do after all.

Sheila Gainsborough was back in town. She called me on her return from London and didn't sound at all pleased that I had so little to report. She insisted on talking face-to-face and asked if I would meet her at Sammy's apartment. I drove over that afternoon.

When I got there the place was unrecognizable. The disorder was tidied and the air in the apartment was scented with beeswax.

Sheila had gathered her blonde hair up with pins and was dressed for serious housework: a red checked shirt-style blouse, the shirt tails tied in a bow at her navel, exposing a couple of inches of pale midriff above the sky-blue Capri pants. She had none of the sophisticated couture she had worn at our last meeting and her face was naked of make-up, other than a quick sweep of crimson around the lips. And she still looked a million dollars.

'I had to tidy the place up,' she said. 'It makes me feel better. Getting it nice for Sammy to come back to, I mean.'

She asked me if I wanted a coffee and I decided to risk it: coffee in Glasgow was typically some chicory sludge from a bottle, mixed with hot water. But Sheila was anything other than typical Glasgow. She returned with a tray encouragingly laden with a percolator, two cups and a plate of pastries. She poured our coffees and sat down opposite me, her knees angled, ankles together, finishing-school style. I thought again about how good a job they had done on her.

She offered me one of the pastries. It was one of those over-sweet things that had become popular since rationing had ended: a doughnut with cream and jam filling – what we used to call a Burlington Bun back home in Atlantic Canada. I didn't know what they called them anywhere else.

'No thanks.' I smiled. 'I don't have a sweet tooth.' I noticed she put the plate back down without taking a pastry herself. That figure was a piece of work.

'The last time we spoke I was really worried about Sammy disappearing . . .' She bit into her crimson lower lip and I found myself wishing she had been biting into mine. 'Now I'm frightened, Mr Lennox. He seems to have vanished from the face of the Earth. And you don't seem to have the slightest clue . . .'

'Listen, Miss Gainsborough. I have found something out. I didn't want to tell you on the 'phone, but do you remember Paul Costello, the guy we came across at Sammy's apartment?'

She nodded. I could see the trepidation in her eyes.

'Well,' I continued, 'I'm afraid he seems to have gone missing too. Same set-up.'

The trepidation became fear and Sheila's eyes glossed with tears.

'I really think you should contact the police,' I said, placing my coffee cup on its saucer and leaning forward. 'I know you're really concerned and, if I'm honest, so am I.'

'But the police ...' She paused and frowned. 'Why do you think they've both disappeared?'

'My theory is that there *is* some truth in what Costello said about this mysterious Largo. I don't think Costello owed him money, the way he claimed, and I don't think this Largo would send heavies here to Sammy's place if he wasn't in some way involved. But Costello denied that too.'

'So what *do* you think is going on?'

'I honestly don't know, but I'm guessing that Sammy and Paul Costello were involved in some kind of deal with Largo and something has gone wrong. If I'm right, that's not necessarily bad news. It could mean that Sammy and Costello have simply gone into hiding. Voluntarily. That would explain why they're so hard to find. That's the way they want it. But it's just a hunch. I think you should go to the police. There's something clearly not right here. Even if Sammy has headed off under his own steam, it would suggest that he's got something to be afraid of.'

'No. No police. If what you're saying is true, then there's a good chance Sammy's broken the law. *Seriously* broken the law. He wouldn't be able to stand prison.' She frowned her cute frown for a moment then shook her head decisively. 'No. No, I want *you* to keep looking for Sammy. Do you need more money?'

'I'm fine for the moment, Miss Gainsborough. The only thing I'd ask is that you tell your agent that I don't work for him. I've nothing to say to him about anything. I deal with you directly. Are you okay with that?'

She nodded. I reached into my pocket for a cigarette, but my case was empty.

'Oh, hold on a minute ...' She stood up and looked about

herself. 'Sammy smokes. I'm sure I found some cigarettes when I was tidying up. Oh yes . . .' She crossed to the dresser against the wall and brought over a silver desktop cigar box. She flipped it open and offered me one.

'They're filtered,' she said apologetically. Then she frowned. 'Look . . . they're the kind you asked about. The butt you showed me with lipstick on it.'

I took a cigarette and examined it. It had two gold bands around the filter. 'Yeah . . . they're Montpelliers. A French brand. There's a lot of them about, it would seem.' I lit the cigarette and drew on it. It was like straining steam through a blanket. I nipped off the filter between finger and thumb and dropped it into the ashtray, pinching the ragged end tight.

'Sorry,' I said. 'Filters are okay for women. But for me they kill the flavour.'

Sheila smiled the smile of somebody responding to something they hadn't listened to. 'So you'll keep looking?' she asked.

'I'll keep looking,' I said, pausing to pick a couple of tobacco strands from my tongue. 'I know you don't want the police involved, but would you mind if I spoke to a couple of police contacts. Strictly on the Q.T. and off the record.'

'What if they get suspicious?'

'The kind of cops I'm talking about don't get suspicious, they just get expensive. Leave it to me.'

We talked for another half hour. I asked if she could remember anything more about the people her brother had been hanging around with, particularly the girl, Claire. I also asked her to think again about the name Largo. I drew a double blank. I asked if there had been any places with which Sammy had a particular attachment: anywhere he may have sought sanctuary in. She tried. She really tried, the poor kid, but she couldn't think of anywhere, anything or anyone that might bring me closer to finding her missing brother.

I left her to her desperately methodical housework. As I was leaving, I said that at least Sammy would be coming back to the place all nice.

The truth was that we both suspected she was simply dressing a grave.

It was on the Thursday night that I got a break. Such as it was. I had been doing the rounds of clubs and bars. Most knew Paul Costello only as Jimmy Costello's son. And the few that had heard of Sammy Pollock/Gainsborough again made the link only through Sheila Gainsborough. I struggled to find any musicians or singers who had heard of them, far less been approached with offers of representation. I worked my way from the few hep joints Glasgow had, like the Swing Den and the Manhattan, to the rougher workingmen's clubs that abounded across the city.

The Caesar Club was one of the latter category. It combined industrial drinking with performers so bad that you *had* to drink industrially to tolerate them. I arrived about nine-thirty.

The Caesar Club was well named. It was the kind of place that left no turn un-stoned, and the acts who took to the stage weren't so much performers as gladiators. I half expected to see Nero in a dickie-bow sitting at the front table giving each turn the thumbs-down. When I walked in there was a comedian on the stage. He had succeeded in warming up the audience in much the same way as Boris Karloff had warmed up an angry peasant mob with torches in *Frankenstein*.

The audience was on the cusp of verbal violence turning physical and, despite the fixed grin above the oversized bow tie, I could see the comic's eyes glittering as they darted desperately around the crowd. I wasn't sure whether he was trying to find just one person laughing or trying to gauge from where the first missile would be launched. I wondered why anyone would choose to be a comedian in Glasgow when there were so many less hazardous career options like bomb disposal, bullfighting or sword-swallowing. I started to feel a deep, real sympathy for the comedian.

Then I heard a couple of his jokes and decided he had it coming.

I knew the manager of the Caesar Club and he pushed an unbidden and unwanted pint of warm stout in my hand and conducted me through backstage.

'This is who I told you about, Lennox,' he said, as he led me along a narrow corridor and shoved open a cupboard door in the hall. I could still hear the audience responding to the comic's act and for the first time understood what baying for blood sounded like.

The cupboard turned out to be the smallest dressing room I'd ever seen; and in my colourful career, I'd seen a lot of dressing rooms. This one, however, was not occupied by a chorus girl but by a small man of about fifty with large brown eyes and no hair to speak of on his egg-shaped head. There was no shade on the bulb that hung from the ceiling and its butter gleam on his pale skin added to the Humpty-Dumpty look. He was dressed in a cheap dinner suit and bow tie. A gleaming trumpet sat on his lap, its case lying open on the shelf that passed as a dressing table. He smiled when I came in.

'You're the gent looking for young Sammy, I believe?'

'That I am. You know where he is?'

'No. I haven't seen him in two weeks. But that's what I thought

I'd tell you about. Two weeks ago, outside the Pacific Club . . . you know, Mr Cohen's place . . . well, two weeks ago I was playing there. Friday night. Anyway, I had finished my stint and was getting the bus home. I was halfway along the street when I heard this commotion, like. Sammy was having some kind of trouble with two men. Youngish fellows, I'd say. Anyway, there was a fair bit of pushing and shoving, that kind of thing. But not a fight, not a square-go, anyway. Not with two against one. Anyway, this other fellow came out of the club. Calmed the whole thing down, like.'

'What time was this?'

'About nine. I was on early.'

'Did you recognize any of them?'

'Not the two troublemakers. I recognized Sammy, of course. The bloke who stopped the tussle looked to me like Paul Costello. You know, Jimmy Costello's boy. They're always hanging around the clubs together. Costello and Sammy, I mean.'

'Did they go back into the Pacific?'

'No. They all got into a car and drove off. They was next to the car when they was arguing. I wouldn't have paid much notice, it's just that it was an odd thing.'

I nodded. A street scuffle in Glasgow was nothing out of the usual. You saw it every Friday or Saturday night. 'What made it odd?'

'I dunno. It was just odd. They wasn't pished, or anything like that. It was more like . . .' He frowned his pale, eggshell brow. Then it hit him. 'It was like they was all agitated, rather than spoiling for a fight. Sammy in particular. It was like the other two had done something wrong.'

'What kind of car did they get into?'

'A big one. White. A Ford, I think.'

'A Ford Zephyr Six?'

'Could be. Yeah, could be. You know who I'm talking about?'

'I've run into them, I think. How well do you know Sammy Pollock?'

'Sammy Pollock?'

'Sheila Gainsborough's brother,' I said, and he looked enlightened. It was becoming pretty clear that all around town Sammy had been trading hard on his sister's name.

'Not that well. I used to see him around. In the clubs, mainly.'

'Did he ever say anything to you about representing you or any other musicians?'

'What do you mean, represent?'

'Did he ever talk about becoming an agent? Or setting up a talent agency with Paul Costello?'

The small man with the glabrous head laughed. 'What would they know about the music game? No, he never said anything to me, or anyone I know.'

'Fair enough.' I thought for a moment. 'Listen, do you have *any* idea of where I might find someone who knows where he is.'

'There's that lass he hangs around with.'

'Claire?'

'Oh, you know her already?'

'No. Know *of* her. I'd very much like to talk to her. Do you know where I might be able to find her?'

'Aye, I do. She's a singer. Not bad, either. Claire Skinner. She sings at the Pacific Club some nights. I think she lives out in Shettleston.'

I took a couple of quid from my wallet and handed it to the trumpeter. From the sounds coming from the main club hall, I would maybe have been better giving him the pocket Webley I'd taken from Skelly.

'Thanks, that's been a help. Good luck out there,' I said and left, wondering how long it would take all the king's men and horses to get there.

I 'phoned Jonny Cohen at home. He said he knew the girl Claire who sang at the Pacific but he didn't know if her surname was Skinner. Nor had he connected her to Sammy Pollock in any way.

'Are you sure it's the right girl?' he asked.

'That's what my source tells me, but who knows? Can you give me an address for her?'

'I can't, but Larry who manages the Pacific for me maybe has one. Or at least he can tell you who he gets in touch with to book her. Call by the club tomorrow night and I'll tell him to give it to you.'

'Thanks, Jonny. I owe you.'

'Yes, Lennox, you do. And Lennox?'

'Yeah?'

'I hope you heard me when I said you shouldn't let this shite distract you from the thing with Bobby Kirkcaldy.'

'I heard you, Jonny.'

Davey Wallace turned up at my office at ten-thirty, just as I'd asked him to in the message I'd left with Big Bob. He was wearing the same too-big and too-old suit that he wore to the Horsehead. He had a red tartany type tie and a white shirt and he had topped the lot off with a wide-brimmed grey fedora that had a couple of decades' worth of shape bashed out of it. At least, I thought, I now knew what a private detective is supposed to look like.

Davey's grin when he walked into the office was impossibly broad and gleeful, making me wonder if I had done the right thing in bringing him in. He was just a kid. And a good kid at that. But it was his choice.

'Now you're clear on what you're doing? And more importantly on what you're not doing?'

'I got it, Mr Lennox. I won't let you down.'

I reached into my desk drawer and pulled out a coarse linen bag. It was heavy, filled with pennies. I tipped some out onto the desk.

'Take this bag with you. You've got enough coppers there to 'phone Australia. If anything happens, call the numbers I gave you and they'll get a message to me as soon as they can.' I tossed the bag in my palm a couple of times, assessing the weight. 'And keep the drawstrings pulled tight when you're not taking money out. This cash bag won't break and it makes one hell of a cosh if you run into trouble. You got that?'

'I got it, Mr Lennox.'

'But I don't want you to take any risks, Davey. Just keep an eye on the Kirkcaldy place and let me know if anything happens. And remember . . . note down times and descriptions of anyone you see coming or going.'

I went back into my desk drawer and tossed a black reporter's notebook over to him. He caught the notebook and then stared at it, wide-eyed, as if I'd just handed him the Keys to the Kingdom.

I drove up to Blanefield and parked the Atlantic along the street from Kirkcaldy's place. It was difficult not to be conspicuous, but the car was far enough away and still had a clear enough view of the entrance to the Kirkcaldy residence. I gave Davey a couple of quid, a packet of cigarettes and a lamppost to lean on. He took the duty so seriously that, when I left him, I found myself worrying that he might not blink until I returned.

I left the car where I'd parked it, giving Davey the keys so that he could take shelter if it started raining. The weather had now definitely reverted to type and the milky sky periodically darkened into a glower: I didn't want to be responsible for Davey contracting pneumonia or trench foot, both of which were possibilities in the West of Scotland climate. Before I left him on sentry duty, I called at Kirkcaldy's house. The boxer wasn't in, but Uncle Bert Soutar answered the door. He was wearing a short-sleeved shirt that exposed arms writhing with tattoos, some of which had unhelpful suggestions for the Pope. If dourness could be measured on a scale, then Soutar was a bass baritone. He nodded glumly and closed the door when I told him that the youth at the corner was with me and not connected to whoever had been carrying out the vandalism.

I knew of course that there would be nothing significant for Davey to report that afternoon. The kind of shenanigans that had been going on with Kirkcaldy were the kind of shenanigans you got up to under cover of darkness.

While Davey was earnestly leaning and diligently watching the Kirkcaldy place, I went to 'Pherson's on Byre's Road for a trim and shave. Old man 'Pherson knew his stuff and I came out with my face tingling and with a parting that made Moses' Red Sea work look sloppy. Afterwards I took a tram back into town and made a few fruitless 'phone calls from my office in pursuit of Largo.

Maybe it was because Jock Ferguson's name had come up in conversation with my tame copper chum Donald Taylor, but, almost on an impulse, I picked up the 'phone and dialled the number for St. Andrew's Square headquarters. Obviously, Detective Inspector John Ferguson knew nothing of my 'accommodation' with one of his junior officers and he sounded surprised to hear from me all right. Surprised and maybe a little distrustful. I have no idea why I bring that out in some people, especially coppers. He did concede he was free at lunchtime and we agreed to meet up at the Horsehead Bar. Ferguson and I hadn't spoken much in nearly a year.

It was one-thirty by the time I got to the Horsehead and the lunchtime crowd had already smoked the atmosphere into a density you could cut with a knife. If I were to describe the ambience of the Horsehead, I would say it was eclectic. There were clerks, uniformed in regulation pinstripe, shoulder-to-shoulder at the bar with workmen in flat caps and Wellington boots. It has to be said that no one could accuse Glaswegians of not being fashion-conscious, and a few of the workies had rolled their Wellies down from calf- to ankle-length as a concession to the warm weather.

I spotted a man in his late thirties over by the bar. He had his back to me but I recognized his tall, angular frame and the dull grey suit he always seemed to wear, year round. Some policemen need a uniform, even after they've transferred to CID. I understand it in a way: the need to take off your job when you got home. I squeezed shoulder first into the bar next to Ferguson. The man who had been standing next to him eyed me with that casual, disinterested hostility that you only seem to find in Glasgow hostelries. I smiled at him then turned to Ferguson.

'Hello, Jock.'

Ferguson turned dull grey eyes that matched his suit on me. Jock Ferguson had anything but an expressive face: it was practically impossible to work out what was going on in his head. I'd seen more than a few men come out of the war with the same absence on their faces. And I somehow had always known that Jock Ferguson had a similar kind of war to mine.

'Long time no see,' he said, without smiling. And without offering me a drink. We were going through the preliminaries. 'Where have you been keeping yourself?'

'You know, keeping my head down. Divorce cases, company thefts, that kind of thing.'

'Still doing work for Glasgow's disreputable element?'

'Now and again. Not as much as before. Things aren't what they used to be, Jock. Gangsters have embraced the free market. I can't compete with the rates your colleagues charge.'

Something set harder in Ferguson's face, but he clearly decided to let it go. Before, he would have laughed off a jibe like that because he knew I was referring to coppers other than him. But this was not before.

'I heard you were asking a few questions about me, Lennox. After that business last year. I could be accused of being paranoid, but that would suggest to me that you think I had something to do with all that shite. Is that what you think?'

I shrugged. 'I just got to chatting with a couple of your colleagues. Are you telling me that you didn't have anything to do with it?'

He held my gaze. Neither of us wished to define what it was that had happened. The truth is that he shouldn't have even known about the events in a dockside warehouse that ended with me having a bullet in my side and someone very special to me lying dead at my feet, her face blown off. Events that would not have taken place if information hadn't been leaked by a copper.

'Anything that happened had nothing to do with me. That's what I'm saying, yes.'

'Okay. If that's what you're saying, then I believe you, Jock.' It was a lie. We both knew it was a lie but it was a form of words that allowed us to move on. For the moment. 'So . . . how are things?'

'Busy. McNab has dumped this train death on me. And he's piling on the pressure. This new smart-arse pathologist has got him farting fire. You know McNab, shite killing shite doesn't interest him unless it's all straightforward and easy, which it usually is.'

I nodded sympathetically. The idea of working for a wroth McNab was a frightening thought. For a second I felt the weight of his hand on my chest. 'So how's the investigation going? Any leads?'

Ferguson snorted. 'Sweet Fanny Adams. We've nothing to go on except the body. And you could carry that around in a couple of buckets. Anyway, you didn't ask to see me to enquire about my level of job satisfaction. What do you want, Lennox? You're always after something.'

Before answering, I nodded over to the barman and ordered a couple of whiskies. He wasn't a barman I knew so I decided not to confuse him by asking for a Canadian Club.

'You know this big fight that's coming up? Bobby Kirkcaldy and the German?'

'Of course. What about it?'

'Well, Kirkcaldy's been getting some unwanted attention. Crap dumped on his doorstep, veiled threats, that kind of thing.'

'Has he contacted us?'

'No. In fact I've only been hired by one of his backers because Kirkcaldy's manager happened to find out about it. Kirkcaldy is doing his best to draw attention away from it.'

'One of his "backers", did you say?' Ferguson raised an eyebrow.

'The point is that something about it stinks. There's this old guy who hangs around Kirkcaldy. A sort of bodyguard-cum-trainer. Like I said, old, but as hard as nails. Goes by the name of Bert Soutar. I was wondering if you could . . .?'

Ferguson sighed. 'I'll see what I can do. But *quid pro quo*, Lennox. I might want something from you in the future.'

'My pleasure.' I smiled and ordered a couple of pies. They

were handed to us on bleakly white plates that were crazed with spidery grey cracks beneath the glaze. It looked like the same kind of porcelain they made urinals from. The pies themselves lay on what the French would call a *jus* of liquefied fat. I had lost weight since I'd first arrived in Glasgow. The presentation didn't seem to put Ferguson off and he squelched into the pie, dabbing the grease from his chin with the paper napkin.

'Was that all?'

'Yeah,' I said and sipped the whisky. 'I believe old Soutar used to be handy with a razor. Bridgeton Billy Boys, that kind of thing. Anything you could find out would be really useful.'

'I can do better . . .' He reached into his jacket pocket and pulled out a non-regulation notebook and pencil. He scribbled something down, tore the page out and handed it to me. 'That's the address of Jimmy MacSherry. He's an old man now but was a real hard bastard in the Twenties and Thirties. Fought the Sillitoe Cossacks, put a couple of police in hospital. Got ten years and the birch for his trouble. He was a Billy Boy and knows anyone who's anyone in that circle. But be careful how you handle him. And it'll cost you a few quid.'

'Thanks, Jock. I appreciate it.' I pocketed the note. Then a thought occurred to me. 'Oh there's maybe one other thing. Nobody else seems to know this guy, but it's worth a try. Have you ever heard of someone called Largo?'

Like I said, Jock Ferguson did not have the most expressive face, but something crossed it that looked as if it had been powered by the national grid.

'What do you know about John Largo?'

'Nothing. Nothing at all, that's why I'm asking. Who is he?'

'Where did you hear the name? You must have heard the name somewhere.'

I looked at Ferguson. He had turned towards me, straightening up from the bar. All of a sudden he became all copper and no acquaintance. After all the asking around, I had in that split second doubled my knowledge about Largo. I now had a full name for him. But every alarm bell that could ring was now ringing. It was clear that knowing the name John Largo was enough to get me the kind of police attention I so studiously avoided. I decided it was best to deliver the goods.

'Okay, Jock, I can see that I've hit pay dirt. But you obviously think I know something I shouldn't. Well, I don't. All I have is the name Largo. I'm investigating a missing person case. It's turned into two missing persons: Paul Costello, Jimmy Costello's son, has also dropped out of sight. But before he did, our paths crossed. He thought to start with I was one of your mob, then he asked me if *Largo* had sent me. That's all of it. I've been asking all around town if anyone knows Largo and nobody I asked did. Until now. So who is John Largo?'

'Now see that . . . See that right there . . . what you just asked . . . if I were you that's a question I would never ask again. John Largo is someone you don't want to know anything about. If ever I've told you anything worthwhile, Lennox, it's this: John Largo doesn't exist. Hear it, accept it and get on with your life. Otherwise you might not have a life to get on with.'

'Oh now wait a minute, Jock. You can't . . .'

'I've got to go. I'll see if I can find anything out about Soutar for you. In the meantime try Jimmy MacSherry.'

Before I could say anything he was gone. I leaned against the bar and looked down at the half-full whisky glass he had left. I knew this was big, big stuff. When a Scotsman leaves a free drink unfinished, you know it's serious.

Bridgeton was the kind of place you felt overdressed if you wore shoes. It seemed that footwear was optional until age twelve;

thereafter you were expected to wear heavy work boots with soles studded with metal *segs* that made a seven-stone youth sound like a Nazi division marching down the street. Like ninety-nine per cent of the population of Bridgeton, Jimmy MacSherry wasn't on the 'phone. So I decided the best thing to do was to go down and do some door knocking. I made sure I had my sap with me. Bridgeton was the kind of place you would feel naked without some kind of means of injuring another human being.

I got a call from Davey before I took the tram down to Bridgeton. There was, as expected, nothing to report other than Kirkcaldy had left for his afternoon session at the Maryhill gym he had always trained in. I had told Davey to stay on the house, not on Kirkcaldy and that's what he had done. I could tell he was worried that I would be disappointed that he had nothing to report, but I reassured him he was doing just fine and he rang off as eager as when I had left him there.

For the rest of the world, a Glaswegian was a Glaswegian was a Glaswegian. They all looked the same, spoke with the same impenetrable patois, worked in the same industrial sweatshop of shipyard, factory or steelworks; they all lived in the same kind of slum. They also shared the same schizoid tendency to be the warmest, friendliest people you could meet while, at the same time, displaying a propensity for the most psychopathic violence. Sometimes simultaneously. Within Glasgow, however, lay a chasm that divided its working class. On the surface it was a religious divide: Protestant versus Catholic. The truth is the divide was ethnic: Scottish Glaswegians versus Irish-descent Glaswegians. And the focus for the biblical hatred between the two communities were the football teams, Rangers and Celtic.

Bridgeton was part of the city's fringes. And it looked pretty much like all the other parts of Glasgow's fringes. The streets were lined with tenements or four-storey apartment buildings.

The building material of choice in Bridgeton had been red rather than blond sandstone or red brick, but it was all pretty academic as all the buildings had been grime-darkened, like every other structure in Glasgow. Occasionally an ember of the underlying colour would glow through the soot, giving a tenement the look of a dark, rusting hulk looming into the sky. Like other parts of the city, the worst of the slums were gradually being cleared to make way for new blocks of flats. The spirit of the Atomic Age had reached Glasgow and soon all of its denizens would enjoy the very latest modern amenities. Like flushing inside toilets.

But Bridgeton was different from the other areas of the city in one way. It distinguished itself in the intensity of its hatred for its neighbour. This was the most ultra-loyalist Protestant, Catholic-hating part of Glasgow.

A few weeks before, as it was on the Twelfth of July each year, Bridgeton had been a mustering ground for the pipe bands, drummers and marchers who celebrated the victory of Protestant King William of Orange over Catholic King James at the Battle of the Boyne. And once they had mustered, they would march triumphantly through the streets of Glasgow. Especially the predominantly Catholic streets. Surprisingly, the curmudgeonly Catholics didn't seem to get into the spirit of things and refrained from joining in with songs containing lyrics like '*We're up to our knees in Fenian blood, surrender or you'll die*'.

But Glasgow was nothing if not a city of balance and fairness, and there was an ultra-republican Catholic, Protestant-hating part of Bridgeton too. The Norman Conks, the Catholic counterparts of the Billy Boys, had been concentrated in the Poplin Street and Norman Street part of Bridgeton. Their speciality, as well as offering the same skills for plastic surgery with open razors as the Billy Boys, was throwing Molotov cocktails made with paraffin or petrol at the marchers on the Twelfth. Or occasionally the odd 'sausage roll': human excrement loosely wrapped in a sheet of newspaper.

I sometimes wondered how Rio could compete with Glasgow's carnival atmosphere.

As I walked through Bridgeton, however, there were no marching bands and little in the way of a carnival atmosphere. In fact, even on a pleasant summer's day, I couldn't imagine anywhere less festive. I certainly was glad I hadn't brought the Atlantic with me. There were no other cars parked in the street in which MacSherry resided, and a knot of five or six children, faces grimy and feet bare, were playing maliciously around a streetlamp. As I walked past one block doorway, a man of about thirty stood watching me from beneath the brim of his cap. He was wearing a collarless shirt and a waistcoat, his shirtsleeves rolled up to expose forearms that looked woven from steel cable. He had his thumbs looped into the pockets of his waistcoat and leaned against the doorway, his heavy-booted feet crossed at the ankles. It was the most casual of poses, but for some reason he gave me the idea he was some kind of guard or lookout.

The only other person I passed was a woman of about fifty who emerged from a house further up the street. She was as wide as she was tall and dressed in a formless black dress. Or maybe it was just the body beneath that was formless. She had a headscarf tied tight around her head and her legs were naked, her stockings having been rolled down into beige bracelets around her ankles. She was wearing dark tartan slippers on her feet. Something had caused the skin of her legs to mottle a purplish red and I suddenly felt the need to foreswear ever touching corned beef again. She walked past me and eyed me with even more suspicion than the shirtsleeved sentinel I had just passed.

I smiled at her and she glowered back. And just when I was about to tell her how pleased I was that Dior's New Look had at last made it to Glasgow.

I found the tenement I was looking for and climbed up the stairwell. It was the weirdest thing about Glasgow slums: you could have eaten your dinner off the flagstone stairs or the doorsteps of each flat. Glaswegians took an inordinate pride in cleaning communal areas – closes, stairs, entrances. There was normally a strict rota, and failure to have a sparkling doorstep or landing would result in the offending housewife becoming a social pariah.

The MacSherry flat was on the third floor. The landing was as spotless as I had expected, but there was some kind of unpleasant smell wafting about in the air. I knocked on the door and it was opened by a woman in her sixties who made the female I'd passed on the street look positively svelte.

'Hello, could I speak with Mr MacSherry, please?'

The fat woman turned from me wordlessly and waddled back along the corridor, leaving the door open behind her. She tortured some vowels in quick succession, which I took to be 'It's someone for you.'

A man in his late sixties or early seventies emerged from the living room and came to the door. He was short, only about five-five, but he was compact and wiry with a heavy head topped with white bristle. There was something about him made me think of an older Willie Sneddon. Except Sneddon's razor scar was delicate needlepoint compared to the criss-cross of ancient slashes on MacSherry's cheek and forehead. Like Uncle Bert Soutar, this was a man whose history of violence was written all over his face, but in a different vernacular.

'What the fuck do you want?'

I smiled. 'I wondered if you could help me. I'm looking for information on somebody. Someone from the old days.'

'Fuck off,' he said, without anger or malice, and pushed the door shut. I stopped it by jamming my foot between it and the jamb. Old MacSherry opened the door wide and looked deliberately down at my shoe and then back up at my face. He smiled. It was a smile I didn't like and I contemplated the ignominy of having the crap beaten out of me by an Old Age Pensioner.

'Sorry,' I said swiftly and held my hands up. 'It's just that I'm willing to pay for the information.'

He looked at my foot again and I removed it from the doorway.

'What do you want to know?'

'Do you know . . . or *did* you know someone called Bert Soutar?'

'Aye, I knew Soutar. What's it got to do with you? You're not police.'

'No, no . . . nothing like that. I represent a group of investors who have an interest in a sporting event. Mr Soutar is involved with this event and we're just doing a check into his background. You see, Mr Soutar has a criminal record.'

'You don't fucking say.' Irony was not his strong suit.

'I do say,' I continued as if I had missed his sarcasm. 'Not that that is, in itself, a problem. But we'd like to know the kind of people we're dealing with. Did you know Mr Soutar well?'

'You said you was willing to pay for information.'

I took out my wallet and handed him a five-pound note, keeping a second fiver in my hand. 'Maybe we could . . .?' I nodded along the hall.

'If you like,' said MacSherry, and he stood to one side to let me in.

The living room was small. Cramped. But again surprisingly clean. A large window with no curtains looked out over the street below and there was a bed recess, a typical feature in

Glasgow tenements, in one wall. The furniture was cheap and worn but there was the occasional item that looked incongruously new and expensive, and I was surprised to see a small Pye television squashed into one corner of the room. It had a set-top aerial sitting on it, its twin extendable antennae each stretching at a wild angle from the other. I understood MacSherry's reluctance to let me into the flat: the mix of new and old was the difference between the legitimately owned and the knocked off.

The fat woman whom I'd guessed was MacSherry's wife left the room. It was clear that business was often conducted here.

'Are you a fucking Yank?' MacSherry had a charming, welcoming manner about him. I guessed I wasn't going to be offered a cup of tea.

'Canadian.' I smiled. It was beginning to make my jaw ache. 'About Soutar . . .'

'He was a Billy Boy. And a boxer. He fought bare-knuckle. Hard cunt. I know what this is all about. It's about his nephew. Bobby Kirkcaldy. That's your fucking sporting event, isn't it?'

'I'm not at liberty to say, Mr MacSherry. Soutar was a member of the Bridgeton Billy Boys about the same time as you, is that right?'

'Aye. I didn't know him that well, though. He was a mental bastard with a razor in his hand, I can tell you that. And with his fists. But then when it got all military, you know, when the Billy Boys started having morning drills and stuff like that, he fucked off. He hated fucking Fenians but he liked making money more. He was still boxing though. It was after he cut them coppers, that was him finished.'

'I thought you said he'd left the Billy Boys?'

'He had. This wasn't a rammy. It was after a match, right enough, but he was breaking into a credit union. He had some fucking mad idea that the mounted polis would be too busy dealing with the rammy. But two coppers caught him in the back close of the building. From what I heard, Soutar got lippy with them and they was going to give him a bit of a doing. That was his biggest problem, too fucking mouthy for his own good. Anyways, he always kept two razors in his waistcoat pockets. The two cops made a move on him and he cut them both. Popped an eye on one. You seen the state of his face?'

'Yes,' I said. 'He must have taken more than his fair share of beatings in the ring.'

'That's got fuck all to do with boxing. Bert Soutar was too light on his feet to get battered like that in the ring or in a bare-knuckle fight. No, that was the fucking polis that did that to him. They half-killed him. Took fucking turns with him. You see, it was a message . . . you don't cut a Cossack.' MacSherry referred to the Sillitoe Cossacks, the gang-busting mounted police squad set up by the then Chief Constable of Glasgow, Percy Sillitoe. 'When Soutar came out of prison he gave up the Billy Boys. Apparently he was a model prisoner inside and got out after six years. And he came out with big ideas. He said he wasn't interested in the Billy Boys any more. He said there was no money in it. And he was finished as a boxer. The beatings he took in prison fucked up his face. He couldn't take any more damage, and couldn't get a licence 'cause of his face and 'cause he was an ex-con. It was about then that he started hanging around with some Flash Harry who filled his head with all kinds of money-making schemes.'

'Who was the Flash Harry?'

'I didn't know him at the time. He wasn't from Bridgeton and I think he was younger than us. Quite a bit younger. But, like I say, flash as fuck. Soutar and this bloke got into the boxing game for a while. Fixing up fights, in more ways than one if you get my fucking drift. Never saw him after that, but I don't think the partnership lasted. Soutar just disappeared and MacFarlane became a big fucking success.'

'MacFarlane?'

'Aye. Small Change MacFarlane. That was the Flash Harry. Became a big-time bookie. Fuck all good it did him considering he ended up having his coupon smashed to fuck.'

I sat and nodded as if I had been processing the information, hiding the fact that a dozen possible combinations of people and events were now running through my head. The flat door was still open and I heard voices out on the hall. The old fat woman and a male voice. Time to go. I stood up and handed MacSherry the other five pounds.

'It's not enough,' he said.

'What?' I put on my best confused expression. I wasn't confused at all.

'Another ten.'

'You've been paid for your time, Mr MacSherry. More than adequately paid.'

He stood up. I heard a sound behind me and turned to see the collarless sentinel had been the voice out on the landing and was now blocking my exit through the hallway. He smiled maliciously at me.

'Another ten. Hand it over. In fact, let me save you a lot of trouble. Just hand over your fucking wallet.'

I weighed up the situation. Sticky. The old guy would have been tough enough to deal with on his own, but the younger man tipped the scales well and truly against me.

I shrugged.

'Okay. I'll give you all the money in my wallet. It's nothing to me. I just claim it back from the investors I was telling you about.' I frowned pensively then made out as if an idea had suddenly struck me. 'Why don't I just get them to come and see you in person. You can sort out remuneration with them. Mr William Sneddon is my employer. Mr Jonathan Cohen is the other investor.' I kept my tone friendly, as if I really didn't mean it as the threat it was. 'I know Mr Sneddon is very angry about people interfering in his business arrangements. So I'm sure he'll take your request for more payment seriously. Very seriously.'

MacSherry looked over my shoulder at the younger guy and then back at me. 'Why didn't you say you worked for Mr Sneddon? Maybe you're just pissing down my back and telling me it's raining.'

'If there's a working callbox anywhere in this shithole, then we can take a wander to it and you can ask him yourself. Or I could simply ask for Twinkletoes McBride to come down here and convince you of my credentials.' I dropped the friendly tone. It was a careful balancing act. Some people don't have the sense to know when to be scared. I'd have bet my last penny on MacSherry being one of them.

He gave a jerk of his head in a signal for the younger man to let me past.

'Thanks for your help, Mr MacSherry.' I turned and walked out of the flat casually and unhurriedly.

But I didn't take my hand from the sap in my pocket until I was out on the street and around the first corner.

CHAPTER EIGHT

By the time I had waited for a tram it was nearly six before I got back to my office. It was turning into another oppressive evening, the air clinging, humid and heavy, and I felt my shirt collar damp at the nape of my neck again. Davey Wallace called me at six on the dot, as agreed. Davey couldn't drive and I told him to stay put and wait in the Atlantic until I came up. I decided I'd probably take a taxi up to Blanefield and get it to take Davey back home. Riding in a taxi was one of the luxuries in life most Glaswegians only ever experienced on special occasions. Before I went up to Blanefield, I 'phoned Sneddon. I told him what had happened at MacSherry's place.

'He knew you was there for me?' he asked.

'Not to start with. But I told him later.'

'Fucking slum rats. I'll arrange a lesson in respect.'

'You better send a mob, then. From what I can see, the old guy still has a crew of sorts. And he has a reputation that must have been earned.' I neglected to tell Sneddon that MacSherry had backed down at the first mention of his name. I was pissed because the old man had tried to turn out my pockets. A lesson in respect, as Sneddon said.

'Aye? Well, I'll arrange a change of scenery for him. I bet he doesn't get out of Bridgeton much,' said Sneddon, reminding me of the promise Superintendent McNab had made me. There was so much local colour here; maybe 'fucking off back to Canada' would do my health a bit of good.

'I did get something interesting out of the whole encounter,' I said. 'Did you know that Bert Soutar went into business with Small Change MacFarlane? Some time around the start of the war?'

'No . . .' I could tell Sneddon was doing the same jigsaw puzzle in his head that I had done in Bridgeton. 'No, I didn't. Do you think it's significant?'

'Well, this hot deal that turned into a fairy story about boxing academies . . . it could be that Small Change was covering up the detail and not the principals. Maybe it *was* something to do with Bobby Kirkcaldy. And maybe the deal was brokered through MacFarlane's old chum Soutar.'

'But MacFarlane was going to broker the deal to me.' I could tell that Sneddon was laying down the fact to see what I would do with it.

'Let's not forget Small Change had his skull cracked like an egg,' I said. 'My guess is it was all about this deal. He was at the heart of it and was playing for the big money, not for some commission. And I suspect Uncle Bert is involved some way.'

'You think he battered Small Change's coupon in?'

'I don't know. Maybe. But I don't see why he would, unless something went pear-shaped with the deal, whatever it was. But maybe it was whoever's been leaving warning messages for Kirkcaldy. One thing I'm sure of is that Kirkcaldy doesn't appreciate the attention we've been giving him. Speaking of which, can I borrow a couple of bodies to take turns watching Kirkcaldy's place. I've just got the one guy and me.'

'Okay,' said Sneddon. 'You can have Twinkletoes. You two seem to get on.'

'Yeah . . .' I said. 'Like a house on fire . . . Thanks. I'll let you know when I need him.'

After I hung up I locked the office and took a taxi down to the Pacific Club. Like the last time I had been here they were just starting to get the place ready for the evening's trade. The manager Jonny Cohen had running the place was a small handsome Jew in his early forties called Larry Franks. I'd never met Franks before but he seemed to recognize me; he came over and introduced himself as soon as I arrived. He had his jacket off and his sleeves rolled up.

'Mr Cohen tells me that you're looking for Claire Skinner.' He grinned widely. Franks had an accent, difficult to place but there was a touch of London in it. And a touch of something much farther away. It was something you encountered every now and then. The war still cast a long shadow and, even though all but one of the Displaced Persons camps that had been spread across post-war Europe were now closed, there were still huge numbers of people building new lives in new places. Whatever Franks's history, it hadn't seemed to suppress his good nature. 'Can I get you a drink? On the house?'

'Thanks, but no. And yes, I am looking for Claire. Jonny said you have an address for her?'

'There you go . . .' Franks grinned again and handed me a folded note he took from his waistcoat pocket. I noticed something on his forearm and he tugged his shirtsleeve down, casually. 'But getting into Fort Knox would be easier.'

'What do you mean?' I unfolded the note; it had an address in Craithie Court, Partick, written on it.

'It's a pussy pound,' he said, matter-of-factly and without a hint of lasciviousness. 'A hostel for unmarried women run by Glasgow Corporation. It's only a couple or so years old. Claire has her digs there. But they've got a matron and she'll have your bollocks if you try to get in. Strictly no gentlemen callers. You'd maybe be better trying to catch her here the next time she's singing.'

'When would that be?' I asked.

'To be honest, it might not be for a week or more. I've got a new combo booked in for the next two Fridays.'

'No . . . I need to see her before then.' I stared at the note for a moment, my mind elsewhere. 'I'm looking for Sammy Pollock. Or Gainsborough, as he seemed to prefer to be known. Claire's boyfriend. Have you seen him lately?'

'That wanker?' Franks grinned. 'No. Not for a couple of weeks.'

'The last time he was seen was here. There was a bit of a disagreement outside the club, about two weeks ago. Did you see or hear any of that?'

'No . . .' Franks pursed his lips pensively. 'No, can't say I did. And nobody mentioned it either.'

'Right, I see.' I pocketed the note. 'Thanks. And thanks for the offer of a drink. I'll take you up on that the next time I'm in.'

'Sure.' His smile was still there but had changed. He was reading my mind and I was reading his. It said: *I don't need your sympathy.*

I walked out of the stuffiness of the Pacific Club and into the stuffiness of the Glasgow evening. The taxi was still waiting for me. I got into the back and told the driver to take me to Blanefield. I sat in silence for the whole journey, thinking about Larry Franks's cheery manner. And the number I'd seen tattooed on the inside of his forearm.

When I got out of the taxi, I could have sworn that Davey Wallace was in exactly the same place, in exactly the same position, as when I'd left him in the morning. We sat together in my Atlantic and he ran through twenty minutes of detailed notes. Twenty minutes of detailed nothing. He was a good kid all right and keen enough to make mustard makers the world over question their calling.

'You free to do the same shift tomorrow?' I asked. 'Maybe a bit longer too?'

'Sure, Mr Lennox. Anytime. And you don't need to bring me up here. I know where it is and I can get the tram.'

'Okay. Meet me up here a bit later. Make it six tomorrow. Nothing's going to happen during the day, I reckon. How about your work? Will you still be okay for the early shift?'

'No problem, Mr Lennox.'

'Good,' I said. Of course it wasn't a problem. Having to cross the Himalayas wouldn't have been a big enough problem to keep Davey away. I gave him a fiver. 'You get off home now.'

'Thanks, Mr Lennox,' said Davey with reverent gratitude.

This was not a good use of my time. I sat watching Kirkcaldy's place for three hours without anything happening. Then Bobby Kirkcaldy arrived, presumably after a day at the gym in Maryhill. He turned more than a thousand pounds' worth of Sunbeam-Talbot Sports, its soft-top folded down, into the drive. Kirkcaldy was a successful professional boxer, but even at that he seemed to be able to stretch his finances impressively. Maybe he had a paper round.

I leaned back in the driver's seat, sliding down to get some support for my neck, and tilted my hat over my eyes. No point in being uncomfortable. It still felt clammy and I had the window wound open, but the air outside was clammy and sluggish and there was no breeze to cool me down. I was going to have trouble staying awake. I turned on the radio but all I could get was Frank Sinatra talking his way through another forgettable tune.

I decided to keep my brain active by going over where I was with everything.

There was a tie-in with Small Change's murder all right. Bobby Kirkcaldy was up to his neck in something that didn't follow Queensberry rules. There was a connection between Small Change and Kirkcaldy through Soutar. Here I was trying to avoid getting any deeper into dodgy dealing and all the time I was being sucked deeper and deeper into Small Change's murder.

In the meantime, my other case – my one-hundred-per-cent *legitimate* case – was getting nowhere. I decided I would try to get in touch with Claire Skinner the next day, but I knew it wouldn't get me anywhere. Sammy Pollock had dropped off the face of the earth. It took some doing, and I was beginning to worry that it was the kind of dropping that could only be done professionally. And then there had been Jock Ferguson's re-action to the name Largo. If it was the same Largo who Paul Costello claimed to know, then it was someone outside the normal gangster circle, yet someone important enough to be instantly recognizable to Glasgow CID.

I wasn't given to much deep personal reflection; maybe because I had seen in the war where deep personal reflection got you: mad or dead. But sitting there in a car outside a prob-ably crooked boxer's house in the countryside outside Glasgow, I suddenly felt homesick.

Blanefield sat above Glasgow. The sun was lower now in the sky and filtered into tones of gold, bronze and copper through the haze above the city in the valley below. I experienced another of my reminiscent moments: Saint John had similar sunsets. The industrial heart of the US lay in Michigan and the dense, grime-filled air would drift north and west, exploding the Maritime Canadian sun into garnet beams and spilling red into the Bay of Fundy. But the similarity ended there. I thought back to those days before the war. Things had been different. It seemed to me people had been different. I had been different.

Or maybe I hadn't.

A car pulled up behind me. A bottle-green Rover. I didn't need to turn around to see that the driver was Twinkletoes. Either that or there was an unscheduled eclipse of the sun. He came around to the passenger door of the Atlantic and tapped on the window. I opened the door and he got into the car, causing me to be impressed with the Atlantic's suspension.

'Hello, Mr Lennox . . .' Twinkletoes smiled. 'Are you well?'

'I'm well, Twinkle. You?'

'In the pink, Mr Lennox. In the pink. Mr Sneddon sent me up here to take over watching Mr Kirkcaldy's place. Singer's going to take over from me until morning.'

'It'll be a long night, Twinkle.'

'I've got the radio,' he said. 'I find jazz has a *molly-fying* effect on my mood.'

'I'm sure it does. Who do you like listening to?'

'Elephants Gerald, mostly,' he said with a smile.

'Who?'

'You know . . . Elephants Gerald. The jazz singer.'

'Oh . . .' I said, trying not to smirk. 'You mean *Ella Fitzgerald*.'

'Do I? I thought it was Elephants Gerald. You know, one of them jazz names. Like Duke Wellington.'

'Duke *Ellington*, Twinkle,' I said. I noticed the smile had fallen away from his face. It was time to go. 'But I could be mistaken. Enjoy, anyway. I'll catch you later.'

I left Twinkletoes sitting in Sneddon's Rover, watching the Kirkcaldy house, reassured by his promise that he would be most *abb-steamy-uzz* in performing his sentry duties. I went straight back to my flat. Again, as I closed the common entrance door behind me, I heard the sound of the television in the Whites' flat being turned off. I headed straight up the stairs to my rooms and set about making myself some real coffee and ham sandwiches with bread that should have been used at least two days before, unless I had intended to use the slices as building materials.

I had just sat down to start eating when I heard the downstairs doorbell ring and Fiona White answer it. There was a brief exchange then the sound of heavy footsteps coming up the stairs. It wasn't that I was inhospitable, but I was not in the habit of receiving callers at the flat. In fact, one of the reasons I had established the Horsehead Bar as my out-of-hours office was because I kept this place pretty much off the radar of everyone I dealt with. So, before I answered the knock on the door, I went to the dresser drawer where I put my sap whenever I hung up my suit jacket and slipped it in my pocket. I opened the door, stepping back as I did so, and found Jock Ferguson framed in the doorway. There was another man behind him. Bigger and heavier. He was stretching a pale grey suit with extremely narrow lapels over huge shoulders and had a straw trilby type thing with a broad blue hatband on his head. He had a big face that was a little too fleshy to be handsome and his skin tone was several summers darker than the locals. The one thing that was missing was a sign around his neck proclaiming *God Bless America*. Seeing Ferguson at my door and in such strange company took me aback for a moment.

'Jock? What are you doing here?'

'Hello, Lennox. Can we come in?'

'Sorry . . . sure. Come on in.'

The big American grinned at me as he entered. He took off

his pale straw hat and revealed the most amazing haircut I had ever seen. His salt and pepper hair had been crew-cut, clipped almost to the skin around the back and sides but bristled upwards on top. What made it truly amazing was the skill of his barber in making it perfectly, absolutely flat across the top. The picture of a hairdressing engineer, scissors in one hand, spirit-level in the other, leapt to mind.

'Lennox, this is a colleague of ours from the United States. This is Dexter Devereaux. He's an investigator, like you.'

'Call me Dex,' said the grin beneath the flat-top.

I shook the American's hand, then turned to Ferguson. 'You said Mr Devereaux is an investigator like me . . .' I asked. 'Or do you mean an investigator like you?'

'I'm a private eye. Like yourself . . .' Devereaux smiled collegially at me. 'I'm here on a private investigation. Criminal, but private.'

'Okay . . . so what can I do for you?' I asked. I realized we were all still standing. 'Sorry . . . please sit down, Mr Devereaux.'

'Like I said, call me Dex . . . Thanks.' Ferguson and the American sat down on the leather sofa. I took a bottle of Canadian rye and three glasses out of a cupboard.

'I take it you guys aren't so on duty that you can't have a drink?'

'Speaking personally, I'm never that much on duty,' said Devereaux. He took the whisky and sipped it. 'Mmmm, nice . . .' he purred approvingly. 'I thought you guys only ever drink Scotch.'

'I'm not a Scotch kinda guy,' I said, and sat in the armchair opposite. Devereaux eyed my apartment, his eyes ranging casually across the furniture, the bottles on the sideboard, the books on the bookshelves. But it was the same apparent casualness of a pro-golfer preparing for a swing.

'You've got a lot of books,' he said turning back to me. 'You got any Hemingway?'

'Nope,' I said. 'No Hemingway. Just like I've got no blended Scotch. So what *is* it I can do for you, Mr Devereaux?'

'Please . . . *Dex*. As for what you can do for us . . . you mentioned John Largo to Detective Ferguson here, I believe.'

'I asked him if he knew him or anything about him.'

'And what do *you* know about John Largo?' Devereaux turned his eyes from me while he sipped the whisky.

'All I know about Largo is his first name is John, and I only know that because Jock here inadvertently told me. And now I know that he's some kind of really big fish, because someone is prepared to fly a twenty-dollar-an-hour private detective across the Atlantic on his account. And that, I'm afraid, is all I know. Other than someone who was a friend of someone who has gone missing knows him. And now he's gone missing himself.'

'Paul Costello. I told you about his father,' Jock Ferguson explained to Devereaux, who nodded almost impatiently, but with his smile still in place. There was something about the exchange that told me all about the hierarchy of this relationship. This may have been Ferguson's town, but Devereaux was calling all the shots on this case. Whoever Largo was, whatever he was into, it was big.

'Who's the friend of Costello who's gone missing?' Devereaux asked, and took another sip of whisky. Again, question and action both done with professional casualness.

'I'm afraid I can't tell you that, Mr Devereaux,' I said, returning his smile. 'Client confidentiality. My client doesn't want the police involved.'

'You're Canadian?' asked Devereaux.

'Yep. New Brunswick. Saint John.'

'That's practically Maine. I'm from Vermont.'

'Really? That's practically Quebec.'

Devereaux laughed. 'You're not wrong there. D'yah know we've got the highest percentage of French Americans in the States. Higher even than Louisiana. That's where my name comes from.' He laughed. 'Vermont–French, I mean, not Louisiana.'

'Yes. I did know that, as a matter of fact. Like you say, New England's just over the border from Saint John. And New Brunswick is bi-lingual.'

'Ah, yes . . .' Devereaux gave a sigh of exaggerated satisfaction at our exchange. I got the feeling that the hands-across-the-water act was about to come to an abrupt end. 'You know, Mr Lennox, it really would be a big help to us if you could see your way to telling us who your client is.'

'Can't do it, Mr Devereaux. As an enquiry agent yourself, you should know that. But that's the only thing I can't do. I'll help you in any way I can. Who is John Largo?'

Devereaux looked into his glass. Jock Ferguson hadn't touched his whisky. When Devereaux looked up, he was still smiling, but the thermostat had been turned right down.

'You can't expect us to trust you, Mr Lennox, if you don't trust us. Let's be honest, I've seen Detective Ferguson's colleagues at work. The police here seem mighty interested in Mr Largo too. If you were taken in for withholding evidence, then it could be a long and painful process.'

'I don't give up my clients, *Dex*. Not for a beating, not for cash, and most definitely not because of threats.' I stood up. 'I think you gentlemen should go.'

Devereaux held up appeasing palms. 'Okay, okay . . . take it easy, colleague. Truth is, I can't tell you too much about Largo. But you're right, he's a big fish. And he's here, somewhere in Glasgow. I've heard all about your Three Kings . . . some half-assed Jock Cosa Nostra crap. Let me tell you ... sorry, I can't keep calling you Mr Lennox – what's your Christian name?'

'Just call me Lennox. Everybody else does.'

'Let me tell you, Lennox, John Largo could snuff out all Three Kings in the bat of an eye. The difference between Largo and the Three Kings is the difference between shark and pond scum. The shark doesn't know or care that the pond scum's there, but he could destroy its universe with a flick of his tail. From what we know about him, John Largo is a step beyond being a criminal. He practically constitutes a threat to the security of the United States. A particularly dangerous, clever and well-resourced threat.'

'So what is he doing in Glasgow?'

'He's spent the last five years setting up an operation that spans the whole damn world. He's put together different elements in different countries, like links in a chain, until the chain reaches here.'

'Let me guess ... this is only the *second* last link in the chain? That's why you're here.'

Devereaux's grin widened. He turned to Ferguson. 'You know, you were right, Jock. He *is* a smart cookie.' He turned back to me. 'Yeah. Your family came from here, right? I mean, you're of Scottish descent?'

'That's right. My folks shipped out from Port Glasgow.'

'Yeah. Along with hundreds of thousands ... millions of others. Russians, Jews, Germans, Poles ... they all came through this port, along with the native Scots who immigrated to Canada and the US. This is one of the big departure points, Lennox, like Marseille or Naples or Rotterdam. Not just for people. Largo has something he wants to get to the States and he has people in New York waiting for it to arrive. People who have the *infra-structure* to make the most of Largo's commercial opportunity.'

I sipped my whisky and nodded. 'Let me guess, these *people* didn't leave for the US from Glasgow. More like Palermo and Naples.'

'Like I say, you're a smart cookie, Lennox. I hope you're smart enough to see the bigger picture. And it's a very big picture.'

'How do I know that you've not been sent over here by our spaghetti-eating New Americans?' I said.

Devereaux gave a laugh that I didn't like. 'Detective Ferguson can vouch for me. And if that's not good enough for you, you can call Superintendent McNab. The City of Glasgow Police are being very supportive.'

'That's sure big-hearted of them,' I said.

There was a pause more pregnant than a Gorbals girl after a weekend in Largs.

'Okay . . . Here's the thing,' I sighed, and said in my best okay-you-got-me-I'm-going-to-give-you-the-goods tone. 'My client is a public figure. Like I told Jock, I'm investigating a missing person. And the person who's gone missing is a relative of my client. A close relative. I went around to his apartment and Paul Costello lets himself in with a key. Costello thinks I'm a cop. When I tell him I'm not he asks me if Largo sent me. We end up having a bit of a heated discussion. I ask him who Largo is and he brushes me off, says Largo's someone he owes money to. That's it. All of it. Then a few days later Costello's pop calls me in and I go through everything I've just told you. Then he tells me Paul's gone missing.'

'Just like your client's relative?' Jock Ferguson took his first sip of whisky.

'That doesn't mean it's connected.'

'What about this Bobby Kirkcaldy?' asked Devereaux. 'Jock here said you're involved in some kind of case with him and it was when you were asking him about Kirkcaldy that you mentioned Largo.'

I waved my hand vaguely in the air. 'No . . . that's not connected in any way. It was just while I was talking to Jock that I thought I'd ask if he'd heard of this Largo. By the way, I have been asking all over town about Largo. No one has heard of him.'

'That's no surprise,' said Devereaux. 'Like I told you, Largo works on a different level.'

'My point is, could we be talking about two different Largos? Like I said, I didn't even have a first name for him until Jock mentioned it. Maybe it's not John Largo at all.'

'It could be,' said Devereaux. 'But we know he's here in Glasgow and your mention of him is the only lead we've had in months.'

'Aw, for God's sake, Lennox . . .' Ferguson suddenly vented his frustration. 'Just tell us who your client is. All we have to do is go around and talk to Jimmy Costello and he'll tell us.'

'Then you'll have got it from him and not from me. And I wouldn't be so sure about Costello as a source of information.' I sighed. 'Look, I've told you all I can, which is about all there is to tell. So why not end the Mexican stand-off and you tell me what you know about Largo and what it is he's involved in and I tell you if it fits with anything else that's been happening?'

Devereaux stood up and put the straw trilby over his perfect, level lawn of hair. 'Maybe we will. Thanks for your time, Lennox. Next time the drinks are on me,' he said with his customary good-natured grin. Which was why I couldn't work out why it sounded to me like a threat.

Ten minutes after they had left there was another knock on the door. Opening it revealed the figure of Fiona White. She was wearing a pale pink shirtwaister dress with capped sleeves. She was also wearing a disapproving look. It was an ensemble I'd become accustomed to.

'Please, Mrs White, come in . . .' I offered, knowing that she wouldn't. She never did. Her pale green eyes glittered coldly but I noticed that she'd put on fresh lipstick before coming up.

'Mr Lennox, I've told you how I feel about policemen coming to the door. After the last time you were arrested . . .'

I stopped her with a held-up palm, as if I were halting traffic. 'Listen, Mrs White, you're right that one of the gentlemen who called was indeed a policeman. But I'm sure you noticed that one of them was American. He's in the same line of business as I am.' I paused to let this impressive fact sink in: I was operating on the international stage. I looked at her face. It had sunk, without trace. 'They didn't come here to arrest me or question me, Mrs White. They came here as colleagues, to ask my opinion on a case. And as regards the last incident . . . I thought we were clear on that. A misunderstanding. A misunderstanding that you, yourself, were instrumental in clearing up.'

She looked at me coldly. I really, really wanted to warm her up, to find the last, faint ember of muliebrity and breathe on it until it caught fire again. And I think she knew it.

'Well, I'd be obliged if you did not conduct business from this house.'

'Detective Inspector Ferguson is a friend of mine, Mrs White. His visits to me are as much social as business. And, as you are aware, I don't have a habit of having guests of *any* kind here.' It was the truth. I never brought women there, and I had done all I could to keep this place separate from everything else that went on in my life. A refuge, almost. I sighed. 'Please come in and have a seat, Mrs White. I'd like to talk to you about a couple of things.'

'Oh?' Something even colder and harder fell like a shutter across her eyes.

I seasoned my smile with a little impatience and indicated

the sofa. Fiona White somehow managed to fill her acceptance brim full with resentment and marched past me. She didn't sit on the sofa but in the armchair, perched on its edge in a stiff-shouldered posture that was no ease and all temporariness.

'What is it you want to talk to me about?'

'I've lived here for two years, Mrs White, and I've paid the rent regularly and without delay. Including the six months last year when I was out of the country. I don't make noise; I don't drink myself stupid and sing the ballads of ol' Ireland into the wee small hours; I don't bring young ladies up to look at my etchings. All in all, I consider myself to be a pretty model tenant.'

Fiona White looked at me silently with the same flinty defiance. If I had been expecting confirmation of my credentials as a tenant, it was not forthcoming.

'It's just that I get the impression that I somehow disappoint you as a tenant,' I continued. 'That you somehow wish that you hadn't accepted me for the tenancy. If that's the case, Mrs White, then tell me now and I'll take it as notice to quit.'

'It is entirely up to you whether you stay or go, Mr Lennox,' she said, a hint of fire now behind the ice. 'I really don't know what you expect me to say. It sounds to me like it's *you* who disapprove of *me* as a landlady. I apologize if my manner offends you. If that is the case, by all means you are free to leave.'

'I don't *want* to go, Mrs White, but I want to feel free to have the occasional caller, or for you to take the odd telephone message for me, without being made to feel that it is a huge imposition for you. Listen, I understand that you would not have chosen to divide your house up and let in a lodger. But you have and I'm here. And if it wasn't me, it would be someone else. I'm not to blame for the circumstances that made this flat available.' I stood up and went over to the sideboard. I took the same bottle of whisky and poured myself a glass. There was a bottle of Williams and Humbert Walnut Brown Sherry on the sideboard and, without asking first, I poured a glass for Mrs White and handed it to her. For a moment she looked as if she was going to shake her head. Instead she took the glass from me wordlessly.

'If you want to stay, then stay,' she said. 'But don't expect me to issue you with a merit badge just because you fulfil your contractual obligations as a tenant.'

She took a sip of the sherry. I could have been imagining it, but I thought I detected something easing in the rigid shoulders.

'I like it here,' I said. 'I told you that. I also like being able to do anything I can for the girls.' I referred to Fiona White's daughters.

'We don't need charity, Mr Lennox. We don't need anything from you.' The thaw had been brief and false. She put the sherry glass down on the table and stood up abruptly. 'If that's everything, Mr Lennox, then I'd better get back to the girls.'

'What is it you resent about me, Mrs White?' I said. 'Is it that I'm a Canadian? Is it my line of work? Or is it simply the fact that I'm here?'

That did it. We moved from a chill in the air to a positive Ice Age.

'And just what is that meant to mean?'

'I mean that I'm here. That I came back. I survived and your husband didn't. Sometimes I think you resent me because I represent everyone who did come back from the war.'

She turned and headed for the door. I went over and placed my hand on the door handle. I was going to open the door for her, but she clearly misread my intent and pulled at my hand on the knob. It was a tight grip: warm, slim fingers strong on my wrist. She was close to me now, her body inches from mine.

I could smell the sherry on her breath. The scent of lavender on her neck. We both froze for a moment, our eyes locked. She was breathing hard. I wasn't breathing at all. It was a second that seemed to last forever, then she snatched open the door and stormed down the stairs.

'Goodnight, Mr Lennox,' she said, her back to me, her voice unsteady.

'Mrs White . . . Fiona . . .'

Reaching the bottom of the stairs, and without looking round, she slammed the door of her flat behind her.

I went back into my flat and poured myself another whisky. Probably to celebrate my diplomatic skills and to commemorate the last time I had been in a situation so charged with sexual tension. I idly wondered what had happened to Maisie MacKendrie, with whom I'd danced at the Saint John Presbyterian Church Social when we were both fifteen.

But that wasn't all I reflected on. I sipped at my whisky contemplatively. I had a lot to contemplate.

Dex Devereaux, for example. And how it was mighty big of the City of Glasgow Police to be so cooperative. To the point of subservience.

CHAPTER NINE

Some people relish the unpredictability of life; the never really knowing what's ahead around the next corner. You wake up in the morning and engage the day, totally and blissfully blind to all of the things that may turn to crap within twenty-four hours. When I woke up, washed and shaved the next morning, I didn't really get much of a chance to reflect on what was going on that was so big it commanded transatlantic interest. Other developments kind of took over my attention.

I got the news in the same way as any other Glasgow citizen. A headline in the *Glasgow Herald*.

SUSPECT ARRESTED FOR MURDER OF GLASGOW BOOKMAKER

I had bought a copy on the way into the office and I stopped for a coffee at my usual place on Argyle Street to read it. The article beneath the headline explained that Tommy 'Gun' Furie, a small-time boxer, had been arrested for the murder of James MacFarlane, a leading Glasgow turf accountant with suspected links to the Glasgow underworld. Reading on, I discovered that Furie was one of the tinkers camped up at Vinegarhill. I read small-time boxer as bare-knuckle fighter and I thought of the edifying spectacle at Sneddon's barn hideaway.

Furie, the article said, was an Irish tinker. A pikey, as Sneddon would have described him. Being an Irish gypsy meant that Furie stood a very good chance of getting a fair trial. Much in the same way that I stood a very good chance of Marilyn Monroe throwing over Joe DiMaggio to come to Glasgow and live in squalid sin with me. Glasgow CID had told the reporter that, although Furie was helping them with their enquiries, they would continue to explore all other avenues of investigation. As I read that, the image of Marilyn washing my smalls in a Glasgow tenement *steamie* leapt to mind.

That seemed to be that.

I wondered how Lorna had reacted to the news – and if the police had had the sense to let her know before she read it in the newspaper. I finished my coffee and walked to my office. Glasgow's weather had reverted fully to type and a greasy drizzle seeped from the steel-grey sky. When I got into my office, I 'phoned Lorna's number but it rang out. Putting the receiver down, I decided to call in on her that evening. It had been a few days since I'd seen her, although I'd 'phoned every day. Each call seemed to elicit a cooler and cooler reception. I felt bad that I hadn't been there more often but everything that had been going on had distracted me. And I still couldn't give her what she wanted from me.

With the distraction of Small Change's murder out of the way, I decided to drop the whole thing about what kind of deal he had had going with Bobby Kirkcaldy. The main thing was to find out who was trying to put Kirkcaldy off the fight. I knew it wasn't anyone in the Schmidtke camp; they weren't due in the country until the end of the week. Of course that didn't mean they hadn't recruited local talent, but somehow it didn't seem feasible, and my money was on finding out who had a bundle riding on Kirkcaldy losing. I spent the rest of the day going from one bookie shop to the next. A tour of the public toilets of Calcutta would have been more edifying.

Lunchtime found me in the East End and I tried a café I

hadn't been to before. It turned out to specialize in viscosity: the bacon, sausage and fried bread I was served with were islands on a lipoid ocean. I decided to spare my bowels the violence and stuck to the coffee. Afterwards, I walked to a telephone kiosk and fed it copper and brass.

I tried Lorna's number again but it still rang out. There was a telephone directory on the shelf, and I went through it until I found the numbers of the three hotels within walking distance of St. Andrew's Square and in the kind of price range that the City of Glasgow Police would usually stretch to. Each time I asked to speak to Mr Dexter Devereaux out of Vermont, USA. Three strikes. I tried the Central Hotel and St. Enoch Station Hotel. No American called Devereaux. It turned out that I should have worked alphabetically: I tracked him down to the Alpha Hotel in Buchanan Street. The reception told me that Mr Devereaux was out on business and was not expected back until the evening. I said there was no message and I pushed the silvered buttons on the 'phone to break the connection. I released them and dialled the number I had for Sheila Gainsborough's Glasgow apartment. Again nothing.

My next call was more successful, if you can call having to talk to Willie Sneddon a success.

'Have you seen the news?' I asked.

'I seen it.' Sneddon's voice was flat. Neutral. 'Fuckin' pikeys. Can't turn your back on the bastards for a second.'

'Tommy Gun Furie . . . from what the papers said it sounds like he was a bare-knuckle boy. You ever come across him?'

'Naw. Not that I know of. Maybes. No names no pack drill and shite. I don't stamp their fucking insurance cards. Anyways, all that shite has got fuck all to do with fuck all. You got anything on Bobby Kirkcaldy?'

I took a moment to absorb the richness of English as it could only be spoken in the Mother Country.

'No. I've spent the day going round bookies trying to find out who's betting against him.'

'They fucking tell you that stuff?' asked Sneddon.

'I've been using your name in vain ... in vain ... no one seems to know of any big bets.'

'Means fuck all,' said Sneddon. 'The really big stuff won't go through fucking street shops. Talk to Tony the Pole.'

'Grabowski?' I asked, but was prompted by the exchange to put more money in the pay 'phone. It was a reminder to be careful what you said from a public callbox. I fired a couple of brass threepenny bits in and hit the A button.

'Grabowski?' I asked again. 'I thought Tony had given up the gambling business as well as opening doors.'

'Naw. Fuck knows he's made enough money to retire, but he's still running the odd book. If anybody's been touting a big bet around town then Tony the Pole will know about it.'

'I'll check it out. Can I keep using Twinkletoes for staking out the Kirkcaldy place? I've got my guy on it early evenings.'

'Suppose. That it?'

'There is something else ...' I hadn't been sure if I was going to voice my suspicions, but I reckoned that Sneddon, as my client, had a right to know what was going through my head.

'What?'

'This may or may not be something to worry about. You know I asked you if you knew someone called John Largo?'

'Aye, what about it?'

'Well, I asked one too many people about John Largo and I got a visit from a police chum of mine last night. He brought company. A Yank claiming to be a private detective from Vermont.'

'And?'

'If he was a private detective then I'm Grace Kelly. He's calling all the shots as far as the City of Glasgow Police are concerned.'

'What's it to me?'

'I don't know. I don't know that it's anything to anybody, but it means two things: some heavyweight American law enforcement is in town and whoever John Largo is he's a big, big fish. And Glasgow's a small pond. Your pond.'

'I take your point. I'll ask around. Have you let Cohen and Murphy know yet?'

'No, but I will. And I wouldn't ask around too loudly. That's what brought me to the attention of Eliot Ness.'

After I hung up from Sneddon I drove out of the East End, across the river and south in the general direction of Cathcart and Newton Mearns.

There was a lot about Glasgow, about Scotland, that itched at me like a nettle rash; but there was also much about the Scots I liked. One of their most redeeming qualities was the way they accepted different shades of Scottishness. Just as it was possible to call yourself an Irish-American, there were identities within Scotland that were unique, but taken as part of the Scottish identity: Italian-Scottish; Jewish-Scottish, the variation that had given birth to a totally unique cultural phenomenon of the bar-mitzvah cèilidh, where yarmulkes and kilts were required dress; and, since the end of the war, there had been a new Caledonian breed: the Polish-Scot.

Tony the Pole Grabowski was one of the thousands of Polish servicemen who had fought alongside the British Army or in the skies above Britain. Many had died defending an island they had only known for months. The vast majority of the British-based Free Polish Army had been stationed in Scotland. I had a soft spot for the Poles: the Polish First Armoured Division had been attached to the First Canadian Army and I had seen them in action. And having seen them, I had counted myself very lucky to have been on the same side as them.

After the war, like so many of his countrymen, Tony the Pole had decided he preferred the pattern on this side of the Iron Curtain and had become a resident alien, then a naturalized British citizen. He had married a Scottish girl and had settled down in Polmadie, in the south of the city. Polmadie was about as picturesque as its name suggested: a maze of tenements and 1930s' Corporation semi-detached houses – mind you, in a city with districts called Auchenshuggle and Roughmussel, Polmadie was positively lyrical. And a semi-detached was a palace compared to a Gorbals slum.

Tony the Pole's day job was as a greengrocer. Being Polish, he hadn't understood that fruit and veg – unless they had been fried or were capable of being fried – were always at the bottom of any Glaswegian shopping list. Maybe that was why green-grocery had remained Tony's day job. It was his night job that had brought in the real cash – Tony the Pole Grabowski opened doors, all right. He had been, without doubt, the best peterman in Scotland. There had not been a safe he couldn't crack, one way or another. But the peterman's life was a perilous one. There was always the threat of the missed foothold, the slip from a drainpipe, the fall. Or the danger of silent alarms, night watchmen, or patrolling bobbies with a soft tread. So Tony, when he had saved enough to keep his family comfortable and before he had been locked into a box himself, had quit the peterman business and had resigned himself to a world of wilting cabbages and wrinkling tomatoes. Except, every now and then, Tony would organize a card game or set up a book on a sporting event. Just to supplement the income from peas and sprouts.

I found Tony the Pole behind the counter of his shop on Cathcart Road. He was a short, squat man with a broad Polish face and an even broader Polish accent. He was balding and had shaved off what had been left of his hair. From the darkening rim that swept from temple to temple, I guessed the time must have been nearer five o'clock than I had thought.

'Hi, Tony . . . whaddya say, whaddya hear?'

Tony laughed at the movie line. He actually giggled, an action at odds with his squat, powerful frame. He was a James Cagney fan and at our first meeting had been entranced by my 'American' accent. Since then, every time I met him, I greeted him with the Rocky Sullivan line from *Angels with Dirty Faces*. I had once tried Bogart from *The Treasure of the Sierra Madre* on him but had withered under his disapproving gaze.,,

'Hey, Lennogs. Vad daya zay? Vad daya hear? It's been a vee vile, *neebour* . . .' Tony's party trick was made all the better because he didn't know that speaking in the Glasgow vernacular and a thick Polish accent simultaneously *was* a party trick. Anyone learning a new language tends to speak in the idiom they are exposed to. As far as learning English had been concerned, Tony had been exposed to the linguistic equivalent of gamma radiation: Glaswegian English. Now, Tony bantered and pattered like a native Glaswegian, yet almost every initial consonant was substituted with v or z. It was as hilarious as it was impenetrable and it cracked me up every time I heard him. But I never let it show.

'Hi, Tony. How's business?'

'Ze ushual. Cannae complain . . . widnae dae much use iv I did . . .' Tony said, the usual mix of Will Fyffe and Akim Tamiroff. Maybe a little Bela Lugosi thrown in. 'Vot's occurin'?'

'I'm looking for a bit of information.'

'Vell you'ff come to ze right place . . . I know my onions.' He laughed his girlish laugh and indicated his counter stock with an open-armed gesture.

We were interrupted by a small woman in a headscarf, pinnie and faded tartan baffies – as carpet slippers, for some reason light years beyond my ken, were known in Glasgow. She was somewhere between thirty and eighty. Glaswegians generally bypassed middle age, taking the direct road from youth to decrepitude. The indeterminately aged woman placed her order and Tony snapped open a bag with the kind of theatricality that only greengrocers and stage conjurors seem to attach to paper bags. He dropped the onions into it and, with the same conjurer's flourish, spun the bag around to seal it.

'Zere you go, hen . . .' Tony beamed as he handed the bag to the woman in slippers. She shuffled from the shop.

'Vad kind of invormation?' he asked after she was gone.

'This is all very discreet, Tony. Just between you and me . . . No one will know that you are my source. I just need to know if anyone's been trying to tout a big bet on the Bobby Kirkcaldy–Jan Schmidtke fight. I mean a serious wager.' I was relying on Tony's good will. No bribe or threat here: it was always easier if your source was poor or yellow.

'Oh aye, here vee vucking go . . . "Between you and me", my Silesian arze . . . You're vorking for one of ze Zree vucking Kings, I'll bet. Who zent you here, Villie Zneddun?' said Tony. It was like having a conversation with Count MacCula.

I ignored the question. 'That's not important, Tony. Has anybody been trying to lay over the odds on Bobby Kirkcaldy losing?'

'Naw. I vould have heard about it. I'd have had to broker it wiz zome o' ze bigger buoys . . .' The skin on his brow corrugated, the limit of his frown indicating the ghost of a long-dead hairline. 'Hold on . . . zere vas something. A couple of wee gobshites . . .' Tony pronounced the insult *ghubzhides*. 'Zey vere in ze Zaracen's Zord . . . about zree veeks ago. Zey vere comin' ze big bollogs . . .'

I knew the Saracen's Sword, the pub Tony referred to. He used it as an informal office much in the same way I used the Horsehead Bar.

'And they wanted to place a bet?'

'Naw . . . no' qvite. Zey made oot zat zey vere just interested in finding oot vat vey it vood vork. Zey vere a couple of vee bambots acting ze big bollogs, like I zaid. I got ze impression zat zey didn't have ze money to lay a big bet, but zey vere expectink to get ze money.'

'Where from?' I asked and only through a monumental effort resisted the impulse to turn my 'w' into a 'v'.

'Vuck knows, Lennogs. I zink zey vere just talkin' shite. Ken vat I mean?'

'But they were talking about placing a bet *against* Bobby Kirkcaldy?'

'Naw . . . I didnae zay zat. Zey didnae zay vat vay zey vanted to bet. Zey just vanted to know who vould take on a big bet like zat. I didnae pay zat much attention tae zem, tae be honest. Like I zaid, zey vere just a couple o' vee vankers talking shite, like.'

'And what did you tell them?'

'Zat it vould be me vot vould broker a big bet like that. Get ze big buoys involved. Me or Zmall Change MacFarlane. But zat vas bevore Zmall Change got his coupon stoved in.'

'Small Change MacFarlane?' I felt a tingle in my scalp.

'Aye . . . 'course I vould normally zend zem to Zmall Change. But ze only bet Zmall Change iz takin' now is who'z next to get it up ze arze viz ze devil's pitchfork . . .' Tony chuckled more than giggled this time.

'Have the police been to see you since the murder?'

'The Polis? Naw . . . zey dinae bother wiz me. As far as zey're concerned I've nae got a record. Zey dinnae know half ze shite I've been up to. And everybody kens zat I'm straight noo.'

'So these two young wideboys . . . do you know who they are? Did you recognize them?'

'Naw. A couple ov vucking Flash Harrys, iv you azk me. Didn't pay much attention to zem, ken vot I mean?'

'Okay, thanks, Tony.' I shook his hand and made to leave. Something occurred to me and I turned back to the short, smiling Pole. 'What do you know about Jack Collins? He was Small Change's partner in a couple of businesses.'

'Aye . . . Did you know he vos also MacFarlane's bairn? Illegitimate bairn? Zmall Change and Mamma Collins had been playin' a vee game ov hide-ze-*kielbasa*, as vee used tae zay back in ze ol' country.'

'Was that common knowledge?'

'Oh aye . . . Everybody knew zat. I've never had vuck all to do vid young Collins, zough.'

'One other thing. Bobby Kirkcaldy has a minder of sorts. Claims he's his uncle . . .'

'Oh aye . . . I ken zat old *skurvysyn* vell.'

'*Skurvysyn?*' I asked. I had been concentrating hard, untangling the Breslau from the Glasgow in each of Tony's utterances, but he'd taken me beyond any recognizable landmark.

'Aye . . . *skurvysyn*. Bad vord in Polish. How do you zay in English? Fucker . . . no. Zat's no' right. Arzehole . . . Maybes. Vanker? No, zat iznae right eezer. Zon of a Bitch . . .'

'All right, I get it Tony . . .' I held my hands up. 'What do you know about him?'

'Just zat he's a bad bastart. Bare kinuckle fighter vay back ven. Zen he vos a fixer. Used to fix boxing matches by scaring ze shite out ov fighters. Bad vee bastart no mistake. But zere's no vay he vould be involved in fixing up Kirkcaldy's fight. Or at least so zat it vent against Kirkcaldy. He kens vat side his vucking bread iss buddered.'

'Thanks, Tony. See you around.'

'Vaddya zay? Vaddya hear? Eh, Lennogs?'

I left the beaming Pole behind his counter. I still hadn't got anywhere, but someone was playing with the light switch in that small, dark room at the back of my brain.

I tried Lorna again from a call box. Still no answer. I was becoming seriously concerned and I decided that once I'd done all I had to do that day, I'd take a drive down to Pollokshields and see what, as Tony would have put it, *voz occurin'*.

I drove up into Partick, parked on Thornwood Drive and walked to Craithie Court. There was a pleasant, late afternoon light and I had that cloyingly melancholy feeling again. The Young Women's Hostel in Craithie Court was off Thornwood at the top of a gentle hill and I had a view down the street, a corridor of sandstone tenements, to where the forest of cranes marked the edge of the Clyde. There were more cars parked in the streets here and cars were beginning to change the shape of the area. For the last six years there had been plans to dig a tunnel under the Clyde to make it easier to move from north to south. Whether the local inhabitants were keen that Govan, on the opposite bank of the Clyde, should have such ease of access to Partick was something I couldn't comment on.

When I got to the Hostel, I knocked on the administrative office door. Difficult though it was to believe, I did have some hard and fast moral codes and rules of behaviour, one of which was that I would never hit a woman. The matron who answered the door was one of the best arguments for my moral stance I had encountered. Burly isn't an adjective normally attached to women, but it stuck to the hostel matron like crap to a shirt-tail and I would never have hit a woman like her for fear she might hit me back. She was dressed in a dark grey suit of tweed so abrasive that I was sure some religious order somewhere must use it for mortification.

'Can I help you?' she asked. I didn't answer right away, mesmerized as I was by the way her eyebrows knitted themselves together above the bridge of her nose and by the rich baritone of her voice. I explained that I was looking for Claire Skinner, and that it was business-related.

'Then you'll have to arrange to meet her somewhere else. No male visitors here.'

Such steadfast but ill-placed guardianship of virginity brought to mind empty stables with locked doors. I brought all of my weapons to bear on Hairy Mary, including my not-inconsiderable homespun Canadian charm. None of them worked on her and she raised an eyebrow, or more correctly one half of her cyclopean eyebrow in weary disdain. I decided, because I had a Plan B up my sleeve, to drop it for the moment. I shrugged as if it had been no skin off my nose but big trouble for someone else and made to leave. She let me. She'd seen that trick, along with all the others, before.

CHAPTER TEN

I drove back into town and parked the Atlantic in Buchanan Street where I could have a clear view of the Alpha Hotel's main entrance. It was sixish when I parked and it was another half hour before Devereaux arrived back. He was dropped off by a marked police Wolseley: if Devereaux was a private detective and the City of Glasgow Police was extending him this kind of courtesy, then I decided it would be a good idea for me to change my brand of cologne. I certainly was doing something wrong.

Devereaux got out of the car and trotted into the hotel. I gave him a couple of minutes to get into his room then locked the Atlantic, crossed the street and walked into the lobby.

The desk clerk was a small dark man of about forty who smiled welcomingly at me despite the fact that he was small, forty and a desk clerk.

'Can I help you, sir?' he asked, still smiling.

'Yeah, you sure can,' I grinned back. I hammed up my accent a bit. Generally Brits couldn't tell me from an American, providing I avoided diphthongs. Americans pronounced diphthongs flatly; we positively yodelled them. Linguists called it Canadian Raising. The Americans just called it Canuck. 'I'm looking for a buddy of mine,' I said, dodging diphthongs. 'Dex Devereaux from Vermont. He's registered here I think.'

'Yes sir. Do you want me to send a boy to his room to tell him you're here?'

'Before we do that, I just want to make sure I got the right Dex Devereaux. If it is he'll have been booked into the hotel from Washington DC, is that right?'

The clerk continued to smile. 'I'm sorry, sir, I can't give out that kind of information.'

'That's okay,' I said. 'I quite understand.' I took three pound notes from my wallet and laid them on the reception desk, my fingers pinning them to the mahogany.

'I believe you are correct,' said the clerk, still smiling, and the notes were gone. 'Shall I send a message?'

'That won't be necessary,' said a voice from behind me. I turned and saw Devereaux standing behind me. He must have been waiting in the lobby. 'Hey there, *Johnny Canuck* ... Your surveillance skills stink,' he said and looped a firm, guiding arm through mine. 'Let's take a walk.'

We headed out of the hotel and Devereaux suggested we take my car. As he did so he waved a hand vaguely in the Atlantic's direction. My guess was that he had spotted it, or me, from the back of the police car that had dropped him off.

'Where do you want to go?' I asked.

'Somewhere quiet,' he replied, without letting the smile drop from his face. 'Where we can talk.'

Ten minutes later we were parked beneath a sheltering arch of trees on Kelvin Way where it dissected Kelvingrove Park.

'Nice day for a walk,' said Devereaux as he got out of the car. I followed, locking up the doors. He led the way into the park and in the direction of the museum and art gallery until we found a tree-shaded bench. Devereaux was in a suit of exactly the same style and cut as he had worn the night he'd called at my flat with Jock Ferguson, except this time it was blue. Several shades too light a blue for a local ever to have worn. I imagined it would have looked okay in the swelter of a New York summer, but amongst the muted tones of tweed- and serge-bound Glasgow, it was the sartorial equivalent of a screeching jazz trumpet played through a loudspeaker.

'So you thought you'd try to find out who booked my hotel room for me?' he said, and placed the straw trilby on the bench next to him, exposing the precision engineering of his flat-top haircut. He took a handkerchief from his pocket and drew it across his brow before putting the trilby back on.

'This is all very Graham Greene,' I said. 'Parleys in parks, that kind of thing.'

'Did you think that was how to work out who had sent me here?' Devereaux ignored my diversion. 'My client?'

'Your client?' It came out almost a snort. 'If you have a client, then their motto is *Fidelity, Bravery, Integrity.*'

Devereaux laughed and eyed me as if appraising me. There was a hint of respect in his gaze. Also a hint of the lion appraising the antelope.

'Yep, Jock Ferguson was right,' said Devereaux. 'You are a smart cookie. Okay, you got me.'

'So what do I call you?' I asked. '*Special Agent* Devereaux?'

'Dex will still do just fine. And what we talked about the other night was all true.'

'So what in hell's name is so important about John Largo that the FBI send one of their finest on a tub all the way over to Glasgow.'

'Actually I flew. To London. I took the train up here. And John Largo *is* that important. Seeing as you're so all-fired curious about me, and seeing as you enjoy an interesting relationship with the local law enforcement, I thought it would be good for

you and me to have a talk without Jock Ferguson present.'
Devereaux stood up and we started to walk through the park.

'You don't trust Jock?' I asked.

'I'm just cautious, that's all.'

'Yet you're prepared to trust me?'

Devereaux laughed. 'Now, there's a question: do you trust a
man who doesn't really trust himself? Well, let me tell you,
Lennox, you're an interesting kind of guy. You'll have guessed
that I've been through everything that's on file about you. War
record. *Post*-war record. I know that you deal with crooks. I know
that you've done the odd crooked thing yourself. And I know
more than you might think I would know about everything
that happened last year.'

I said nothing. He probably did know more than I'd like. More
than Jock Ferguson knew; or was sure that he knew.

'Like I said, I saw your war record. I know what it was like
to have your kind of war. I was with the First Ranger Battalion.
That's one of the reasons I put myself forward to come over
here ... I know Scotland. I trained here with the British
Commandos before Omaha Beach.'

Again, I said nothing. Everybody had a war story.

'I also know about the ...' Devereaux paused, looking somewhere in the park's trees for the right word. ' ... *difficulties* you
got into towards the end of your war service. The accusations
about black-market dealing. And I know all about your German
associate ending up face down in Hamburg harbour.' Devereaux
stopped in the path and turned to me. 'Do you know what I
see, Lennox? I see a man who can be trusted for the best reason
of them all. Money. I don't know what schemes Ferguson has
going. Maybe none. But it looks to me like every second cop in
this city is on the take. I'd be pretty sure that Largo has a couple
in his pocket. So here's the deal: I'll pay you for anything I can

use to get Largo. You give me the goods that lead me to him and I'll pay you a thousand dollars. That's over and above anything you make on the side from the cases you're investigating. It should also be enough to resolve any conflicts of interest, should they arise.'

'That's an interesting offer, Dex . . .' All of a sudden I felt comfortable using his first name: promises of large sums of money tended to make me more amenable to widening my social circle. 'But, to be honest, a lot of people have been paying me to find people. So far my batting average has been pretty lousy.'

'You don't need to find him, Lennox. Just get enough to point me in the right direction.' He led on and I followed. A woman in a flared shirtwaister dress and winged sunglasses pushed a pram the size of a taxi past us. Devereaux lifted his hat to her and I followed suit. We were pretty elegant for a couple of New World Joes.

'You still haven't told me why he is so important,' I said. 'What did he do: steal George Washington's wooden teeth from the Smithsonian?'

'When we met at your apartment the other night, I told you how Largo has built up a chain of supply across three continents. It's a very, very impressive operation. But what's even more impressive is the vision behind it. You and I saw all kinds of hell in the war, I'd say, but John Largo has a vision of the future that would give us new nightmares. Have you heard of a narcotic called heroin?'

'I've heard of it,' I said. 'It was used in the war instead of morphine. I've heard of people getting hooked on it, but it's less addictive than morphine, I believe. That's why they used it.'

'That's where you're wrong. That's where everyone behind

heroin got it wrong. It was created as a less addictive alternative but it actually creates a higher dependency among those who use it. That's not been a problem. Here in England it's still legal and a prescribed medicine. If your kid has a cough that won't go away, the doctor will write you a script for a dose of heroin drops. In fact, the authorities here only started to keep a record of heroin addicts this year. There are just short of four hundred recorded addicts in Britain. Almost all are doctors or connected to the medical profession. You don't have a problem here. But in the States we do, and it's getting bigger. Heroin has been controlled since the Harrison Act and we made it completely illegal more than twenty years ago.'

He paused as a couple of young men in shabby business suits walked past.

'I work out of the Bureau's New York office. Last year, in Harlem, New York City, we saw a rapid spread of the illegal supply of heroin. This summer we have an epidemic on our hands . . . an epidemic of negroes injecting themselves with this stuff.'

'So this is Largo's business. He's the one who's supplying it to the blacks?'

Devereaux shook his head. 'John Largo is supplying the people who supply the negroes. The Syndicate. But Largo's not the only one supplying the Syndicate. Glasgow isn't the main supply port, and Largo isn't the only exporter.'

'Who's the competition?' I asked.

'Corsicans. Between you and me there's a rumour that Uncle Sam did a deal with the Corsican Mafia to keep the commies out of Marseille. Uncle Sam in the form of the CIA. The flip-side of the deal is that the same Corsicans are running heroin from French Indochina to Turkey and into Marseille and supplying the stuff to the New York Syndicate. The story is that

Largo uses a different route and the stuff ends up here in Glasgow. Then it's shipped to the States.'

For a moment, I considered what Devereaux was saying. I leaned back on the bench, hooking my elbows over the back and tilting the brim of my Borsalino to let the sun bathe my face.

'So why are you here and not in Marseille? Sounds to me like Largo is small fry in comparison to these Corsicans.'

'He's not. Anything but. Largo represents serious opposition, and the Corsicans don't take kindly to opposition. Trust me, John Largo has more to fear from his swarthy islander competitors than he does from law enforcement. Fact is the Syndicate is largely made up of Neapolitan and Sicilian families. There's some kind of animosity between the Italians and Corsicans. The Corsicans are the wrong type of Guinea or something, I guess. And Largo has been undercutting their prices. So, he's slowly been carving out a bigger share of the US market.'

'How did you find out about him?'

A couple of young women walked past and we again raised our hats. The girls laughed in a stupid way and walked on. No class, I thought. The one nearest to me had on a white linen skirt so lightweight that the sun shone through, outlining her thighs and hips. No class but nice ass.

'Six months ago I got a lead,' said Devereaux. 'The Italians don't talk because of their omertà, but they have to work with others. In the Syndicate and out of it. They've been setting up a network of coloured middlemen throughout Harlem. One of them was a guy called Jazzy Johnson, who also happened to be one of my snitches. Johnson wasn't able to pass on information of any quality because they never told him anything more than the barest minimum he needed to know. But what made Jazzy a good snitch was the way he was all ears and he told me everything he could pick up. One of the things he overheard was a conversation about an overdue shipment that was coming from Glasgow, and the name John Largo was mentioned.' Devereaux shrugged. 'That's it ... not much to go on, but at least I was able to put the name to a figure we knew was operating in Europe. Still not much information there except he was an ex-soldier ...'

'Ain't we all?' I interrupted.

'Sure, but Largo is supposed to be some kind of ex-professional. You know, career-type soldier.'

'Which army?'

'Don't know. US, Canadian ... maybe even British. The start of the supply chain has to be out in the Far East and it could be that John Largo started out in some Brit colony like Hong Kong. Or fought the Japs rather than the Krauts. Wherever he did his fighting and whoever he did it for, the rumours are that he is one deadly son-of-a-gun. There's been a lot of blood spilt across Asia and Europe just setting this thing up.' Devereaux stopped again and looked around the park. 'Say, do you think we could do this wet?'

I looked at my watch. 'The pubs are open. I know a place near here ...'

There tends to be an architectural style or design vernacular that unites buildings used for a common, specific purpose. Glasgow bars seemed to be themed *eternal gloom*. Where there were windows, the glass was frosted or misted for the twin purposes of concealing the earnest business of Scottish drinking from the outside world and to attenuate any sunlight into an insipid milky-white bloom.

We didn't speak further about Largo or the FBI all the way through the park and onto the main road. Instead, we talked about Vermont and New Brunswick. Different sides of the border but pretty much the same way of life and pretty much the same way of looking at life. A few heads had turned in our direction when we entered the gloom of the bar, but we were ignored once we had ordered a couple of whiskies and sat over at a corner table away from the smattering of other customers.

'So your informant. Can't he find out any more about Largo?'

'He can't find out anything about anything any more.'

I raised an eyebrow but Devereaux shook his head. 'Bar fight. The same old crap . . . about a woman, or a spilt drink, or a remark. He took a knife in the ribs.'

'Oh, I see,' I said, and a fleeting thought that Glasgow was maybe twinned with Harlem fleeted. 'And you have no other leads?'

'You got all I got.' It was the first time I'd seen Devereaux close to gloomy. But it might just have been the pub.

'Listen,' I said, 'don't get me wrong, I'm not haggling . . . but a thousand dollars isn't much for the FBI to be offering for information leading them to someone as big, and someone who you have so few leads on, as John Largo.'

'We have other priorities. Commies, mainly. Between Hoover and McCarthy we've spent the last five, six years chasing red spectres and letting the Syndicate get away with murder. Literally. The other thing is my bosses don't put the same impor-tance on Largo as I do. They see the French Connection, as they call it, as the biggest threat. And, to be honest, this problem isn't a problem as far as a lot of my superiors are concerned so long as it's in Harlem. Upper Manhattan or Nassau County and we'd have a task force set up with a million-dollar budget. But Harlem . . . it's just niggers.'

I took a breath and let it go slowly. It all fitted. 'You can keep the reward money,' I said. 'If I find anything out about Largo

I'll give it to you for free. Like I said, I've got a lot of people paying for my time to find people I can't find.'

Devereaux stared at me as if he was unsure if I was serious. 'Why, Lennox?'

'You liked this coloured guy? Jazzy?'

'He was a cheap hoodlum.'

'You liked him though?'

'I guess.'

'The reason there's only a thousand up for this reward is because it's your money, isn't it?'

'No one else sees the big picture.' Devereaux sighed. 'These people are stuck in a shithole of a place and heroin gives them a holiday. It's supposed to be the most incredible feeling, puts you in a different place a universe away from your troubles ... but it turns your brain to mush and makes you its slave for the rest of your life. And that, my friend, means that it offers the criminal opportunity of the century. There's no way that it's going to stay in Harlem or Watts or Englewood. And even if it does, I didn't join the FBI to watch people rot to death to make a buck for organized crime. Like I said, everything I told you in your apartment was true. My investigation here *is* private. Or semi-private. The Bureau agreed to pay my transport and accommodation and give me some kind of official sanction as far as the City of Glasgow Police are concerned. But if I don't come up with the goods ... literally come up with the goods, then I have a long and happy career in filing and archiving to look forward to.'

'What do you mean "literally come up with the goods"?'

'The New York Police Department have had to deal with all of the consequences of what's happened in Harlem over the last two summers. Consequences on the street. It means that NYPD beat cops have become our best source of information.

That information tells us that there's been a hiccup in supply. About three weeks ago a shipment was supposed to arrive. It didn't. There are a lot of itchy customers on the street as a result and, last I heard, it still hadn't arrived. Which is why I'm here. There's been some kind of wrinkle and I reckon that John Largo is here in Glasgow with iron in hand. Let's just hope it's a big wrinkle and I have enough time to find him.'

'What about the movement of the stuff itself. Have you spoken to the port authority? There's a chance you'd be able to track any iffy shipments. I have a contact . . .'

Devereaux held his hand up. 'You've got this all wrong. This isn't illegal gun shipments . . .' He shot me a meaningful look: he really did know more than Jock Ferguson about what had happened last year. 'What you've got to remember about this stuff is that you don't need a freighter to bring it over. It's small and it can be hidden anywhere and in anything. A suitcase of this stuff in its pure form would be worth a hundred thousand dollars.'

I thought about what he was saying for a moment. 'Does the City of Glasgow Police know any of this?'

'Some. They're not that interested in the heroin. They're just very keen to be seen to help Uncle Sam.' Devereaux smiled wryly. 'We just saved the world, you know.'

'That you did,' I said, leaving the bitter Scottish beer and sipping at the whisky chaser. 'That you did . . .' I looked at my watch and suddenly had an idea. 'Do you have your FBI badge with you?'

'Sure . . .' Devereaux frowned. 'I have it with me all the time. Why?'

'Because you could make someone's day for me.'

I gave Devereaux the lowdown on the way up to Blanefield. I

told him about what had been happening with Kirkcaldy and the forthcoming fight with the German title holder. All of which was just background for why I had really brought him up there.

'I really appreciate you doing this, Dex,' I said, as we pulled up behind the bottle-green Rover. Sneddon was allowing it to be used as an almost permanent observation post. Davey Wallace took the early evenings, Twinkletoes until one in the morning, then Sneddon would provide another thug to watch the place until daybreak. Davey still approached his duties with fierce dedication, taking notes of absolutely anything and everything that happened. He had looked more than a little intimidated by Twinkletoes at their first meeting. However, Twinkletoes had been positively avuncular with Davey. Which had been even more scary.

I tapped on the window of the Rover and Davey swung open the door and stepped out. I half expected him to stand to attention.

'How's it going, Davey?' I asked.

'Fine, Mr Lennox, just fine,' he said. He cast a glance across to Devereaux who stood beside me. 'I'm sorry, but there's really nothing to report. I've not taken my eyes off the place though. You can trust me on that, Mr Lennox.'

'I know that, Davey. I've brought someone up to meet you. I've been telling Dex here about how you work for me part-time and what a great job you've been doing.'

'Dex Devereaux ...' The American said earnestly, almost sternly, and before he shook Davey's hand he reached into the inside pocket of his jacket and pulled out a leather wallet. He flipped it open and gold flashed in the evening light. 'Special Agent Dex Devereaux, FBI.'

It took all of my willpower, but somehow I suppressed a smirk at Davey's reaction. He stared at Devereaux's FBI shield, eyes wide, open-mouthed, mesmerized. It seemed to take an eternity before he looked past the badge to Devereaux's face. Devereaux pocketed the shield and shook Davey's hand.

'Mr Lennox has told me you're doing a darned fine job for him here. Darned fine. It's always good to meet a fellow investigator. Keep up the good work, Davey.'

'Dex is over here carrying out an investigation for the FBI. But that's strictly between us, Davey,' I said as gravely as I could manage.

'Oh, yes . . . I wouldn't say a thing, Mr Devereaux . . .' Davey spoke like a child giving his very best promise. It was the child-likeness of it that troubled me. He was only a kid. I was pretty sure I had placed him in no danger, but I couldn't be absolutely sure. 'You can trust me not to say anything,' he said with the same boyish earnestness.

'I know I can,' said Devereaux. 'We *are* colleagues, after all.'

'I'm sure you have a lot of questions for Dex,' I said, offering them both a cigarette before lighting one for myself. 'Is Bobby Kirkcaldy in?'

'Yes sir,' said Davey. 'He came back with his uncle from the gym about an hour and a half ago.'

'Why don't you two have a chat while I go and see if there's anything else to report.'

As I left them chatting, I saw Devereaux take his shield out again and hand it to Davey. At the same time I liked Devereaux and resented him. He reminded me of some of the men I'd met in the war. Men who saw all kinds of shit yet somehow managed to keep their humanity and sense of honour intact. There hadn't been many of them. And I hadn't been one.

The door was answered again by Uncle Bert Soutar. He was his usual charming self and, after I said I wanted a word with Kirkcaldy, he turned his back on me and walked along the terra-cotta-tiled hallway.

Bobby Kirkcaldy wasn't in the lounge this time. Soutar led me further along the hall until there was no hall to lead me along. He opened the door and a few steps took us down into what must have originally been intended as a built-in double garage and workshop. Instead it had been converted into a gymnasium: three benches; a rack of weights and some free dumbbells in one corner of the concrete floor; a couple of heavy punch bags hung like giant pendulous sausages from robust ceiling chains, and a speed ball on a wall bracket. Bobby Kirkcaldy was in the centre of the gym, dressed in what looked like longjohns with boxing trunks over them. The air was filled with the sound of it being sliced repeatedly by Kirkcaldy's skipping rope. His feet made only the smallest of movements but looked as if they were not actually in contact with the ground at any time. He ignored me as I came down the steps, finishing his set before wiping his face with the towel he had wrapped around his neck.

'Well?' he asked unceremoniously, breathing hard. I was surprised at how out of breath he was: I'd seen him go the distance in the ring without breaking much of a sweat. I would have been surprised if he had neglected his fitness this close to a fight.

'I just wanted to check that everything's okay. As you know we've got someone watching the house most of—'

'The kid?' It was Soutar who interrupted me. Maybe that was how his face got the way it was – interrupting people. 'What the fuck is he going to do if someone starts any shite? He looks about twelve.'

'Oh no,' I said in an offended tone. 'I don't hire anyone under thirteen unless it's for chimney sweeping.'

Uncle Bert took a step closer to me.

'Bert . . .' said Kirkcaldy in a low tone, causing Soutar to check himself and allowing me once more to consider the ignominy of being beaten up by a pensioner. Kirkcaldy turned to me. 'You can call him off. Nothing's happened for weeks and I'm getting pissed off being under surveillance. If I needed that I'd've gone to the police.'

'Listen, Mr Kirkcaldy, I'm just doing my job. Mr Sneddon has an interest in you and I'm just protecting that interest. If you say there's been no more trouble, then fine . . . I'll report back to Sneddon and take instructions from him. In the meantime, it's a free country and if Mr Sneddon wants to park his car outside on the street and have someone look after it, then there's nothing anybody can do.'

'You done?' There was no aggression in Kirkcaldy's voice. He was cool. Always. That was what made him deadly in the ring.

'Not quite. This is all very strange, if you don't mind me saying so. You've been getting warnings and threats and you don't tell anyone about it until your manager just happens along at the wrong time and sees it for himself. And since I first got involved in this, you've gone out of your way to make out that there's nothing going on.'

'There's not. And I didn't mention it because it means fuck all. It was obviously someone trying to put me off. It didn't work. It was never going to work, and they've given up.'

'What about you, Gramps?' I turned to Soutar. Deep within the folds and creases and pads of puffed flesh, his eyes glittered hard and black. 'What do you think? Do you think it's someone trying to spook Mr Kirkcaldy? I mean, I'm asking you for your expert opinion.'

'What the fuck is that meant to mean?' he asked nasally.

'I mean fight fixing. You know a thing or two about that. I was talking to an old *amigo* of yours . . . Jimmy MacSherry. He was reminiscing about the old days.'

'Do you have a point?' asked Kirkcaldy.

'Just that Uncle Bert here has had a colourful past. Am I right in thinking that you were involved with a bookie? Rumours of fight fixing?'

'You should mind your own business . . .' Soutar hid the threat in his tone with the subtlety of a turd hidden in a teacup.

'But it *is* true, isn't it?' I said, pushing my luck. 'You got involved with a kid on the make. My guess is he became a bookie. Small Change MacFarlane?'

'What the fuck has that got to do with anything?' Kirkcaldy moved closer. It wasn't a threat: he was preparing to stop old man Soutar in his tracks if he moved to have a go at me.

'I don't know.' I shrugged. It was true. 'Maybe nothing. MacFarlane's dead and they've got his killer. But maybe something. And if there is, I'll find out.'

I left them in the gym and made sure that I let myself out. There was something about the idea of taking the walk back along the hall with Soutar behind me that gave me an itch between the shoulder blades.

I walked back up to where the cars were parked. I could see Devereaux was still holding court with Davey, who continued to hang on every word.

'Problem?' asked Devereaux as I came up to them. He obviously had a talent for reading faces. Or minds. The FBI probably ran classes in it at Quantico.

'Dissatisfied customer. I would appear to be over-delivering my service.'

We left Davey buzzing and I drove Devereaux back to his hotel.

'Thanks for doing that, Dex,' I said, as Devereaux got out of the car. 'Davey's got nothing. He's stuck in a shitty home, with a shitty job with shitty prospects. You've made his year.'

'You're welcome, Lennox. He's a good kid. But now you owe me.'

'Anything I hear, you hear.'

'Okay, Lennox. Look after yourself.'

I watched Devereaux, a huge man in a loud suit and a straw trilby, cross the street to the hotel. Whatever else the FBI taught its agents in Quantico, how not to be conspicuously American wasn't part of the curriculum.

After I dropped Devereaux back at his Buchanan Street hotel, I parked and walked a few blocks to the Imperial Hotel. I wasn't after another drink.

May Donaldson and I had an arrangement.

May was a divorcee. Glasgow was not New York or London high society and the Glaswegian view of divorce was less than sophisticated. It didn't matter that she had been blameless: any divorce, for any reason, and in any class, placed a woman well and truly on the outside of Presbyterian respectability. May and I had done a few rounds together, it was true. But I liked to think that I had never actually *used* her. I also liked to think that Santa Claus really existed. I found May where I knew she would be, tending bar in the lounge of the Imperial Hotel. May had a knockout figure but a forgettable face, often wreathed with a kind of sadness or weariness. When I walked into the bar she was wearing a conservative white blouse and black skirt, the hotel's required uniform. The aim was to put the title *waitress* rather than *barmaid* in the minds of patrons. May had poured me a bourbon before I reached the bar.

'What's up, Lennox? You got a job for me?' she asked with a smile that didn't reach her eyes.

'Yep ... but not the usual,' I said. May did the odd job for me where she would turn up at a prearranged time and lie, fully clothed, beneath the covers in a hotel bedroom. Next to her would be a fully clothed middle-aged male. I would walk in with a member of the hotel staff and a couple of months later we would all speak of the event in a divorce courtroom as if it hadn't really been the pantomimed sham that everyone knew it was. The British allowed divorce, but in a British way: bureaucratic, long-winded and more than a little shoddy. Which suited me fine. I had made a lot of money from staged infidelities to support divorce cases.

'Oh?' May looked at me with so much suspicion in her expression that she clearly thought I was going to offer to buy her mother for the white slave trade.

'Don't worry, nothing dodgy. I'm trying to contact a young woman who lives in one of the Corporation hostels. There's a matron there who won't let me in and I can't park myself outside until she shows.'

May arched an already arched eyebrow.

'It's not what you think,' I said. 'I've got a missing person case and this girl is maybe the last one to see my guy before he disappeared. I'd like you to call on her and ask her to meet with me so I can ask her a few questions. If she can tell you where to find the guy then that'll do just as well.'

'When?'

'When do you finish here?'

'My shift ends at nine.'

I looked at my watch. It was eight-fifteen. Of course, I could have stayed and drunk my bourbon and chatted to May until her shift ended, but that would have been awkward for both of us. 'Okay, I'll pick you up then.'

I drank half the bourbon for appearances' sake, paid for it, and headed back to my car. Considering May and I had been intimate on a number of occasions, I found something depressing about the sterile, businesslike exchange I'd just had with her. But then, when I thought about it, our intimacy had often been sterile and businesslike.

I tried Lorna again from a callbox at the corner of Bath Street. Still nothing. I looked at my watch again. I had this business with May and Sammy's putative *inamorata*, Claire, to sort out. It would be ten before I could head out to Lorna's.

I killed the half hour and went back to pick up May. She came out wearing a lightweight coat and smart black hat. They looked new but I'd seen them on her more times than I could remember. While the rest of society was coming out of austerity, a divorcee in Glasgow working behind a bar had to learn to stretch her wardrobe.

I put the radio on as we drove to Partick. Mel Tormé was singing 'Harlem Nocturne' and it made me think of everything Devereaux had told me about his bosses, who were convinced that Devereaux's particular Harlem nocturne wouldn't play in Peoria. They were wrong and Devereaux was right.

The Velvet Fog sang, and saved both of us the effort of conversation. I don't know what it was that was going on between May and me, but it was mutual. It was as if we were both on the brink of becoming other people. Putting a past behind us. And each represented an embarrassing reminder to the other of who they had been.

We were halfway to Partick when May confirmed my thesis. 'I've met someone, Lennox,' she said tentatively. 'A widower. He's older than me but he's a good man. Kind. He's got two children.'

'Does he come from Glasgow?' I asked. If she said no, I would know that the chump was a ticket out of the city. May had made it very clear in the past how much she hated Glasgow. In the past, in the pluperfect, and in the present perfect continuous.

'No. He has a farm in Ayrshire. You know that my ex-husband was a farmer?'

'You mentioned it,' I said. Several drunken times, I thought. 'Does he make you happy?'

'He stops me being unhappy. That's enough for me. We need each other. I get on well with his kids and they're at an age where they need a mother.'

'Okay ...' I smiled at her. 'I'm happy for you, May. Really. I take it there's a reason you're telling me this?'

'I can't do any more work for you. After tonight, that's it. George doesn't know that I've done these divorce cases with you and he can't find out. We're going to make a clean break, get right away from the past.'

'To Ayrshire?' I couldn't keep the puzzlement from my voice. 'That *is* the past. To be specific it's the eighteenth century.'

'No,' she said coldly. 'Not Ayrshire. You'll laugh at this ...'

'Okay, try me.'

'Canada. We're emigrating to Canada. They're looking for farmers there.'

I didn't laugh. In fact, I was surprised at my reaction. Something sharp and unpleasant bit me in the gut and I realized it was envy.

'Where in Canada?'

'Saskatchewan. Near Regina.'

We pulled up outside Craithie Court. I switched Tormé off mid croon. 'I really do wish you all the best.'

'The other thing, Lennox ... it would be best if you didn't call round to the flat any more.'

I placed my hand on hers. She stifled the instinctive recoil, but not quickly enough for me not to sense the tensing of her fist to pull away.

'It's all right, May. I understand. I really hope it works out for you. We'll make this our last job, okay? I won't call round any more.'

She smiled. It would have been nice if her smile had been tinged with sadness, but the idea of not seeing me again seemed to cheer her up no end. I have that effect on some women. I went over with her again what to say to Claire Skinner and gave her Sammy Pollock's name again. She got out of the car and went into the Hostel. When she didn't come back immediately, I took it as a good sign.

It was half an hour before she re-emerged and got back into the car, her face flushed and her expression dark.

'Drive around the corner,' she said without looking at me. 'She's probably watching the car.'

I did what May told me. 'What's going on?' I asked when we were parked again.

'I don't know, Lennox, but whatever it is, that girl in there is terrified. She said she wouldn't come out to talk to you. She says she knows nothing about where Sammy Pollock is and she wouldn't tell you if she did know. It's not that she's being tough about it, it's just that she is so terrified.' May frowned. 'I don't know what you've got involved with, Lennox, but you better be careful. Someone has that poor girl scared half to death.'

'Okay . . . I guess I'll have to wait until she has a spot at the Pacific Club and have another go at her then.'

'You'll be lucky. I get the feeling she's keeping a low profile.'

'You okay?'

May looked at me for a moment, sighed then smiled. 'I'm fine. It's just she was very . . . *agitated*. I thought she was going to go for me.'

'Sorry. I didn't think . . .'

'Forget it . . . it wasn't anything I couldn't handle.' Suddenly, May's attention was drawn to something through the windscreen.

'Look . . .' she said.

'Is that her?'

I followed May's eyes to the junction about two hundred yards ahead, to where a young woman in her early twenties was hurrying across the street, coming from the direction of Craithie Court. From this distance she appeared to be quite attractive. My experience of Glaswegian women was that they were usually only ever attractive from a distance, or through bourbon-tinted glasses. The woman up ahead was not quite slim with a slight heaviness around the waist and ankles. She had a pale grey jacket draped over one blue-bloused arm and everything about her movements suggested urgency.

'You haven't seen her before?' May seemed surprised. 'Yes, that's her.'

We watched as she made her way along the street towards the corner.

'Can you drive, May?' I asked. It was odd, but it was one of the thousands of things about May that I didn't know.

She shook her head. I took out my wallet and handed her everything I had in it apart from a couple of one-pound notes. It amounted to just over thirty pounds and I thrust it into her hands.

'That's for helping me out tonight. I've got to go after her so that's to cover your taxi fare home too. Thanks, May.'

'That's far too much, Lennox.'

'Consider it a wedding gift,' I said. I got out of the car and May followed. 'I'm sorry that you have to get a cab home.'

'That's okay,' she said.

I looked impatiently up the road to the corner around which Claire Skinner had just disappeared from view. I turned back to May. It was as if she was trying to frame a thought, put something into words.

'It's okay, May,' I said. 'See you around.'

She nodded in an odd way, her eyes avoiding mine, said 'Thanks' and 'Bye', turned abruptly, and walked briskly back down Thornwood Road towards Dumbarton Road and out of my life.

I jumped back into the Atlantic. The chances were that Claire Skinner hadn't spotted my car outside the hostel. And my face was totally unknown to her. My fond farewell to May had cost me too much time to follow Claire on foot: I had too much distance to cover. And once I had covered it, things would get tricky: it's never easy to follow by car someone who is on foot, without being detected. But I guessed that Claire would jump onto a bus or tram, or hail a taxi. I had no idea where she was going, but I was pretty sure whom she was going to see. I picked her up again when I turned the corner. Her trot had slowed to a brisk walk, still a determined effort on a muggy summer's evening in Glasgow. I saw her check her watch, but I was pretty sure this was no prearranged appointment: she had been spurred into action by May's unwelcome intervention.

I caught up with her and had to drive past her at normal speed. I decided to pull over farther up the street, dump the car, and hoof it. A car travelling at walking pace would be far too conspicuous. I pulled over to the kerb and did a quick check of where I was. Fairlie Park Drive. I was about to get out of my car when she walked briskly past without looking in my direction. There was a telephone booth at the corner with Crow Road and Claire stepped into it. She made a short call before stepping back out and waiting outside the 'phone box. I noticed her feet, small beneath the slightly too thick ankles and doing a little side to side dance step. I decided to sit tight. The mountain was maybe on its way to Mohammed. After about ten minutes, I saw her wave furiously at something. A black taxi pulled over and she jumped in. I waited until the cab passed me and put another car between us before I pulled out.

The taxi headed south out of the city. We passed through Pollokshields, reminding me that I'd have to return there later, then Pollokshaws, Giffnock and Newton Mearns. One of the things I could never get used to about Glasgow was the way it was this concentrated, dense knot of stone, brick and steel, factories and furnaces, tenements and bristling cranes; and then suddenly you were in open, almost empty countryside. We were on the main road south, a grey-black scar on a wrinkled blanket of green that stretched as far as I could see on either side. This was the main Carlisle road and it meant I was able to conceal myself in traffic: something that became more difficult when the taxi pulled off onto a B-road. Another turn took the cab onto an even narrower country road. This was a road to nowhere else and you needed a reason to have made that turning. I held back, allowing a gap to open up between the Atlantic and the cab. The road traced the edge of a flooded quarry that looked up at the sun like a mud-brown eye.

I had lost sight of the taxi around a bend. It didn't concern me because there was nowhere for it to go. A little bit of acceleration and I could bring it back into view. But when I turned the bend I was suddenly faced with the rear of the cab, pulled into a farm gate. I drove on without looking in its direction and only once I was past did I see Claire Skinner disembark and hand some notes to the driver. Clearly not waiting for change, she turned, opened the gate, and headed up what looked to me like a farm track.

Bingo.

I continued along the road until I reached the next bend. In my rear-view mirror I saw the taxi struggle to make a three-point turn and head back in the direction of the main road. I drove around the next bend, a sharp turn to the left. A little further on there was a copse beside the road. Bumping the Atlantic onto the grass verge, the two driver's side wheels still on the tarmac, I felt reasonably sure I had concealed my car from the farm track and presumably any buildings at the track's end.

I made my way on foot through the clump of trees until I was at its edge and had a clear view across the fields. The sun was low and rich in the evening sky, softening edges and warming tones. I spotted Claire's head for a second before it disappeared from view where the path dipped between its banks and I couldn't see her – which meant she couldn't see me. For how long, I didn't know: the path could soon incline back to become level with the surrounding fields.

I broke out from the cover of the trees and ran across the field, angling my trajectory across the grass to aim for the field-height stretch of path behind the point at which I had last seen Claire Skinner. The lush green grass in the field was ankle height, but the ground beneath was reasonably firm, having been dried out of its normal sodden state by the recent atypical spell of sunshine. Siberia has permafrost; Scotland has permasog. My rush across the pasture was watched disinterestedly by a handful of black-faced, dead-eyed sheep. I wasn't hurrying in order to catch up with Claire – my guess was that there would be only one destination at the end of the lane – but rather to keep out of her sight by getting to the path before she emerged from the hollow and had a view of the field.

Vaulting over the dry-stone wall, I dropped down onto the lane, a thin grey ribbon of dusty earth between grassy banks. There was something about the lane and the evening light that made me feel I should be in a collarless shirt, sleeves rolled up and with a scythe over my shoulder. But that wouldn't really be me: as a character I always thought of myself as more Leslie Charteris than Thomas Hardy. Ruddy-cheeked farm girls and frothy ale weren't my thing. Although I'd probably give the ruddy-cheeked farm girls a go.

I put these bucolic musings out of my head and made my way along the lane at a steady, unhurried pace. There was no sign of Claire Skinner until I came to a bend in the lane. I could see her up ahead, about a hundred yards distant. I ducked behind the cover of the grassy bank and watched as she headed towards a farm cottage tucked into a tangle of bramble and bush. Scotland's latitude made for long summer evenings, but the sun was low now and I would have expected to see a light from inside the cottage. There was none. Claire knocked on the door and had to wait for a minute or so before someone unseen to me admitted her.

I watched the cottage for five full minutes, just to make sure it wasn't going to be a flying visit. Seeing as Claire had dismissed the taxi at the lane's end, and the fact that we were in the middle of nowhere, my guess was Claire had no plans to make the return journey to Glasgow that night.

I considered my options. I would have a long loiter if I waited until it got truly dark before approaching the cottage; but in any kind of light I would be visible on the path a hundred yards away. Time enough to put a party together and shout 'surprise!' when I came in through the front door. I didn't know what I was dealing with and it would be best to check it out unseen first.

Backtracking up the farm lane, I climbed over another stone wall and took a long, wide sweep around to the side and rear of the cottage where I was sure I'd be obscured by the bushes and brambles. It was my only option, but I felt exposed up on an elevated field and silhouetted against a shield of sunset sky. It took me five minutes to get into position around the back of the cottage. As I drew close, I could see that this was a camp-out. Much of the glass in the windows was cracked or broken and what wasn't was fogged with grime. What I guessed had been a small vegetable garden at the back was now waist-high overgrown and I gently had to scythe my way through it, pushing the vegetation as quietly as possible from my path. By the time I reached the back door, I could hear voices from inside – this was not somewhere you would feel the need to whisper. The voices were urgent. Two voices. One male, one female.

Edging along the rough stone wall, I reached one of the small, grimy windows and peered in. I snapped my head back immediately when I realized that Claire Skinner was sitting directly in front of the window, with her back to it. I wasn't able to see where the man was, but I could hear him talking. Then I heard Claire saying exactly what I'd been waiting for her to say since I had first started to follow her.

The name 'Sammy'.

Chapter Eleven

They both turned abruptly when I entered. Claire stood up so suddenly that the old chair she'd been sitting on crashed onto the grubby floor. The young man stood up too.

I had been wrong about there being no light on: a kerosene lamp sat on a table improvised from a crate, but its wick was turned so low that its light was dim and weak. Bright enough, though, for me to see that this was the kind of place you could call a hovel if you raised the tone sufficiently. A tumble of bedclothes and a large army-style knapsack were piled onto a low-slung camp bed in one corner, a primus stove sat next to a half dozen unopened cans on another crate. Empty cans and bottles lay piled in another corner. You had to be really scared to hide out this much.

I barely recognized Sammy Pollock as the cocky, smooth youth with the expensively barbered hair in the photograph Sheila Gainsborough had shown me. His dark hair was now lank and greasy and his jaw hadn't seen a razor for several days. He looked unwashed and tired. There again, the facilities here were not all they could be. But there was something more to the tiredness that dulled his expression and draped itself around his frame: it was the high-tension, electric exhaustion of a man on the run.

'Nice place you've got here,' I said. 'Fixer-upper?'

Sammy slipped a hand into his jacket pocket.

'Did Largo send you?' he asked.

'Largo?' I asked and smiled. I leaned forward and turned the flame on the kerosene lamp up. 'Do you mind?' I asked. 'I'm doing a piece for *Better Hovels and Gardens* and I'd like to have a good look at the place.' As I did so, I became aware that there were four of us in the room: me, Claire, Sammy and a two-and-a-half-feet-high, very green, very oriental demon. Or dragon. Or devil. Whatever he was, he was an ugly son-of-a-gun, for sure. He grinned at me, his long tongue lapping between jade fangs. Sammy saw me looking at it.

'Take it,' he said. 'Tell Largo to leave me alone. I won't go to the cops. I won't do anything. Just take it and go.'

'Thanks for the offer,' I said, 'but it would clash with my colour scheme. I'm not here about ornaments, I'm here for you.' Whatever it was he had in his jacket pocket, he closed his hand around it. I tutted and shook my head. 'Don't even think about it. Sammy. You're a big boy, but not big enough.'

'Who are you?' asked Claire, staring at me with wide, terrified eyes.

'It's okay, Claire. I'm the guy who wanted to talk to you about Sammy. I was hired to find him by his sister, Sheila Gainsborough. She's been worried about him.'

Both their expressions changed and a sense of enormous relief filled the small, filthy cottage. The same kind of relief as if someone had found a whole bunch of lifeboats that no one had known about immediately after the *Titanic* had hit the iceberg. 'I'm sure Paul Costello has told you all about me,' I said. 'Paul and I had a little chat before he followed you out of the limelight. Where is Costello, by the way?'

I got my answer. Someone was kind enough to switch out all of the lights so I could enjoy the firework display in my head better. After the fireworks, I went somewhere deep and dark and timeless.

I woke up in hell. Or at least that was the first thought I formed after my vision started to come together again. The demon I was looking up at hadn't been carved out of jade. It was made of much sterner, tougher material.

'What happened?' I asked, even though I knew that Singer was incapable of answering. He helped me up to my feet. I was still in the cottage. Sammy, Claire and the little green god weren't. Instead Twinkletoes McBride stood, hunched over because of the limited headroom. He looked like he was holding the whole roof up. Which probably wouldn't have been a challenge. Willie Sneddon was there too, eyeing me maliciously and smoking a cigarette.

'There's an ashtray somewhere,' I said as Singer eased me down into a sitting position on the crate-cum-table. 'Don't get ash on the carpet ... I've just done the spring cleaning.'

'You never tire of the wisecracks, Lennox?' asked Sneddon.

'I find them comforting in challenging times.'

I held my head in my hands, trying to keep it still and stop the pounding in my skull. I gingerly felt the back of my head. The skin hadn't been broken but there was half an egg tucked behind my ear and it hurt like hell. I'd been sapped from behind. The kind of blow with a sap that can kill a man. I pictured the sap swinging through the air behind me and when I followed the imagined hand, arm and shoulder behind it, it led me to Costello's face. I'd catch up with young Costello sooner or later. Then it would be party season.

I looked up at Sneddon and frowned; a thought suddenly hit me, which was becoming a habit. 'How did you find me?'

'Singer's been on your tail for a while. Quiet, like,' said

Sneddon. Then with a malicious grin. 'He's good at that . . . quiet.'

'Why d'you have Singer tailing me?'

'Let's call it insurance. I get all worked up about you maybes experiencing a crisis of interests.'

'How did he—'

'He had someone with him. Tam. Always does. He got Tam to drive into the nearest village and 'phone me. The rest he writes down for me. He said two men and a tart came out of here like bats out of hell. When Singer and Tam saw you didn't, they came in and checked. Thought you was dead.'

'How long have I been out?'

'An hour. We've just arrived. We was looking for you anyway.'

'Oh?' I said. Then I saw Twinkletoes' expression. It worried me. Anything other than a smile on Twinkletoes' face worried me.

'I'm sorry, Mr Lennox,' said Twinkletoes. 'It's Davey . . .'

'Davey Wallace? What about him?'

'Someone gave him a doing,' said Sneddon in an I-couldn't-give-a-shit tone. 'A really good doing.'

'He's in the Southern General, Mr Lennox,' said Twinkletoes in a doleful baritone. 'It's not right. Not right at all. It's *egg-gree-jus*, that's what it is . . . fucking *egg-gree-jus*.'

'Is he going to be all right?'

Sneddon shrugged.

'How'd it happen?' I tried to shake some of the fog out of my head. When I did, I kept seeing Davey's eager, youthful face. Whatever had happened to him, I was responsible.

'I need to go.' I stood up but gravity objected.

'I'll drive you,' said Twinkletoes as he caught my fall like I was a kid on skates for the first time.

'My car . . .' I said weakly. 'It's around the corner of the road. Parked by some trees.'

Singer pointed silently to himself and held out his hand. I handed over my car keys and nodded. It could have been my imagination, but these days there seemed to be less menace in his lurk.

By the time we reached the hospital, the sky had turned a velvety purple. At this time of year it never got truly dark. Glasgow's Southern General Hospital had started off as cavalry barracks, then became the Govan Poorhouse, then a lunatic asylum, before being converted for its current use. It had somehow managed to maintain the charm of its previous incarnations and its jagged Victorian architecture was as welcoming as Castle Frankenstein.

The linoleum-floored corridors we made our way along were quiet and I did not hear distant cries of 'It's alive! It's alive!' echoing off the porcelain wall tiles. The strictly observed visiting times were over and we were confronted by a matron only slightly less forbidding than the one I had encountered at Craithie Court. She had the same singular eyebrow, with the added twist of facial hair on her upper lip that was in danger of becoming a Ronald Colman moustache. I wondered where they all came from and decided that perhaps Baron Frankenstein did have a part-time job here after all. I anticipated another frosty rebuttal, but Sneddon gained our admittance by handing the matron our special pass: a nice new, crisp, folding special pass with a picture of Her Majesty on it. Matron Karloff tucked the twenty into her apron and bustled off down the corridor, her ugly flat shoes squeaking on the linoleum.

Davey was in a room on his own. I assumed Sneddon was behind that and I was grateful to him, although I guessed that it had less to do with concern or feelings of responsibility towards Davey and more to do with keeping me sweet so I'd deliver everything I could find out.

Someone had done a real number on Davey. His head and jaw were bandaged, framing his face like a mask. And it was more like a grotesque mask than a recognizable face, puffed and swollen until the eyes had become slits between thick pads of bruised flesh. It looked like his nose had been broken but, thankfully, whoever had attended him in the hospital had made some effort to set it straight. His lips were split and the lower lip had ballooned up like Maurice Chevalier's on a bad day. There were stitches in his upper lip.

'Davey, it's Lennox. Are you all right, son?'

Davey turned his head to me. His distended lips twitched and I realized he was trying to smile. That simple act caused a tidal wave of rage to swell up inside me.

'Who did this, Davey?'

'I'm sorry, Mr Lennox. I let you down.' Davey's voice was strained through clenched teeth and I realized that his jaw had been busted and wired shut.

'You didn't let anyone down. Who did this?'

'I didn't see them. They came up behind me and clobbered me. When I was on the ground they gave me this kicking. Then I passed out. That's all I remember, Mr Lennox.'

'Okay, Davey . . . okay. You take it easy. Anything else broken?'

'Just my jaw . . . and some cracked ribs. The doc says I must have a steel skull. He says he doesn't think there will be any permanent damage.'

'That's good, Davey. We'll have you out of here and on your feet in no time. I owe you a bonus.'

'You don't need to do that, Mr Lennox. Just tell me that you'll let me work for you again.'

'Sure, Davey. Sure I will.'

'Mr Kirkcaldy came to see me.'

'Bobby Kirkcaldy?'

'Aye . . . it was him what found me. He 'phoned for the ambulance and that.'

'I see. Did he see who attacked you?'

'No. He only came along later.'

'I see.'

'I lost my book,' said Davey through the wired cage of his teeth.

'What book?'

'The one you gave me, Mr Lennox. My notebook that I wrote everything down in.'

'Don't worry about it, Davey. I'll probably find it in the car or on the ground up there. It's not important.'

'I'm sorry . . .' Now Davey's voice sounded distant. He made a soft, detached groaning sound.

'You rest, Davey. I'll be back to see you tomorrow.'

'Promise?' he asked and sounded like a kid. In that moment I remembered that he was alone in the world. No parents. No brothers or sisters that he knew about. A Barnardo's kid out in the world on his own. The thought restoked the fury in my gut. A fury that was directed in equal shares at whoever had done this to Davey, and at myself for having put the kid in that position.

'I promise, Davey. I'll see you tomorrow.'

We left Davey to sleep, and outside in the corridor I had as coherent a conference with Sneddon as I was capable of having. I told him to put men on watch on the Kirkcaldy house twenty-four hours a day. I asked if they could look around for Davey's notebook, more to put the kid's mind at rest than anything else. Given that Singer had followed me all the way out into darkest Renfrewshire without me spotting him on my tail, I suggested he be put on following Kirkcaldy. I wanted whoever clobbered Davey, and Sneddon was itchier than ever to find out what was going on with Kirkcaldy. He didn't care about people getting hurt: he had invested in Kirkcaldy and didn't want his money to get bruised.

We headed back along the gloomy, porcelain-tiled corridors towards the exit. My head hurt like a bastard and the lurching in my gut was turning into determined heaving. I stopped off in the washroom and only just made it to the cubicle before I vomited. After I finished retching I went over to the wash-hand basins and splashed cold water on my face. When I looked into the mirror I saw a wraith with deep blue shadows under its eyes set into a bleached face. No wonder the ladies found me so damned attractive. The harsh hospital lighting threw up the hard angles of my face: the sharp, high cheekbones and the arch of my brow. The faint scars on my cheek, the reminders of an encounter with a German hand grenade, seemed more noticeable. I smoothed my black hair back with the palms of my hands. A plastic surgeon had had to do a bit of tidying up after my adventure with German munitions and it had left me with taut skin that accentuated my features. One thing I got a lot, especially from women, was that they thought I looked a little like the actor Jack Palance. Women seemed to like my face. I'd been told I had a handsome face but it had a touch of cruelty in it. That's why they liked it and that's why I hated it.

'You fucking coming?' Sneddon was at the door of the washroom.

'Sure,' I said, sniffing and drying my face with a paper hand towel. 'I'm coming. I've got work to do.'

I took one more look at the face in the mirror; it seemed to me it looked a little more cruel.

Singer drove me back to my digs in the Atlantic. Halfway there, I had to get him to pull over to the kerb so I could throw up again. I felt dizzy and sick, and had that feeling of unreality that comes with concussion. It wasn't the first time I'd been clobbered on the head and it probably wouldn't be the last, despite a doctor warning me that my skull had had just about all the punishment it could take.

It was just before eleven-thirty when Singer parked outside my flat. He helped me to the door. I thanked him and he nodded: we were bosom chums now. He went back out onto the street and climbed into the green Rover that Twinkletoes had followed us in. I didn't go up to my room right away. There was silence from the Whites' flat so I was as quiet as I could be as I dialled Lorna's number. I let it ring a long time. Still no answer.

I went up to my rooms and poured myself a whisky. It was a mistake: the first swallow made me retch. I was getting too old for this kind of malarkey. I decided that I'd probably have to have my head examined in the morning; not an unusual state of affairs but this time not metaphorically.

Before the war, when I'd been a kid in New Brunswick, I'd been handy with a pencil or paint brush and had given serious thought to studying art at the college in Halifax. Then the war had come along. Fact was that I was still handy with a pencil, and before I did anything else I took a clean sheet of paper and a pencil from the sideboard drawer, sat down and sketched out what I could remember of the jade figure I had seen in the farm cottage. When I was finished my head hurt even more but I was satisfied with the image I'd drawn. Not exact, but it was my memory rather than my abilities that let me down.

When I was finished, I drank some water from the tap, splashed my face again and pressed a damp towel against the egg behind my ear. I needed to pull myself together. I shaved and changed my clothes; my suit bore the traces of country life and I needed to feel freshened up. I drank some more water, this time swallowing more than the recommended dosage of aspirin with it: a stomach ulcer was the least of my worries at the moment.

I hit the street again just before midnight, climbed wearily into the Atlantic and drove down to Pollokshields.

When I got to Lorna's house, Benny Goodman was 'Stompin' at the Savoy'. In fact, he was stompin' so hard I could hear him from the drive as I pulled up. The front door was unlocked and I let myself in. There was no sign of Maggie, Jack Collins, or any other semi-detached members of the MacFarlane dynasty.

I found Lorna in the living room, dancing with the air along to the full-volume Benny Goodman record. In Lorna's case it should have been 'Staggerin' at the Savoy', and I hooked an arm around her waist and guided her over to the sofa. I discovered she had been clutching a hidden dancing partner to her breast. I pried the tumbler full of malt from her grasp and eased her down onto the chesterfield.

'Well, hi, handsome.' She breathed fumes that could have fuelled a jet into my face and smiled at me in an unfocussed, cold sort of way. It was a look I was used to in Glasgow: Scottish truculence is a craftsman's work, filtered through peat and sheep droppings and distilled till it's a hundred proof. 'Long time no see.'

I went over to the record player and tore the needle from its groove. Benny stopped stompin' and I hoped the neighbours hadn't already 'phoned the police.

'This doesn't help you know, Lorna,' I said, placing the Scotch on the side table and out of her reach.

'Nor do you. *You* don't help much, do you, Lennox?' She pushed at my chest as if ridding herself of a great annoyance. 'So what do I owe the pleasure of your company?'

'I read the papers. I wanted to see how you are.'

'Well you've seen. You may go . . .' She approximated a regal wave of dismissal.

'Not until you've sobered up, Lorna. I'll make some coffee.'

'Fuck the coffee. Fuck you, Lennox.' It was the first time I'd heard Lorna utter a profanity. 'Oh . . . is that what you want? You want me to fuck you, Lennox? We have such a deep and meaningful relationship, don't we, sweetheart?'

'Lorna, be quiet. I've been trying to get in touch with you all day. I didn't realize you were working so hard on tomorrow's hangover. I'll get you some water while the coffee's on.' I went through to the kitchen, filled the kettle and put it on the stove. Ditching the malt in the sink, I rinsed the glass and brought it back to Lorna, filled with water. Lorna looked at it disdainfully but I sat next to her and waited until she had drunk it all down.

'I'm sorry, Lorna. I should have been here more often,' I said, and meant it. 'It's just that I've been tied up with a few things, including looking into some of the deals your father was into. I thought that I might find out something about his death. But that all seems redundant now. Have the police spoken to you about the arrest?'

Another dismissive wave. Less regal this time. 'They showed me a photograph. Asked if I'd seen him before.'

'Had you?'

She shook her head sullenly. 'Some bloody gyppo. He must've followed Dad home from Shawfields a few times to learn his routine. Then waited for him . . .'

'Is that what the police told you?'

'They told me nothing. They talked to Maggie for a while and then Jack.'

'Jack Collins?'

'Yes ... He's family,' she said with what I took as a bitter laugh. There again, everything about her was bitter.

'The gyppo must've broken in and waited until . . .' She started to cry. 'Daddy . . .'

I put my arm around her and she pulled away.

'Have you eaten?'

She shrugged. I went through to the kitchen and made the coffee and some toast. Again I had to overcome her resistance before she drank the coffee and ate the toast. I took some coffee too and managed to keep it down. The aspirin was beginning to work on my headache: like a butterfly trying to wear away a cannonball with its wing.

We sat for an hour, saying nothing, me topping her up with coffee. Eventually the inevitable happened and she had to run for the toilet. When she came back, her face was grey-white and the streaked make-up stood out like flaking paint. We made a handsome couple. I made her drink more coffee. Gradually, her voice became less slurred and her hatred of me less intense.

'Why did they want to talk to Jack Collins?' I asked eventually.

'About Dad's business. If there could be a connection with his death. He knew all kinds. Like you do.'

I let the dig go.

'Do they suspect Collins of being involved in any of this?'

She shrugged a loose, drunken shrug. 'I dunno. Jack wouldn't have anything to do with anything like that. Jack's a good boy . . .'

I wasn't going to get much sense out of her so I guided her upstairs to her bedroom. I laid her down on the bed and she grabbed my jacket by the lapels, pulling my face close to hers. She reached her mouth to mine. I gently eased her back onto the bed.

'Stay with me, Lennox. Sleep here tonight . . .'

'Okay,' I said. It was a reflex action, like kicking your leg when a doctor hits your knee with that little rubber hammer.

It was Maggie MacFarlane who woke me up. I looked up at her, blinking. There was just too much sun streaming into the room for my bruised noggin to cope with.

'You look terrible,' she said. No smile. Just a hard, cold stare.

I eased myself up into a sitting position on the sofa. We were in the living room. That irritating chivalrous streak had shown itself again and I'd camped out on the sofa. To get my gallantry into perspective, I don't think either Lorna or I had had it in us to perform a horizontal tango. So here I was on the sofa: cramped, aching and in a foul mood. I looked at my suit trousers: they had more wrinkles than a Nepalese octogenarian and I congratulated myself on the smart move of changing clothes before I came over.

'Where have you been?' I asked, stretching.

'What the hell is that to do with you?'

'I came over last night and found Lorna completely plastered. She could have done with a little step-maternal support. You know that they've arrested a traveller for Small Change's murder?'

'Of course.' Maggie remained frosty, which was far from her usual demeanour. 'The police told me. So it was robbery after all.'

'Did anyone suggest it wasn't?' I asked.

'I think I should go up and see Lorna,' said Maggie, dodging the question.

'I'll go,' I said, removing my restraining hand from her forearm when she looked at it as if I had been a leper. With Blackwater Fever. And a Celtic supporter. 'I promised I'd look after her.' Walking to the door, I added over my shoulder: 'And how is your stepson? Or half-stepson? I get confused.'

'What are you talking about?' It was there in her voice: something tight and a little unsure of itself. I turned to face her.

'Young Jack Collins, the debonair gad-about-town. I'm guessing that's who you were with last night? I know he's Small Change's illegitimate son.'

'I think you should mind your own business and stay out of other people's,' said Maggie. The words were hard but the tone was softening. Like an expert sailor changing tack, she had worked out she needed to approach this breeze carefully. 'Listen, Jack's a good kid and he treated Small Change . . .'

'Like a father?' I helped out.

'Well, yes. There's nothing improper going on.'

'If you say so,' I said. I didn't have time for this. 'I better see Lorna.'

It wasn't a pretty sight. She had thrown up in her sleep onto the bed sheets and I had to help her to her feet and into the bathroom while I stripped the bed. It took me an hour to get her straightened out before I could leave. She cried a lot: the shame of the unaccustomed drunk. You didn't see it much in Glasgow.

I got back to my digs about ten a.m. The day was off to a great start: as I walked up the path Fiona White came out of the main door. She eyed me up and down, taking in my creased suit and probably sickly-looking face. It would have done no good to explain that I was actually concussed rather than hung over and I raised my hat to her as she walked past without uttering a word.

Once I was freshened up again I drove up to Blanefield and knocked on Kirkcaldy's door. There was no one home so I came back into town to the Maryhill address I had for his gym. It was in an old building in Bantaskin Street: a much bigger, less sophisticated and sweatier affair than the set-up he had in the basement of his house. Old Uncle Bert was there too; he showed a fidelity to his nephew that would have made Blackfriar's Bobby look like a fly-by-night. Kirkcaldy was sparring with a padded-helmeted partner in the ring. Bert came over to me and was the most amenable I had seen him. Which still was on the hostile side of chilly.

'We saw what happened to yon laddie of yours,' he said through his nose. 'That was bad. Bobby's upset that the boy was looking out for him when he got the beating.'

'I appreciate it,' I said. 'And I appreciate Bobby taking the time to call into the hospital to see him. Were you there when Bobby found him?'

'Aye, we were both on the way back from here. The lad was lying by the car, all battered to fuck. Somebody must have belted his coupon from behind then kicked the shite out of him.'

'You reckon?'

'That's what it looked like, poor kid. You want to talk to Bobby? He can't really tell you any more than I can but you're welcome to wait.'

I shook my head. 'It's okay. Tell him I called by to say thanks.'

'I'll do that.'

It was turning into an unproductive morning. I called around at Jimmy Costello's. His two goons, Skelly and Young, were sitting at the bar when I went in and eyed me contemptuously, a look I was getting used to. Skelly was still wearing the marks of our recent tango. I asked Jimmy Costello if he had heard from Paul. He told me he hadn't and I could see that he was telling the truth.

'Why you asking?' he said. 'You got a lead?'

'No, I've got a bump on the back of my head and I'm pretty sure it was your son who gave it to me. I tracked down Sammy Pollock but left my rear exposed, to coin an expression.'

'Why would Paul do that?'

'Maybe he's not convinced that I really am just interested in tracking down Sammy. Do you know anything about a stolen jade statuette? Of some kind of oriental dragon or demon?'

'No . . .' I guessed that this was Costello's automatic response to being asked about stolen goods so I pushed him. 'Listen, Jimmy, it's important. I think Paul and Sammy Pollock have bitten off more than they can chew. Now, do you really not know anything about a stolen jade figure?'

'I swear, Lennox. If Paul knows anything about it then he's never said fuck all to me. Not that that surprises me. We don't talk much.'

I talked to Costello for another half hour and just went around in the same old circles. As I was leaving, I saw Skelly shoot me another filthy look. The bump on my head gave another, bigger throb and it crossed my mind that it maybe hadn't been Paul Costello who had bushwhacked me. I crossed the bar and pulled Skelly clean off his stool. His loyal pal backed away from me.

'You got a problem with me, shitface?' I chose the route of diplomacy.

'I'm not the one with the problem,' said Skelly, pulling the tailoring from my grasp. 'And I don't want any trouble.'

'So I have a problem . . . is that what you're saying.'

'I'm not saying anything. Like I said, I don't want any trouble.'

'Then just watch your manners when you're around your betters, Sonny.'

He turned a sullen back on me. There was no fight in him, but that didn't mean he wasn't handy enough with a sap in dim light and from behind.

I left him to his sulk and ignored Jimmy Costello's impatient glare. I was pushing my luck, I knew it, but I had a sore head and was in a bad mood and everyone I dealt with seemed to be either lying to me or hiding something.

A promise is a promise. I called in to see Davey at the lunchtime visiting hour. He was pleased to see me but I could tell he hurt like hell. I wasn't far behind him. We talked and I joked with him and all the time I felt that old dark fury kindle itself deep in my gut.

After I left the hospital, I 'phoned Sheila Gainsborough and asked if I could meet her, either at her apartment or my office. It was important, I told her, and not something that could be discussed over the 'phone. I got my message across and she agreed to meet at her apartment. But I would have to give her an hour to sort things out. She gave me the name of a café around the corner from her building and said we could meet there. The decorum was unnecessary and ill-advised but I was too beat-up to argue.

I drove into the West End, found the café in Byres Road and took a table by the window. It was one of those Italian places, where they made an opera out of making a cup of coffee with a steam-hissing machine that sounded like it should be pulling the eleven-fifteen to London out of Central Station. At least the coffee was good.

Sheila Gainsborough arrived five minutes late. She looked

flustered and apologized for the delay. She took her scarf off and everyone in the café made a big show of not staring at her. Staring would have been much less obvious than the clumsily stolen glances. A waiter who looked as if he'd come straight off the boat from Naples but sounded like he'd come straight off the ferry from Renfrew took her order for a coffee.

'You have news?' she asked urgently. Her cheeks were flushed and, despite my gloomy mood and aching head, the thought of how nice it would be to make her cheeks flush crossed my mind.

'Like I said on the 'phone, Miss Gainsborough,' I said quietly. 'We should do this at your flat or my office. Like it or not, you're a celebrity, and every ear in this place is flapping. You never know when someone's a reporter or a copper.'

She took the point and we drank our coffee in haste and silence. Afterwards, we walked the few blocks to her apartment. Most of the dwellings in the area were tenements, townhouses or the occasional villa. Sheila Gainsborough's place was a rupture in the grimy Victorian and Georgian façades: an Art Deco block that would have been about thirty years old. One of the interesting things about Glasgow was the richness and variety of its architecture: Victorian, slum, Art Deco, slum, Contemporary, slum . . .

It was a classy place. Sheila led me into a huge, bright foyer that made you feel you'd stepped straight into the mid-Twenties. A uniformed commissionaire, who had an ex-military bearing but was of a vintage to have fought Kaiser rather than Führer, saluted us and we took the elevator to the top floor.

'You want a drink?' she asked, as she dropped her bag and scarf onto a chair in the hall. 'You look like you could do with one.'

'I could do with one, but it would probably finish me off.' I moved into the lounge. Everything in the flat was clean and orderly. The furniture, like the architecture that housed it, was Art Deco and was simple and tasteful – in that subtle way that tells you simple and tasteful is more expensive. There was a huge picture window, unbroken except for a couple of widely spaced, thin, white mullions. It gave a view over the city towards the university and Kelvingrove.

'Please . . .' she said, impatiently gesturing for me to sit. I sat. I think if Sheila Gainsborough had told me to jump out the window, I'd have done it. She remained standing, clutching her hands in front of her. 'Is this about Sammy?' she asked anxiously.

I held my hands up. 'Sammy's okay. I saw him last night.'

'Thank God he's safe . . .' she almost gasped. Tears of relief glossed her eyes.

'I'm sorry, Miss Gainsborough, but I don't think he is safe. I saw him last night and he was all right, but he's in trouble. And he's very scared.'

'Then why in God's name didn't you bring him with you?'

'Because, Miss Gainsborough, someone smacked me over the back of the head and put my lights out. Sammy and his girlfriend – and his handy associate – scarpered while I was counting sheep.'

Her face fell. I felt sorry for her, but there wasn't a lot I could do to put a positive sheen on it.

'I'm afraid that Sammy has gotten involved in something heavy,' I said. 'Something out of his league. You remember Paul Costello? The guy who was wandering in and out of Sammy's apartment, seemingly at will?'

Sheila nodded.

'I rather suspect it was young Mr Costello who put my lights out. They're in this together. Whatever this is.'

'I knew Sammy was getting in with the wrong sort . . .' She frowned her cute frown again. 'Where did you find him?'

'Sleeping rough in a derelict farm cottage in the middle of nowhere's back of beyond. I only found him because I spooked a girl he's involved with – Claire Skinner – and was able to follow her.'

'Sleeping rough?' Her eyes glossed with tears again. 'What do we do now?'

'I keep looking. I think there's a chance he'll get in touch with you. He looked hungry and tired. My guess is he'll need money. If he gets in touch, I need you to let me know. No matter what he says, you've got to tell me. Got it?'

'I've got it.'

'When I was out at the cottage, there was something odd. A statuette of a dragon. Looked like it was made of jade. Chinese by the look of it. Mean anything to you?'

She shook her head. 'Do you think they stole it?'

'I'm pretty sure they did. I don't know if that's why they think the devil himself is after them or not. I really don't know, but it would be a good guess.'

'Where on earth would they have stolen something like that from?'

'I don't know. But I maybe know someone I can ask.'

Chapter Twelve

Surprising though it might seem, I was the bookish type. I read a lot. I would read almost anything, by anyone, on any subject. I only really drew the line, as I had pointed out to Devereaux, at Hemingway.

Glasgow was the kind of city that liked to make a show of its knowledge. The University was a collection of grand and imposing Victorian buildings but the most strident statement of the city's erudition came copper-domed: the Mitchell Library sat imposingly right at the heart of the city and was all Corinthian pillars. The original design of the building hadn't included the St. Paul's style dome, but the City Corporation councillors had insisted on it. Now the Mitchell Library shouted to the rest of Scotland and the world, 'See . . . we *do* have books!'

I waited in the main hall of the library. A smallish man with prematurely greying hair approached me.

'Hello, Lennox,' he said, and pump-handled my arm. Ian McClelland was an enthusiastic kind of person. His easy-going exuberance cheered me up every time I met him. Despite his impeccably Celtic name, McClelland was an Englishman, from Wiltshire, who had taken the usual upper-middle-class route of top public schools and Cambridge. He was probably the only person I knew who had any idea how to hold a fish knife. What the hell he was doing in Glasgow was beyond me.

McClelland was a political science lecturer and specialist on the Far East and we'd met at a university function. I had been conjugating verbs with a young female French lecturer at the time. The romance hadn't lasted, but the friendship with McClelland had. He dressed like an academic but didn't for some reason look like one. On more than one occasion I had had suspicions that McClelland, who had spent a lot of time out in the Far East, had been at one time or another and to one degree or another involved with the intelligence services.

'How's it going, Ian?' I asked in library tones. 'Corrupted any young female students lately?'

'Only their minds, old boy. Only their minds. You said on the 'phone this is about a jade figure?'

We had attracted the frowning attention of a couple of academic types at one of the desks, bent over their research. McClelland steered me to another desk where he had laid out several reference books.

'Yes,' I said, once we were seated. 'Ugly as sin. All fangs and big staring eyes. I think it was a dragon. It seemed to have cloven hooves, like a goat. It was maybe a demon. Here ...' I pushed the sketch I had done into his hands.

'The dragon is a major folkloric figure in China.' McClelland frowned as he examined the picture. 'But what you've drawn here isn't a dragon, it's a *Qilin*. The hooves give it away. Giraffe's hooves. You say this is made out of jade?'

'Unless the Chinese make their gods out of green Bakelite.'

'I can understand you thinking it was a dragon. There are a lot of jade dragons about. How tall did you say it was?'

'About a couple of feet, give or take.'

'Then it could be worth a tidy sum.'

'How much?'

'It's impossible to say without seeing it. It depends on the quality of the jade – and that varies enormously. And, of course, it is frequently faked. If it's real solid jade, then a thousand. Maybe two. Was it a deep emerald green?'

'The light wasn't good. I saw more its shape than anything, but it was green.' I set my head to working again on what I had seen, but my head was still taking a tea-break. 'No ... maybe not emerald green. Paler. Milkier. Why?'

'Imperial jade has a wonderful translucence and a deep emerald green colour. It's rare and extremely valuable. But the piece you've described could be anything. Maybe not even jade.' He caught my frown. 'Not what you thought?'

'Fifteen hundred quid isn't enough for the kind of grief this thing seems to have caused.'

He shrugged. 'Is it stolen?'

'Let's just say I'm trying to return it to its rightful owner in the hope it'll get someone off the hook. A very big, very sharp hook.'

McClelland asked me if he could keep the sketch for a few days and I said he could. The mugginess in the air hit me when I stepped out of the stone-cooled interior of the library. I found a call box and 'phoned the hospital but the officious nurse on the other end of the line said she wouldn't give me any information because I wasn't a relative of Davey's.

I spent the afternoon nursing my headache and pondered whether I really should get my head checked out. A couple of hours' rest seemed to help it though, so I decided to skip it. I called police headquarters and got put through to Dex Devereaux.

'Hey there, *Johnny Canuck*, how y'doin'?' Devereaux's American accent seemed amplified on the 'phone.

'Fine. I wanted to ask you something. How much is each shipment Largo's been sending to the States? I mean size or weight.'

'We're talking about forty pounds a shipment.'

'That's not a lot.'

'In cash terms it is. Heroin is worth a hundred-and-fifty bucks a gram. That works out at nearly five hundred dollars per pound weight. Each forty-pound shipment Largo sends over is worth twenty thousand bucks. I don't know what that is in limey money. The exchange rate I got was two dollars eighty cents for a pound sterling so work it out yourself. This stuff is literally worth twice or three times its weight in gold.'

'So it would be reasonably easy to hide it in other stuff and lose it in a ship's cargo manifest,' I said, imagining a small rank of ugly jade demons.

'I told you that already. It's like the A-bomb. Small package but big punch when it hits the streets. What you got, Lennox?'

'Maybe nothing . . . A hunch . . . that's all at the moment. But I think part of Largo's last shipment was stolen by some of the local boys. Amateurs who are scared out of their wits. It means I might be able to give you Largo *and* some of the dope.'

'Lennox, if you're sure about this . . .'

'I'm not, Dex. I'm not sure of anything. Like I say, a hunch, and it would waste your time chasing it. If it turns out to be worthwhile, I'll hand over everything to you and you can lead the local police by the hand to make the arrests. But I need to get someone out of the picture first. Thanks for the gen, Dex. I'll be in touch.'

I hung up before Devereaux could pressure me any more. I was putting a picture together in my head and I needed to concentrate. I also needed time to follow up a few things.

There was one thing getting in the way of everything: Small Change MacFarlane's murder. It nagged and nagged at me and I couldn't work out why. I had all but accused Maggie MacFarlane of a bedclothes entanglement with Jack Collins, but I had no reason to imagine it as anything more than that. I somehow couldn't cast Jack Collins as a smitten Walter Neff, and Maggie, although she was a satisfying piece of art, was no Barbara Stanwyck. I had asked Lorna, as subtly as I could, about insurance policies and a will. Both Maggie and, to a much lesser extent Collins, would benefit right enough, but the lion's share went to Lorna. Under Scottish Law, Maggie, as the surviving widow, would have a reasonable case in challenging MacFarlane's provisions but, according to Lorna who certainly was not free from suspecting her stepmother, Maggie had made no suggestion that she would.

But it all still bothered me.

I'm paid to stick my nose in. More often than not, I'm paid to stick it in where noses aren't welcome. My most irritating habit was sticking my nose in where it wasn't welcome when I wasn't being paid for it. When I walked into the Vinegarhill camp, my nose had never felt so shunned. I was seriously concerned that it was going to be put out of joint.

I had performed an act of faith parking the car in Molendinar Street, trying not to think what odds Tony the Pole would give me against it being in one piece, or even being there, when I got back to it. The traveller camp was set up on a barren, grubby walled square, entered by a double iron gate, permanently open, next to the sugar works. There were a handful of modern touring, car-drawn caravans, but the vast majority were the traditional vardo or burton wagons: painted, horse-drawn jobs with arched roofs, that went hand-in-hand with everybody's romantic image of gypsies. The rough humps of bender tents domed between some of the wagons.

There was no enticing odour of simmering goulash or

impassioned violin-playing to accompany my arrival. These travellers did not hail from the Hungarian plain or Carpathian mountains, unless the Hungarian plain and the Carpathian mountains had a view of Galway Bay. And the most romantic thing I saw were two unleashed mongrels copulating over by the works' wall. A handful of kids without shoes rampaged about the camp, and I was aware that a couple of young men had moved in behind me as soon as I had entered the yard.

That would normally be my cue to reach for my sap but, in a place like this with people like these, it would have been an inadvisable move. A painfully inadvisable move. Instead, I would have to talk my way out of here, like the cavalry captain with the white flag sent into the Indian encampment to parley. I strode across to where an older man leaned against a wagon, smoking a pipe. As I did so I passed a vardo wagon with the shutters drawn and deep crimson ribbons wrapped around the shafts and tongue.

'I'm looking for Tommy Furie's father,' I said, when I reached the old man. 'Could you tell me where I could find him?'

'The *Baro*? What do you want with him? Who the fuck are you?' The old man stopped leaning and took the pipe from his mouth. He spat a greeny viscous glob which splashed close to my shoe. Jimmy Stewart or Randolph Scott were never treated like this.

'Like I said, I want to talk to him. And I'm pretty sure he'll be very keen to talk to me. Now, do you know where I can find him or not?' I was aware that the two youths had positioned themselves behind me, at either shoulder. The old man jerked his head in the direction of one of the modern-style caravans, the largest on site. I nodded and walked over to it, leaving my honour guard behind.

Sean Furie was a big man in his fifties. He was tall, and had probably been heavily muscled when younger, but had turned to fat. His full head of jet black hair was without a trace of grey and was oiled and combed back from a huge face. He and Uncle Bert Soutar had obviously gone to the same place for their nose jobs. The difference with Furie was that the tip of his nose was swollen and red and river-mapped with purplish capillaries. Romany rosacea, I decided to call it – the effects of bare knuckle and bare alcohol.

I told him who I was and what I wanted to talk to him about. I braced myself for his reaction, but it took me off guard anyway. Furie was remarkably soft-spoken and politely asked me into his caravan. There was a distinctive odour inside the caravan. Not dirty or unpleasant, just distinctive. The caravan seemed huge in comparison to the vardos I'd seen outside. It was wood-panelled and had a small kitchen, a lounge, and a room closed off by a door. I assumed the bedroom lay through there.

Sitting at the far end on a built-in sofa was a large, dark-haired, doleful-looking woman in her forties. We sat and, without word or glance, she stood up and left the wagon, squeezing past me to reach the door. It was an accustomed exit; it was clear that when Furie had business to do, the womenfolk left. He offered me a whisky and I took it.

'I saw some ribbons tied onto one of the wagons as I came in. Red ribbons.' I decided to be conversational. It often paid to ease into the main business. 'Is that a celebration thing?'

'You could say . . .' Furie gave a bitter laugh. 'We'll have the same on this wagon soon. When they hang my boy.'

'Oh . . . I see.'

'It symbolizes death,' explained Furie. 'And mourning. Red and white are the Romany colours for mourning.'

'Who died?'

'I don't know. It's a Nachin family I don't know.'

'Nachin?'

'Scottish gypsy. We're Minceir, from Ireland. The travellers from England are called Romanichals and the ones from Wales are called Kale. But everyone here is either Minceir or Nachin.'

'I see,' I said. I lit a cigarette and offered him one, which he took but tucked behind his ear.

'They're going to hang my boy for something he never done, Mr Lennox,' Furie said in his soft brogue. 'It's a fit-up, that's what it is. Then you'll see the red ribbons on this caravan.'

'Tommy hasn't even stood trial yet, Mr Furie, far less been found guilty and sentenced. If he didn't do it, then they'll find it difficult to prove he did,' I lied.

'Well, he never done it. But that's just what you expect me to say anyway, isn't it?' he said. 'You think that I'd deny it even if I knew he done it. We're all liars and thieves, after all. Isn't that right?'

'I didn't say that.'

'But you was thinking it anyway, wasn't you?'

'As a matter of fact I wasn't. I don't know anything for sure. But there's something bothering me about MacFarlane's murder. Maybe your son is being framed for it, but if he is, who by and how?'

'He's a traveller. That's all the reason they need.'

'With the greatest respect, no, it isn't. There's much more to this than your son being the wrong type in the wrong place at the wrong time. What do the police say happened?'

Furie ran through it all. Tommy Furie had been one of the boxers whom Small Change MacFarlane had been involved with developing. Reading between the lines, Small Change had been organizing bare-knuckle bouts and running a book on them, and it struck me that there was maybe another reason behind Sneddon wanting me to find any hidden log kept by the deceased bookie. I wondered who had started the regular bouts out at Sneddon's recently acquired Dunbartonshire farm. Sean Furie explained that his son had started to work as a sparring partner at a couple of the gyms and that Small Change had gotten him a number of legitimate ring fights. Small Change was notoriously tight with his cash and there had been a dispute over payment for a bout. Tommy Furie had complained to Small Change, several times, and in front of witnesses.

'He was at the gym that night that MacFarlane was murdered,' said Sean Furie. 'It was one of his regular nights. He got a 'phone call at the gym telling him to go up to MacFarlane's house to collect the money he was due for the fight.'

'MacFarlane 'phoned him?' I asked.

'No. It was someone who worked for him. Or so he said. Tommy didn't get a name. Or can't remember. Tommy's a good boy, but not too clever.'

'I see,' I said, trying to hide my surprise at the revelation.

'Tommy went up to the house. He'd never been there before but had the address like. So he went up. Got the tram there and back. He said no one answered when he knocked but the front door was open. He went into the room and found MacFarlane on the floor. Dead. Tommy's not as tough as you'd think and he panicked. On the way out he knocked over a lamp and picked it up to put it back.'

'So the police have his fingerprints on the lamp?'

'Aye, they have.'

'What else do the coppers say they've got on him?'

'The tram conductress remembered him on the way back. All agitated like. And they've got his fingerprints at the house. In the room where MacFarlane was murdered.'

'That's it?'

'It's enough,' said Furie, 'to convict a *pikey*.'

'No it's not. What does the lawyer say?'

'To plead guilty so he doesn't get hung.'

'Brilliant ...' I shook my head. 'I suggest you get another lawyer.'

With the kind of thing I had planned – the kind of thing that could end you up on the wrong side of a set of sturdy bars – preparation was everything.

I had a small black holdall, which I brought through to the living room and placed on the table. Taking a double page out of the *Glasgow Herald*, I laid it out next to the holdall. I put a set of heavy-duty wire cutters, a pair of black leather gloves and a black turtleneck sweater into the holdall. I had two corks saved from empty bottles. Taking one at a time, I lit a match and set light to them, allowing them to smoulder for a good while before blowing them out and setting them down to cool. In the meantime, I placed the rest of my toolkit in the holdall: a pair of black plimsolls, a bicycle lamp, a short crowbar-style tyre lever and both my saps.

Once the charred corks had cooled I folded them neatly into the sheet of newspaper and placed them in the holdall. I paused for a moment to reflect on my highly professional selection of equipment. If I were to be stopped by a policeman curious enough to look in my bag, there was enough in there to get me a three-month stretch for intent.

I had deliberately chosen a darker suit, which was probably too heavyweight for this time of year but appropriate for what I had planned for later.

I had a lot of time to kill before I could put my plan into action, but I had to load the stuff into the car now rather than have Fiona White hear me leave the house in the dead of night.

I dumped the bag in the trunk of the Atlantic and drove to

the MacFarlane place in Pollokshields, picking Lorna up about seven. I took her to the Odeon Cinema in Sauchiehall Street, where we watched Gregory Peck in *The Million Pound Note*. A trip to the pictures may have seemed inappropriate, but I was trying to take her mind off her troubles, if only for a couple of hours.

Lorna didn't say much before, during or after the picture and thanked me politely without inviting me in when I dropped her off. As I was leaving, I noticed Jack Collins's Lanchester parked in the drive.

Willie Sneddon was a man of habit. Exact habit. Sometimes peculiar habit.

I had arranged to meet with him at the Victoria Baths, where he regularly took a steam bath and swim. The Victoria Baths was a temple of sandstone, marble and porcelain in the west end of the city. It had a swimming pool beneath an Italianate cupola, Turkish baths, steam room, massage tables and a lounge. It was a private club but members could sign in guests. A lot of the guests who were signed in here were Corporation councillors and officials, senior cops and the odd MP. Most left with their pockets heavy. There were allegedly more planning permissions, and public house and club licences granted here than in the City Chambers.

I waited for Sneddon in the foyer. I never swam in the Baths myself, and certainly never in any of the municipal pools, ever since I discovered that 'swimming pool' and 'urinal' are synonyms in Glaswegian. At least I had company while I waited: Twinkletoes McBride was already there, intimidating the staff and passing bathers. It was purely unintentional and passive; he was intimidating sitting down.

'How's it going, Mr Lennox?' he asked cheerily, when he looked up and saw me; then with an alarmingly sudden change to grave asked, 'Any news about wee Davey?'

'They won't tell me anything because I'm not a relative but I went in to see him today. He's bearing up.'

'You find out who did that to wee Davey and I'll sort the fuckers out, Mr Lennox. Big toes too. And don't worry, I'll do it *gracious*.'

'I'm sorry?'

'*Gracious* . . .' Twinkle frowned. 'No charge . . .'

'Ah . . . you mean *gratis*.'

'Aye. That. They have it coming . . . what they did to Davey was *reppy-hen-stable*.'

I formed the word *reprehensible* in my mouth but kept it there: there was no point in correcting him further. And, as I'd already mentioned to Sneddon, I was rather attached to my toes.

'I appreciate it, Twinkle,' I said, and smiled.

'My pleasure. How's everything else going?' Twinkletoes was leaning forward, elbows on knees, turning his smile to me. It was a huge wide smile in a huge wide head between huge wide shoulders. Twinkletoes was friendly bulk that could be turned into unfriendly bulk at the flick of a switch. 'I heard you was going around with a posh bit of skirt,' he said.

For a moment I thought he meant Sheila Gainsborough. Then I twigged. 'Oh, yes . . . Lorna MacFarlane. Small Change's daughter. She does have a bit of class. Unusual around here. A bit of class and a little sophistication. I go for that in a woman.'

'Aye? Personally I go for big tits and a fanny tighter than a Fifer's fist.'

I didn't get a chance to frame an answer before the Victorian stained-glass panel doors that joined the foyer to the main part of the baths swung open and Sneddon, in an expensive wide-shouldered camel sports coat, tieless and with his shirt's top button undone, emerged pink-faced and flanked by another of his heavies.

'Sorry, am I interrupting something?' he asked facetiously, noticing that I was somewhat lost for words.

'No ... I was just getting a few romantic tips from Charles Boyer here.'

Sneddon went across to reception and scribbled into the log that lay open on the desk.

'I've signed you in,' he said. 'Let's go and get a drink. Twinkle ... you and Tam wait here. I won't be long.'

Sneddon led me through into a large clubroom. It was the kind of place where they could have cut down on the decorating costs by simply wallpapering it with five-pound notes. If anything, it was more over-the-top than the Merchants' Carvery. The furniture was all polished hardwood and leather and the velvet drapes were a deep crimson. The walls were dressed in flock wallpaper – burgundy red fleur-de-lis against cream damask – so thick you could vacuum it. A vast onyx-type marble fireplace dominated one wall. I imagined that this was what hell looked like if you had a first-class ticket.

Sneddon led the way to a corner at the far side and sat down on two-and-a-half cows' worth of red leather. I sat across the coffee table from him, on the rest of the herd. There were deep red velvet drapes behind us and I felt as if we were in a crimson cave.

'Listen, Mr Sneddon ... you've hired me to do a job. But you can't ask me to do a job and then give me only half the story. You're holding back vital information. I understand that you've got your interests to protect and there are some things I'd probably be better off not knowing, but in this case it means I've been up more blind alleys than a Blythswood Square floozy.' I paused while a burgundy-jacketed waiter came over with two malt whiskies on a silver tray. I waited until he had gone before continuing. 'The police have got Tommy Gun Furie for Small Change's murder. And it looks to me like a set-up. More than that, it looks to me like a very well-thought-out set-up. Timing was everything with this. Tommy Furie was summoned to MacFarlane's by someone calling the gym he trained in. Someone knew he was going to be in the gym at that time on that night and that they could get a message to him. My guess is that Small Change was still alive when they made that 'phone call and they only killed him after they knew Furie was on his way. Which means they were pretty confident that they could reschedule the whole thing if they had to. That would suggest that they were very familiar with Small Change's routine.'

'So why does this mean that I've been holding back on you? Are you saying I had something to do with Small Change getting topped?'

'No. But I *am* saying that this appointment book you asked me to look for has nothing to do with bare-knuckle fights. Big money bare-knuckle fights. And if I'm right, then you have more to worry about than whether the police put you in MacFarlane's house for a meeting. Tommy Gun Furie was one of the fighters MacFarlane lined up for you. And right now his own lawyer is telling him he'll be lucky not to take a short walk to a long drop through a trapdoor in Barlinnie prison. He's going to tell the coppers everything he can to try to save his neck. Literally. And somewhere along the line your name is going to come up. The only way out of it is for us to find out who really did kill MacFarlane and why.'

Sneddon looked at me with a steady gaze: the steady gaze of a crocodile looking at an antelope.

'Okay,' he said at last. 'There was some stuff I was trying to keep to myself. But it doesn't get the pikey out of the frame. If anything, it points to him having done it. Small Change MacFarlane and me were in business together. We were fixing up fights. But not what you saw out at the farm – the usual bare-knuckle shite with a couple of fucking pikeys slapping each other around. Although you're right that Small Change helped me organize those too. We had something different going on.'

'What?'

Sneddon didn't answer for a moment, instead seeming to look around to reappraise his surroundings. 'I've seen the way people look at me in here sometimes. Even when I'm walking my dog in the street where I fucking live. They look away. Avoid looking me in the fucking eye. They think people like me, Cohen and Murphy are the scum of the earth. We scare them. But I'll tell you this, it's them that scare me.' He paused when the waiter returned to our crimson cave to replace our empty whisky glasses with full ones.

'You should see the so-called ordinary man in the street when people like me serve them up with what they want,' said Sneddon when the waiter was gone. 'They're the fucking monsters. I have an interest in a whorehouse in Pollokshields, not far from MacFarlane's house. Discreet. One of the girls got beaten up so fucking bad we thought she'd die. Cost me a fortune getting her treatment without it being official. You should have seen the fucker that did it to her. A wee, bald, fat cunt that looked like he wouldn't say boo to a goose. But when he was in there with the girl he turned into some kind of fucking monster.'

'You turn him over to the police?' The question was out and stupid before I thought it through.

'Aye, right. That's just what we done. What do you think we done? Twinkletoes sorted him out with some transport. A fucking wheelchair.'

'What's this got to do with your deal with MacFarlane?'

'Like I said, you have no fucking idea what ordinary people want. The worse it is, the more they want you to dish it up to them. You're not going to believe this, Lennox, but I read a lot. History, that sort of shite.'

I shrugged. It didn't surprise me: since I first encountered Sneddon, I had sensed a hidden, dark intelligence about him. The Smart King.

'I read a lot about ancient Rome. There was no difference between the Caesars and Rome and the Kings and Glasgow. They even had a triumvirate. Three Kings. You can learn a lot from history.'

'I don't know,' I said. 'Personally I think there's no future in it.'

Sneddon didn't laugh – not at my joke and not ever that I could recall. 'I've read a lot about the Colosseum. It used to be packed right to the top. Ordinary people turning out to watch blood and death. The fucking crueller the better. Do you know they used to make fucking children fight with swords, to the death? Or that the comedy turn was to put blind people into the ring? They'd slash and hack each other to bits, but it would take a fucking age for one or both to die because they couldn't see each other. And the public fucking *loved* it.' He paused to sip his whisky. Silver-suited and manicured, against the crimson of the booth he looked like a clubbable Satan. 'Nothing's changed,' he continued. 'We started to draw in big money from the bare-knuckle fights. The more brutal the fight the bigger the crowd the next week. So we started to put on special fights. At special prices. Only regulars were invited to buy a ticket.'

'What made these fights special?' I asked, though some horrible ideas had already flashed across the screen of my imagination.

'They was no-holds-barred. No weapons, but apart from that

everything was allowed – kicking, choking, gouging, biting. It started off small then just got bigger and bigger. The more blood, the bigger the crowds. And the higher the ticket price.'

'Okay,' I said. 'Let's have it . . . what happened?'

'Someone got killed . . .' Sneddon shrugged as if a human being's death was an inconsequence. 'A pikey. Something happened in his head and there was fucking blood everywhere, from his nose, his ears . . . even his fucking eyes . . .'

'Let me guess . . . he ended up catching a train . . .' I shook my head. It had been there in front of me all the time.

Sneddon made his usual crooked mouth shape to approximate a smile. 'You're a smart fucking cookie, aren't you, Lennox. You make all of the connections. Yeah . . . he was the pikey that got mashed by the train. So no one's the wiser.'

'That's where you're wrong.' I put my glass down and leaned forward. 'There's a keen-as-mustard new pathologist on the job. Very keen on what they call forensic science. He worked out that your pikey fighter wasn't some drunk caught on the rails. Even proved that he'd been in a fight before he died.'

'So fucking what?'

'So you've got a problem. Or another problem. The City of Glasgow Police are treating it as murder. Believe me, they'd much rather have chalked it up as an accident, but because of this sharp new pathologist they can't.'

'Fuck.' Sneddon's face hardened. Which was surprising, because there wasn't much scope for further hardening. 'I knew we should have minced the bastard. But I didn't want Murphy knowing nothing about this.'

I nodded. Hammer Murphy, one of the other Three Kings, owned a meat-processing plant in Rutherglen. It was well known that several bodies had been disposed of through the plant's mincer. The Three Kings had an agreement whereby Murphy, for a fee, provided the same service for Sneddon and Cohen. Not for the first time I considered vegetarianism.

'You should have told me all of this at the start,' I said. 'It would have made things easier.'

'Murder. Fuck. And for once it wasn't . . .' Sneddon shook his head self-critically. It was like watching a golfer who had missed what should have been an easy putt. The thought flashed through my head that murderers maybe have a handicap system too.

'You say he was a traveller?' I asked.

'A pikey, aye . . . What about it?'

'Well, that means there's maybe no official records of his existence. No birth certificate, no war record, no National Insurance number. No paperwork means he didn't exist officially and that makes it more difficult to tie him in with anything. I think you sit this one out.'

'What about his family?' asked Sneddon glumly.

'They're not going to go to the police, I'd say. It looks to me like they've already said their goodbyes.'

'How the fuck do you know that?' asked Sneddon. 'You don't even know who they are.'

'When I called in at the Vinegarhill site there was a vardo – you know, a gypsy caravan – all dressed up with red ribbons. Deep red. That's their colour for mourning, not black. Of course, it doesn't mean it's your boy. What was his name?'

'Gypsy Rose Lee . . . How the fuck would I know? He was just a pikey.'

'Go back to the fights. What was Small Change MacFarlane's involvement in them?'

'He set them up and ran the book on them for me. He took a percentage of the winnings and I provided the venue, and the muscle to collect unpaid bets.'

'He supplied the fighters?'

'Aye, kind of. He arranged for them to be supplied. The deal was he paid for that out of his cut.' Sneddon sighed wearily. 'It was Bert Soutar who found them for Small Change.'

'Soutar?' For a second I was deafened by the sound of pennies dropping. 'Oh, I see ... so Bobby Kirkcaldy had a stake in this too?'

'In the background, aye. Kirkcaldy's a good fighter and he'll batter this Kraut on Saturday. But when me and Cohen put money into him, we said he was to get checked out by an independent doctor. Turns out his heart's fucked. Arrhythmia, they call it. Two, three, more big fights and then he'll have to give the fight game up. The Board of Control know fuck-all about it like. They're not exactly on the ball. But Kirkcaldy likes having money, so wherever there's a pie, he has his finger in it.'

'So that's why he was so out of breath ...' I said more to myself than Sneddon, remembering the toll Kirkcaldy's skipping workout had taking on him in his basement gym. That would be why he had been doing so much training there, instead of in the city gym: no one to see him struggle for breath.

'Then Kirkcaldy or Bert Soutar will have a name for the dead traveller?' I asked.

'Maybes. Maybes not.'

I leaned back into the plush red upholstery and sipped at the whisky. It all made sense.

'So it didn't occur to you at all that it was the tailers who were making all of these symbolic threats?'

'Pikeys? Because of the one that got killed? No, it didn't. It didn't even cross my mind.'

'I find that very difficult to believe.'

Sneddon leaned forward, as if about to share a great confidence with me. 'I'd be very careful before you call me a liar, Lennox. Very fucking careful.'

I said nothing for a moment, doing the discretion/valour equation in my head.

'So Soutar supplied fighters for these contests and Small Change organized them and ran your book. What about Jack Collins? He was the real fight arranger as far as Small Change was concerned.'

'Naw. We did have dealings with Collins, but that was for proper boxing matches. What I told you that night I hired you was true. We was putting together proper bouts and running a few half-decent fighters. That was what Collins managed. And that pikey kid who's supposed to have done Small Change in . . . he was moving up out of bare-knuckle and was turning into a tasty boxer. All that's fucked now anyway.'

'Do you still have Singer on Bobby Kirkcaldy's tail?' I drained my whisky and stood up.

'Aye . . .'

'Good. He needs to be watched like a hawk.'

'Where are you going?'

'I've got paperwork to do.'

Finding a place to park out of sight of the main road, under a dank railway arch, I sat for half an hour, smoking and listening to the steel sounds of the Clyde. It was quieter and cooler during the night, but the shipyards and repair docks never really slept. This was no man's land, between the tenements and the docks. No one would come down here unless they had a reason. That was both good and bad for what I had planned. There would be very few people to spot my car tucked away from view; but those few people would either be up to no good, like me, or trying to catch the up-to-no-good. The last thing I needed was a patrolling bobby to happen across the Atlantic.

A train thundered over the rails above me and its rattles echoed damply in the arch. I put out my cigarette and took my stuff out of the trunk. Taking my suit jacket off, I pulled the turtleneck jumper over my shirt and I changed my shoes for the plimsolls. I unwrapped the charred corks from the newspaper and rubbed them all over my face. If that patrolling bobby were to catch me now, I'd have to convince him I was auditioning for a blackface minstrel show or face those three months in Barlinnie. Locking up the car, I pulled on my leather gloves and made my way out from under the arch. I ducked behind a bush and watched while an elderly dockworker cycled along the cobbled road that lay between me and the bonded dockside area. He pedalled so slowly that I wondered how he could remain upright with so little momentum carrying him forward. After what seemed an age, he disappeared from sight around the distant corner.

The streetlamps threw meagre pools of light onto the cobbles and I ran between them, bent over, across the road and down into the ditch on the far side. I was about three hundred yards away from the gates and the watchman's shed when I took the wire cutters from the bag and snipped at the steel wire fence, folding it back like curtains and crawling through, hidden by the long, uncut grass.

I made my way along the inside of the fence, still keeping low because I would still be visible from the road until I reached the area where I remembered the Nissen huts to be. There was only one lamppost and the Nissens loomed darkly, with little to distinguish one from another. I didn't want to use the bicycle lamp out in the open and it took me five minutes to find the sign *Barnier and Clement*. The front door was reasonably solid, but this was an office rather than a store, and the padlock that secured the door fell away with a sniff of the crowbar. I caught the padlock before it hit the ground and let myself into the Nissen.

Normally, I would have switched the lights on: a fully illuminated room attracts less attention than a torch flashing around; but out here in the dark of the warehouse area, switching the lights on would have been as inconspicuous as a lighthouse on a clear night.

The offices seemed pretty much as I had seen them when I had called and asked to see Barnier. I went over to the filing cabinets and was soon saying a little appreciative prayer for Miss Minto. Her filing was meticulous and easy to follow. It took me only twenty minutes to find what I was looking for: a ship's manifest order and duplicates of a ship's insurers claim form with a Lloyd's Register stamp on it.

I smiled. The last thing Barnier would have wanted was for an insurance claim to be put in, but this had to be seen as a scrupulously legitimate business.

I laid the manifest on the desk and shone the bicycle lamp on it, running my finger down the list of items. There it was, as bold and innocent as could be:

ITEM 33a. 12 VIET KYLAN NEPHRITE JADE FIGURINES. CRATED. DESTINATION: SANTORNO ANTIQUES AND CURIOS, GREEN-WICH, NEW YORK, NEW YORK

Except there were only eleven now. KYLAN. When I had first turned up without an appointment, Miss Minto had thought I was there about the 'key lan'. And they weren't Chinese. They were *Kylan*, not Chinese *Qilin*. They were Viet, from French Indochina. Alain Barnier was an established importer from the

Far East, exactly the kind of link that John Largo needed in his supply chain. Except now Barnier was a weak link. Taking notepad and pencil from my bag, I wrote down the details of the shipment, put all the paperwork back in the files and the files back in the cabinet.

I heard a sound outside.

I killed the light from the bicycle lamp and crouched down. Grabbing my sap from the bag, I scuttled under the lidded reception counter to the door. There was a small window next to it and, pressing myself against the wall, I stole a peek through the window. I saw the watchman's back as he walked through the pool of light from the lamppost and out of sight. I waited for several minutes, straining my neck to watch through the window, before deciding it was safe to put my sap back in the bag, go back to the files and switch the lamp back on.

Barnier was my way to Largo. If I kept tabs on the Frenchman, there was a chance he would lead me to Largo. Or at least take me a step closer. I needed an address. Again I blessed homely, unfriendly Miss Minto, who had channelled all of the sexual and social frustration of the spinster into a fanatical efficiency. Her address book was not tabulated or indeed a proper address book. Instead it was a hardcovered notebook into which she had written all of the company's most important contacts. It was impressively obsessive: not a name was out of perfect alpha-betical order. Barnier lived some distance out of town on the Greenock Road, in Langbank. He was on the telephone and I noted both address and 'phone number. I found myself wondering about the mysterious M. Clement, and after I got the address of the *Barnier et Clement* French office in Cours Lieutaud, Marseille, I looked up and found the name Clement: Claude Clement lived somewhere called Allauch. I wrote down both addresses and put my notebook back in the bag. A worth-while night's work.

It was just as I had put everything back in my bag that I heard the footsteps outside the door.

CHAPTER THIRTEEN

I had already switched off the bicycle lamp and put it back in my bag. I dropped down behind Miss Minto's desk and tucked myself into the knee-hole. There was no point in trying to go out through the door: whoever it was I had heard was out there. Again, I played out all my options in my head. It could simply have been the watchman again, making a second round of this part of the bonded area; or it could have been that the watchman had noticed the missing padlock and twisted bar on the door and had called the police.

I slowly unzipped my holdall. Just enough to put my hand in and rummage around until I found my sap. This was potentially a situation where I couldn't win; if it was the elderly watchman, I'd have to use my sap judiciously. Too hard a blow and I'd end up facing a murder charge. Added to which, although I had an unpleasant propensity towards violence, I avoided using it against the totally innocent. If it turned out to be a copper, then I'd have to hit him hard and run for it. Hitting a City of Glasgow copper usually turned out to be a much more painful experience for the attacker; the boys in blue liked to hold a little reception for you in the station. Allegedly, it normally involved being stripped naked and wrapped in a soaking wet blanket. For some physiological reason beyond my ken, the wet blanket stopped bruising when twenty or so Highland lads set in about you with their boots and truncheons. The second painful element came judicially: police assault usually combined a prison sentence with corporal punishment. The birch. You would be tied to a table and thrashed with some dried foliage. Quaintly traditional but incredibly painful.

I considered my options and huddled beneath the desk. I heard the door opening. A torch probed the recesses of the Nissen hut for a moment. It switched off and the neon strip light above me fizzed and crackled into life.

'You was right, Billy.' The voice had a Highland lilt to it. A copper. Option two. I guessed 'Billy' was the elderly night watchman. 'Someone's broken the lock.'

A pause. I remained absolutely still beneath the desk, controlling my breathing, ignoring the thunder of my heartbeat in my ears. All my time in Glasgow, I had avoided being charged with a criminal offence. I would do time for this. Unless I dealt with the copper and the night watchman.

'All right . . .' the unseen Highlander called out into the Nissen hut. 'This is the police. I know that you're in here.' No you don't, I thought . . . I could tell from the tone of his voice. 'Show yourself now and don't make any bother.'

Silence. I sat tight and silent. The sap was gripped so tight in my hand that I could feel the heartbeat in my fingers keeping time with the pulse in my ears.

'Come on now . . . let's not be having any silliness . . .' Again the voice had the sound of someone who thought they were speaking to an empty room. I heard wood on wood: the lid on the reception counter folding over. He would be stepping through it, his baton drawn. Scottish police batons were made of Caribbean *lignum vitae* – one of the densest and strongest woods on the planet. Bone-crackingly and muscle-deadeningly hard. Whatever I did, I was going to have to avoid a blow to the head. I heard his boots now. He was at the desk in front of mine. He moved forward. One step. Two. His breathing, slow and deliberate. Not frightened. He moved something around. A chair or something. Three. Four. He was next to my desk, but couldn't see me. Yet.

'Nothing looks like it's been disturbed,' he said. 'Maybe you frightened them off, Billy. Don't look like there's anyone here now.' His boots ground grittily on the floor. He was looking around himself. Don't look under the desk, I beamed the thought to him. Whatever you do, you big Teuchter bastard, don't look under the desk.

'Billy, you go and telephone the number you've got for the proprietor,' he lilted. 'I'll stay here until he arrives.'

'All right, Iain ... I'll do that.' An older voice. Eager. Acquiescent to authority. Good, I thought, one less to worry about. But I'd have to make a break for it past the copper.

I heard the night watchman close the door as he left. The copper was still standing there only inches away from me. My mind sped through the options open to me. Barnier would take at least half an hour to get here, but there was no guarantee that another copper wouldn't arrive in the meantime.

Suddenly, the desk above me creaked. I almost bolted from my hiding place but kept calm: he was sitting on the edge of the desk. There was the sound of a match being struck, then the smell of cigarette smoke. I heard a muted ping: a telephone being picked up. Dialling. The unseen policeman asked to speak to the duty sergeant and told him that he was attending an attempted break-in and gave the address. An *attempted* break-in. The idiot hadn't searched the place properly but had decided there was no one on the premises. I silently offered heartfelt thanks to the City of Glasgow Police for recruiting from the Highlands.

My heart picked up a pace. I knew that I had to act as soon as he put the receiver down. He didn't think there was anybody here and I could catch him off guard. But I was in the worst possible position from which to launch an attack. I hung onto every word he said into the telephone.

'All right, Sergeant,' he said. I heard the Bakelite clunk of the receiver in its cradle.

I was about to make my move when I heard the sound of pencils hitting the floor. There was a creak as the cop stood up from the edge of the desk. I guessed he had knocked the pencils off the table. Instead of rushing, I eased myself out from under the desk, making no sound. I turned and straightened myself up slowly. He was a uniform all right, and he was bent over, cursing poetically as only Highlanders can, gathering up the pencils. He stood up again and turned towards me.

He didn't even have the time for surprise or shock to register on his face. I fetched him a blow across his left temple with my sap and he dropped to the floor. There was more calculation in that blow than Einstein had put into the theory of relativity: if I killed a copper then I'd hang. And if they couldn't trace me, some other mug would swing for it. Justice had to be seen to be done. By the same token I needed him incapacitated long enough for me to make a getaway.

Looking down, I saw that he was stunned, rather than out cold. Perfect. I grabbed my bag, vaulted over him and out of the door, switching off the lights as I did. Anything to confuse my dazed sheep-botherer.

I saw 'Billy', the flat-capped night watchman, illuminated by the single lamppost, about a hundred and fifty yards off. He froze when he caught sight of me. I turned in the other direction and shouted to an imaginary associate already out of sight.

'Run, Jimmy! It's the watchy!' I yelled, doing my best

Glaswegian impersonation. I raced off towards where I'd cut the hole in the fence. I lobbed my bag over and commando-crawled through the gap I had cut.

I checked behind me: there was no sign of the constable and the elderly watchman would not risk chasing after two Drumchapel desperadoes.

I sprinted along the cobbled road and dived behind the bushes next to the railway alcove. One more check backwards: nothing. I took off the sweater and wiped my face with it, getting as much burnt cork off as possible. I threw my burglar kit into the boot of the car, put on my suit jacket and jumped in behind the driver's seat. Keeping my lights switched off, I reversed out onto the main road. I drove slowly, with the lights still off until I reached the end of South Street. Only then did I pick up speed and switch the lights on. I drove into the countryside and out of the City of Glasgow Police jurisdiction. Ironically, I took the Greenock Road and passed only one car travelling in the opposite direction. At that time of night it was no surprise that the roads were dead and I wondered if the car I'd passed had been Barnier on his way in from his home in Langbank.

An idea flashed through my head: I would be passing Langbank and it was the one time I knew for sure that Barnier would not be at home. And I did have all of my housebreaking kit with me. I shook the idea from my head. I had no idea if Barnier lived alone or not, added to which I had had quite enough jolly japes for one night. I drove past Langbank and turned south onto a single track road that led through woods and fields. I found myself on the edge of a reservoir, its silky, still water reflecting the velvet clouds. There was a farmhouse at the head of the reservoir and I drove along the water's edge until I was at the opposite end. Parking the car under some trees, I made a pillow out of the sweater I had worn. Despite the discomfort and the adrenalin still pumping through my system, I was asleep within minutes.

When I woke up I bad-temperedly tried to plunge back into sleep and recapture the dream I'd had: something about me and Fiona White and a new life in Canada. Or had it been me and Sheila Gainsborough? The aches in my neck and the insistent jabbing of the handbrake in my side forbade my return to my dream.

I creakingly unfolded myself. Looking in the mirror in the too bright morning light, I could see the burnt cork still ingrained in the creases and lines of my face: I looked like I was wearing Donald Wolfit's stage make-up. Rolling up my shirt sleeves, I walked across the road to the reservoir's edge. I scooped up some water and rubbed vigorously at my face and neck.

Once I was sure I was clear of all traces of my nocturnal adventures, I drove back into town. As I did so, I was pretty smug with myself. It was no small thing to have clobbered a copper, but I was convinced that by now Billy, the elderly night watchman, would have sworn on his mother's grave that he had *seen* two burglars and one had been called *Jimmy*. The bobby I had tapped would only have gotten a fleeting glance of my cork-blackened face; and I was sure he would be only too willing to swear that 'there must have been two of them' to take him down.

Obfuscation could be such a satisfying pastime.

But the smug smile was wiped off my face as I passed my digs in Great Western Road. There was an immaculately polished, black Wolseley 6/90 parked outside, gleaming in the morning light. I was particularly impressed by the super sheen the garage had managed to get on the rectangular plate across the car's radiator: silver letters against a dark blue background, spelling out the word POLICE.

I drove on and around the corner until I reached the newsagents, where I bought a copy of that morning's paper before driving back, parking just around the corner. I dumped my jacket in the car, took off my tie and rolled my sleeves up. I ambled towards my flat, trying to look as casual as I could. It was probably the innocent act that the coppers had seen a thousand and one times, but I needed to make it look as if I had been at home all night and had just taken a morning stroll to pick up the paper. It all fell down, of course, if the police car had been there for anything more than half an hour.

As I drew near, both rear doors of the police car swung open. Superintendent Willie McNab emerged from one side, Jock Ferguson from the other. I put my best surprised face on, which was probably as convincing as the last time I had used it, when on my birthday my mother had presented me with the sweater I'd seen her knitting for three weeks.

'Gentlemen . . . what can I do for you?'

'You're an early riser, Lennox,' said McNab sourly.

'You know what they say: birds and worms and that sort of thing.'

'Get in the car, Lennox.' McNab stood to one side and held the door open. I imagined it would be the first of many doors that would be closing behind me. My mouth was dry and my heart pumped madly, but I kept as much of an outer cool as I could.

'Can I get my jacket?' I jerked a thumb in the direction of my lodgings. As I did so, I could see Fiona White's face at the window of her flat.

'Go with him . . .' McNab said to Ferguson, who shrugged and followed me in.

'What's this all about?' I took the opportunity of having Ferguson on his own as we climbed the stairs.

'You'll see . . .' he said. And I knew I would.

We didn't head towards police headquarters in St. Andrew's Square. Instead, as I sat crushed between McNab and Ferguson in the back seat of the police car, we headed out towards the river and the bonded warehouses.

'Where are we going?' I asked, as if I had no idea. We took a turn down onto the cobbled road and past the railway arch where I'd hidden the Atlantic.

We didn't stop.

Instead, we drove on until we saw a uniformed constable with zebra-striped traffic cuffs over his tunic. He seemed to be standing on an unbroken piece of grass verge, but as we drew nearer he signalled us to turn in. The barely discernible mouth of a largely overgrown, cobbled access road, just wide enough for the Wolseley, opened up for us and we bumped our way down to the shore. The lane widened into an open area as we reached the water. This had obviously been a working quay, but the Luftwaffe had made a good job of making it inoperable for the rest of the century. Vast concrete blocks, like broken teeth, thrust out of the overgrown grass, rusting metal cable projecting, twisted, from their broken ends. At one corner of the site an earthmover sat, its shovel resting heavily on the ground. On what looked like it had originally been the quay's loading area, four police cars and an ambulance, which must have struggled to negotiate the lane, huddled close to the water. Whatever this was, it didn't look like it was about my break-in to Barnier's office.

McNab and Ferguson led me over to where the other vehicles were parked.

'He was found here this morning by workers clearing the site for more bonded warehouses,' said Ferguson. 'We reckon he's been dead a day at least.'

'Who? What's this got to do with me?' I asked, genuinely confused. I saw that the rear of the ambulance was open and there was a body inside, covered with a grey blanket, lying on the ambulance stretcher.

'What's it got to do with you?' McNab sneered at me. 'That's what I want to know. According to our leads, you've been looking for this fellah for the last week or so. Now he turns up dead.'

My gut gave a lurch. I did a little time travelling into the future and imagined myself in front of Sheila Gainsborough, trying to find the words to tell her that I'd found her brother all right. Dead.

So John Largo was no spook. No shadowy figure without substance. And he had caught up with Sammy Pollock at last.

McNab pulled back the blanket. 'You know him, I take it?'

'You take it right,' I said with quiet resignation as I looked down at the body. The quiet resignation was to disguise my surprise. And my relief. 'That's Paul Costello.'

Costello's eyes were wide open. There were grains of dust and dirt on them and looking at them made me want to blink. His face was bleached of colour and his hair dishevelled. The paleness of his skin was in stark contrast to the vividness of the gaping wound that arched, like a clown's smile, across his throat. He was very, very dead.

'Why were you looking for Costello?' asked McNab. He snapped the blanket back over the dead face.

'His father Jimmy asked me to,' I answered honestly, if not wholly. 'Paul Costello went missing a few days ago. Without warning and, more importantly, without cash.'

'Aye,' said McNab, his voice loaded with suspicion. 'Inspector

Ferguson here said you told him that when he came up to see you with that Yank, Devereaux.'

'That's right.'

'And that was because you were bandying the name Largo about. So tell me, is this Largo's work, d'you think?'

I looked at the blanket-draped corpse. 'I honestly don't know. But if Largo is as big and as dangerous a crook as Dex Devereaux seems to think, then my guess would be yes.'

'Aye? Well thanks for your valuable insight, Lennox. Next question: who the fuck is this celebrity client of yours? The relative of the other missing person?'

I sighed. 'Like I told Inspector Ferguson, I can't compromise client confidentiality.'

'Client confidentiality my arse . . .' McNab took a step closer to me. I didn't need to look to know his hands had already balled into fists. Whatever happened here would be only the beginning.

'If I tell you, will you keep her out of it? Unless there's a direct involvement, I mean?'

McNab laughed. An ugly, mocking laugh. 'Do you think that I have to *negotiate* with the likes of you, Lennox? I'll do whatever the fuck I want, talk to whoever the fuck I want. This is a murder enquiry, you clown.'

'And then some. Let's face it, Superintendent, someone is playing a very big game in this town. Bigger than anything the local talent is capable of putting on. Now you can walk all over me and feel like the big bollocks, and I'll do exactly what you want and walk away from the whole thing. No skin off my nose. But if we work together you could end up getting the credit for breaking the biggest case this city's seen in years. Remember that Dex Devereaux can't make the arrest here . . .' I looked meaningfully at Ferguson. 'Yes, Jock, I know Devereaux's FBI. I knew the moment you brought him into my place.' I turned back to McNab. 'I'm not being funny, but this case involves things you don't understand. You don't understand them because this kind of crap has never washed up in Glasgow before. Okay ... here it is: my client is Sheila Gainsborough, the singer. Now you can let me deal with this side of it or you can dirty her carpet with your size tens. But, if you do, then count me out.'

'I'm a *policeman*, Lennox.' McNab looked at me as if inspecting something noxious that he'd just scraped from his shoe. 'Doesn't that mean anything to you? I don't have to wheel and deal with the likes of you. I've got hundreds of officers I can rely on. *Real* policemen. Not Canadian gobshites.'

'Okay,' I said and shrugged. 'Your call.'

'Just a minute ...' Jock Ferguson stepped between us. 'Lennox has got a point, sir. And we *don't* have someone like him we can call on.'

'He works for fucking crooks, for God's sake, man. How do we know that he's not delivering information to them instead of us?'

'I *am* working for one of the Three Kings,' I admitted. 'But not on this, on something else. And the job I'm doing for him is legitimate private investigation work. I know you have a low opinion of me, Superintendent. I don't blame you, sometimes I share it. But I'm not a crook. Anyone who hires me knows I won't break the law for them.' I stopped. It was a pretty speech. I particularly liked the bit where I'd sworn my adherence to the law. Apart from the laws pertaining to breaking and entering and police assault, that was.

'Sheila Gainsborough?' McNab asked. 'How the hell did you get a client like that?'

'I move in the best circles, Mr McNab. Now, can I deal with the Sammy Pollock/Sheila Gainsborough side of things?'

McNab examined me long and hard. 'For the meantime, Lennox. But just remember this is a murder investigation now.'

I looked back at Paul Costello's body. So I wouldn't be getting even with him, after all.

'I'm not likely to forget,' I said.

McNab remained at the scene while Jock Ferguson and I got back into the polished Wolseley squad car.

'I'll take you back,' he said. 'I've got a stop to make on the way, if that's okay.'

'I'm glad of the lift,' I said.

I didn't remain glad for long. We only drove a little way along South Street before turning into the gates that led to the Nissen hut offices of various importers.

'This won't take long,' said Ferguson as we pulled up. Outside the office of *Barnier and Clement Import Agents*. 'Some stupid break-in. I wouldn't be involved if it weren't for the fact that some stupid flatfoot got himself clobbered.'

'No rush.' I smiled. Which was an impressive achievement, because a small, elderly man in a worn tweed jacket and a flat cap was looking at me through the rear window of the police car. Billy the night watchman stood, rolling a scrap of tobacco in a cigarette paper. Even though I hadn't seen him close up, I recognized his stooped frame and wide, scruffy flat cap. I hoped he wasn't about to return the compliment. I was sitting in the back of the car, with the uniformed driver in front. It made me look like an arrested suspect. I had been sure Billy wouldn't identify me: he had only seen me from a distance. But with the visual clue of me seemingly in custody he might make the connection.

'I think I'll stretch my legs,' I said to the driver and stepped out of the car, lighting a cigarette. As I did so, Billy seemed to peer at me, as if examining me more closely. He walked across to me, a little uncertainly, the meagre roll-up unlit between his lips. At least he wasn't shouting for help from the police. His eyes were narrowed under the brim of his scruffy flat cap.

'Excuse me, officer,' he said. 'Would you spare me a light?'

'Sure,' I said, suddenly, explicably cheerful. I struck a match for him. 'Lots of excitement today . . .'

'Aye,' he said with a bright mournfulness. 'Too much excitement for me.'

'What, the break-in?' I asked.

'Aye . . . Those hooligans really clobbered yon young polisman.'

'Did you see them?'

'Aye . . . But not good. To tell the truth I forgot my spectacles. Brand new ones and all, off the National Health. Two pairs I got. And the one night something happens that I need to see, I leave the bastards at home.' He shook his head and I resisted the impulse to kiss him. 'But I seen them all right. Running away. Two of them.' He leaned forward conspiratorially. 'Teddy Boys. Them Teddy Boys is nothing but trouble. Them two was lucky I didn't catch up with them.'

I smiled. This time it was a genuine smile. A heartfelt, thankful, joyous smile. It had been one hell of a morning so far: a rollercoaster of emotions. Everything that could have come along to shake me up, had. All I needed now was the copper I had sapped to turn up, the blow to the head I'd given him somehow bestowing a photographic memory. There again, he was a Highland copper: a photographic memory is no good if there's no film in the camera.

But he wasn't going to turn up. Unfortunately, as I looked over the cap of my new best night watchman friend, I saw the next best thing arrive.

Striding with resolute purpose up from the main gates and

heading towards the offices, a small but sturdily built woman with her hair in what could only be described as an aggressive permanent. Miss Minto.

I could see her taking in the police cars and guessing that something had happened that threatened her little but jealously guarded realm of absolute order. The last thing I needed was for her to spot me; or casually ask in front of Jock Ferguson what I was doing there.

'Excuse me,' I said to Billy, turning my back to the approaching Miss Minto and ambling as casually as I could between the Nissen huts, as if I had been going around the back to check for damage. I heard her determined steps behind me on the gravel, then on the wooden steps into the office. Doing a swift about turn, I flicked my cigarette away and headed back to the car. It was now the best place for me to keep out of sight. I just hoped that Miss Minto did not re-emerge from the office and spot me in the police car.

Leaning forward between the seats, I rested my elbows on the seat backs and supported my head in my right hand, hopefully concealing my face from the office doorway. As an excuse for invading his territory, I engaged the police driver in small talk. It was an effort: he was only marginally more chatty than Sneddon's mute bodyguard, Singer. After what seemed an age, Jock Ferguson came out of the office and over to the car.

'Sorry about that,' he said. 'I'll give you that lift now.'

'No problem,' I said cheerily. 'I would have thought that by now you would be above investigating simple break-ins, Jock.'

Ferguson shrugged. 'The bastards clobbered a cop. That changes everything. 'No one puts one of ours in the infirmary and gets away with it.'

'Quite right . . .' I said, and tried to think ahead. But not too far ahead.

Chapter Fourteen

It took me a little while and another conversation with her supercilious agent, before I finally arranged a meeting with Sheila Gainsborough. Telling her that the person her missing brother had gone missing with had turned up dead was the kind of thing you had to do face to face.

I met her again at her apartment. She took it well, or at least as well as it could be taken, and much better than I had anticipated. I suspected there was an element of blind wishful thinking on her part; or maybe it simply didn't occur to her that her brother might be just as dead as Paul Costello but no one had found the body yet. It was a thought that was never far from the front of my mind.

For my part, I played it all down, as much as you can play down a sliced throat. It also didn't occur to her that eventually the police would want to talk to Sammy. It was only a matter of time and lack of results before they would start to look around for the most convenient possible suspect. That's when Sammy's name would be pulled out of McNab's hat and I would be elbowed out of the way.

I had things to do and places to be, but I could see that Sheila Gainsborough was in a fragile state, so I gave her all kinds of assurances that I would double my efforts now that the stakes were higher, and that I would definitely bring Sammy back in one piece. Making promises to women was something I did all the time – especially ones like that, where there was every chance I wasn't going to be able to deliver on it.

After I left Sheila, I went to a telephone kiosk and rang Ian McClelland at the University. We did the usual banter thing and then I got down to business.

'Ian, could you tell me what a Baro is? In a gypsy or tinker context?'

'Gosh, Lennox, it's not really my field, but I could check it out. What was the context?'

'I was meeting with someone, a gypsy, and another gypsy referred to him as the *Baro*.'

'Okay, I know someone I can ask . . .' said McClelland.

'Could you ask the same people what significance a wooden box with pieces of wood and red and white wool might have as well? About nine inches square, I'd say.' I described the box Lorna told me had been delivered to her father shortly before his death. 'The wool was rolled up into a ball.'

'Certainly, old man. In fact I'm just along the corridor from the very person. Can I call you back in ten minutes?'

'Sure,' I said. 'What about the description and drawing of the dragon I gave you?'

'As I thought, it's a Chinese *Qilin*.'

'Actually, you're wrong . . .' I sounded rather smug. 'Not a *Qilin*, it's a Vietnamese *Ky-lan*, if my information's correct.'

'Probably is,' said McClelland. If he was impressed with my knowledge of the finer points of oriental mythology, he hid it well. 'It is a Sino-Vietnamese character. It looks fierce but it's one of the good guys. It brings you luck and wealth and looks after the good and the honourable.'

'I can tell,' I said. 'My luck's been just dandy since I first saw him.'

*

As good as his word, Ian McClelland called back ten minutes later.

'A *Baro* is a clan chieftain,' he explained. 'A real bigwig in Romany circles. And I hope you didn't find that box you were talking about . . . the one with the wool in it.'

'No I didn't . . . why?'

'It's a *bitchapen* . . . it's a kind of gift, but not the kind you want to get. Everyone in the gypsy tribe touches it and passes on everything ill or evil into it. It rids them of ill-fortune but whoever finds the *bitchapen* gets the lot.'

'Thanks, Ian,' I said. 'That makes a lot of sense.'

I met up with Dex Devereaux for a drink in the bar of the Alpha Hotel. I told him about Sammy, Paul Costello, Claire Skinner, their little jade demon friend and the charming country retreat they all shared. But for the moment I kept my suspicions about Alain Barnier and his possible connection to John Largo quiet. I had one very good reason to keep quiet: the big American was a good guy, but, at the end of the day, he was a copper. The last thing I needed was the City of Glasgow Police connecting me with Barnier. They may not have been the Brains Trust, but it wouldn't take much thinking to place me at the Barnier and Clement office on the night of the break-in with a sap in my hand and a semi-conscious Highlander at my feet.

Maybe they would pick up Billy the night watchman's glasses for him. The City of Glasgow CID must have had a leading neurologist working for them: they had a remarkable record of suddenly curing witnesses of bad vision and unreliable memory.

After I said goodbye to Devereaux, I drove up to see Lorna and check how she was. Again, she responded as passionately as a bank manager and Maggie MacFarlane was positively frosty. There was no sign of Jack Collins when I called. Lorna made some tea and we sat in the lounge drinking it, me doing my best to say the right solicitous things and Lorna remaining sullen and unresponsive, her expression one of barely concealed resentment. She knew I was going through the motions and would have given anything for a way out. And we both knew that if the roles had been reversed she would have been the same. Neither of us had signed up for emotional involvement.

I spent the next two days keeping tabs on Alain Barnier. Because I had so many other things to juggle, including squeezing in a daily visit to Davey, it was an *inter alia* kind of surveillance and therefore pretty hit or miss.

What made following the Frenchman especially difficult was that he was hardly a creature of habit. On average he would only spend two or three hours of each day in the office, and not always the same two or three hours. The rest of the time he spent doing his rounds of clients, mainly hotels and restaurants. Wines and spirits were not his sole stock in trade: he also did a fair amount of visiting antique dealers, a handful in Glasgow and several more in Edinburgh.

Following Barnier was time-consuming and seemed largely pointless, but there was always the chance that he would lead me somewhere that would be one step closer to John Largo. Although, as Barnier went about his mundane daily business, I found myself doubting that this debonair, cultured and educated Frenchman could have anything to do with an international peddler of narcotics.

I was maybe getting cocky, but I actually took to parking the Atlantic under the same railway arch that I had used on the night of the break-in. From there I could see the gates into the bonded area and pick up Barnier's Simca whenever he left his office. He emerged at three-thirty in the afternoon; leaving early was something he did quite often, squeezing in a few client calls before driving home to Langbank.

It may have seemed like a pointless exercise, but I followed him anyway. An ugly jade demon and a dead gangster's son were pointing me in that direction. And then there was the gut feeling I had about the Frenchman too: I liked the guy but every time I thought of him it was like someone prodding something that had been curled up for a nap in a room somewhere at the back of my brain.

One afternoon I waited outside the bonded docks until about six. When Barnier's Simca pulled out through the gates, I followed. When he drove west towards Greenock, I guessed we were heading straight to his home in Langbank. I had to hold back as far as I could without losing him. The road ribboned along the side of the Clyde and, despite this being the main road that connected Glasgow with its satellite town Greenock, there were practically no other cars in either direction. We passed the point where I had turned south and camped out in my car by the reservoir. Then, surprisingly, the Simca drove past Langbank and out towards the west. I couldn't imagine what business an importer of fine wines and oriental curios could possibly have in Greenock.

He drove towards the town and I lost him where the coast takes a sudden sweep southwards. I accelerated a little and nearly missed his turning. Port Glasgow had a vast sugar works and the hill above it had been named Lyle Hill. Why Tate didn't deserve recognition was something I didn't know. Driving up the sweep of Lyle Hill I passed Barnier's parked Simca. I drove on, not even slowing down until I was around the bend in Lyle Road, out of sight of where he had parked. I pulled over and took a set of binoculars out of the glove compartment. I had to scrabble up the hillside to get a vantage point from which I could watch Barnier. The leather soles of my Gibsons slipped on slimy grass and I came down onto my knees several times, cursing the damp, dark staining on my suit trousers. Glasgow was a city with a heavy-industrial attitude to everything and I had found out to my cost that laundries in the city approached the dry-cleaning of my best suits with a delicacy that make steel-smelting look like needlepoint.

I made it to the top of the hill and seemed to be on the edge of a golf course. There was brush and some meagre trees to give me shelter and I looked down at where the road swept around the edge of Lyle Hill. The view was breathtaking: out across the Clyde to the mountains of the Cowal Peninsula. Immediately below was Greenock on one side and Gourock on the other. And, further out, the Tail of the Bank. This had been the departure point for my parents when they took me, as a baby, to start a new life in Canada.

But what struck me most about what I was looking at was the fact that Barnier had stopped at the monument that commanded the best of the view. The memorial was in the form of a vast white ship's anchor, the shaft of which thrust dramatically up into the sky. But instead of having the usual rode-eye at the top, the anchor shaft had two beams cross it, one shorter than the other. A Cross of Lorraine. As a piece of civic sculpture, it could not have been more dramatic. And I knew something about what it commemorated.

I watched Barnier. It was difficult to tell if he was waiting for someone or if the monument had some particular significance for him. He stood as if reading the inscription on the base. Then he turned and leaned against the border rail, with his back to me, and seemed to be gazing out over the Firth of Clyde. He stood there for a good ten minutes before turning and heading back towards his car. I cursed inwardly. I had been sure he was going to meet someone, and the monument seemed an ideal place for a rendezvous. But I had probably just watched too many Orson Welles movies.

I scrabbled down the side of the hill as fast as I could to get back to the Atlantic. If Barnier turned back down the hill then I would have to hurry or lose him. As I scrambled, fingers of tree branch snagged at my suit to impede my descent. My hat came off a couple of times and it was only by some nifty goal-keeping that I saved my Borsalino from the mud. I burst out from the green web of bushes and onto the road, a few feet from where I had parked the Atlantic.

You see it all the time in Westerns. The settlers look up from the pass and spot the menacingly still and silent silhouettes of mounted Apaches or banditos up on the hillside looking down on them. The Badlands.

Port Glasgow was Scotland's equivalent of the Painted Desert, and when I came out onto the road again there were three Teddy Boy Comancheros waiting by my car. My gut feeling was that there was nothing professional or organized about this encounter: it had nothing to do with my tailing of Barnier and was just your run-of-the-mill Scottish small-industrial-town thuggery. I reckoned that they were all about nineteen. They clearly identified themselves with the emerging Teddy Boy fashion, but none of them had been able to put together a complete assembly. Instead one wore the thigh-length jacket, one had drainpipe trousers and the jacketless third thug had had to settle for a bootlace tie.

Between them they had enough oil in their hair to lubricate a battle ship and an array of skin conditions impressive enough to keep a dermatologist on a stipend.

'This your car, pal?' the youth with the Teddy Boy jacket asked. He was clearly the leader; maybe that was why he'd got the jacket. He was leaning against the wing of the Atlantic and looked relaxed. A bad sign. Confidence in any kind of physical encounter is half the battle. The other two just looked at me with a dull-eyed lack of interest, as if this was something they did every day, which it probably was.

'Yeah, this is my car,' I sighed, brushing the worst of the leaves and mud from my suit trousers.

'We've been looking after it for you,' said one of the others. I had to concentrate hard: I hadn't brought my Greenock phrase-book with me. It had taken me years to understand the Glasgow accent. But Greenock was beyond the pale.

'I appreciate that,' I said with a smile. I took my keys out of my pocket and headed to the door. No rush now. I was going to have to let Barnier get away. I had more immediate problems. The leader in the Edwardian jacket slid along the wing and positioned himself in front of the door.

'Well, it's like this. You could've come back here and found your tyres all flat and fuck knows what else. But we was here to make sure nobody touched it. So we think that you should maybes give us a couple of quid, like.'

His two mates took up position on either side of me, squaring their shoulders. Not much to square.

'Yeah?' I said. 'Very enterprising of you. But the trick is to ask for the money first, Einstein.'

He furrowed his brow. Not anger, just uncertainty about the insult. I realized he didn't have a clue who Einstein was. I was going to have to learn to keep my references simple. I sighed and reached into my pocket and the frown on his pimply brow eased. It shouldn't have.

They were just kids. I knew that and I didn't want trouble. But I knew they would have beaten the crap out of me so they could empty my pockets and probably steal the car, given half the chance. In the army, I learned that if there's a threat, you have to neutralize it. And I'd done more than my fair share of neutralizing. So I decided to feel sorry for them later.

I drew the sap out of my inside pocket and, again in a single, continuous movement, backhanded the lead Teddy across the temple with it. The youth on my right lunged forward and I jabbed out the hand I held my car keys in. The key split his cheek and chipped against his teeth. He screamed and staggered back, clutching his bleeding face. The third thug reached into his pocket and started to pull out a razor. I swung the sap at him, not taking time to aim properly. By luck it caught him on the side of his weak chin and he dropped stone-out. The first guy started to ease himself up from the ground and I dissuaded him with the heel of my Gibson across his mouth. The thug with the keyhole in his cheek was running back down the hill, still clutching his face and crying.

Pulling the lead hooligan out of my way, I got into the Atlantic and headed back down Lyle Hill. Halfway down I passed the running, crying youth. I rolled down my window and, beaming a smile at him, asked him if he needed a lift. I guessed he preferred to walk because he just stared at me wildly, turned on his heel and started running in the opposite direction, back up the hill.

I pulled over to where Barnier had parked. The monument was set in a rectangle edged with railings and a gate repeating the cross of Lorraine motif. I got out and stood, taking in the view for a moment before reading the inscription on the base of the monument:

THIS MONUMENT IS DEDICATED TO THE MEMORY OF THE SAILORS OF THE FREE FRENCH NAVAL FORCES WHO SAILED FROM GREENOCK IN THE YEARS 1940–1945 AND GAVE THEIR

LIVES IN THE BATTLE OF THE ATLANTIC FOR THE LIBERATION
OF FRANCE AND THE SUCCESS OF THE ALLIED CAUSE

On the other panels, specific Free French vessels were
mentioned: the submarine *SURCOUF*, the corvettes *ALYSSE* and
MIMOSA. But, as everyone knew, while the monument may have
been officially dedicated to all of the Free French sailors who
had been based in Scotland during the war, it had a very special
significance for a particular group of Frenchmen. And related
to a particular event. Something that had happened before the
Free French forces were officially formed. Something that
happened right here, within sight of the spot where the monument now stood.

And Alain Barnier seemed to be connected to it.

I didn't see the road as I drove back to Glasgow. And I didn't
think much about what had brought me to Greenock. Someone
was poking away again at that curled-up sleeping thing and
had switched on the light in the room at the back of my brain.
I saw a name. *Maillé-Brézé*.

But the ghosts of dead French seamen weren't the only things
that were nagging at me. I should have been happy that I had
stopped beating on the three thugs as soon as they no longer
represented a threat to me. That I had displayed an element of
restraint. Even a few months earlier, once I had the advantage,
I would have given them a serious hiding. A hospital hiding. I
should have been happy. But I wasn't.

The truth was that I had still enjoyed it.

CHAPTER FIFTEEN

It was a good seat. It wasn't ringside. It wasn't two, three or even four rows from ringside. But as I sat there in my black tie and tux, I had a pretty good view of the fight even if I had an even better view of the back of Willie Sneddon's head as he sat ringside with his guest, a Glasgow Corporation councillor and head honcho of the Planning Department. The only thing that impeded my view was the curtain of tobacco smoke that hung in the air. It hung more heavily over the front two rows. The cigar class rows.

I sat next to my dates. Sneddon had been able to swing an extra couple of tickets for me and I had done my own little bit of suborning hospitality. Jock Ferguson was the kind of copper usually immune to inducement, but he had leapt at the chance to see the title fight. And it would do me no harm to patch up the bridge between us a little. Everyone knew, because the movies told us so, that the FBI was incorruptible, and anyway Dex Devereaux was not, officially, a peace officer while on this side of the Atlantic. So he had nothing to lose by accepting my invitation.

It had been remarkably easy to get the tickets from Sneddon. As soon as I told him I wanted to sweeten a couple of coppers, he handed over the tickets without a word of complaint.

I sat there and watched as the fighters – Schmidtke first,

then challenger Kirkcaldy – made their way into the ring. Schmidtke was a German and there remained a huge anti-German sentiment throughout Britain. But despite all of the problems of poverty, sectarianism, violence and drink that afflicted them, Glaswegians were a warm bunch. I had been brought up in Atlantic Canada amongst open, friendly people. Maybe that's why I liked it here. In any case, there was no booing or jeering when Schmidtke entered the ring, just a polite, restrained applause. There was an explosion of cheering and whistling as soon as Kirkcaldy entered the ring. There is no greater passion in Glasgow than pride, and Kirkcaldy was their boy.

As the bout began, I felt strange sitting there with the know-ledge that only I, Sneddon and Bert Soutar had: that Kirkcaldy was stepping into the ring with a time bomb ticking away in his chest. I watched him move fluidly and without effort, just as he had the last twice I had seen him fight – without a hint of any deficit of stamina. It was not the most exhilarating of fights. Schmidtke seemed to be pacing himself, and both boxers were out-fighting, each keeping his opponent at a distance and weighing up any potential strategic weakness. It was not Schmidtke's usual style and the second round was as unin-spiring as the first. Both fighters seemed over-cautious and unwilling to open up.

When the third round went the same way, I could sense my fellow spectators becoming restless. I could understand why Kirkcaldy was circumspect about launching any kind of energy-sapping onslaught, but I couldn't see why Schmidtke was holding back. Unless Schmidtke's thinking was that if it ended up going the distance, there was always the tendency for a split decision to go the title-holder's way.

But, there again, there was always the chance that Kirkcaldy had come to an arrangement that would allow him to end his career with a championship belt.

It was in the eighth round that I guessed I had been wrong. The German came out of his corner with the same tentativeness as in the previous rounds. His head low and defence tight.

It was the simplest of errors: Kirkcaldy swung an uncharacteristically loose right. It wasn't so much that Kirkcaldy telegraphed the hook, as announced it with a gold-edged invitation complete with the times for carriages. The German answered the RSVP with an arcing hook that hurt me just to watch it connect. It lifted Kirkcaldy off his feet and he shoulder-slammed the canvas. Half of the spectators, including Jock Ferguson, leapt to their feet and there was a deafening explosion of shouts. The referee backed the German towards his corner with a hand to the chest and started counting out Kirkcaldy. The Scotsman shook the crap out of his head and stood up swiftly, bouncing on the balls of his feet and nodding to the ref. Once you'd kissed canvas, if you wanted to avoid a technical knock-out, you had instantly to convince the referee that you were okay, usually with an overdone display of bright athleticism. The ref backed Kirkcaldy into a neutral corner and checked his eyes before retaking the centre of the ring and indicating, with a gesture like drawing curtains, for the fighters to come together and recommence the match.

The German's massive shoulders dipped and rose as he came out of his corner. There was a new energy in them. Kirkcaldy tried to outflank every new attack, but the German just kept driving him into the ropes, raining in vicious hooks.

I could see it now: Kirkcaldy's face was pale, almost white, the lividity of the bruises around his eyes stark against his whiter skin. He launched an attack to drive Schmidtke back, but the German stood planted, rooted to the canvas, his bulky arms working like pistons, driving one blow after another into Kirkcaldy's body.

Again it was clumsy. Schmidtke caught Kirkcaldy a legal hair's breadth above the belt. Kirkcaldy dropped his elbows, bringing his guard down. Two successive jabs to his face, followed by a vicious, ugly bolo punch stunned the Scotsman. Then Schmidtke made his delivery. The dazed Kirkcaldy was probably the only person in the auditorium who didn't see it coming: every single ounce of Schmidtke's weight behind a roundhouse right that seemed to take an age to connect. But it did. Right on the side of Kirkcaldy's jaw and the Scotsman went limp and crashed into the canvas. The German had his hands above his head grinning a gumshield grin and jumping on the spot before the referee had finished his count.

Everybody was on their feet, shouting, cheering and some booing now: less with hurt nationalistic pride and more with suspicion that they had just been witness to amateur dramatics instead of professional boxing.

I stood too, but I wasn't applauding. I was watching the referee, Uncle Bert Soutar, and a fat, middle-aged man in a dinner suit and with a leather Gladstone bag crouched over Kirkcaldy. Even the German had stopped his triumphal dance.

The noise of the crowd was still deafening, but I felt as if a curtain had been pulled between me and them; as if I was the only person really seeing what was happening in the ring.

'Christ . . . he's dead . . .' I said, my voice so drowned out by the crowd that I barely heard it myself.

'Waddya say?' Dex Devereaux shouted, still clapping, leaning in towards me.

I still watched the scene in the ring. Bert Soutar and the doctor were now helping Kirkcaldy to his feet. Kirkcaldy nodded vaguely to them, and Schmidtke, with a relief I could feel four rows back, embraced his defeated opponent. Kirkcaldy was helped from the ring to the cheers and jeers of the spectators.

After the fight, Dex Devereaux, Jock Ferguson and I made our way to the exits. I had hoped to talk to Willie Sneddon, but I'd lost sight of him. My guess was that he would not be a happy bunny. No matter what other schemes Kirkcaldy had come up with and cooperated with, he had cost Sneddon money. Costing Sneddon money was not something it was advisable for anyone to do. I did see Tony the Pole though. I excused myself from Ferguson and Devereaux for a moment.

'Whaddya say? Whaddya hear Tony?' I said smiling.

Tony didn't smile back. 'Iz a fugging dizgraze, Lennogs,' he said gloomily, ignoring our traditional greeting. 'A load ov fugging bollos. Whit vaz zat like?'

'Not a good night for you, Tony?'

'Ziz fuggin carry-on haz cost me a fugging vortune.'

'I suppose none of the local bookies will be happy with this result.'

'Naw? You'd be zurprized, Lennogs. Not everythink iz vat it zeems. Zere's at leazd vone baztart iz goin' home happy.'

'What do you mean?' I asked, almost yelling to be heard. But Tony the Pole had been collared by a punter energetically waving a betting slip.

'Azk Jack Collins aboot zat. Aye . . . you go an' azk Jack Collins . . .' Tony called, before turning his attention back to his punter. I left him to it and rejoined my guests.

I took Ferguson and Devereaux to the Horsehead Bar. It was well past closing time and Ferguson made a point of finding interesting something far off and down the street while I gave my coded knock. There were as many as twenty regulars inside the pub. Big Bob was on the bar.

'We're not looking for waiters, Lennox,' he said, grinning inanely and taking in our dinner suits and black ties. 'What'll you be having then?'

'You know Inspector Ferguson, don't you Bob?' I asked.

Bob eyed Ferguson and sighed. 'On the house, *obviously*.'

I indicated a quiet table in the corner for Ferguson and Devereaux to take their drinks over.

'For fuck's sake, Lennox,' said Bob when they were out of earshot. 'Who the fuck you going to bring next ... the chief constable?'

'I wouldn't do that, Bob. I always take him to the Saracen's Sword ... classier joint. Anyway, I thought this was the nightshift canteen for the City of Glasgow Police.'

'Aye, a dozen or so bluebottles who think their uniform entitles them to limitless free fucking beer. If I start on the management ranks it'll be handouts as well and I'll be truly fucked.'

'Don't worry, Bob,' I said. 'Ferguson is a straight copper.'

'Aye? They're the ones you've got to watch.'

Ain't that the truth, I thought, as I took my drink and joined Devereaux and Ferguson in the corner.

'So,' said Devereaux. 'What did you think of the fight?'

'I really thought our boy would have given that kraut bastard a run for his money,' said Ferguson. 'But it was a bit of a walkover in the end.'

'You?' Devereaux nodded in my direction. 'What did you think, Lennox?

I shrugged. 'You never can tell with these things.'

'Really?' said Devereaux. 'I think someone *could* tell the way that fight was going to turn out.'

'A fix?' Ferguson looked up from his beer. 'You think it was rigged?'

'Four, five rounds of dancing around each other, then the door's left open for a couple of killer punches? You bet it was rigged,' said Devereaux.

'But Kirkcaldy's on his way to the top. Everyone thought he had a good chance of picking up the European belt tonight. Why would he throw a fight?'

Devereaux shrugged. 'Maybe there's something we don't know about him. Maybe he owes money. Maybe he hasn't got the future everyone thinks he has.' Devereaux seemed to examine me for a moment. 'You're not saying much.'

'Me? Nothing much to say, Dex. I'm a bit pissed off that the fight was such a disappointment, that's all.'

After a while we got off the subject of the fight, which I was thankful for. That little nugget of exclusive knowledge about Kirkcaldy's heart condition kept rolling to the front of my mind. And from the front of my mind to the tip of my tongue was a short trip. Especially when I'd tied on a few.

I wasn't thankful for long. Devereaux leaned forward and spoke to me in low tones when Ferguson had gone to the toilets.

'Jock told me that they're giving you quite a bit of licence with this Costello killing,' said Devereaux. 'How much do they know about it being tied in to John Largo?'

'Nothing. I don't know for sure that it is.' It was the worst kind of lie, an obvious one, and Devereaux gave me a look. I sighed. 'Okay, it could be that Largo killed Costello or had him killed. But I want to get my client's brother out of this. Like I said, then I'll give you Largo on a plate. Once I have Sammy, I'll get him to talk. He's my ... *our* ... best hope of getting Largo.'

'Okay, Lennox. Anything you say.'

'What's that meant to mean?'

'It means you're holding out on me.'

'Am I? What?'

'Alain Barnier.'

That stopped me in my tracks. Thankfully it was at that point that Jock Ferguson re-emerged from the toilets.

'We ready?' he asked.

Devereaux drained his whisky. 'We're ready.'

It had been raining while we had been in the Horsehead. The stonework and the cobbles on the street outside were the oil-sleek black of a Glasgow night. I had arranged to give Jock Ferguson a lift home.

'I'll drop you off at your hotel first,' I said to Devereaux.

'It's okay,' he said, squeezing his considerable bulk into the confines of the Atlantic's back seats. 'I'll come along for the ride. See a little more of Glasgow by night.' It was a *fait* that could not have been more *accompli*. I shrugged and dropped in behind the wheel.

Jock Ferguson, normally on the lugubrious side of funereal, was positively chipper on the journey back. The evening and the drink had combined to open a door in his personality. I wondered if that was who Ferguson had really been before the war. And I wished I could find as easy a way back to my pre-war self. There again, the bottle was the key most men used.

After we dropped Ferguson outside his anonymous semi, Dex Devereaux swapped seats and took the front passenger seat.

'Okay Johnny Canuck . . . Let's go for a drive,' he said cheerlessly.

The rain started again: intermittent, thick, greasy globs on the windscreen. The streets were empty of cars and our only obstacle on the way back to his hotel was a drunk in the middle of the road, one foot anchored as if glued to the asphalt. I gave him a blast of my horn but he waved his arm vaguely and cursed incomprehensibly at me. I swerved around him and drove on.

'This town sure has an interesting relationship with booze,' said Devereaux. Then he sighed. 'I suppose if most of the crime you deal with is related to drunks, then it doesn't stretch the grey matter. And these guys here . . . I mean the City of Glasgow Police – and no offence to Jock Ferguson – but these guys aren't the brightest of cookies.'

'I've made the same observation myself. In the past,' I said, keeping my eyes on the road. 'Why don't you say what it is you want to say, Dex?'

'Okay . . . like I say, these guys aren't big thinkers. If they were, I reckon you'd be in a lot of trouble by now.'

'And why would that be?'

'Come on, Lennox.' Devereaux laughed. 'Paul Costello's body is found half a mile away from a break-in and they don't even think to see if it's connected. Do you know the kind of beating you'd get if these guys found out you tapped that uniform?'

'If you're so convinced I did, why don't you tell them?'

'Listen, Lennox, if you get antsy with me, I might do just that. But I'm not interested in giving them you. I'm interested in you giving me Largo.'

'I don't have him to give,' I said. We were on a quiet street and I pulled over to the kerb.

'Yet,' said Devereaux.

'Yet.' I sighed and rested my wrists in the basin of the steering wheel.

'But you're getting close. And you should have told me about Barnier.'

'You seem pretty well informed without my help.'

'Ferguson told me about the break-in. Actually, he was being a gripey pain in the ass about it. He said it was a French importer with an office in Marseille who got broken into. You see, it's difficult for these guys to hold two thoughts in their head concurrently . . .'

'They need a lie-down if they hold them consecutively,' I said.

'Well, the only thing they've got stuck in their heads is that a uniformed cop got cracked across the head. This town isn't so different to the States. There's a blood price to be paid if a cop gets hurt. But, like I say, they can't see past that. No one is asking why the hell someone would break into an importer's office where there's nothing to steal except paperwork . . . in the middle of a bonded warehouse area filled with whisky, luxury goods, cars and god knows what else.'

'Maybe they'd run out of paper clips and the stationers was closed.'

'Cut the crap, Lennox, or I might just begin to feel the need to pay some professional courtesy to my Glasgow colleagues. What have you got on Alain Barnier?'

'I think he's a front for your boy. Or at the very least he's behind the murder of Paul Costello, directly or indirectly. Costello and Sammy Pollock have stolen at least one of a consignment of twelve jade statuettes. My guess is that each statuette is packed with happy snow for your Harlem negroes.'

'How did you find out about the statuettes?'

I told Devereaux about my trip to the disused farm cottage, the jade demon and somebody, probably the recently deceased Paul Costello, putting the lights out for me.

'That's why I turned over Barnier's office, and I was right. I found the manifest for twelve Vietnamese jade demons.'

'Vietnamese?' Devereaux turned in his seat, pivoting his shoulders around.

'Yeah. So what?'

'Indochina is the source of the heroin that's turning up on

the streets. It could be that your frog Barnier doesn't know what he's shipping. It's likely the heroin's been packed into statuettes at source. Maybe Barnier has just been asked to ship these things, not knowing what's inside them.'

'I'd like to think that,' I said. 'But, for a wine merchant-cum-curio importer, Alain Barnier is pretty handy in a fight.' I told Devereaux about what had happened outside the Merchants' Carvery. 'I've been following him for the last day or two.'

'And?'

'And nothing. The only thing remotely illicit I've caught him doing is visiting a married woman in Bearsden while her husband's at work.'

Devereaux sat quietly for a moment. 'You say he has a history of importing from Indochina?'

'As far as I know, yes.'

'Then he must have strong connections and contacts there. The place is a mess. The French have fucked up good. Dien Bien Phu has been a disaster. A turning point. The French are going to clear on out of it, you know.'

'I guess.'

'And when they do, the Commies will take over. The French are going to leave the back door wide open for them.'

'It's a long way away, Dex,' I said. 'It's a French colonial problem.'

'Not now. Now it's our problem. There's going to be another Korea out there, take my word for it. In the meantime, it's chaos. And chaos is the best environment for someone like John Largo to operate in.'

'But you don't think Barnier's directly involved?'

'I didn't say that. It *could* be that he doesn't know what he's shipping. Or it could be that, for all we know, Alain Barnier *is* John Largo.'

'It's unlikely,' I said. 'Barnier is established here. The other thing is he looks too much like an international criminal mastermind. The sharp clothes, the French accent and the goatee beard . . . I think John Largo would keep a lower profile.'

'So don't I,' said Devereaux, then grinned at my puzzled expression. 'You'll have to learn Vermontese. It's what we say when we mean "so do I". You know the other thing it could be . . . maybe John Largo is like Robin Hood. A kind of *composite* character. Maybe John Largo is more an organization than a criminal. Maybe Barnier is *part* of John Largo.'

'He has a partner. A guy called Claude Clement. Here . . .' I took my notebook from the side pocket of my dinner jacket and copied the addresses onto a blank page, tore it out and handed it to Devereaux. 'I found that when I was stealing paper clips. Maybe Barnier and Clement are in this together. So what now?'

'I'll get onto Washington, see if we've got anything on Barnier or this other guy. In the meantime I suggest you keep tabs on him. I also suggest you give me everything you get, as soon as you get it. Otherwise I might just offer McNab or Ferguson my professional insight into who clobbered their beat boy. And, remember, I've still got a thousand dollars if you lead me to Largo. Don't hold out on me again, Lennox.'

'There is one more thing,' I said. I had just remembered it myself. Taking out my notebook again, I scribbled a second note and handed it to Devereaux. 'That's the address in New York the jade demons are being sent: *Santorno Antiques and Curios*.'

'Thanks.' He took the note and put it in his pocket without looking at it.

We didn't talk much after that. I drove him back to his hotel and waited to make sure he got in; it was three in the morning and it took an age before an elderly night porter opened up for him. Devereaux turned and gave me a half wave, half salute and disappeared into the hotel. I sat for a moment, staring at the closed oak door. I had given Devereaux everything. Almost everything. I hadn't mentioned the visit to the Free French naval monument. It probably wasn't anything, but I needed to check it out for myself first. I was deep tired. Tired to the bone. There were so many thoughts buzzing about my head but my brain had pulled the shutters down and turned the sign around on the door.

Thinking would have to wait until morning.

CHAPTER SIXTEEN

First thing the next morning, I made another trip to the Mitchell Library. This time it wasn't to meet with anyone. I was looking for a very specific piece of information.

I was aided in my search by a rather accommodating librarian who fell for my helpless hunk act. She was a brunette, about thirty, and was dressed in a vaguely bohemian way, or as bohemian as the formality of the city library would allow, with her dark hair loose. I had spotted her from across the main library. She had been supporting an impressive array of heavy reference books in her arms and in turn supporting an equally impressive bust on the books. She looked to me like a free-thinking type: I found an open-minded attitude an asset in a woman. We hit it off right away. It could, of course have been our shared bibliophilia, but my guess was it was more likely to be my very obvious and profound appreciation of her best assets.

In any case, her cooperation made my search faster and more efficient than if I'd stumbled around myself. It took me forty-five minutes to compile the newspaper articles, service reports and casualty lists that I needed. Of course, there were details that I couldn't get to: Britain was a secretive state, and nearly ten years after the end of the war there were details of the conflict that remained locked away in Whitehall basements, where they would remain for another eighty years at least. But

I found enough to be getting along with; I also managed to get the home address of my brunette research partner as well as very specific times I could call: along with the vaguely bohemian dress, she wore a wedding band on her left hand. I guessed her husband was neither bohemian nor open-minded.

She left me at one of the desks with all of my research materials. I was focussed on one event and I spent two hours going through newspaper accounts and official reports on the disaster. But it was the casualty lists and service lists that interested me most. Finally, I found what I was looking for: Alain Barnier had been a junior officer on the *Maillé-Brézé*. It would explain the Frenchman's attachment to this part of the world. It would also explain his visits to the memorial on Lyle Hill.

But, as I looked at Barnier's name on the page, it left more unexplained than explained.

I read through back issues of the *Greenock Telegraph*, covering the earlier years of the war. There had been a lot of French sailors stationed in the area during the war and I scanned every mention of the French forces. They were mainly the usual flag-waving, *forget-Napoleon-we're-all-pals-now* pieces. The Scots had a very different relationship with the French than the English had: there had been the *Auld Alliance*, the Franco-Scottish–Norwegian treaty that had preceded the British Act of Union, and to which the Scots romantically attached great importance. The relationship between the French sailors and the locals had been generally positive. There was certainly not going to be anything negative said about it in the wartime press.

But I did find something significant in the court records. Three Greenock dockyard workers, exempt from military service because of their reserved occupation, had appeared in the town's sheriff court charged with breach of the peace, assault and police assault. Apparently the three locals had been involved in a melee in the town. The local police, and provosts of the *Gendarmerie Maritime* had had to break up a major brawl that had spilled out of a Greenock bar and into the streets. The date was significant: 5 July, 1940 – two days after the British Royal Navy had attacked the French fleet at Mers-el-Kébir to stop the ships falling into German hands. Ten ships had been sunk and nearly 1300 French sailors killed. It had been a diplomatic disaster and had left the French asking 'with friends like these . . .'

It didn't take massive skills of deduction to work out that tensions had been high and some loudmouth must have said something to get a fight started between the French sailors and the locals. Of course, it didn't need to be that. In the West of Scotland you didn't need much of a reason for a fight, and seeing as many of the local girls had earned, with much enthusiasm, the epithet of *matelots' mattresses*, the good old standards of sexual jealousy and booze were always available for the potentially pugnacious.

I was about to move on when a statement by one of the witnesses drew me back into the report. A group of French sailors had found themselves surrounded by a mob of locals. They were rescued by a group of local police and French naval provosts made up of naval gendarmes and *Fusiliers Marins*. The witness's statement described how some of the French provosts had used 'some kind of fancy foot-fighting' to drive back the crowd.

I asked my librarian if she could photostat the report for me and, after a little gentle persuasion and much Lennox charm, she agreed. But I would have to pay for the materials and call back for the prints.

It was nearly lunchtime and I made my daily trip to see Davey at the hospital. His face was becoming slightly more recognizable but, if anything, he seemed less chipper than he had been right after the attack. After you've taken a beating, it takes a while for the pain to settle itself in, to find the little corners it wants to occupy; to soak itself deep into your muscle and bone. Usually it invites shock and depression as roommates. It was clear that young Davey Wallace's broken body was now fully let.

It suddenly occurred to me that I had been so obsessed with what had happened immediately before the attack on him that I hadn't asked Davey if anything unusual had happened earlier in the day, during his watch.

'Did you find my notebook, Mr Lennox?' Davey asked through his cage of wired-shut teeth – that was another thing to dampen your spirit a week or so after a beating, having to be fed through a tube because your teeth are wired shut. Whoever had done this to Davey had opened an account with me and I was due them a lot of interest.

'No, Davey,' I said. 'There was no sign of it where the car was parked.'

'I've been thinking about that notebook, Mr Lennox. I have a lot of time to think, here. I don't lose things. I'm very careful that way. Even with what happened to me, in all of that confusion. That notebook was in my jacket pocket. It should still be there and it's gone now. Whoever duffed me up took it. I think I saw something or someone that I didn't take seriously and they thought I'd made a note of it.'

'What?'

'I've been racking my brains about it. It's been doing my head in.' Davey paused to wince. Some pain, somewhere inside, had moved about a bit, just to remind him of its tenancy. 'Like I said, I've had lots of time to think about it. But nothing special happened that day. The only thing that came to me was the car that I saw.'

'Someone who went into Kirkcaldy's place?' I asked. I lit a cigarette and held it to his lips.

'No. Two people in the car, but I didn't really get a look at them. Just a glimpse of the driver as he passed. I thought they were going to park and go into Mr Kirkcaldy's house, but the car drove on by. I know it's daft, like, but I got the idea that they maybes saw me parked and watching the house and decided not to stop.'

'It's not daft, Davey. It's instinct. If Dex Devereaux was here he would tell you that every detective, every FBI man needs it. Did you see what make of car it was?'

'I don't know much about cars,' said Davey melancholically, again as if he had let me down. 'Makes and that. But that's why I was asking about the notebook. I wrote down the registration number. It was a big car, but. Fancy, like.'

'What colour was the car?'

'Red,' said Davey. 'Deep red. A sort of winey colour?'

'Burgundy?'

'Sorry, I don't know . . . is that winey colour?'

'Do you know what a Lanchester looks like? Or a Daimler Conquest?'

'Sorry, Mr Lennox, like I said, I don't really know anything about cars.'

'That's okay, Davey. You've done fine. Just fine. I have a hunch about who it might have been in the car. And it *is* important. Thanks, you've been a big help.'

I left Davey, his mood lightened by my praise. I dialled Lorna from a pay 'phone in the hospital. Her tone remained distant and cool, but I tried to sound as chatty and informal as possible, hiding the real reason for my call: a casual question camouflaged in the deep foliage of small talk.

'No,' she said in reply. 'Jack isn't here at the moment. He doesn't spend *all* his time here you know.'

'Have you any idea where he might be?'

'I don't know. At work, probably. He has an office above the boxing gym in Maryhill. Why? What's the sudden interest in Jack?'

'Nothing,' I bluffed. I wondered for a second how many boxing gyms there could be in Maryhill. 'I just wanted to talk to him about the fight last night.'

I moved the conversation on to how she was and if she wanted me to come up to see her that night. She said she was having an early night: the doctor had given her something to help her sleep. Maybe that explained, I thought, why Lorna had begun to sound so distant. But her coolness was more than pharmaceutical. Maybe I was losing my touch. How women, once exposed to my charms, could then go on to resist them had always dumbfounded me. But, somehow, they seemed to manage just fine.

It's odd how things just seem to come together: red ribbons tied to a gypsy vardo wagon, an off-the-cuff remark made by Tony the Pole, the colour of a car remembered by Davey Wallace, a reference to a *Fusiliers Marins* officer in a Greenock court report, a guardedness in Lorna's answer.

I was spreading myself too thin working two cases at the same time, both of which had grown into something much bigger than it had first appeared. To start with, I had thought that finding Sammy Pollock was going to be a straightforward job and not interfere with my getting to the bottom of the Bobby Kirkcaldy thing. But I should have known that nothing in this life is straightforward. The truth was that I had suspected for a while that there had been some kind of connection between them. There was an oddly coincidental chronology here. Sammy

Pollock's disappearance had been coincidental with two things: the theft of one or more of Alain Barnier's jade *Ky-lan* demons and the untimely demise of Small Change MacFarlane.

Willie Sneddon was the kind of man my dad would have described as 'so crooked they'll dig his grave with a corkscrew', and I still had reason to doubt that Sneddon had told me all there was to tell about his involvement with Bobby Kirkcaldy. But I had no reason to doubt the truth of what he *had* told me. And that included the fact that somebody or something had terrified Small Change MacFarlane immediately before Sneddon had met with him that day.

Now, for me, a coincidence was kind of like Socialism: a nice idea, looks good from a distance, but when you get up good and close you can't really bring yourself to believe in it. I was pretty convinced that MacFarlane's murder was connected to at least one of the cases. MacFarlane was a backroom player, a money man with his finger in almost as many pies as Sneddon. But, unlike Sneddon, MacFarlane could get his fingers burned. There was a picture coming together in my head. Like a Picasso it was pretty ugly, jumbled, and didn't make any sense to me.

My immediate and main problem was how to keep tabs on two pilgrims at the same time: Alain Barnier and Jack Collins. Then I had an idea, but first I needed to speak to Collins.

It was basically two small offices on the upper floor of a two-storey building, the lower floor devoted to a boxing gym. It was an older building that was crumbling a bit around the edges. I passed the door to the gym and climbed the stairs to the offices.

When I walked in I was greeted by a secretary who I guessed hadn't been hired for her shorthand skills. Her hair was the kind of blonde that comes out of a bottle and her figure was the kind that comes out of a teenager's wet dream. She parted crimson lips and flashed white teeth at me and showed me into the inner office.

Jack Collins sat behind a desk and a dense screen of blue-grey cigarette haze. When I went in, he had been running a finger down a ledger column and yanking at the crank handle of an adding machine. He was in shirtsleeves, his cuffs kept clear of ink and paper by arm garters positioned above his elbows and just beneath his biceps. Seeing Jack Collins close confirmed my first impression of him: he was smooth, expensively tailored, and groomed to an exceptional degree for a city where *panache* was defined by beating the coal dust from your flat cap before you took a girl up a darkened alley. He was a lean man, his face long, and his features elegant if a little too fine. His thick black hair was immaculately combed back from a broad, tanned brow, and he sported a pencil moustache that was so neat that he must have trimmed it on the hour.

'Someone to see you, Jacky,' said the blonde secretary over my shoulder.

'Senga,' he said wearily, looking past me. 'How many times have I told you to get their names first?'

'I'm Lennox,' I said helpfully.

'I know,' he replied, looking back to 'Senga' and making an impatient gesture of dismissal. 'It's okay, you go back to whatever it is you have to do. Close the door behind you.'

'Sorry about that,' he said. 'I'm training her up at the moment.'

'I can imagine that would be taxing,' I said, and sat down opposite him. He stubbed out a cigarette and lit another immediately. 'Sorry,' he said, and pushed the packet towards me. 'Help yourself.'

'No thanks,' I said, and took my cigarette case out and lit one of my own. 'I don't smoke filters. They're French, aren't they?'

I nodded to the ashtray bristling with filter stubs. Each had two bands of gold around them.

'Yes. Montpelliers. I don't usually smoke them but I got a job lot from an importer friend of mine. You're the chap who's been seeing Lorna, aren't you?'

'Your half-sister . . . yes.'

He stared evenly at me. Cool and unruffled. 'You know about that?'

'That you're Small Change MacFarlane's son? I'm sorry, but it's not the big secret you think it is. Half of Glasgow knows.'

'I see. What can I do for you, Mr Lennox?' Still relaxed. Collins was either extremely cool or he had been expecting my visit.

'I've been looking into a few things concerning Bobby Kirkcaldy. I thought you might be able to cast some light on them.'

'Really? Why me?'

'You know something, Jack . . . Do you mind if I call you Jack? You know something, Jack, I'm quite a philosophical cove. I reflect on the nature of things. One of the things I've been reflecting on is the nature of coincidences.'

'Oh?' He put on an unimpressed act. Or maybe it wasn't an act.

'Yeah . . . Just like nature abhors a vacuum, I abhor a coincidence,' I said.

'What kind of coincidence do you have in mind?'

'Well, for a start, you are the semi-secret and completely illegitimate son of Small Change MacFarlane. The population of this city is over two million, yet your father's murderer just happens to train in the gym downstairs. In fact, his defence is based on the claim that he got an anonymous telephone call to the only place with a 'phone where he could be reached. In the gym downstairs. And then there's Bobby Kirkcaldy, who's famous for his rigorous training regimen. And where does he train? In the gym downstairs. Then, of course, there's the fact that every bookie in town is smarting because Bobby Kirkcaldy folded in the middle of a fight that he was expected to win easily. Every bookie, that is, except you.'

'I'm not a bookmaker.'

'Not officially, but you and Small Change had a real MacFarlane and Son thing going. I'm guessing that you've taken over his book. That's why there was no paperwork worth a damn for the police to find. My God, you must have moved quickly. And I have to say your grief over your father didn't impede your business acumen, did it?'

'You're becoming very offensive, Mr Lennox. And what makes you think that I didn't lose out? Everybody expected Bobby Kirkcaldy to walk that fight.'

'A friend of mine seemed to think that there was someone in the know. Someone who didn't so much hedge his bets as get Capability Brown to landscape them.'

'You shouldn't believe everything Tony the Pole tells you,' said Collins with a sneer. He was a bright boy, right enough.

'I don't *understand* everything that Tony the Pole tells me. And before you go pointing fingers, I did a lot of asking about and everyone says it was you who scooped on the fight. There are a lot of fingers pointing at you.'

'What is it you want from me, Lennox?' He leaned back in the chair, elbows resting on the arms, slender fingers inter-locked beneath his chin. A pose of contrived concentration.

'What I want is to know what exactly you, Small Change and Bobby Kirkcaldy have gotten yourselves involved in. I was hired by Willie Sneddon to find out who was trying to intimidate Kirkcaldy and to look after his investment. Now, after that sham last night, it looks to me like whoever it was succeeded and

Sneddon's investment has gone down the pan. Either that, or a deal of some kind has been done to get you all off the hook. What I want to know is with whom.'

Collins watched me as I talked, still cool and unflustered. I had to resist the temptation to walk around the desk and kick the chair from under him.

'If what you're saying is true, what's it to you? Why should you care? You've run your errand for Sneddon. Fight's over, the outcome is what it is, whether Sneddon likes it or not.'

'Well, first of all, I have a funny feeling that it wasn't some disenchanted gypsy brawler who killed Small Change. Secondly, even though you seem to be taking it remarkably well, the bottom has fallen out of Lorna's world and I feel I owe her something. And thirdly . . .' I stood up and leaned knuckles on his desk, pushing my face towards him. 'And this is the thing that really riles me . . . There's a kid lying in the Southern General taking his lunches through a straw, all because there was a chance he saw you arrive to talk with Bobby Kirkcaldy. And that's where it gets puzzling. It was no secret that Kirkcaldy and Small Change did business. And you were Small Change's partner in at least one enterprise. So what I'm wondering is who was in the car with you and why he didn't want to be seen arriving that night.'

'Listen, Lennox . . . if you're really interested in clearing up Jimmy's death, like you say you are, then I'm grateful for it . . . though it looks pretty much to me like the police have got their man. But putting that aside, do you think I would really have anything to do with killing Jimmy? Like you said, he was my father, whether it was public knowledge or not, and he looked after me. There were lots of things we were going to do together. He had big plans for me. Why would I have anything to do with his death?'

'I don't think you did. I don't think you were responsible for his death and I don't think you wanted his death. But I *do* think you're scared. And I *know* Small Change was scared witless before he died. Whoever had him scared has got you toeing the line, for fear of getting the same treatment.'

'This is shite, Lennox. God knows where you're getting this stuff. I wasn't anywhere near Kirkcaldy's house that day or any other.'

'What day? I didn't say when it was. And I didn't say whether it was day or night.'

Collins gave a small laugh. 'Look, you're not tricking me into saying anything because there's nothing for me to say. You're barking up the wrong tree.'

'Really? I think different. But, like you say, I've got nothing to back it up. Yet. When I do, it will be interesting to see who your biggest problem is: the police or Willie Sneddon. But, in the meantime, you think things over. If you decide you need my help to get yourself out of whatever it is you've gotten into, give me a call.' I pointedly tossed my card onto his desk. He pointedly didn't pick it up.

CHAPTER SEVENTEEN

Bantaskin Street, Maryhill, was hardly Sunset Strip, Hollywood, and observing a building from a car is less than inconspicuous when yours is one of only three cars in the street. It meant I had to park around the corner, some distance from the gym, leave the Atlantic, and carry out my surveillance from a tenement corner.

I hadn't really expected to get anything worthwhile out of Collins. The whole exchange with him hadn't been to find out what he knew, rather to hint at what I knew. Which was less than met the eye. If my hunch was right, it would take Collins only the time it takes to make a 'phone call and arrange a meet before he'd come hustling out of the side door of the gym. I'd guessed ten, but in fact it was nearer twenty minutes before he emerged and crossed the street to where he had parked his Lanchester–Daimler. I sprinted back to the Atlantic and came around the corner just in time to see the tail of his car as it took the junction into Cowan Street.

I had hoped for a car to intervene between me and Collins's Lanchester, but Maryhill Road was pretty much empty of anything but trams and buses. I had to hold back. Collins would have checked the street before he got into his car, satisfying himself that I had gone. But that didn't mean he wouldn't be checking his rear-view mirror a little more frequently than usual.

Thankfully, his burgundy Lanchester was the kind of colour you couldn't miss, and I reckoned I could keep tabs on it from a distance.

Collins led me up Maryhill Road and through Milngavie. I smiled smugly, for no one's benefit but my own: we were heading for Bobby Kirkcaldy's place in Blanefield. But we didn't. Instead we passed through Strathblane and Blanefield and headed further north and into Stirlingshire. I couldn't complain about my work not being varied. Over the last two weeks I had seen more Scottish countryside than a Bluebell Tours bus driver.

We were the only cars on the road now and I held right back, allowing myself to be guided by the blood fleck on the horizon that was Collins's Lanchester as it breached a hill or took a corner. There was nowhere for him to go, which made me feel relaxed about following him but perplexed about where he might lead me.

We were now out into that part of Scotland that was gently scenic rather than dramatic, but the mountains ahead reminded me that we were becoming ever more remote. When I turned the next corner I found that I had lost sight of Collins completely, so I gunned the Atlantic a little until I reached the next bend. Still nothing. I stopped reflecting on the view, dropped a crunching gear and floored the accelerator. I took the next bend a little too fast and the rear tyres protested. Still no Collins. I took the next stretch as fast as the last, braking hard at the corner. This time there was a long, open expanse ahead of me where the road dipped between trees and rose gradually again, stretching out towards the mountains. I slowed down. No Collins, and there was no way he could have cleared that stretch before I made the corner.

It took me a while to find a place where I could get turned around. The Atlantic objected a little as I floored the accelerator again, heading back up the hill and around the bend. Slowing up on the straight, I checked every farm gate and track, peering through the dense clumps of trees. I passed what looked like the entrance to a house, but couldn't see the building itself because of the trees and bushes that lined the road, just a sweep of dirt and gravel driveway. I drove on for another five hundred or so yards, checking for signs where Collins could have turned off. Nothing. It had to be the entry into the house. I found a lay-by of sorts and parked so I could steal up the driveway on foot and have a nosey-around. This was becoming a bit of a habit and I was becoming more gumboot than gumshoe. As I headed along the road to the entrance to the driveway, I wondered if I should trade in the Atlantic for a tractor.

It was a long driveway. Tree-lined and curving, so you couldn't get a glimpse of the house till you were nearly on it. It turned out to be a big Georgian type. Bigger and classier even than Sneddon's newly acquired country retreat and fight venue. But when I drew closer I could see that most of the windows were shuttered and a door to the side was boarded up. Another empty house. But not another derelict. This had all the look of a home boarded up while the owners were away, or one that was between owners. The driveway opened out into a huge semi-circle in front of the house. No blood-red Lanchester. In fact, no cars at all. I could have saved myself some time and driven up to check it out. There was clearly no one here, least of all Collins. I'd lost him. But it still made sense for me to check the house out. And it still made sense for me to be cautious as I did so.

I decided to get off the drive: the gravel was crunching under every footfall and everything else around here seemed to have taken a Trappist vow. I walked across a broad triangle of lawn that was yearning for a long-lost mower and around the side of the house. The first couple of windows I found – the usual tall, elegant Georgian jobs – had the internal shutters closed over. But when I got around to the back, I found an unshuttered window, its glass as black as obsidian. I peered in through it, pressing my face to the glass and shielding my eyes with my hands, but it was no good: the interior was so dark I could see nothing.

I straightened up. There, reflected in the dark glass, was a face next to mine, standing behind me. A battered, indeterminately old face that looked like it had been used as a punch bag for decades. The name 'Uncle Bert' formed itself in my head and I started to turn, but something that felt like steel slammed into my back, right above the pelvis. The pain exploded through my gut and I felt as if my kidney had exploded. The punch had caught me exactly where I was still tender from my encounter with Costello's goons outside the Carvery.

I spun around and swung wildly at the old man. He blocked my punch with his forearm, and his fist, still feeling like steel instead of muscle and bone, rammed into my solar plexus. Every bit of air pulsed out of my lungs. I stopped defending myself. I stopped thinking. Once more, all of my being was concentrated on the simple effort of breathing. He pushed me back and to the side so I collided with the wall.

Uncle Bert took his time, holding me in place with one hand and pulling his other fist back to deliver a right that we both knew would send me sleepy-bye-byes. He had braced his legs to deliver the maximum power and I swung my foot up as hard and as swiftly as I could manage. My foot went through between his legs but my shin slammed into his groin. He doubled over and I grabbed his ears, hoisted him up and smashed my forehead into his face. The good old Glasgow Kiss.

I pushed him away from me. Blood was pouring from his nose and I fully expected him to crumble; but Uncle Bert was an old pro and came straight back at me. I scrabbled in my pocket for my sap and swung it at him, catching him on the temple. It sent him sideways but again, amazingly, his feet remained planted and he didn't go down. I backhanded him with the sap. He went down on one knee and I kicked him in the face. He fell backwards onto his back. I staggered forward, pulling air into my empty lungs and bent from the pain in my kidney. All the hate and the rage was back: I stood to one side of him and raised my foot, aiming to smash my heel into his ugly, old battered face.

There was a shot. I staggered back.

Chapter Eighteen

I looked down at my body, then down at Bert Soutar sprawled on the ground at my feet. Neither of us was hit. When I looked up I saw Bobby Kirkcaldy, his face carrying the evidence of his defeat the night before, standing with a Browning in his hand. He'd obviously fired a shot into the air, but I now found myself looking at the business end of the automatic.

'Against the wall, Lennox,' he said, his voice still disconcertingly calm. Gentle. 'Uncle Bert, you okay?'

Soutar got to his feet slowly, eyeing me with malice. I knew what was coming and so, clearly, did Kirkcaldy.

'Leave it, Bert,' he said. 'We'll do this in the garage, like we said.'

Soutar grabbed me by the collar of my suit jacket and pulled me from the wall. He took up position behind me and guided me with vicious shoves around to the back of the house. The drive arced round the far side of the house to a whitewashed outbuilding. It looked like it had, at one time, been a stables, but had since been converted into a garage. There was a dormer window above it suggesting that the attic had been the chauffeur's accommodation. There were two huge double doors, and I reckoned you could easily have parked four cars inside it. I studied the structure carefully, for two reasons: the curiosity of the condemned man about his place of execution; and because

I wanted to work out any possible escape routes well in advance.

Soutar kept the shoves going and I considered dancing with him again. He was a tough old bird, all right, but I'd do my best to snap his neck before his nephew got one off. I could always hope that Kirkcaldy was a worse shot than he was a boxer.

'All of this because you fixed a fight?' I called over my shoulder. 'I've got to give it to you, Kirkcaldy, you take your petty larceny very seriously.'

'Shut up and walk . . .' Uncle Bert gave me another shove. It was beginning to become rude.

'We've got a friend waiting for you,' said Kirkcaldy, and laughed in a dark, vicious way. He went ahead of us and opened one of the doors into the garage.

Just as I had expected, there were two cars in the garage: the sleek, carmine droplet of Collins's Lanchester and Bobby Kirkcaldy's open-top Sunbeam-Talbot Sports. What a chump, I thought bitterly to myself. There I was thinking I was all smart and devious, stirring up Collins so he would lead me to Mr Big. Yep, I had had it all down pat, except that the delay in Collins leaving his office had been to give Kirkcaldy time to make the fifteen-minute drive from Strathblane to this place, and get himself settled in. All Collins had had to do after that was lead me by the nose. It served me right; I was beginning to believe my own advertising.

The garage was even bigger inside than I had guessed. The two cars took up less than half of the space. Jack Collins stood in the middle of the free area of floor.

'I told you he'd follow me,' he said with a contempt I could have found hurtful.

'Okay, so you're pissed off that I'm doing my job. But like I said outside, this doesn't smell right to me. You're going to too much trouble just to cover up a fixed fight. Why the artillery?' I asked, nodding to the Browning in Kirkcaldy's hand.

'Maybe you're right, Lennox,' Kirkcaldy said. 'Maybe there's more going on than you can understand.'

'Try me,' I said. 'I'm an understanding type. But first of all, indulge my curiosity as a fan . . . why throw the fight last night?'

'What makes you think I threw it?'

'Oh, come on. I was there. And I've seen you fight several times before. If you could flatten McQuillan the way you did, then Jan Schmidtke should have been a walkover. You threw the fight all right. Is your heart really as bad as that?'

'As a matter of fact it is,' said Kirkcaldy, in a matter-of-fact way. 'Congenital defect. I've had it since birth but didn't know about it. It's only over the last six months that I've had problems with it. The quack says I've to take it easy, take the stress out of my life. Maybe I should start with you, huh, Lennox?'

'So I'm guessing you made a killing on the fight?' I asked.

'Jack here arranged it all for us. It actually started off as Small Change's idea. No really big bets. Nothing that would get noticed too much, but lots of them, spread out across all the bookies. And each bet placed by a third party who couldn't be connected to Collins, far less me.'

'Very sweet,' I said. 'But you weren't the only ones in the know. Two young Flash Harrys tried to broker a big bet against you winning through Tony the Pole.'

'That's something I don't know about,' said Kirkcaldy as casually as he could manage. If he had been as poor at throwing a feint in the ring, then his prematurely terminated career would have terminated even more prematurely.

'Who were they?' I pushed my luck. Seeing as I was at gunpoint in an outbuilding in the middle of nowhere, where a shot would go unheard far less unnoticed, I felt I was just as well pushing it.

'I told you, I don't know anything about them or anybody else laying bets.'

I decided to move on before Kirkcaldy's pants caught fire. 'I'm sure your little scheme will have raked in a lot of cash. But not that much. Not enough for this kind of grief. And it doesn't add up to something worth killing Small Change for.'

'Small Change's death has got nothing to do with us. Nothing at all. And it's got nothing to do with the fight scam either.'

'No . . . I believe you didn't kill Small Change, but the fight scam *does* have something to do with his death. Maybe Small Change came up with the idea of you throwing the fight to start with, but when he did it was simply to get you out of the fight game with a little pension. You must have told him about your heart condition. But the real reason you needed to pull it off was because you needed to pay someone off quick. Someone who was going to give you the same treatment that Small Change got.'

Kirkcaldy didn't say anything, but exchanged a look with Uncle Bert.

'You see, Bobby, I'm a studious sort. I spend a lot of time up at the Mitchell Library expanding my mind. One direction I've expanded in is the traditions and customs of our travelling cousins. Take the ones up at Vinegarhill. Now, to start with, I thought they were just Irish travellers, but it turns out they're *Minceir*, proper Romanies from Ireland . . . the real Gypsy McCoy, you could say.'

Kirkcaldy said nothing.

'They've had a long and difficult history, gypsies,' I continued. 'They've been in Britain for centuries, you know. Did you know that we actually sold them to Louisiana to work as slaves for freed blacks who had their own small plantations? Or that we used to hang them just for being gypsies? It's made them an unforgiving bunch. They're big on vengeance and blood feud.'

'What's that got to do with anything?' Kirkcaldy said, but again I could see behind the expression.

'I don't know what you did. That's the one piece that's missing for me. You see, like I said, I've been reading up on gypsy customs. And I met Sean Furie, whose son is up for Small Change's murder. Now, to start with, I thought Furie was more Blackrock than Bulgaria, but it would seem he's the real thing. He and his mob follow gypsy customs and law. Furie himself is a *Baro* – that's a kind of clan chieftain. The kingpin gypsy. And as a *Baro*, Furie will also sit as a judge on the *kris*, the half-arsed court arrange-ment they have going. One of the things the *kris* does is sit in judgement on fellow gypsies or even on *gaje* as they call non-gypsies.'

'Very fucking interesting,' said Bert Soutar. 'Consider my hori-zons expanded. Now get over against the wall.'

I decided to stay where I was for the moment. 'It *is* inter-esting. You see, one of the things the *kris* sits in judgement on is if one of their own is killed by someone else. Murder, say . . . or a careless accident. Then they can issue a sentence on the accused and the only way he can get out of it is to pay a *glaba*. Blood money.' I paused for a moment. Less for dramatic effect and more to check my surroundings again. There were a couple of small, grimy windows over by the rear wall. A clutch of old and rusting garden tools, including a small hand scythe mottled with reddish-brown flecks. A shadow fell across the grime-dimmed window and passed on. There was someone else here. Outside.

'Anyway,' I continued, 'here's the way I see it: you, good old Uncle Bert, and young Collins here, are all under sentence of death. And death, though it's bad enough, isn't as scary as the kind of death you'll have at the hands of the gypsies. Now I don't know if Furie's son carried out sentence on Small Change or not, but you fellas have a pretty good idea what's ahead of you ... unless, of course, you hand over a large *glaba* ransom.'

'So what are we supposed to have done?' asked Kirkcaldy.

'Well, it's pretty obvious at first sight. Uncle Bert here supplied that young pikey fighter for the bare-knuckle fight. Then he dies. So Soutar, Small Change and Collins are held responsible. Small Change meets a sticky end by having his skull pulped with a statue of his favourite greyhound, and you start getting traditional gypsy symbols of death dropped on your doorstep. I was supposed to work it all out. Well I have. But what I don't get is why ... the gypsy boy went into the fight of his own free will, knowing the risks, and took his chances. So why does his clan hold you responsible?'

'You're not as smart as you think you are, Lennox,' sneered Jack Collins. His face was white and drawn. The coolness had gone. He was afraid. It was either what I had been saying, or he knew he was about to witness something unpleasant. I did my best to believe it was the power of my oratory.

'Shut up, Collins,' said Kirkcaldy. 'Against the wall, Lennox. And keep your hands where I can see them.'

'So this is it?' I asked. I noticed I wasn't breathing hard and I didn't feel my heart pounding. That was what happened, I guessed, when you'd thought you were going to die so many times before. When you'd seen so many others go before you. 'So you're going to kill me over a gypsy curse and an amateurishly fixed fight? No ... this doesn't make sense. I'm missing something here. Who was it in Collins's car outside your house? And why are the gyppos really after you?'

My back was to the wall now, but, as I'd backed up, I'd angled my steps so I ended up next to the scythe. A rusty garden implement against a gun and two experienced fist fighters. They don't stand a chance, I thought to myself.

'Show him . . .' Kirkcaldy barked the order at Collins and indicated his car with a jerk of his head. Collins went over to the car and opened the trunk, lifting out something wrapped in a blanket. He carried it in his arms like it was a baby. He laid it on the floor and unwrapped it for me to see. It was the *Ky-Lan* demon statuette. It had been broken into two pieces. The fake jade was less than an inch thick. The contents spilled from the broken sculpture: tightly wrapped waxed paper bricks.

I sighed as something tied itself into a knot in my gut. I knew what Kirkcaldy having it meant. 'Sammy Pollock?'

Kirkcaldy smiled, and it reminded me of the way Sneddon smiled. 'Just like everything else in Glasgow, Lennox, the Clyde is unpredictable. You dump two bodies at the same time in the same place and one washes up and the other sinks without trace.'

'He didn't deserve that, Kirkcaldy. He was just a kid.' I thought about how Sheila Gainsborough would take the news. I hadn't earned my fee on that one, that was for sure. But, there again, it wouldn't be me who'd be breaking the news to her. I gave a bitter laugh.

'What's so fucking funny?' asked Kirkcaldy.

'Just that I was working two cases that I never connected. I'm not as smart as I thought I was.'

'You're smart, Lennox. Too smart. But you should know by now that nothing happens in this city without it being tied into everything else. And before you get all huffy about Pollock, remember that he brought it on himself. He wanted to play with the big boys. He ended up way out of his depth.'

'I don't think you're far behind him. You having that stuff

means you don't just have a bunch of irate gypsies after you. Have you heard of John Largo?'

'I've heard. And I know this is his stuff. But he's still looking for Pollock and Costello. We happened on this by chance. We're in the clear.'

'Not that in the clear. I found you.'

'No you didn't. All that you said to Collins here was smoke and mirrors. You were grouse-beating. Except now it's the grouse with the gun on you. Anyway, you're not going to be telling anyone anything.'

That's that then, I thought. If there was one thing you couldn't accuse Kirkcaldy of, it was ambiguity.

'How did Costello and Pollock get their hands on the jade demon? There was no way they could have known what was in it.'

'That's where you're wrong. Young master Pollock was a young man of cosmopolitan tastes. Bohemian, you might say. He was a bit of a hashish smoker and had experimented with opium. No other bastard in this city would have realized the value of refined heroin, but Pollock knew all right. But that was as smart as he got. He was no master criminal and he thought he was dealing with Al Capone when he got in tow with Paul Costello. But Costello was a wanker and as much out of his depth as Pollock was.'

'So how did they get their hands on this?' I asked. The three of them – Soutar, Collins and Kirkcaldy – were all facing me now, with their backs to the doors. Kirkcaldy had left the door open a few inches and I could have sworn that I had seen it move. My shadow at the window was maybe not another accomplice after all. I pinned my hopes on a guardian angel.

'Paul Costello was always looking for a score,' Kirkcaldy continued and I made a gargantuan effort not to cast a glance at the garage doors behind him. 'I think he was trying to prove he could be a real player, like his Da. Fuck all chance of that. He didn't have the brains to blow his hat off. Sammy Pollock was supposed to be the thinker. Talk about the blind leading the blind. Anyway, they did a couple of night-time jobs. They got two other guys in with them. Their first score was a warehouse with cigarettes. French shit. They didn't have a clue how to move the stuff on, other than going round the clubs and pubs themselves. Complete amateurs. You don't pull a job unless you've done a deal in advance with a fence who'll move the stuff on. Not only did these wankers have no deal, they didn't even know a fence.'

'So they went to Small Change?' It was all fitting now.

'Aye . . . he took the stuff off them for peanuts. Now Small Change was no Fagin, but he did handle the odd dirty merchandise now and again. Especially if there was decent money to be made. But only if it was something special and there was a high brokering margin to be made.'

'It still doesn't explain how Pollock knew to steal the jade dragon.'

'Pollock and Costello had help on their jobs. Two guys who worked for Costello's Da and a pikey who provided extra muscle,' said Kirkcaldy. Again something fell into place for me.

'The five of them did the cigarette job,' Kirkcaldy went on. 'All the stuff came from the warehouse used by that Frog, Barnier. Before they get to the cigarettes, they have to open a few crates to check before they hit the jackpot with the fags. The genius pikey cracks open a jade statue by accident and sees it's full of packets. He tells Pollock and Pollock jumps to the conclusion that it's hashish. So they take the statue as well and get away scot-free. But when Pollock gets home and opens one of the packets, he realizes they're all in the deepest shite. He realizes it's not hashish but heroin, and pretty high grade. He takes a sample from one brick, puts the brick back and glues the statue back together. He takes the sample straight to Small Change. Small Change doesn't know the slightest thing about narcotics, so he comes straight to yours truly.'

'So these two guys you said were working for Costello,' I said, 'I'm guessing that they did a deal with you and Small Change and then delivered up Sammy Pollock and Paul Costello . . . So what went wrong?' I kept my eyes fixed on Kirkcaldy's and ignored the figure I saw on the edge of my vision slipping in through the doors and edging, crouched down, along the wall and behind the cars.

'The pikey works out there's something more to the job and starts asking for more money or he'll talk. Except he doesn't know that I'm involved now. He also happens to be a bare-knuckle fighter who Uncle Bert has fixed up with a few fights at Sneddon's place.'

'And he just happens to die during the fight?'

'Aye . . . funny that.' Kirkcaldy smiled coldly. 'Quite a coincidence. Particularly as Uncle Bert gave him some special medicine before the fight. Told him it would make him fight better and not feel the other bloke's punches. The last bit was right. The stupid pikey bastard took it. The other fighter was able to beat the shite out of him and then he started bleeding like fuck. From the beating or the drugs I don't know.'

'And your problem's solved.' I tried to stay relaxed and natural, when all the time I was mentally measuring the distance to the rusting scythe and waiting for the figure hidden behind the cars to make his move.

'Naw . . . that's when our problems just began. Turns out that the pikey is Sean Furie's son . . . the brother of the one up for Small Change's murder.'

'So that's the *glaba* you have to pay . . .' I said. 'A *Baro*'s son won't come cheap.'

'It takes more than a bunch of pig-arsed Irish gyppos to scare me. It's a nuisance that I don't need at the moment. I can't sell the heroin yet and I needed to raise money to buy the knackers off.' He jerked his chin in the direction of the broken statuette. 'This is the biggest business opportunity I've ever had. This stuff's going to be big here . . . Have you seen Glasgow on a Saturday night? Half the city gets totally fucking stocious. Thousands of men out of their skulls on booze. No one drinks for the taste and Christ knows they don't drink for the social fucking aspect. Do you know what they want? They want a holiday. They drink because for a few hours they can step outside their lives. If cheap whisky or red biddy gives them a day trip to Largs, this stuff is two weeks in fucking Monte Carlo. This . . .' He bounced the package in his hand, as if assessing its worth. 'This is the future, Lennox. This is Glasgow's future. We won't be able to get enough of this stuff to keep up with demand. I'm fucking telling you, this stuff was made for Glasgow. Because this stuff makes Glasgow go away. Anyway, talking about making things go away, enough chat . . .'

Kirkcaldy pulled the carriage back on the Browning. The three of them faced me. Collins looked even paler. He had known from the moment he left his office to lead me up here that this was what was going to happen. Bert Soutar twisted his thin lips underneath his busted-up nose. He was going to enjoy this.

For some reason that I couldn't fathom, Fiona White's face came to my mind. Maybe it was the fact that she was about to have a vacancy to let.

There was a terrible grace to it. I had guessed it would be Singer who was behind the car. After all, it had been me who had suggested he was put onto tailing Kirkcaldy. He moved out from behind the car without a sound. It was Collins's startled cry that caused Kirkcaldy and Soutar to spin round. I saw Singer's hand move swiftly up and make a short arc in the air. Collins made a gurgling sound and blood started to pulse from his neck where Singer's razor had slashed him.

I lunged for the scythe. Kirkcaldy heard the rasp as I tore it from the wall and he spun back, swinging the gun around. The scythe sliced into his wrist and the gun fell to the floor. I rushed forward and swung the scythe again, this time its tip sank into Kirkcaldy's back and he screamed in a way that didn't sound human. I saw that Singer and Soutar were now desperately wrestling with each other: Soutar's iron grasp on Singer's wrist, stopping him from bringing the razor down to his throat. I threw down the scythe and snatched up the automatic Kirkcaldy had dropped. I didn't even think about it. I put two rounds into the side of Soutar's head and he went down. Lifeless. His dead grip pulling Singer down on top of him.

The whole thing would only have lasted four or five seconds, but now Soutar lay dead, Collins was on his back, shivering and twitching the last of his life away, Kirkcaldy was on his knees, clutching his hacked-open wrist.

'Thanks, Singer . . .' I said. 'If you hadn't come along, I'd be dead.'

Singer straightened himself up and nodded. He was out of breath but I thought I detected a hint of a smile in the corners of his mouth.

We left the bodies in the garage. I wrapped a handkerchief around Kirkcaldy's hand and we put him in the passenger seat of his Sunbeam-Talbot Sports. Tucking the Browning into the waistband of my trousers, I gathered up the jade demon, wrapped it back into its blanket and put it into the boot of my car. I knew Kirkcaldy wouldn't give me any more trouble, so I told Singer to follow me in my Austin Atlantic. We stopped at a telephone box by the side of the road and Singer watched Kirkcaldy as I 'phoned Willie Sneddon. I gave him a brief outline of what had happened and told him there were a couple of consignments of meat for Hammer Murphy's mincer, and where to find them.

We drove back into Glasgow, all the way Kirkcaldy trying to do a deal with me, offering all kinds of riches if I helped him get out of this mess. As I drove along the Clyde and into the Gallowgate, I promised I would; that I knew people who would sort him out.

Singer parked outside and waited for me. I drove into the enclosure at Vinegarhill. The old guy I'd seen before ran across to Sean Furie's caravan and hammered on the door. Furie nodded to me and I nodded back. Neither of us paid any heed to Kirkcaldy's begging. I threw the keys of his car onto the ground and he fell out of the car and started to scrabble in the dust for them, but they were too far away and the ring of gypsies that had formed was already closing on him.

When I dropped Singer off at Sneddon's place, I thanked him again. He nodded once more and got out.

I was tired and I was aching but I had three 'phone calls to make. It was getting dark, darker than it had been for weeks, and there was something in the late evening air that spoke of a colder season on its way. I parked by the side of the Clyde and took the shattered jade demon out of the trunk and carried it down to the water's edge. I took a couple of the waxed-paper bricks out and held them, one in each hand. I was always looking for a way of making a buck. Here, in my hands, I had an entire retirement fund. I guessed I would even get a tidy finder's fee if I returned the narcotics to Largo. I also knew that it was only a matter of time before Kirkcaldy's predictions came true and the streets of Glasgow would be awash with the stuff. But there was some money that was just too dirty, even for me. I took my lock-knife from my pocket and, one by one, cut open the bricks and shook out great clouds of white powder. I watched the clouds of white powder drift away on the evening breeze, and the wrappers as they drifted away on the dark, sinewy surface of the water.

I made my calls from a telephone box on the corner of Buchanan Street. The first was to someone everybody seemed to think of as a phantom: I told John Largo that he had an hour before I told Dex Devereaux where to find him. Without going into the specifics, I told him that all accounts had been set straight and he had no scores left to settle in Glasgow. I recommended an immediate change of climate. Probably somewhere sunny.

The second call was to Jock Ferguson at home. I told him to meet Dex Devereaux at his hotel in half an hour and that it would mean he would get the John Largo collar.

My third call was brief and to the point. I tried ringing Jimmy Costello at the Empire Bar. He wasn't there but I got him at the Riviera Club. He asked me impatiently what I wanted. I understood his impatience: he had asked me to find his son for him and he had turned up dead. I was making a habit of it.

'Are Skelly and Young there?' I asked.

'Aye, so fucking what?'

'They're there right now?'

'Aye . . .' His impatience grew. 'I'm looking right at them.'

'Then you're looking right at the men who killed Paul. Or at least gift-wrapped him for someone else to kill. And don't worry, all other accounts have been settled.'

'If you're fucking lying . . .'

'I'm not. Skelly and Young stitched up Paul and Sammy Pollock for money. That's a fact. What you do with that fact is up to you.'

There was a pause at the other end of the line. I could hear a band in the background. The melted-together sounds of many people talking and drinking.

'I'll deal with it,' said Costello, and I knew that he would. 'Lennox?'

'Yeah?'

'Thanks.'

I was as good as my word to Largo and stood outside the Alpha Hotel for half an hour before I went in and asked for Dex Devereaux. The night porter had been very reluctant to let me in and even more reluctant to disturb Mr Devereaux.

'It's very important,' I said and pushed a couple of pound notes into the pocket of his waistcoat. 'Tell him I have the address he's been looking for. Mr Largo's address.'

I sat down and waited. It took less than ten minutes for a dishevelled Dex Devereaux to appear in the lobby. Dishevelled except his flat-top haircut, which looked as precision-engineered as ever. I handed him the note with the address.

'You sure about this?' He held up the note.

'That's him. That's his address.'

I left Devereaux, passing a flustered Jock Ferguson as the night porter let me out and him in.

'Dex'll explain,' I said elliptically. I was in an elliptical frame of mind. I had another call to make. The one I dreaded most. I got back in the Atlantic and drove out to the West End, to Sheila Gainsborough's apartment.

*

It was two weeks later that I met John Largo. Dex Devereaux had been as good as his word and had paid me the thousand dollars for the information, but when they had arrived at Largo's place, he had flown the coop. He must have been warned off, Jock Ferguson had said to me, without a hint of suspicion.

Largo was waiting for me, hanging back in the shadows, as I came out of the Horsehead Bar. He kept his hand in the patch pocket of his suit jacket and I suspected he was holding something more than his change. That was okay. I understood his caution.

'I wanted to thank you,' he said.

'What . . . for turning you in?'

'For giving me a chance. How did you find me?'

I took out my cigarette case and offered him one. He took it with his left hand, keeping his right in his pocket.

'You're too sentimental,' I said. 'I followed you to the Lyle Hill monument. I guessed there was some connection to the *Maillé-Brézé*. So I did some checking.'

As I had explained to Devereaux in the lobby of his hotel, the *Maillé-Brézé* had been a French Navy destroyer. It had been anchored at the berthing point at the Tail of the Bank, at the mouth of the Clyde Estuary and beneath the spot where the Free French monument now stood. The Tail of the Bank had been the gathering point for the Atlantic convoys: a bustling knot of merchant vessels and their heavily armed escorts. And it had also been where the *Maillé-Brézé* had been berthed in April 1940. The French destroyer had only just set out to sea when two torpedoes were accidentally launched onto the ship's own deck. The torpedoes had exploded midships with a force that had shattered windows in Port Glasgow and the broken vessel had blazed and smoked with many of its crew trapped in the forward mess hall. Despite the efforts of the Port Glasgow fire brigade, when the *Maillé-Brézé* eventually sank to the bottom of the Firth, it took sixty-eight of the two-hundred-strong crew with it. I had never met anyone connected to the disaster. Until now.

'I found your name all right . . .' I said. 'I mean I found the name Alain Barnier. But it was amongst the list of missing. I had no list of survivors to check.'

'Alain was a friend of mine.' Largo smiled. His face looked completely different without the goatee beard. And his hair was now as dark as mine. 'In a way, it was my way of commemorating him . . . keeping his name alive. But how did you trace my name?'

'Remember the fight in Port Glasgow? A couple of nights after the French fleet was sunk at Mers-el-Kébir?'

'Ah . . .' He nodded. 'Of course . . .'

'When I first came to your offices, Miss Minto corrected me when I said the name *Clement* the English way. There are a lot of names that are spelt the same in French and pronounced differently.'

'And, of course,' he concluded the thought for me, 'there are many words that are spelt differently but sound the same . . .'

'Dex Devereaux had an informant who heard mention of your name. He just reported it how he heard it, *John Largo*. But when I was going through the court records, I found the statement given by Capitaine Jean Largeau of the *Fusiliers Marins*. After that I guessed your career must have become so colourful that you adopted the name Alain Barnier.'

'It was prudent at the time. I have another name now. And another port. You have succeeded in making Glasgow –' he struggled for the right word – '. . . *untenable* for me.'

'I can't say I'm sorry about that. I don't approve of your business, Jean.'

Largeau shrugged the same Gallic shrug that he had as Alain Barnier. 'America is corrupt, my friend. I did not create the corruption, I merely profit from it. And I do not force these blacks to use my goods. I supply a need.'

'They're going to hang the gypsy boy, you know,' I said, changing the subject. 'The boxer, Tommy Gun Furie.'

Largeau made an expression of incomprehension.

'For Small Change MacFarlane's murder. He pled guilty, on his lawyer's advice, but they're going to hang him anyway. Which is a shame, because I don't think he killed Small Change.'

'Ah ...' Largeau shook his head slowly. 'I'm afraid I'm not familiar with the case. But with these itinerant people, they are normally guilty ... of something.'

We talked for a few more minutes. Two men standing chatting outside a Glasgow bar. We wished each other well and he took his hand from his pocket to shake mine. I left him standing there and drove off. When I looked in my rear-view mirror he was gone.

I don't know why I didn't turn Largeau in to the police, or at least why I gave him a chance of getting away before I did. I think it was probably one of those *there but for the grace ...* moments. The war had done things to us both and I had very nearly turned out the same way.

But I hadn't.

Epilogue

Maggie MacFarlane, the Merry Widow of Pollokshields, took the disappearance of Jack Collins with the same stoicism as she had her husband's demise. I guessed I would never know just how much she knew about, or was involved with, his business dealings. Jack Collins wasn't mentioned once when I called up to see Lorna and there seemed to be some kind of peace between the two MacFarlane women. I reckoned it had about the same chance of lasting as the new armistice in Indochina.

I told Lorna that if she needed anything, I was there for her. It was goodbye and we both knew it. She was a big girl and could look after herself – one of the things that had brought us together was that we had both been carved from the same wood – but I was beginning to question how I handled women.

Willie Sneddon coughed up my fee in full. I had gone up to see him with Singer and we had told him the whole story. Or I told him the whole story and Singer backed me up with nods every time Sneddon looked to him for confirmation. Sneddon took his losses on the chin, but made his displeasure clear when I told him what we had done with Kirkcaldy instead of handing the boxer over to him. But Sneddon was better off out of it: a few days later the papers were full of the discovery of Bobby Kirkcaldy's body, which, they reported, had been subjected to a protracted and brutal assault. I braced myself for a visit from

Jock Ferguson or, worse still, Superintendent Willie McNab.

There was a sudden outbreak of infectious amnesia in Glasgow: the witnesses who could place Tommy Gun Furie near Small Change MacFarlane's place on the night of the murder recanted. The charges against Furie were dropped. I found myself wondering how many of the witnesses had been getting doorstep deliveries.

Against her injunction, I called around to May Donaldson's later that week. I waited outside until she got home from work and I was sure she was alone. Her face darkened when she opened the door to me.

'Lennox, I told you . . .'

'Don't worry, May,' I said. 'I'm not staying. I just came to give you this . . .' I handed her a white vellum envelope. It was a nice envelope. Classy-looking. Her eyes grew wide when she opened it.

'What's this?'

'It's five hundred pounds. Consider it a wedding present. Another wedding present. You deserve a good start.'

'I can't accept this, Lennox. You know I can't.' She held the envelope out to me but I pushed it back.

'Yes you can. It's something I earned and I'm not happy about what I did to earn it. Don't worry . . .' I said, reading her look. 'It's not dirty money. In fact I was paid from the coffers of global law enforcement.'

'Still, I really can't take it . . .' she protested, but with significantly less enthusiasm. 'How do I explain this to George?'

'Tell him you've inherited something from a relative you didn't know about. I'll send you a letter with my official heading on it, if you like.'

She looked at the envelope with the bulge of money pushing

it wide. It looked like some split-open vegetable. A cash crop.
'Lennox . . .'

'Okay,' I said. 'There is something I'd like you to do for me.
Maybe I should come in and explain . . .'

I was waiting when Davey Wallace got out of hospital. The
swelling had gone down but his face was still a dark spectrum
of bruises. He walked slowly but gingerly, as if treading on hot
coals. I guessed that anything but the gentlest footfall would
jar through his cracked ribs. Somehow, he managed to grin his
usual grin at me. That hurt more than if he'd swung a punch
at me.

I held open the car door for him. He got in and we drove
across the city. Davey told me that he didn't want me to worry
about him and that he would be ready to do work for me again
in a couple of weeks. And he would have plenty of time, he told
me: he'd been laid off from the yard.

I didn't say anything. Instead I drove down to the river and
parked on a scruffy patch of cleared bomb-site. I helped Davey
to the water's edge and we sat on a wall beneath the bristling
black branches of shipyard cranes. A puffer belched blackly as
it drifted past us.

We sat there for more than an hour while I talked, without a
break. I talked about my home in Canada and about the war. I
talked about when I'd been Davey's age and everything I thought
the world had held for me. I talked about things that I hadn't
talked about to anybody before, and I told Davey that. I talked
about Sicily and Aachen, about the friends I'd seen die and the
enemies I'd killed. About the bad things I'd done because you had
to do bad things in war, and the bad things I'd done even when
I didn't have to do them. I laid out my life for him. And for me.

When I finished, I handed him an envelope. The same classy,

vellum type I had given May. I told Davey about Saskatchewan, about open prairies and hot summers and snow as deep as your chin in winter. I told him he should quit watching gangster movies and watch more Westerns.

'Two friends of mine are moving out there. May and George. They've got a huge farm out there and they'll need someone to help out. There's a ticket in there for you to travel with them and five hundred pounds in sterling. That goes a long way in Canadian dollars, Davey.'

'Why are you doing this, Mr Lennox?'

'Because you're a good kid, Davey, and I was a good kid once. Or I like to pretend to myself that I was a good kid once. You deserve something better than this . . .' I gestured to the black, oily Clyde, to the cranes around us, to the dark city behind us. 'I've put a letter in there as well. It gives my folks' address and details in New Brunswick. I wired my dad and he said he'll stand as sponsor for you if immigration need it.' I put my hand on his shoulder. 'But you won't. Canada wants good kids like you.'

'I don't know what to say, Mr Lennox. If there's anything I can ever do . . .'

'What I want you to do is have a good life. Marry one of those strong, pretty Ukrainian-Canadian girls with sky-blue eyes, rosy cheeks and butter-coloured hair they've got in Saskatchewan and have a dozen blond kids.'

Davey sat silently in the car on the way back, the white envelope on his lap. He didn't speak until I pulled up outside his digs.

'I'll never forget this, Mr Lennox. Never.' His face was determined. Almost grim.

'Good,' I grinned. 'I don't expect you to. Maybe one day I'll come out and visit.'

*

After I left Davey, I drove back to Great Western Road. Something churned in my gut and I knew it was because, out there by the river, I had faced things with Davey that I hadn't faced since the war. It had liberated me and burdened me all at the same time. But at least, for once, I knew for sure what my next move was going to be.

I parked the Atlantic outside my digs, walked up to the door, unlocked it and stepped into the hallway. But I didn't go up to my flat.

Instead, without hesitating, I knocked firmly on Fiona White's door.

ACKNOWLEDGEMENTS

I would like to offer my heartfelt thanks to the following people for their help and support: Wendy, Jonathan and Sophie; my agent Carole Blake, my editor Jane Wood, as well as Jenny Ellis and all at Quercus; my copy-editor Robyn Karney; Louise Thurtell at Allen and Unwin; Marco Schneiders and Helmut Pesch at Lübbe Verlag, as well as all of my other publishers around the world; also to Colin Black and Chris Martin.